Edward Herries

Memoir of the Public Life of the Right Hon. John Charles Herries

in the reigns of George III., George IV., William IV. and Victoria - Vol. 2

Edward Herries

Memoir of the Public Life of the Right Hon. John Charles Herries
in the reigns of George III., George IV., William IV. and Victoria - Vol. 2

ISBN/EAN: 9783337334130

Printed in Europe, USA, Canada, Australia, Japan

Cover: Foto ©Andreas Hilbeck / pixelio.de

More available books at **www.hansebooks.com**

MEMOIR

OF

THE PUBLIC LIFE OF THE RIGHT HON.

JOHN CHARLES HERRIES

IN THE REIGNS OF GEORGE III., GEORGE IV.
WILLIAM IV. AND VICTORIA

BY HIS SON

EDWARD HERRIES, C.B.

WITH AN INTRODUCTION BY SIR CHARLES HERRIES, K.C.B.

IN TWO VOLUMES—VOL. II.

LONDON
JOHN MURRAY, ALBEMARLE STREET
1880

CONTENTS

OF

THE SECOND VOLUME.

CHAPTER VI.

CHAPTER VII.

CHAPTER VIII.

CHAPTER IX.

MEMOIR OF J. C. HERRIES.

CHAPTER VI.

AFTER the conclusion of the Ministerial peace (or suspension of arms) Mr. Herries went abroad, and returned
to England in October 1827 with partially renovated
health. The notices found among his papers of occurrences previous to the renewal of hostilities in the
Cabinet are scanty and for the most part unimportant.

As to his financial administration, we are not able
to say anything. We gather, however, from a paper
belonging to a later period what was the nature of the
policy which he had in view, and which met with the
concurrence of the First Lord of the Treasury and Mr.
Huskisson :—

'Being convinced that the accumulated wealth of
the nation ought to contribute in a greater proportion
than it had done to the support of the burdens of the
country, consisting in so large a degree as they did of
the charge of accumulated debt,' and that 'the very
great preponderance assigned in our system of taxation

to the duties derived from manufactures and consumption was not only impolitic but unsustainable,' he intended ' to propose a property tax by way of commutation for some of the then existing taxes which were most obstructive to the interests of the country, and consequently most detrimental to it in its growing rivalry with the manufactures of the Continent, and also most obnoxious to public feeling.'

That he continued to enjoy the undiminished confidence of the mercantile and moneyed class may be gathered from the following letter, addressed to him on November 26 by a great commercial notability of that time, Mr. Hart Davis, member for Bristol in several Parliaments :—

' I am in almost daily communication with two or three of the largest holders of English stock, and I observe that the great fear operating in their minds is not so much the political state of the world as the expected Finance Committee, which they fear may be so formed as to recommend measures of finance of a very novel character. . . . The great stockholders above referred to put *all* their trust in you, and I can assure you with truth that they would not at this moment hold any English stock if you were not the Chancellor of the Exchequer.'

The attention of the Cabinet, however, must have been devoted less to financial than to foreign affairs, and especially to that constant vexation of all Cabinets, the Eastern Question. Of the deliberations of the Ministry on this subject not much is known ; but it appears that differences of opinion existed among them, similar to

those which seem to have divided their successors under
the Duke of Wellington as to the mode of carrying out
the treaty of July 6 for the pacification of Greece.
There were some who desired to give that treaty an
extended, and others, a restricted, application.

As an illustration of conflicting views and arguments
the following paper in Mr. Herries's handwriting may
be not devoid of interest.   It is docketed in pencil :—

‘ Mem. of grounds of opposition to a proposal made
by Huskisson to press the operations against Turkey to
the extent of our becoming parties to a plan for invading
her by Russia.—Made between the time when we first
heard of the battle of Navarino and the receipt of further
explanations on the subject.   N.B. Huskisson’s proposal actually made before the news of the battle : ’—

‘ The question is whether we shall now, without
further delay, accede to the proposal of Russia that the
Porte should be distinctly threatened by the allied
Powers with an invasion of Wallachia and Moldavia, if
she does not submit, within a specified period, to the
terms prescribed by the mediating Powers ; and, further,
that if the invasion of the provinces by the Russian
troops shall take place, it shall be with the common
consent of the three Powers, and with an agreement
between them that they shall only be held by Russia for
the object of the Triple Treaty and as a means of enforcing it, and shall be evacuated on the attainment of
that object.   The grounds upon which our acquiescence
in this proposal is recommended, are—

‘ That Russia will be no longer controllable by
us and by France if we refuse to do so, and that the

invasion of Turkey will, in that event, be undertaken by Russia without any restrictions upon her further proceedings ; and much stress is laid upon the expectation that Turkey will submit under the influence of such a measure.

'This argument has obviously more reference to the importance of averting the danger which we apprehend from Russia than to that of securing the object which we seek to obtain for Greece.

' The objections to the proposal are that it leads directly to war in the event of the continued refusal of the Porte to submit; and we must first consider its consequences in that view of the alternative, whatever expectation we may entertain of the effect of intimidation on the Porte.

' We must regard this step as being in effect the first declaration on our part of an intention to enforce by war (commencing by a territorial invasion by Russian troops) the terms with respect to Greece which the Treaty of July was intended to secure.

'In every former stage of the proceedings on this subject, Great Britain has most distinctly and emphatically asserted that the mere refusal of the Porte to accept the mediation of the allied Powers would not by Great Britain be considered as a just cause of war.

'It must, on the other hand, be admitted that the Treaty, where it contemplated the contingency under which we might be called upon to concert ulterior measures for the enforcement of its objects, must have had war in view as one of the measures then to be made the subject of consideration.

'We are, therefore, as yet perfectly free to determine whether a war with Turkey merely for the purpose of enforcing a satisfactory arrangement between that Power and its subjects is a fit course to pursue ; and, then, it is open to us to consider whether, if we do adopt it, the mode of aggression suggested by Russia is the best.

'As it has hitherto been maintained in our diplomatic communications that the refusal of the Porte to accept our mediation should not be considered a ground of war, what are the reasons or circumstances which should now induce us to declare it to be a ground of war ?

'Is the battle of Navarino an event which would justify such a change of principle? Without further information upon the origin of that battle we certainly are unable to solve that question. The battle of Navarino may have sprung out of circumstances affording just ground of complaint, and perhaps even of war, against Turkey ; but it *may* also be quite otherwise, and the blame of it may be on our side. At present, therefore, it should rather operate as a reason for awaiting further intelligence before we take any new decision in this matter, than as affording a ground for such a decision as is proposed to us.

' This view is greatly strengthened when we consider that the battle of Navarino must, in all human probability, have produced at Constantinople some strong decision one way or the other, of which we shall, within a short time, receive information.

' Either the Porte will resent that action violently and do some act which will itself be a just cause of war on our part; or it will be intimidated and submit to the terms prescribed to it.

'The intermediate course of continuing passively sulky and obstinate seems almost impossible.

'In either of the two former cases we shall get out of our present embarrassing position without having committed ourselves to a measure of war upon grounds on which the opinion of the country will, to say the least of it, be much divided. If the Porte submits, we shall have triumphed without having broken through the pacific professions which we have hitherto maintained : if she gives us new ground for war by aggression or insult, we shall enter upon it without any inconsistency with those professions.

' Supposing the Porte to adopt the third course, then we shall still be in the same position as we now are with regard to our ulterior measures.

'If it be contended that Russia will take such offence at our even suspending our decision upon her proposal that we may incur the risk of seeing her break from our alliance and invade Turkey without our concurrence, it must at once be manifest that that supposition implies a conviction of such bad faith on her part, and such uncontrollable ambition to accomplish her ultimate designs upon Turkey, that the project of restraining her by the terms of the alliance must be utterly hopeless. It must be observed, then, that we ourselves shall be acting under the conviction that her fidelity to her engagements can only be depended upon so long as everything is done that can suit her purpose ; for she is unquestionably bound to us in good faith not to take any steps against Turkey for the *pacification of Greece* except in concert with us; whether those steps which are prescribed in the Treaty or such others as the three Powers may agree upon.'

From a passage in the Diary of Mr. Greville (Dec. 13, 1827) it would seem that he had been made acquainted by some member of the Cabinet with the plan propounded by Mr. Huskisson, who, although desirous to bring Russian arms into Turkey, does not appear to have been a very ardent Philhellene ; for, if we are to believe Greville, in a conversation with the latter he spoke ('Diary,' Sept. 15) irreverently of Greece as a 'humbug.' According to Lord Palmerston's 'Journal,'[1] a proposal made by him in December for sending a land force to the Morea 'to sweep the Turks from Greece' did not meet with Huskisson's approval.

It may be supposed that these discussions were not conducive to harmony in a Cabinet composed of discordant elements, the prolonged co-existence of which in the same body was soon found to be impossible. The inevitable dissolution of the Administration was precipitated by circumstances never hitherto clearly explained.

We have mentioned the strong desire of the Whig section of the Cabinet for the introduction of Lord Holland, and the no less strong repugnance of the King (with whom the Prime Minister agreed) to his admission, which, as anyone possessing a grain of political sense must have perceived, would have been inconsistent with the basis of the Government. Such a step

---

[1] *Lord Dalling's Life,* &c., vol. i. p. 288.

would have implied, not only the abandonment, but the reversal, of the Canning programme, to which Lord Goderich and his colleagues professed to adhere. It was morally impossible that Lord Holland should consent to desist from the advocacy of the views—wholly opposed to those of Mr. Canning—which he had constantly and vehemently sustained on many questions of the first importance, and notably on that of Parliamentary reform. Equally certain was it that, unless the Cabinet was to become nothing but a sort of club of individual office-holders, who might or might not occasionally exchange a few casual remarks on the state of public affairs, every question could not be left an open one, like that of Catholic Emancipation. It followed, therefore, of necessity, that the bringing in of Lord Holland involved the adoption by the Cabinet of the principles which he represented, or, in other words, the conversion of a coalition Ministry, pledged against Reform, into a Whig—and an advanced Whig—Ministry, in favour of Reform. And there cannot be a doubt that such was the object in view.

For a while the importunities of the Whig members of the Government ceased, and the matter was allowed temporarily to rest. By-and-by, little by little, a change came over the spirit of the central division of the Cabinet. The so-called Canningites—described by Lord Dalling as neither Whigs nor Tories—began, gradually and insensibly, to drift away from the principles Mr. Canning had always maintained, and towards the principles he had always resisted. Day by day, drawn by the Whig current, they dropped out of their course a little to leeward. But the Chancellor of the Exchequer did not drift. He never drifted. Throughout his whole life he 'kept station,' because throughout his life his 'principles were fixed, his views defined.'

At length the time arrived when it was deemed expedient to give an outward and visible sign of the silent progress of conversion by stamping a decidedly Whig character upon a Cabinet not originally intended to be Whig, and the pressed Premier urged the King to accede to the demand which three months before he had advised his Majesty to reject.[2]

Lord Palmerston (who in his 'Autobiography' strangely omits any allusion to this business), in a letter to his brother of December 18, 1827 (Bulwer's 'Life'), mentions that Lord Goderich, after having unsuccessfully offered a verbal recommendation for the admission of Lords Holland and Wellesley, 'wrote the King a letter again urging the matter,' and stating that 'without such an addition of strength to the Government he felt himself unable to make himself responsible for carrying on the King's service; and unless his advice was adopted he begged leave to retire. To this Lansdowne and Huskisson were parties, and they were prepared to abide by the same alternative. But then Goderich added to this letter a postscript, which nobody saw, and in which he stated that he felt himself, from domestic circumstances affecting the health of one most dear to him, wholly incapable of continuing to perform the duties of his station.'

---

[2] This appears from Mr. Planta's letter to Huskisson of August 21—'To this proposal Lord Goderich has no inclination to accede, and the King has decided objections to it.'

Neither in this letter nor anywhere else does Lord Palmerston say—as he might have said, for it was the fact—that the steps taken by the Prime Minister on December 8 and 11, in concert with some of his colleagues, were kept concealed until the 13th from others who, as was well known, would have protested against them.

So that we get at this : Lord Lansdowne and Mr. Huskisson took part with Lord Goderich in a course of action leading necessarily to the immediate dissolution of the Government in the not improbable event of the King's refusal to comply with demands put forward without the knowledge, and against the wishes, of some of its principal members ; and the Prime Minister then took, on private grounds, a separate course, tending to the same result, without the knowledge of those who thought they were in his particular confidence.

The manner in which the secret action of a portion of the Cabinet became at last known to other members of it, and the resolutions taken in consequence of the tardy discovery, will appear from a record left by Mr. Herries, and from his correspondence, which show that a persistence on the part of Lord Goderich and some of his colleagues to force Lord Holland upon the King (and they could no longer have receded) must have broken up the Government at no distant date. It would have had the effect of driving out the Tory element of the existing mixed Cabinet, which would thus have come to an end. The vacant places could only have been filled up from the ranks of the Whig party, and the result would have been a Whig Administration, such as the King did not wish to have, and Parliament would not have supported. The conclusion is unavoidable, therefore, that, from this cause alone, the days of the Goderich Ministry, at the close of December 1827, were numbered.

But there was another embarrassment which was made the immediate and ostensible cause of its destruction.

It has been clearly pointed out that the appointment of a Finance Committee, announced by Mr. Canning for the session of 1828, was a measure which originated with Mr. Herries. He proposed it to Mr. Canning, as he had already done to Lord Liverpool; and this fact was positively affirmed by him without contradiction in the House of Commons.[3] The Committee was his child, and therefore he was in a peculiar degree interested in its success. That his special connection with the plan, independently of departmental considerations, was recognized, is shown by the circumstance that one of the conditions of the compromise suggested by Mr. Huskisson on August 30 was that Mr. Herries, as President of the Board of Trade, should have the management of this Finance Committee, which, when he was Chancellor of the Exchequer, became a matter belonging to his own particular department. No one having any ordinary sense of propriety can fail to perceive that nothing relating to this business ought to have been done without previous concert with him.

Great, then, was his astonishment, and equally great his displeasure, at learning casually, in the course of

[3] Speech in Ministerial explanations, February 18, 1828.

conversation on other matters, that steps had been taken, without his knowledge, towards the formation of the Committee, Mr. Tierney, who was not called upon to act in any way in the matter, having taken upon himself to select for the chair a prominent member of the Whig party, and induced both Lord Goderich and Mr. Huskisson—the leader in the House of Commons—inadvertently to assent to the choice of Lord Althorp, without previously consulting the Chancellor of the Exchequer. It is not to be supposed that Mr. Huskisson and Lord Goderich had the least intention to give offence to their colleague, although they were undoubtedly too hasty in sanctioning the proposal of Mr. Tierney, with regard to whom we cannot conscientiously express the same opinion. On the contrary, looking at the personal animosity recently displayed by him towards Mr. Herries, on the one hand, and, on the other, at the want of any good reason for his interference in an affair in which he was not directly concerned, we are drawn to the conviction that one of the motives for his action was a desire to give offence, and, by rendering the position of the Chancellor of the Exchequer untenable with credit, to push out of the Cabinet the man whose entrance into it he had strenuously endeavoured to prevent. .

What ensued may best be told in Mr. Herries's own words, preserved in the following

STATEMENT AND CORRESPONDENCE.

' On November 28 Mr. Herries, having occasion to communicate with Mr. Huskisson on some business depending between the Treasury and the Colonial Office, learned, in the course of conversation, from him that Lord Althorp had been thought of as the chairman of the Committee of Finance.

'Mr. Herries expressed thereupon the favourable opinion which he entertained of Lord Althorp, and observed that, so far as his own personal feelings were concerned, such an appointment would by no means be unsatisfactory to him. But the proposition came upon him by surprise; and he did not understand, when the subject was first mentioned, that it had been formally considered, entertained, and acted upon.

'Mr. Tierney came in just at this time, apparently for the express purpose of communicating with Mr. Huskisson on the subject of the Committee of Finance. Some remarks which fell from him conveyed the impression of something like a final agreement with Lord Althorp, after a negotiation with Lord Spencer on the subject. But they were not addressed to Mr. Herries; they passed between Mr. Tierney and Mr. Huskisson.

'Some discussion then took place concerning the subjects which it might be proper to refer to the attention of the Committee of Finance; this was terminated by the entrance of Mr. S. Bourne.

'Mr. Herries's first reflection upon what had transpired in this interview, after he returned home, satisfied him that the step which had been taken was highly inexpedient, and that the manner in which it had been adopted, without communication with him, was not only irregular, but very derogatory to the character of the office which he held.

' He determined accordingly to communicate immediately with the head of the Government upon the subject.

' He could not see Lord Goderich before the following morning. To him Mr. Herries stated what he had learned, and at the same time the grounds of his objection and complaint against it.

' He was then, however, told by Lord Goderich that his lordship also was aware of the proceedings with respect to Lord Althorp; and Lord Goderich informed him that when, on a late occasion, he had enquired of Mr. Huskisson whether Mr. Herries had been consulted in the matter, and was informed that he had not, he (Lord Goderich) had expressed the greatest regret and surprise. But it appears that no communication of the proceedings was even then immediately made to Mr. Herries.

' On the same day Mr. Herries wrote to Mr. Huskisson on the subject; but before the letter was despatched he received a request that he would call on Mr. Huskisson. This message was the consequence of what Mr. Herries had said to Lord Goderich.

' In the interview which followed Mr. Herries stated his objections to the measure adopted, and to the manner in which it had been executed.

' When he returned he despatched the letter already written, with a note, stating that, notwithstanding the verbal conference, it appeared right to him to send as a written protest the letter which he had stated, in the conference, that he had previously prepared.

' This letter was answered by a short note from Mr.

Huskisson, stating that Mr. Herries had some right to complain of Lord Goderich and himself, but adding that he still thought, for certain reasons, that it would be advisable to have Lord Althorp in the chair of the Committee. This note was accompanied by the copy of a letter from Mr. Huskisson to Mr. Tierney, suggesting the propriety of entire forbearance from any further steps on the subject of the Committee.

'*Mr. Herries to Mr. Huskisson.*

' " (Private and confidential.)

' " Downing Street: November 29, 1827.

' " My dear Huskisson,—I send you the letter which, as I told you, I had written, though not closed, when you sent to let me know that you were alone. It is right that you should have my written protest against the course which has been pursued. I am quite sure that you cannot think differently from me upon the subject of the ground of complaint which I have against it.   Truly yours,

' " J. C. HERRIES."

' " My dear Huskisson,—When you mentioned to me yesterday what were your views with respect to Lord Althorp as chairman of the Finance Committee, I was not aware of the length to which the negotiation with him had proceeded, nor did I know until this day that it had been some time in progress.

' " When Mr. Tierney came in and referred to the communications which he had had with Lord Spencer as well as with Lord Althorp, I was indeed made aware of the fact that the business was understood to be actually settled.

' " I did not, however, think it a fit opportunity for making any other remark than what I then said (and with great sincerity) as to my personal respect for Lord Althorp.

' " But I felt at once (and reflection has since made me feel much more strongly) that the commencement, progress, and termination of this arrangement without the slightest communication with me must place me in a very awkward position.

' " A further reflection has also tended to satisfy me that, in the present state of parties and the present situation of our Government, the choice is not a happy one. The alarm and distaste of those who are opposed to Finance Committees as instruments of too extensive and dangerous reforms will not be diminished by the appointment of Lord Althorp, who is regarded as the most prominent member of the most reforming party in the House.

' " It appears also that the steps which have been taken are not confined to the chair of the Committee. Other persons have been communicated with, and, as I understand, have received promises of being nominated as members of it in the same manner, without any intimation of these proceedings to me.

' " I have been speaking to Lord Goderich this day on the subject. I think he entirely concurs in my view of the matter, and entertains the same feelings as myself upon it, so far at least as relates to the irregularity of the course which has been pursued. What can now be done to set matters right again I do not know, but I will call on you and talk the matter over as soon as I can find an opportunity of seeing you. Truly yours,

'" J. C. HERRIES.

'"Downing Street: November 29, 1827."

' *Mr. Huskisson to Mr. Herries.*

'" (Private.)

'"S. P.: November 30, 1827,
8 A.M.

'" My dear Herries,—I wrote to Tierney before I left the office last night—indeed, before I received your letter.

'" I enclose to you a copy of what I said to him.

'" I retain my opinion that upon a balance of inconveniences and advantages Althorp will be safer in the chair than a leading personage in the Committee, kept at a jealous distance by the friends of Government.

'" But this was no reason for communicating with him at present.

'" In respect to yourself I must admit that both Goderich and I must take some blame to ourselves for not having sooner informed you of what Tierney had mentioned to Goderich on the subject; but I am sure you will acquit both of us of anything intentional in this delay.   Yours very truly,

'" W. HUSKISSON.

'" I am going to Claremont in the expectation that we shall have no message till *Sunday*."

' Mr. Huskisson to Mr. Tierney.

' " (Private and confidential.)

' " Downing Street : November 20, 1827.

' " Dear Tierney,—There might arise so much serious embarrassment from its becoming known that particular names had been pointed out as members of the Finance Committee, as well in respect to the manner in which their claims and pretensions would be canvassed prematurely out of doors (as we say) as to the sort of applications which it would bring upon me and other members of the Government, that I am sure you will excuse my suggesting to you not to hold out expectations to any of the individuals who were thought of or mentioned yesterday as persons to be put upon the Committee. Indeed, it will, I am sure, be the safest course, where so many jealous and conflicting feelings may be excited in the different parties into which the House is split, for the members of the Cabinet to abstain from all discussion upon this matter, except strictly among themselves.

' " Upon reflection I incline to think this, at least for the present, would have been the most prudent line even in respect to Althorp; but I am sure it is very desirable, in respect to others, that no further step in advance should be made in this business till we come nearer to the time of meeting Parliament, and have had an opportunity of talking it over more fully among ourselves. Yours very faithfully,

' " W. Huskisson."

'Here the matter rested. Mr. Herries remained in expectation for some days of receiving a communication concerning the course which it might be proposed to pursue, or the measures to be adopted for undoing those which had been taken. But there were other matters of extreme and urgent importance then occupying the attention of the Cabinet; and the arrangement of the Finance Committee was obviously one which might be postponed for some time. He felt confident at least that no further step would now be taken without consultation with him.

'It was within about a week of this time that Mr. Herries received intimations of some projected changes of great importance in the Government; they were vague as to the purport of the proceedings going on, although not doubtful as to the fact of some measures being actually on foot. In this state of anxiety and surmise he remained in daily expectation of receiving some intimation from the head of the Government of the nature of those proceedings, but nothing was made known to him on the subject until after Lord Goderich's resignation had taken place. He then found the apprehensions which he had been led to entertain fully justified. Negotiations of the most pressing nature had been carried on, with the concurrence of a part of the Cabinet, for effecting a material change in its composition, which had ended in the retirement of Lord Goderich.

'His return took place on December 19, and, as it then appeared to Mr. Herries, without any settlement concerning the projected changes, although he soon afterwards discovered that he had formed that conclusion erroneously.

'The proper time appeared, therefore, to be now arrived for calling upon Lord Goderich to come to a decision respecting the Finance Committee.

'Mr. Herries's general views and principles on the subject had been stated to Lord Goderich in the conversations which had passed between them.

'He therefore addressed to him the following letter, which led to the correspondence annexed to it :—

'"Downing Street: December 21, 1827.

'"My dear Goderich,—It is now full time that some further steps should be taken with respect to the Committee of Finance.

'"It would, I believe, naturally be my duty to bring that subject under the consideration of the Cabinet ; but, after what has passed (and I advert to it with much pain), I feel that it is not at present in my hands. I must, therefore, learn from you, as head of the Government, what is the course intended to be pursued for the formation of this Committee and the regulation of its proceedings.

'"What has hitherto been done in this matter has taken place without consultation or communication with me, although it would seem to belong principally to my department of the public business. A negotiation has been carried on, and completed by Mr. Tierney, with your sanction and that of Mr. Huskisson, for the nomination of the chairman of the Committee.

'"The Government is, I presume, fully committed to

the individual fixed upon for the purpose, and to the noble family of which he is a member ; and this proceeding, as I am given to understand, has been adopted with a view, in a great measure, to a political object, and as being calculated to strengthen the hands of the Administration.

' " I doubt much whether that view be correct, and whether the calculation be a just one. But I have an objection to the arrangement upon a much higher ground. I conceive that, in order to derive in the utmost possible degree from this important measure all the public benefit which it is capable of affording, and at the same time to avoid the inconveniences to which it is liable, all political views of the narrower kind—all those which are connected with particular parties and influences only—should be utterly discarded in the formation of the Committee.

' " It appears to me that these objects would be best secured if the Committee were composed of the most eminent individuals of the several parties in the House of Commons, and the chair filled by some person of high character and respectability, either entirely unconnected, or connected as little as possible, with any of the political parties into which the House is divided.

' " Whether this be a proper view of the subject, and whether, if it be so, you could yet proceed upon such a principle, you and Huskisson are best able to judge. I do not feel that I could act in it upon any other. In order, therefore, to relieve you from any difficulty, as connected with my situation, respecting the course which you may deem it expedient to pursue, I beg to assure you that if, by putting my office into other hands, you can more satisfactorily execute this difficult and delicate measure, you may command my most ready and cheerful resignation of it. I place it (and I beg it to be understood as being done in the most friendly manner) entirely at your disposal. Yours, &c.,

' " J. C. HERRIES."

' " Downing Street: December 24, 1827.

' " My dear Herries,—I received your letter of the 21st instant on Saturday evening. I agree with you in thinking that the time is at hand when it will be necessary to consider the question of the Finance Committee in all its bearings, both as to its character and composition and as to the mode in which its duties can best be performed for the public good and with credit to all parties interested. When Huskisson returns to town, which will be in two or three days, this matter must be taken in hand and brought to a final issue.

' " In the meantime I owe it both to you and to myself to explain what you seem greatly to have misunderstood, viz. the degree to which I was a party to anything like a settlement of the question with respect to the chairman of the proposed Committee.

' " I thought, indeed, that I had already explained verbally to you that, as far as I was concerned, nothing had passed but some casual conversation between Mr. Tierney and myself; and I certainly was greatly surprised when I learned that any step whatever had been taken in the business.

' " The facts of the case, as regards myself, are as follow :—Some weeks ago Mr. Tierney, having to call upon me upon some other business, mentioned incidentally that he thought it would be a very good thing if the confidence of the Government were shown to Lord Althorp in respect to the Finance Committee; and upon my stating that I thought he ought to be a *member* of the Committee, Mr. Tierney explained that what he suggested was to place him in the chair. I stated to Mr. Tierney that that was a proposition which ought to be well considered before any decision could be taken, but that personally I had a regard for Lord Althorp, arising out of old friendship and esteem. There the matter ended at the time; and, as we were all occupied with other matters (I think it was in November), I took no further notice of what I considered to be a loose suggestion. A few days after Mr. Tierney spoke to me again in the Cabinet Room, and I then answered that to whatever the members of the Cabinet in the House of Commons might think advisable upon the subject I should not object, not anticipating that anything could be acted upon without such a communication with all of them, and not myself supposing that the matter pressed for an immediate decision.

"'When I afterwards learned that Mr. Huskisson had, in consequence of a communication with Mr. Tierney, acquiesced in the idea, and that some sort of communication had been made to Lord Althorp, the first thing I did was to enquire of Mr. Huskisson whether he had spoken to you, and whether you were a party to the arrangement; and I found, to my great surprise, that you had never heard anything of the proposition and were in no way a party to it.

' "I have thought it right to state these circumstances, because you appear to think that I was aware of the communication (whatever it may have been) which was made to Lord Althorp *before* it was actually made to him.

' " With respect to the latter part of your letter, in which you place your office at my disposal, I can truly say (what I am sure you can easily believe) that I cannot conceive a case in which it would be a *convenience* to me that you should retire ; but at all events I should hope that you will not take any final step upon that subject until we shall have had an opportunity of giving to the whole question the fullest and most unreserved consideration.   Yours, &c.,

' " GODERICH."

' Two personal communications,[4] by desire of Lord Goderich, took place upon this subject between Lord Goderich and Mr. Herries, one on December 29, 1827, and another on January 2, 1828.   Nothing materially bearing on this question took place in these interviews, beyond what is noticed either in the preceding or in the following portion of this correspondence.

' " Downing Street : January 4, 1828.
' " My dear Herries,—Having had much communication with Huskisson on the subject of our recent correspondence respecting the proposed nomination of Lord Althorp to be chairman of the Committee of Finance, I have distinctly ascertained from him, and now think

---

[4] Memoranda of these conversations will be found at the end of this statement.

it right to tell you without reserve, that he feels it to be quite impossible for him to acquiesce in giving up that nomination : it is clear, therefore, that such a decision of the question would at once dissolve the Administration. I cannot but feel that your resignation, on the other hand, would in all probability have the same effect. It becomes, therefore, indispensably necessary, both on public and private grounds of the greatest urgency, that I should distinctly understand from you whether it is your fixed determination to resign the seals of the Exchequer unless Lord Althorp's nomination be abandoned. I would not press you for an answer in so strong a manner were it not for the near approach of the meeting of Parliament, and that infinite embarrassment to the King's service and to the public interests would arise if this matter were not brought to a speedy determination ; and the King would certainly have the right to complain if he were not apprised of the state of things as long before the meeting of Parliament as possible.

' " There certainly has been an unfortunate misunderstanding upon this subject, and I deeply regret upon every account that I was not aware on Wednesday, December 19, when I stated to the Cabinet my readiness to go on, provided they continued to entertain their former sentiments towards me, that this point, respecting the Committee of Finance, was likely so soon to bring the Government, and especially myself, into jeopardy.

' " That, however, cannot now be helped, and I have only to hope that you will let me know your determination, in order that I may regulate my own conduct. Yours, &c.,   ' " GODERICH."

'" Montreal: January 5, 1828.

' " My dear Goderich,—I received your letter of yesterday at this place last night.

' " You inform me that, after much conversation with Huskisson, you have ascertained that he feels it impossible for him to acquiesce in giving up the nomination of Lord Althorp to the chair of the Finance Committee, and that a decision of the question to that effect must at once dissolve the Government.

' " You add that you think my resignation would in all probability have the same consequence.

' " Upon these grounds you desire to know distinctly whether I should resign the Exchequer seals if that nomination were persevered in.

' " In answer to this question allow me once more to refer you to my letter of December 21, and also to request your recollection of what passed between us in the two interviews which I have since had with you upon this subject.

' " In both those interviews I distinctly explained to you that I felt it to be imperative upon me to abide strictly by the terms of my letter, and that I must consequently leave it entirely to you to dispose of me, with reference to the conditions therein stated, in such manner as might appear to you to be the most expedient for the public service and for the interests of your Government.

' " It is scarcely necessary for me to repeat on this occasion the declaration which I have already several times made to you, and which I distinctly made to Huskisson also, that, far from feeling even the shadow of any personal objection to Lord Althorp, I should, on the contrary, have had much satisfaction in transacting business with him as Chairman of the Committee, on account of the esteem and respect in which I hold his character, if his appointment could be made consistent with the public principles upon which it appeared to me to be indispensable that the Committee should be formed, in order to be productive of the utmost possible benefit to the public.

' " As to the soundness of that principle, I have not understood that you differ in the least degree from me ; nor have I heard that it is disputed by anyone else.

' " With respect to the regret which you express on account of your not having been aware, on December 19, when you stated your willingness to go on with the Government, that the ' point now in question was likely to bring the Government, and especially yourself, into jeopardy,' permit me to observe, that if I had been in your confidence with regard to the important steps which you had taken before the 19th, and also as to the arrangements connected with the resolution then announced (but which arrangements were at that time only made known to some and not to all of your colleagues), I should have been better enabled (as I should sincerely have desired) to study your personal convenience with respect to the best time for urging a settlement of the question of the Finance Committee.
Yours, &c.,   ' " J. C. HERRIES."

‘ “ Blackheath : January 5, 1828.

‘ “ My dear Herries,—The more I reflect upon this unfortunate question respecting the Finance Committee, the more I am convinced that the view which you have taken up is founded upon a misconception both of the circumstances themselves, which took place at the end of November, and of the consequences which would result from placing Lord Althorp in the chair of that Committee. I am quite convinced that there was no *intention* whatever of treating you with disrespect, or of exposing you to the embarrassment of not being in your proper place in all that relates to a matter so closely connected with your own department.

‘ “ It is certainly unfortunate that anything whatever was said to Lord Althorp before it was settled that something should be said ; but it by no means follows from that circumstance that the Government ought to be placed in jeopardy, if it can be avoided, especially at a moment so peculiarly inconvenient to the King’s service and the public interests as the present must necessarily be. Now as to the appointment itself, I must say that it appears to me that you greatly over-rate the objections and difficulties.

‘ “ Lord Althorp is a man of perfect honour and integrity, and if he consented, with the approbation of the Government, to take the chair of that Com-mittee, it cannot be supposed that he would do so without giving his fair and honourable confidence to the Government. I do not mean that he would or could compromise his own opinions ; but I am persuaded that neither hostility nor mischief would enter into his views or feelings in discharging his duties. I wish very much that you would well consider this matter before you decide to withdraw from the Government under circumstances which would cause so much embarrassment.

' " If I thought I was counselling anything discreditable to you personally, nothing would induce me to lay this view of the case before you. But we all owe much to the King and to the public good, and although I feel more and more the extent of the sacrifice which office requires, and the pressure, bodily and mental, which it imposes, I feel that we ought, if possible at all events, to meet Parliament to justify our measures, and then leave it to Parliament to take what course they may choose in deciding upon our fate. Yours, &c.,	' " GODERICH."

' " Montreal: January 5, 1828.

' " My dear Goderich,—Before I received your letter, of which I return you a copy (as you desire), I had despatched an answer to yours of yesterday, which reached me last night.   But having no messenger here, I sent it by a conveyance, which may perhaps not be expeditious in the delivery of it.

' " The effect of it was precisely the same as what I have stated to you twice verbally, when we discussed the unpleasant subject of the Finance Committee.

' " I will not reply to what you have now written to me until I have done what you desire—again very carefully considered the matter.

' " Of one thing, however, I wish to assure you, lest a misapprehension should, on that point, remain on your mind. I am not actuated by the least feeling of offence or disgust in the determination which I adopt. I was unquestionably hurt, and very much so, when I first learned what had been done, on account of the slight which appeared to have been put upon me in my *official character*. But I have too much friendship for Huskisson to entertain a belief, or to harbour any suspicion, that he would intentionally do me any wrong. I need not say that the same observation would apply to yourself in the strongest manner, independently even of the explanation which you have given me of the small part which you had in the business. In short, my conduct will not be governed by any unpleasant feelings towards any individual in this matter.

' " J. C. HERRIES."

' In consequence of Lord Goderich's request, another interview on this subject took place on January 7. The same arguments and observations as had been urged and answered in the former interviews were repeated, and little more occurred deserving of particular notice, except that Lord Goderich laid stress upon the circumstance that, after all, no positive or definite engagement had been made with Lord Althorp, and that the negotiation could hardly be said to have been carried beyond the ascertaining that Lord Althorp and his friends would be satisfied by the appointment if it were offered. To this Mr. Herries answered by some observations, the substance of which will be found in the following letter, written in consequence of Lord Goderich's particular request to receive an answer in that form to his last letter. It was sent to him very soon after the termination of the interview :—

'"Downing Street: January 7, 1828.

'" My dear Goderich,—I have, as you requested in your last letter (and as I promised in my answer that I would), carefully reconsidered the subject of my letter of December 21.

'" I regret to be compelled to state that the reconsideration so bestowed upon it has not conduced to any alteration of the judgment which I had previously formed and communicated to you.

'" The question at issue, and upon which *your* judgment—not *mine*—is to be formed, is obviously not the mere nomination of Lord Althorp. That nomination cannot be treated as an insulated point, disconnected from the circumstances under which it was determined upon and the manner in which it was settled ; nor (which is of much more importance) can it be fairly considered without reference to the principles by which I have stated that I think every step, in the formation of the Committee of Finance, ought to be guided.

'" In your last communication to me you gave me to understand that I had been mistaken in supposing that a conclusive engagement with Lord Althorp had been made. It appears, from your view of the matter, that little more had been done than to ascertain that Lord Althorp would undertake the office. If such be the case, I cannot but observe that it renders the

positive determination of Huskisson to adhere peremp-
torily to that choice, and even to refuse all discussion
of the reasons upon which I think a different course
ought to be pursued, not only more unintelligible
to me, but more difficult for me to acquiesce in. I
should have thought that it might upon such grounds
have still been an open question.

'"Let me take this opportunity of renewing the
assurance which I have already given you that your
determination, as the result of your judgment in the
matter, to advise the King to confide to other hands
the seals which I now hold, will not have the slightest
tendency to diminish the friendship which I feel both
for you and for Huskisson, nor to abate the sincere
wishes which I entertain for the future success of your
Administration.

'" I feel that where parties of such unequal weights
are placed by an unfortunate concurrence of circumstances in two opposite scales, there ought not to be a
moment's hesitation (with reference to the interests of
the Government) in so disposing of me as to retain the
invaluable services of our common friend. Yours, &c.,

'"J. C. HERRIES."

'*Memorandum of a Conversation with Lord Goderich
between 11 and 12 o'clock on December* 29, 1827.

' Lord Goderich began by stating the embarrassment
in which he was placed by the letter which he had
received from me on the subject of the Committee of
Finance. He appeared to be in doubt as to the sense in

which he should understand it, and expressed a wish
to know from me whether he was to conclude that I
had determined upon resigning my situation in consequence of what had been done.   In putting the question in this mode he referred to his explanation by
letter of the part which he had himself taken in the
affair, and which he conceived I had materially misunderstood.

'It appeared to me sufficiently clear that his object
was to draw from me the declaration that my resignation was to be considered rather as final than contingent,
and tendered on account of what had already been done,
without opening for any other course that might now
be adopted.

'I met this mode of treating the subject by recalling
to his attention the terms of my letter, and by pointing
out to him that it was in his power upon that letter to
dispose of me as he might judge best for the interests of
the public and those of his own Government.   It was
for him to judge whether I could usefully for both
objects continue in my situation, and that the question
must be decided materially with reference to what he
himself might think it right to do with respect to the
engagement with Lord Althorp.

'I insisted strongly upon the public and personal
objections to the measure which I had before stated, and
I availed myself of his declaration that the matter had
been conducted and concluded without his own knowledge to impress upon him that he was therefore the
more clearly at liberty to decide upon it now in such
manner as for the public interest might seem the best.

'From the manner in which the conversation was conducted on his part it was very obvious to me that he was above all things anxious to avoid this difficulty (personal to himself) by drawing from me some definitive and unqualified expression of a determination to resign. But I resisted carefully—but with the fullest and most candid explanation, and, as I think, the fairest and most honest statement of the real case—all these endeavours. I made him clearly understand that my resignation, so far as he might leave it to my own choice (confessing that he was clearly empowered by me to leave me no choice in the matter), must be contingent only upon his perseverance in the measure into which he had been drawn by others. But I left him no reason to suppose that if that course were persevered in my determination would be susceptible of change. He appeared himself to be unable to imagine that I could, consistently with my own character, with what was due to my office, and what was due to the public interests in the view which I took of them (and the correctness of which, be it observed, he never once attempted to dispute), continue to hold the office which I fill.

'The conversation was continued by many lamentations on his part, and expressions of the embarrassment and difficulty in which he was placed—being repetitions only of what he had said to me on many previous occasions.

'In the course of these I took the opportunity of desiring to know whether I had distinctly understood him on the subject of the prospective change in the Government. He then repeated to me that the King had assented to the introduction of Lord Holland " at Easter," he first said, and then, correcting himself, " before Easter." I asked him if Lord Wellesley was likewise to be introduced. He said, hesitatingly, " Yes, he thought so ;" but he added that he had been very ill-used about Lord Wellesley ; that Lord W. had been forced upon him on several occasions, and rather strangely on this occasion ; and that it was not an act of his own choice. All this was uttered in an uncertain and hesitating and confused manner, as if more the expression of his own ruminations than intended as a distinct communication to me. I took the opportunity, however, of telling him on my part, very distinctly, that I feared that these measures were all pressed upon him by persons out of the Cabinet in communication with a part of ourselves, and that I was afraid he would in the end experience all the evils and misfortunes which had attended all other parties or persons who had been governed by the suggestions of Mr. Brougham.'

' *Memorandum of a Conversation with Lord Goderich this Morning.*

' January 2, 1828.

' He sent to me about eleven o'clock to request I would call upon him. I did so very soon afterwards.

' After some remarks upon indifferent topics he said he had desired to see me again on the subject of the letter which I had written to him concerning the Committee of Finance.

' He reverted to the difficulties of his situation, and repeated his lamentation on the hardship of being placed in it, against his own choice and inclination, to serve the purposes of others.

'I allowed him, without contradiction or interruption, to pursue the strain of these lamentations.

'He then came to the particular difficulty which my letter created, and asked me in the same terms as he had done in the last conversation on the same subject, "What was he to do ? How was he to understand it ? How was he to act upon it ? I must be sensible," he said, "that it was absolutely necessary for him to come to some decision in a matter which might concern the existence of the Government."

'He pressed me, in short, precisely in the same tone and manner as on December 29 last, to declare categorically whether I was determined to resign my office or not.

'I treated the question in the same way as on the former occasion. I desired him to look well at my letter, which had nothing ambiguous or obscure in it, and to act upon it as he might judge best for the public service and most consistent with his duty to the King and his Government. I observed to him that he had said nothing to induce me to alter the opinions expressed in my letter, either by explaining the conduct of the persons mentioned in it (except so far as concerned the extent of the sanction which he had given to their proceedings) or by controverting the principles which I had laid down in it ; and I could therefore only reiterate my adherence to what I had therein declared to be my conviction and determination.

'He then said that the other parties remained equally

convinced that the course adopted by them was right, and that they were determined not to yield, so that probably they might resign if it were determined to make any change in it.

' I observed that in that case we were fairly at issue, and it must be for him to decide as he thought best and to act upon my letter accordingly.

' In the course of the conversation he stated that he thought I was mistaken as to the extent to which the parties in question were pledged by their proceedings. It appeared to him that, after all, they had only sounded Lord Althorp, and that they could not be understood as having so completed the arrangement with him as to be positively bound by it.

' I immediately availed myself of that declaration to point out to him that, in that case, his decision would be perhaps less difficult, and certainly less embarrassing. It appeared that he could set aside the nomination of Lord Althorp without much inconvenience.

' He then, however, denied that he could do so, observing only that there were cases in which an understanding between parties could not be set aside without giving as much offence as by the violation of a more formal engagement.

' I was, therefore, left to conclude that, whether as an understanding or as a compact, the arrangement was deemed by Huskisson and Tierney irrevocable.

' Our discussion (if such it can be called) continued some time, with many words on his part and very few on mine, but made no progress towards an agreement. I steadfastly refused to make any declaration beyond that which the letter contained, or to adopt any step by which the matter would be taken out of his hands.

'He hinted that he supposed, if I resigned, some of the minor adherents of the Government would follow me. I took no notice of the hint.

'The conversation at one time diverged from the point immediately in question to other topics connected with the state of the Government. I observed to him among other things that the change proposed to be made by introducing Lord Holland appeared to me most unwise at this particular moment, independently of the objections that might be urged against it upon more general grounds, because I was convinced that, in the present temper of the country, and as the Parliament was now composed, there would be at least five votes alienated by that junction for every vote conciliated by it. He made no answer to that remark.

'He said he had communicated my letter to Huskisson, but not to Tierney. I told him he was of course quite at liberty to communicate it to both of them, or to anybody else.

'He had said in a former communication that Huskisson denied the correctness of some part of the letter, but did not say of what part. He made no remark of that kind on this occasion.

'He complained of the "Times" newspaper, to which I adverted as having announced the determination that some of us (I supposed myself, of course, among the number), who were not liberal and enlightened enough, should be turned out as soon as Don Miguel's departure should have left the King more at leisure. He said significantly "there was something about the ' Times ' which required explanation ; he should not allow that system to go on."

'I did not leave him without strongly impressing upon him that he owed it to me and to my office well to consider the situation in which he allowed me to be placed. Whatever there was difficult and unpleasant in the dilemma which my letter occasioned to him, he must admit that it was not created by any act of mine, and that I could take no other course than that which I had adopted. He admitted fully that I was justified in what I had done, and that I could hardly have acted otherwise. In short, he objected in no respect, either on this occasion or in the former conversation, to my conduct in the business.'

Mr. Huskisson, thinking, or persuaded by others, that he was too far pledged to be able creditably to draw back from the sort of engagement he had unwarily allowed himself to be led into by Mr. Tierney, refused to give way, and declared it to be his intention to withdraw from the Government. But, as appears from the explanations given by him in the House of Commons, he was induced by the solicitations of Lord Lansdowne and others to suspend the actual transmission of his resignation, and to ask Lord Goderich instead ' whether the proffered resignation of the Chancellor of the Exchequer might not be accepted.'

It is also evident, from the memoranda of conversations between Mr. Herries and the Prime Minister, and from their correspondence on this subject, that attempts were made to draw an absolute and final resignation from the Chancellor of the Exchequer, who was left for several days in total ignorance of Mr. Huskisson's[5] announced determination to retire.

But he persisted in adhering to the line he had taken, and in leaving the question whether he was or was not to remain in office to be decided upon by the head of the Government.

While the perplexed Prime Minister was lamenting over the difficulties that beset him, a new cause of strife was suddenly introduced into the distracted Cabinet.

Letters from Lord Bexley mention a proposal made by Sir James Scarlett, then Attorney-General, one of the Whigs who had joined Mr. Canning, that a measure should be brought forward for the repeal of the Foreign Enlistment Act of 1819. It is not conceivable that a question of such political importance could have been raised at such a moment except in concert with some members of the Cabinet, who must have looked forward to one of two results—either the adoption of the proposal by the majority of their colleagues, followed by the certain secession of the dissentients, or its decided rejection, followed by their own retirement. If, now, the line previously taken on this question by the Whig party on the one hand, and by Mr. Canning with the Tories on the other, be considered, the connection between the strange move made by the Whig Attorney-

[5] His declaration that he no longer considered himself as a member of the Government was made on December 29, just before a meeting of the Cabinet at which Mr. Herries was present; but the fact of Mr. Huskisson's resignation was not made known until January 5 to Mr. Herries, who afterwards learned its date for the first time from Mr. Huskisson's speech on February 18.

General and the contemplated change in the composition and system of the Government will become apparent.

The condemnation of the heretical pravity of the Foreign Enlistment Act (destined at a future time to be rendered more stringent by a Liberal Ministry) filled for many years a large space in the Liberal *syllabus* of damnable Tory errors, and was to be accepted as an undoubted Whig dogma under pain of major excommunication.

The degree of detestation in which this Act was held was the measure of the degree of Whig orthodoxy as taught in Holland House. He who was not convinced by the eloquence of Sir James Mackintosh,[6] exhorting the House 'to exclaim with the brave barons of former days, *Nolumus leges Angliæ mutari!* '—not convinced by the arguments of Lord Holland,[7] demonstrating that, as the consequence of the passing of the Bill then under discussion, 'the State' would be 'converted into a prison for the confinement of its subjects'—not convinced by the oratory of ardent champions of freedom, as understood and practised in South American republics, that, because British buccaneering was unimpeded in the reign of Queen Elizabeth, filibustering ought not to be prevented by the Government of King George—was deemed a friend to tyrants, and an enemy to the sacred cause of revolution all over the world.

Lord Holland, who was about to be brought into the Cabinet at the end of 1827, had been the leader of

---

[6] Speech in the House of Commons, June 10, 1819.
[7] Speech in the House of Lords, June 28, 1819.

the opposition to the Foreign Enlistment Bill in 1819 ; and Lord Lansdowne, the person most active in the negotiation for his admission, had warmly supported him in the debate on the occasion above referred to.[8]

Lord Althorp, the unfortunate treaty with whom concerning the Finance Committee caused so much embarrassment, had been the mover of the repeal of the obnoxious Act a few years before, and Mr. Tierney, who set that treaty on foot, had vehemently condemned the Bill at the time of its introduction.

Who can fail to see a clear connection between all these facts, and to draw from them the conclusion that the abrogation of the neutrality legislation[9] so resolutely

[8] Lord Lansdowne's speech in the House of Lords on June 28, 1819, was not in a very high tone. Two of its principal arguments against the Bill were that it would (a) deprive several half-pay officers of the means of profitably employing their activity, and (b) check the development of a rising branch of British industry.

[9] It seems to be generally forgotten that Bills for the repeal of the Foreign Enlistment Act were passed by the first reformed House of Commons in the two successive sessions of 1833 and 1834, but were, fortunately for us all, burked in the House of Lords. Let anyone having the least amount of historical knowledge, of political judgment, and of imagination, considering also what a vast store of latent fanaticism exists in England, ready at any moment to be evoked by any stump orator, and how profound is our insular ignorance of international rights and duties, picture to himself the certain consequences to this country of the efforts, had they been successful, of the Liberal party, in the first instance to defeat, and afterwards to annul, the wholesome, wise, just, and necessary measure propounded and carried by a Tory Government for the fulfilment of our obligations towards other States. There is hardly a nation in the world which would not have suffered, from the cupidity of British adventurers and the frenzy of British partisans, an accumulation of unendurable wrongs calling for vengeance. With regard to the United States particularly, if, through fraudulent evasions of the law, we were exposed to the imminent peril of a conflict ruinous to both countries, what would have happened had there been no law to evade? Instead of one or two semi-piratical cruisers stealthily fitted out, whole fleets would have been openly equipped for hostile operations, and, with regiments on board, levied,

combated by the Whig party, was intended to be a principal part of the new system to be inaugurated by the advent of Lord Holland.

The filibustering policy of that nobleman and his friends never was, and, as we have a right to assume, never would have been, the policy of Mr. Canning, who warmly supported the Foreign Enlistment Act in its origin, and steadily maintained it afterwards, because he thought that the neutrality of England ought to be a real, not a sham, neutrality.   If he had believed that it was the duty of his country to pour out her blood and treasure on behalf of communities whose misgovernment, discord, and convulsions have never ceased to offend civilization ; if he had thought (as, fortunately for present and future British income tax payers, he and his colleagues did not think) that Great Britain was under any obligation to enter upon a tremendous conflict with France, backed by all the great military Powers of Europe, in defence of an impracticable constitution in Spain, he would have counselled open, not covert, hostilities.

Never would he have connived at so mean and so iniquitous a course as State neutrality with private belligerency—unofficial war under the disguise of official peace.

The following selection from correspondence illustrates the Ministerial crisis :—

armed, and trained in England, would have sailed from our ports to engage in a quarrel in which no Englishman had a shadow of right to interfere. The certain result would have been a desperate war, which might have lasted for many years.

Mr. Herries to Lord Bexley.

'Downing Street: December 28, 1827.

'My dear Lord Bexley,—I send, in the same box with this, a letter upon the unpleasant subject of our distractions in the Cabinet.

'Pray read it with a recollection of the difficult circumstances in which I am placed, and let me have the benefit of your calm and excellent judgment when we meet.

'The more I think of the proposal which has been forced upon the King, the more I wonder at the imprudence of urging it at this period, and without any consultation with us.

'I cannot imagine any motive but mere party interest (and that ill understood) for this proceeding.

'What really public object could it promote ? It could not be supposed that Lord Holland could bring any useful addition of knowledge or ability to the Government in the management of our domestic concerns ; and it will hardly be pretended that his principles and opinions as to our foreign policy and Continental affairs, proclaimed and disclosed as they have been in various ways, are of a nature to smooth the difficulties in which our foreign relations are at this time involved. It would not be impossible, I think, to prove the contrary.

'I am sorry to hear that the King is distressed and unwell in consequence of all these things. Mountcharles (who, by-the-bye, went to him to disclose that *he should go out of office if Lord Holland came in*) gives a bad account of him in that respect. I fear he will have no peace till he makes a strong Government, either Whig or Tory. The mixed Cabinet requires a firmer hand and sounder judgment to govern it than he can, I fear, at present command. Most truly yours,

'J. C. HERRIES.'

Mr. Herries to Lord Bexley.

'Downing Street: December 28, 1827.

'My dear Lord Bexley,—I have carefully and anxiously reconsidered all that has passed between us on the subject of the proposed change in the Cabinet, which has been consented to, as I understand, reluctantly, and after much objection, by the King, upon a very pressing requisition on the part of Lord Goderich. This requisition was made without any previous communication with us, and it appears that there existed no intention of even communicating to us at present the prospective arrangement adopted as the result of it. Had it not been for a surmise on your part by which you were induced to require a categorical explanation from Lord Goderich, we, and others of our colleagues, would, I apprehend, at this moment have been unapprised of it, although it was well known to another portion of the Cabinet. Having, however, already expressed my opinion upon the subject of these partial confidences in the Cabinet, I shall at present say nothing more on that topic, but submit to you what occurs to me upon the proposition itself.

'In order to judge of the effect which may be pro-

duced upon the existing constitution of the Government
by the introduction into the Cabinet of a leading and
most influential member of the extreme Whig party,
it is necessary to advert to the principles upon which
that Government has been formed, as well as to the
manner in which it is at present composed.

'The present Cabinet consists in part of persons
avowedly attached to the political principles which
have prevailed in the Government of this country
during the last forty years (with the exception of a
very short interval), and in part of individuals
previously accustomed to act in systematic opposition
to those principles and to that Government upon all
the most important questions of domestic and foreign
policy.

'Of these individuals, however, it must be added
that they were distinguished from the majority of the
party with which they habitually acted by the greater
moderation of their principles and proceedings, and by
a greater approximation on many topics of public
policy to the opinions held by the persons who exercised the power of Government.

'The union of these moderate Whigs with the Tories
was first accomplished by Mr. Canning, and in forming
a Government embracing these varieties of political
persuasion it was distinctly laid down by him that the
ruling character of the Government should be the
same as that of Lord Liverpool. The members of the
opposite party who joined Mr. Canning accepted office
under that express explanation and condition. The
Government thus constituted was therefore essentially

Tory, although composed of persons who had not all of them theretofore been classed under that political distinction.

' The death of Mr. Canning changed nothing in the principle on which the Government was constituted. That principle was, on the contrary, confirmed and enforced by the declaration of the King to his Ministers when he appointed Lord Goderich to the office of First Lord of the Treasury.

' The principle so laid down and so confirmed is in point of fact no other than the principle of Mr. Pitt's Government, transmitted through his several successors (with the exception of Mr. Fox's short Administration in 1806) to Lord Liverpool, Mr. Canning, and Lord Goderich. It is in that character that it challenges the confidence and support of the country, and if that character be abandoned, its Pittite or Tory adherents, both in and out of office, are not only absolved from their engagements towards it, but their reputation for consistency and uprightness in their public conduct is perhaps materially implicated by the support which they may continue to give to it.

' Public character in this country is the creation of public opinion only: it makes the general estimation, for worth and ability, in which the men who take part conspicuously in the management of public affairs are held, and determines usually the place in the service of the State which they may aspire to occupy. There is no point upon which the public opinion is more severely exercised than on that which concerns the consistency between the professed opinions and the real conduct of public men. Upon this subject the public are greatly and justly jealous. Changes of political principles and of party connections are scarcely tolerated even where they are accompanied by declared conviction and distinct recantation; but where there is anything like a mysterious compromise for the sake of the advantages of office, the conclusion is fatal. The compromise is designated a political juggle, and the actors in it are considered with less respect than even avowed apostates. For my own part, I acquiesce in this mode of judgment, because I think the principle a just one and the severity of its application useful to the public service.

'Now, I apprehend that the Tory members of the present Government will be in great danger of incurring the penalties of that judgment if they do not take measures to avert, or rather to avoid, it upon the introduction of Lord Holland into the Cabinet.

'The principle of the Government being such as I have stated, it is obvious that any person of the same political opinion as Lord Liverpool might be added to it without inconsistency or compromise, but that it would be impossible without the one or the other to bring into it an individual of diametrically opposite opinions, and more especially if he should be a person of great eminence, whose opinions, frequently and vehemently asserted, are universally known to be entertained in an extreme degree.

' Such is the case with respect to Lord Holland, who, through a long, active, and conspicuous political career, has espoused the principles and doctrines of the Whig party in the utmost length to which they have ever been carried; and who, even so late as the month of May last, took an opportunity of solemnly declaring that on whatever side of the House he might sit he would never fail to *vote for Parliamentary reform*, nor refuse to *move*, whenever called upon to do so, the *repeal of the Test and Corporation Acts.*

'The consequence of the accession, at this time, to the King's Councils of a person thus pledged to these political opinions must, I think, upon the grounds which I have stated, be destructive either of the principles of "*Lord Liverpool's Government*" or of all public confidence in the political professions of the individual himself. The one or the other must be renounced. Coincide they never can. I will not for a moment suppose that Lord Holland will abnegate the principles which he has so long maintained, and some of the most prominent of which, as subjects of special difference between him and "Lord Liverpool's Government," he has so recently re-asserted. If the head of the Government is equally steadfast in his adherence to the "principle of Lord Liverpool's Administration," there must arise disunion highly detrimental to the public service; if otherwise, discredit.

'In the country, too, and in Parliament, it would be worse than idle to expect that, after such a junction, the Government should any longer be considered as representing both the great political parties in the State. The accession of Lord Holland would necessarily be the signal for the adhesion of all the Whigs, ultra and moderate, to the Government; and equally so for the entire and hostile separation of the Tories from it, whereby those members of it who are professedly attached to the "*principles of Lord Liverpool's Government*" would be placed in a very unfavourable and false position. They would, in fact, be under the necessity of carrying on a contest in alliance with persons whose principles do not coincide with their own against the political party with which, in principle, they are identified. This state of things would, in my apprehension, be productive alike of public inconvenience in the conduct of our affairs and of personal discredit to the subservient minority in the Cabinet.

'The consequences of these degradations of public men in the public opinion extend much beyond the circle of their own personal interests. They produce a general depreciation of all political character in the eyes of the country. I think I may safely say that the last, or rather the present, coalition in which the Whigs have been subordinate has lowered that party in the public estimation. If the Tories act a similar part and show themselves also disposed to compromise their principles, then all respect for those who are entrusted with the management of public affairs must be greatly diminished.

'These observations and arguments are applicable generally to the members or supporters of "*Lord Liverpool's late Government*," who now form a part of the present Administration. But the position and circumstances of each individual will render them applicable in various degrees, and with various modifications, to his own particular case.

'My position is marked by striking peculiarities

whereby I am certainly placed in a painful dilemma between conflicting obligations. I can most truly affirm, however, that an attachment to the honours and advantages of office (which I do not affect to underrate or to despise) forms no part of that difficulty, and adds no perceptible weight to the embarrassment under which I am compelled to form my decision.

' The manner in which I was placed in the situation which I now hold—so far above my pretensions and so much beyond my wishes—has laid upon me a debt of gratitude to the King and to those who then advised him which must induce me to contribute every effort in my power to the support of the Government of which I was thereby made a member. But, on the other hand, the very circumstances which impose that obligation upon me constitute also a peculiar ground for more than common solicitude on my part to maintain above all suspicion the consistency and independency of my public character. It is in a most especial manner due to the King, who so graciously and firmly insisted upon my appointment, against the endeavours of a party which opposed it on the ground of my political principles, that I should uphold those principles without spot or blemish, and that I should take care to afford no ground for the misconstruction by which it was attempted on that occasion to attribute my appointment to private and personal rather than to public motives. Such a misconstruction would be greatly promoted by any act of apparent subserviency on my part, such as would be indicated by conduct inconsistent with my avowed principles and opinions and by a readiness to hold office upon terms

at variance with those under which I accepted it.
Whenever, therefore, such changes shall take place in
the policy of the Government, or in the composition of
the Administration, as must lead, in the judgment of the
public, *to the abandoning or compromising of the "principles of Lord Liverpool's Administration,"* my sense of
what I owe to the King, to the country, and to my own
honour will leave me no choice but to resign my office.
Believe me, my dear Lord Bexley, ever truly yours,

'J. C. HERRIES.'

On January 5, 1828, Mr. Herries's private secretary,
Mr. Spearman, wrote to him thus, communicating recent
confidential information :—

'—— called soon after you were gone. He had
just seen Brougham, and he came to report the conversation he had had with him. He said that B. was in
high spirits, and was quite satisfied that they were all in
the right course ; that Lord Holland would certainly
come in ; that none of the present men would go out on
that account—that *one* of them might indeed go, but no
more. —— asked him if he thought the Government
could be carried on by the Whigs ; to which Brougham
replied that he did not doubt that the present men,
reinforced as they would be, could carry it on perfectly
well ; to which —— rejoined, " Take my word for it,
Brougham, that *you* have broken up the Government."
Holmes has been here this morning. He saw the Chancellor late last night. The Chancellor was yesterday
again with Lord Goderich. He repeated then to Lord
G. and to Huskisson his determination upon the subject

of the Government—that he was determined immediately to communicate with the King, in order that the
state of the Government might not come upon H.M.
unawares ; and it was then settled that Lord Anglesey
should accompany the Chancellor to the King. In
about an hour, however, he received a letter from Lord
Anglesey, declining to go with him on the ground of
his ill health.

'He apprehends that Lord A. or some other person
is therefore to go alone and without him ; and he thinks
it is still hoped that a patched-up Government will be
attempted, but he expressed his intention of taking care
to prepare H.M. beforehand for the intended visit if
he did not immediately go down himself. He appears,
from Holmes's account, to be now deeply intent on submitting his own views and of breaking with the Whigs;
for Holmes says that he will make known to the King
that he will not serve with them.

'It is said, among other things, that Grant will
remain if it be a patched-up Government, and will
succeed you. . . .'

The 5th of January seems to have been a busy day
with Ministerial correspondents.

We find two letters of that date from Lord Bexley,
who wrote :—

'Dear Herries,—I met the Lord Chancellor at Lord
Dudley's, and he spoke to me two or three times on the
falling state of the Government, which he said was
breaking down from two distinct causes, viz. the Finance Committee and Lord Holland's appointment. . . .

'I did not profess to the Chancellor more than a general knowledge that things were going ill from the causes he mentioned. I called his attention to a box I had seen just before dinner, containing a proposal from Scarlett to repeal the Foreign Enlistment Act and the two Libel Acts of 1819. He agreed with me that nothing could be more foolish, and I have written strongly to Goderich on the subject. I do not think the Chancellor has seen the King, who is in bed with the gout.

'Dudley thanked me for my letter on the Greek question,[1] and said he agreed with me, but that he found both Lieven and De Roth much out of humour at our backwardness. I suspect we shall hear that the Russians *have* passed the Pruth. Under these circum-stances I think your line is clear not to resign, but to let the King (or Goderich, if he will take upon himself to do so) decide between you and your opponents. I believe, however, it will end in a break-up without any distinct cause avowed. Yours sincerely,

'BEXLEY.'

'My dear Herries,—Since I wrote by your mes-senger I have met the Chancellor at Don Miguel's. He told me he had intended to go to the King, to represent the state of the Government to him, but that he would not go alone for fear of misrepresentation, and that Lord Anglesey had declined to go with him. He asked me

---

[1] Mentioned in a previous letter, dated January 1, in which Lord Bexley says, 'I have written Dudley a very *pacific* letter upon the Greek question, and I think we may certainly be of some use in supporting a moderate and prudent line of conduct, to which, indeed, some of the Cabinet, who may not always think like us, seem sufficiently inclined.'

whether Lord Goderich had given any answer to your letter about the Finance Committee. I told him I understood that you had seen him twice, but that he had said nothing distinct, only lamenting the hardship of his own situation. The Chancellor said that was all he did when he was with him. He quite approved of my having written to Lord G. about Scarlett's proposition, upon which I think we are as likely to split as anything, for if it is pressed in Cabinet I shall desire our respective opinions may be laid before the King. I omitted this morning to mention that the Chancellor told me yesterday that Tindal [2] would resign if Lord Holland was appointed. Our conversation this morning was very short, as Mountcharles and Villa Real came in to conduct us to the Prince. . . .'

Mr. Herries to Lord Lyndhurst.

The same date.

' My dear Lord Chancellor,—After what you said to me at our last meeting I would of course take no step without previous communication with you. I then told you of my conversation with Goderich on the same day. I now send you a letter which he has written to me, and the answer which I propose to make to it, if you see no objection to it arising out of the state of our affairs in other respects which I may be ignorant of. It seems to me that the object of Goderich's letter is to draw from me some positive and unconditional declaration, which he may make use of in order to dissolve the

---

[2] Sir Nicholas Tindal, Solicitor-General, afterwards Lord Chief Justice of the Common Pleas.

Government on grounds convenient to him and those who are advising him. In my answer I endeavour to keep firmly upon the condition of the public principle involved in my letter of December 21, and so to compel him to make the decision with respect to me upon that principle alone. . . .'

Lord Lyndhurst to Mr. Herries.

'George Street: Sunday.'[3]

'Your letter to Goderich went last night. I rather think Goderich is acting for [or from] *himself*, and I am pretty confident not by the advice of either Dudley or Huskisson. We shall cut a pretty figure after all that has passed, both publicly and privately, when we meet Parliament, according to the wish of Goderich expressed in his last note,'

Mr. Spearman to Mr. Herries.

'Sunday Morning.

'It appears to me that they are now trying to make it appear distinctly that you would go on with Lord Holland and the Whigs if it were not for the Finance Committee; and if they can get you to give up that point and go on to Parliament, when the Government would assuredly be broken to pieces, they will turn round and say that you never would have refused to serve with Lord Holland on principle, and that you

---

[3] Lord Lyndhurst's letters to Mr. Herries, of which we find several, never bear the date of the month or year. Their handwriting is in general deplorably difficult to read.

only take advantage of the breaking up. They are cunning enough, God knows.'

Lord Bexley to Mr. Herries.

'Foot's Cray Place: January 7, 1828.

'My dear Herries,—I have read your correspondence with Lord Goderich with more regret than surprise. I have for some time been convinced that the Government could not hang together, but it is painful to me to think that its downfall should be occasioned by your act or mine. At the same time I do not think that under the circumstances you could take any other course than you have done. I do not enter into particulars, as I mean to see you to-morrow morning ; and I feel that, with a view to my own conduct, it may be necessary for me to have some conversation both with you and with Lord G. . . .'

On the following day Lord Goderich, in consequence of the intervention of the Lord Chancellor, drew the King's attention to some at least of the Ministerial dissensions ; and the King, who seems to have been then for the first time made aware of the differences between the Chancellor of the Exchequer and the Secretary of State for the Colonies, cut the knot, which the Premier had been unable to untie, by charging the Duke of Wellington with the formation of a new Cabinet.[4]

---

[4] Although it is not our business to correct all the grievous errors with which Mr. Walpole's book abounds, we cannot refrain from protesting against his description, quite unworthy of a serious history of England, of the last interview between Lord Goderich and the King. He sets down as

matter for record a bit of facetiousness current among the wags of the day,
and communicated to Lord Colchester in a letter of gossip from his son.
'His Majesty offered him [Lord Goderich] his pocket-handkerchief.' Mr.
Walpole ought to have known that George IV., whatever may have been
his failings, was, at any rate, not a vulgar buffoon, and that the retiring
Premier, whatever may be thought of his capacity as a statesman, was a
refined gentleman, not to be addressed with insolent personalities.

CHAPTER VII.

Formation of Wellington Cabinet—Herries Master of the Mint—Correspondence—Mysterious incident — Ministerial explanations in Parliament—
Attacks upon Mr. Herries, and successful defence—Subsequent statement
of real causes of breaking up of Goderich Cabinet—Refutation of Lord
Palmerston's posthumous slanders.

MR. HUSKISSON agreed to become a member of the new
Government on condition [1] that Mr. Herries should not
continue to hold the office of Chancellor of the Exchequer, although he did not refuse to be his colleague
in the Cabinet. It was, besides, thought desirable that
there should be nothing to connect the new Ministry
with the questions which had disturbed its predecessor.

For these reasons the Duke of Wellington deemed
it expedient to put into the Exchequer a person who
had not been a member of Lord Goderich's Cabinet—
Mr. Goulburn—offering to Mr. Herries instead of it the
Mint, vacated by Mr. Tierney, who, together with his
purely Whig colleagues, Lords Lansdowne and Carlisle,
was left out of the new Government.

If Mr. Herries had been made aware (which was
not the case) of Mr. Huskisson's stipulation, he would
probably not have accepted the offer made to him by
the Duke of Wellington ; and we incline to the opinion
that he would have done better if he had, even without
such knowledge, refused to take a seat in the new

---

[1] See *Wellington Correspondence.*

Cabinet as the holder of an office having no administrative importance. But it is impossible for us, calmly considering the matter after a lapse of fifty years, correctly to appreciate all the motives which led him to a different decision. Among them must principally be reckoned the persuasions of friends, and a reluctance to show anything that could have been construed into ill-will towards the Tory leaders, to whom he desired to give his political support.

A few letters—all that remain—relating to this subject may be here inserted.

'Lin. Inn Hall: Saturday
(probably January 12).

' (Confidential.)

' My dear Herries,—The arrangements are going on *but slowly.* Should anything occur material to be communicated to you before Monday, I will send by your messenger. I will take care that no misrepresentation shall be made with effect as to the course which you pursued. No such attempt has yet been made, nor is there any prospect of it. Ever yours,   ' L.' [2]

' Sunday, 2 o'clock.

' My dear Herries,—I cannot give you any information upon the subject of the proposed arrangements, because we have agreed to preserve in the progress of them the most absolute secrecy. What I wish to know is whether the state of our Exchequer, Treasury, &c., will admit of the postponement of Parliament for a week. You must feel that this would, under existing

---

[2] Lyndhurst.

circumstances, be very desirable.   Pray send me a full
and a speedy answer.   Ever yours,   ' LYNDHURST.'

' George Street : Monday.

' My dear Herries,—Pray write me a line and let
me know how matters stand ; or if you wish to see me
I shall be here *from* four o'clock.   Ever yours,   ' L.'

' George Street : Tuesday.

' My dear Herries,—I have been with the Duke
to-day to Windsor, and the King has desired me to
make a communication to you.   Can you make it convenient to call here this evening at nine o'clock ?   Ever
truly yours,   ' LYNDHURST.'

On the back of this note there is the following
memorandum in Mr. Herries's handwriting :—

' Tuesday, January 15, 1828.

' I went to him at nine o'clock this night.

' He surprised me much by informing me that very
shortly before I arrived he had received a communication which rendered it impossible for him to tell me
then what he had been commissioned to state to me ;
but he promised to come to me to-morrow.   He did
not fix the time.

' I suppressed the vexation which I felt, and after
talking over some other matters left him.   My reason
for not appearing to resent this versatility and mystery
towards me was that the whole was professed to be
done in the King's name.   I could not, therefore, with
propriety speak my sentiments upon it.   I wrote a note

to Arbuthnot, complaining confidentially, and I sent to request Holmes to call upon me.' [3]

'Apsley House: January 15, 1828.

'My dear Herries,—I am grieved that for one single moment you should have had an atom of annoyance.

'I had known that the Chancellor was to talk to you; but it was for reasons which, when known, could not affect your peace of mind for a single instant. The Duke of Wellington went from Windsor to S. Saye to take leave of Don Miguel, and I fear that before he

[3] How is this mystery to be explained? It may be assumed that the communication, which arrived only just in time to prevent the Lord Chancellor from delivering the King's message, could have come from no one but the Prime Minister. The King would hardly have had time to make it even if he had changed his mind—a most improbable supposition. But the Duke of Wellington having been at Windsor with Lord Lyndhurst, the message must have been given in his presence or with his cognizance, and consequently with his approval. If he had seen any grounds for objecting to it he certainly would have stated them at once. It is to be presumed that the two Ministers returned to London, as they had gone to Windsor, together, and that, in the course of their two or three hours' drive, no reason for delaying the execution of the King's commands being suggested to the Lord Chancellor, none presented itself to the mind of the Duke, whose later injunction can only be attributed to the intervention of a third person. Who this influential counsellor may have been, or what his motives, it would be idle to conjecture. The conclusion, however, is safe that he was a man of more cautious temperament and less straightforward habits than the Duke of Wellington. Perhaps also he was not so well disposed towards the individual principally interested. We do not pretend to know what was the real nature of the message. The mode of its intended transmission, and the fact that it did not reach its destination, sufficiently demonstrate the inanity of the fictions invented by Lord Palmerston and others about secret communications between George IV. and Mr. Herries, to whom the King could easily, if so minded, have caused his wishes—whatever they were— to be conveyed, without risk of impediment, through the private channel of Sir William Knighton. In this business there were, undoubtedly, concealment and intrigue, but not on the part of the King or of his ex-Chancellor of the Exchequer.

comes up to-morrow I could not venture to write to
you respecting the subject about which the Chancellor
had to talk to you.   You may rely upon my friendship
that I would not leave you in suspense for a moment
if there was anything which regarded your honour or
your peace of mind.   I do assure you that in the breast
of no one is there towards you *the most distant suspicion
or distrust.*   On the contrary, everything that I have
heard spoken of you in every quarter has been most
gratifying and satisfactory ; and so you will thoroughly
agree with me when I see you and tell you what the
Chancellor had been desired to say.

'I cannot bear to appear mysterious ; but believe
me as a friend that you will be entirely satisfied when
I explain the whole to you as soon as we meet, and I
will take care to see you the very instant that I am
able.   Ever, dear Herries, most truly yours,

' C. Arbuthnot.'

'I cannot bear to leave you in suspense.   I think
I shall tranquillise you entirely by saying that, it being
understood that the Whigs mean to make a storm in
Parliament about the Finance Committee and Lord
Althorp, it has been thought very necessary that the
new Government should have nothing to do with a
discussion to which it has been a stranger.   You may
see there is nothing to worry you.'

' Wimbledon: Saturday.

' My dear Herries,—I will be in George Street at
four o'clock on Monday, and everything shall be prepared for the fatal ceremony.   I wish I could also get

out of *my* turmoil, but it cannot be. Brougham means, I am told, to *lead* the House of Commons. He says the lead can't be conferred like a *place or dignity*. Ever yours,

'LYNDHURST.'

A premature and surreptitious publication of the list of the new Cabinet in the 'Morning Chronicle' gave rise to an unpleasant incident, to which, as it speedily passed over without any consequences of the slightest importance, we should not have alluded if an undue prominence had not been given to it elsewhere. It chanced that one day Mr. Herries inadvertently left lying on his writing table, when he went for a few minutes into another room, a memorandum of the composition of the new Ministry. During his short absence a visitor was ushered in, who, reading the names and offices in the paper on the table, made a note of them for communication to the 'Chronicle.' This unlucky accident (and that it could have been nothing but mere accident ought to have been manifest, because the 'Chronicle,' which had libelled him outrageously, was obviously the very last journal to which Mr. Herries would have thought of conveying any information) roused the anger of the Duke of Wellington, who displayed his irritation in the hasty and somewhat intemperate tone not unfrequently perceptible in his correspondence. 'I assure you,' he wrote in a letter of January 21, 'that there never was an event comparatively so trifling in itself that will produce such important consequences on the destinies of this country as will the premature disclosure in the newspapers of the names of the new-formed Ministry, notwithstanding the precautions and the pains I took to prevent such disclosure.' If any ordinary mortal had written this sentence it would be treated as an absurd exaggeration ; for certainly the most sensitive politicometer could never have indicated the slightest disturbance of the destinies of this country from the pre-official printing of the names of the new Ministers in an Opposition newspaper.

The unreasonableness of the great Duke's wrath is apparent from the following letter, showing that the list had been sent right and left by the 'whip' of the Tory party some days before it appeared in the 'Chronicle : '—

'Holmes called about five minutes after you were gone. He says there will be a very strong neutral bench.

. . . . . .

'Dawson called on Holmes last night, and not finding him at home, left for him a *confidential* list of the new Administration. It corresponded exactly with that in the "Chronicle." Holmes wrote him an answer expressing his thanks for the *confidential* list, for which, indeed, he said that he was the more obliged because it confirmed the accuracy of the list which *he* had sent on Thursday to Mr. Harrison at Brighton, and which he believed would be found to have been published at Dublin on Saturday last. He did not add to Dawson, however, that he had sent the list to Dublin on Thursday. How particularly absurd, therefore, to make such

a clamour about the publication of what was so generally known. . . . Ever truly, yours,

'A. Y. SPEARMAN.

'Tuesday, January 22, 1828.'

Soon after the meeting of Parliament explanations,
which, however, were not, and perhaps could not have
been, complete, were furnished by the persons principally concerned in the strangely involved transactions
which had preceded the fall of the Goderich Cabinet.
They are to be found in ' Hansard,' and need not therefore be repeated in detail.

Mr. Herries concluded an elaborate statement on
February 18, with a peremptory and unequivocal denial
of accusations made against him, openly out of doors
and covertly in the House of Commons, of having con-
spired with the King, or with the leaders of the Tory
party, or with both together, to upset the Government
to which he had belonged. He declared that he had
never had any communication respecting his resignation
with any individual out of the Cabinet, and that he had
'received no advice from any person whatever before
his letter of December 21 was written.' He added that
he believed that 'in the quarter alluded to not one single
circumstance relative to those transactions was known
till the communication of them was made to the other
House by Lord Goderich,' and ended by saying, ' There
is not a shadow of reason, or the slightest foundation,
for the base statement that has gone abroad.'

His clear explanations produced a very favourable.
impression upon the House. No better evidence of
their effect can be adduced than the following letter

from a gentleman always distinguished for his judgement, tact, and high sense of honour—Mr. Villiers,
afterwards known to the world as the Earl of Clarendon
—who, although not at this time directly engaged in
party politics, had Whig connections and inclinations:—

'I cannot go to bed, my dear Mr. Herries, without
offering you my hearty congratulations upon your
triumph. I have long and eagerly desired that you
should have the opportunity which this night has
afforded of stating the simple truth, because I felt sure
that universal approbation of conduct like yours must
be the immediate consequence.

' You needed not the applause of this night to confirm to yourself the conscious feeling of your own
integrity, but there is no man that must not feel pride
at complete vindication from unjust and malignant
attack, and I believe that you yourself cannot feel more
joy than I do at the result of to-night's debate and at
hearing as I did all round me such marked expressions
of satisfaction. No one that I have heard speak upon
the subject thought you said a word too much about
Lord G. If you erred at all it was certainly not on
that side. Ever yours sincerely,

'GEORGE VILLIERS.' [4]

In the course of his speech, in which he elucidated
all that had taken place concerning the Finance Committee, Mr. Herries said that it was impossible to
suppose that his proffered resignation was of sufficient

---

[4] The writer of this letter, who heard the debate, was not a member of
the House of Commons.

importance to cause the breaking up of the Government;
that, owing to circumstances which had shaken the
Government to its foundation before his letter of December 21 was written, its fall was apparently inevitable;
and that occasion was taken of this letter for doing
that which sooner or later must have happened without
it. He added unguardedly in the heat of the moment—
' I say that I know it was so acted upon '—an expression
which he afterwards qualified by the explanation that
he meant that he drew the positive conclusion from the
circumstances that it must be so. The solid grounds
for this assertion have been already set forth, but it was
met by Lord Goderich with a positive denial in the
House of Lords.

Then burst out all the fury of disappointed faction.
In a succeeding debate in the House of Commons on
the 21st the man who had been guilty of the ' inex-
piable wrong ' of hindering the realization of Whig
aspirations stood at bay against a throng of fierce
assailants, who stormed at him with threats, taunts,
gibes, and insinuations, going to the very verge of personal insult, from which he had to compel more than one
speaker to draw back. Among the foremost of the at-
tacking party was Mr. Thomas Slingsby Duncombe, one
of the most celebrated of the Radical reformers of his
day. His speech on this occasion (February 21), like
his previous discourse on the 18th, which is said to
have ' made a great sensation,' was composed and put
into his mouth, as we learn from Mr. Greville,[5] who

---

[5] Mr. Greville's comments (vol. i. p. 130) on these speeches are instruc-
tive. ' And what are the agents who have produced such an effect? A

seems to have had a hand in its concoction, by the Honourable Henry, afterwards Lord, de Ros.

Called upon to substantiate by proof the declaration which had been contradicted, Mr. Herries refused to enter into any further explanations, and confined himself to the reiterated expression of the conviction he entertained. That conviction was well founded; but its soundness could not have been demonstrated without a revelation of the whole of the secret history of the Cabinet in which Mr. Herries had lately sat along with some of his present colleagues then by his side. He must have told all that he had learnt concerning the series of underhand intrigues (no other description can be given to those proceedings) for the transformation of the Ministry—intrigues in which Mr. Huskisson had taken an active part, and of which Lord Palmerston had at any rate been cognizant; he must have made known to the House the information he had been able to gather as to what had passed between Lord Goderich, some members of the Cabinet, and the King, in December, but not alluded to by Lord Goderich himself in the House of Lords; and, moreover, in order to make all this matter clear, he must have gone back to the period of the formation of Lord Goderich's Cabinet, and spoken of the pressure then put upon the King for the admission of Lord Holland. Obviously he could not make

man of ruined fortune and doubtful character, whose life has been spent on the race-course, at the gaming-table, and in the green-room; of limited capacity, exceedingly ignorant, and without any stock but his impudence to trade on; only speaking to serve an electioneering purpose, and crammed by another man [and what a man!] with every thought and every word that he uttered.'

such revelations. His tongue was tied ; and he found himself in the position in which we suppose many a public man in England is placed, who is obliged to submit to attack without employing in his defence all the weapons he possesses.

His statements, however, which he could not confirm by proof positive, were mainly borne out by declarations, already adverted to by us, which were made by Mr. Huskisson in his speech on February 18, to the effect, that by the advice of some of his colleagues he (Mr. Huskisson) had endeavoured to induce Lord Goderich to act upon Mr. Herries's letter of December 21 by making the contingent offer of resignation contained in it absolute. And this course was suggested, said Mr. Huskisson, as the best means of preventing the dissolution of the Cabinet.[6] The futility, therefore, of the allegation, that the downfall of the Administration was caused by the conditional resignation of the very man whose positive dismissal was deemed necessary for its preservation, becomes at once apparent. Consequently Mr. Herries was warranted in affirming, as he did, that his resignation was not, and could not have been, the true cause of the break-up, for which it was made to serve as a colourable pretext. The following paper in justification of his assertion was afterwards drawn up by him.

---

[6] In the same speech Huskisson said : ‘Before the 26th of December . . . there had occurred many circumstances which tended materially to impair the strength, and shake the stability, of the Administration.’

STATEMENT BY MR. HERRIES OF THE EVENTS WHICH LED TO THE DISSOLUTION OF THE ADMINISTRATION OF LORD GODERICH.

'As it appears to be probable that no further explanations in Parliament will now be given on the subject of the dissolution of the late Government, concerning which Mr. Herries expressed in one House an opinion widely different from that which was pronounced by Lord Goderich in the other, it appears right to Mr. Herries that he should state, for the information of his own friends (but without comment or argument) such of the grounds upon which *his* declaration was founded, as appear to him to be amply sufficient to justify it.

'Lord Goderich has so described the late change in the Administration as to leave a very general, if not an universal, impression on the minds of the public that it was produced entirely by the differences on the subject of the Finance Committee. And he has afforded room, by the manner in which he has noticed these differences, for the imputation of blame, by implication, to Mr. Herries, in respect of the time and mode in which his resignation was proffered.

'Mr. Herries, on the other hand, has declared his entire conviction that his resignation was too slender a matter to be of itself a sufficient cause for the termination of the late Government ; and he has, at the same time, asserted his knowledge of other causes which, in his judgment, produced the event, and under the operation of which the more unimportant incident of the Finance Committee became merely the occasion of it.

'That declaration was grounded upon the following facts :—

'In the early part of last December, Lord Goderich proposed to the King (with the knowledge and concurrence of only a part of his colleagues) the introduction of Lord Holland and Lord Wellesley into the Cabinet, upon the ground of an indispensable necessity for some addition of strength to the Administration.

'The proposal not having been acceded to, it was urged again by a letter on December 11, in which it was intimated that Lord Goderich could not be answerable for carrying on the government if it were not adopted.

'On December 13 these proceedings became known, after a Council held at St. James's, to several of the Ministers who had till then been ignorant of them. The retirement of Lord Goderich was made known at the same time, and was understood to be occasioned by domestic circumstances, which at that time pressed anxiously upon him, and the representation of which had formed part of the letter to his Majesty.

'On the 14th Mr. Herries expressed to Lord Goderich the great pain which the information had given to him. He regretted that a measure affecting so materially the character, and even the existence, of a mixed Administration, such as was then established, should have been adopted without an equal confidence and communication with all its members. He also stated his decided conviction that the junction with Lord Holland would have been fatal to the Government, as then constituted, if the proposition had been acceded to.

'Mr. Herries said enough on that occasion (although he considered the Government as being dissolved) to leave no doubt upon the mind of Lord Goderich that he, Mr. Herries, would not have continued in his situation if the intended coalition with one of the most distinguished opponents of the political principles upon which the then existing Government was founded had been carried into effect.

'An interval followed, during which some steps were taken unsuccessfully for supplying the place of Lord Goderich in the Administration. It was terminated by his return on December 19.

'The members of the Government being assembled on that day were informed by Lord Goderich himself that the difficulties which had occasioned his retirement, and which had in some degree been misunderstood, were removed, and that if his colleagues had no objection to it, he was then ready to resume his station, such being his Majesty's pleasure. Lord Goderich adverted at the same time to the proposition which had been submitted to the King for strengthening the Administration, but the particulars of that proposition were not stated, nor were the names of the parties declared, who were the subjects of it.

'It was on that occasion observed by Mr. Herries that if any change was still in contemplation which might be productive of a difference of opinion among the members of the Government, it would be better that it should be communicated at that time than made known at a later period when any discussion or dismemberment of the Administration, consequent thereupon, might occur under circumstances very inconvenient for the public service, as, for example, in the midst of the active business of a session of Parliament.

'This observation was met by a declaration from Lord Goderich in general terms that he had no intention of altering *the principle* of the Government, whereby Mr. Herries was satisfied, and pressed the subject no further.

'A noble lord [7] then present, who had been unacquainted with the circumstances which had occasioned the recent occurrences, was, as well as Mr. Herries, impressed by this conversation with the belief that no change was then intended in the composition of the Government. But he was induced afterwards to consider that some more explicit information of Lord Goderich's intentions was necessary; and at an interview which he obtained for that purpose two days after the meeting, he was informed that Lord Goderich was positively pledged to bring Lord Holland into the Administration at an early period.

'The noble Lord made this known to Mr. Herries, and stated that he had expressed in strong terms his opinion and feelings on account of the want of confidence shown towards him, and also upon the injurious effects of the late occurrences upon the credit and character of the Government.

'He added that he had declared to Lord Goderich that he reserved his determination as to any steps

---

[7] Lord Bexley.

which he might think it right to take in consequence of the measure to which Lord Goderich was pledged, until the King's domestic engagements at Windsor connected with the reception of Don Miguel, should be terminated.

' Mr. Herries afterwards saw Lord Goderich on the same subject, and obtained the same information from him. He again stated his opinion of the inexpediency of the course about to be pursued, and declared his intention of following the example of his noble colleague in postponing any step thereupon which might break in improperly at that time upon his Majesty's arrangements.

' In the meantime, and before those engagements were concluded, Lord Goderich received other communications of great importance as to the state of his Government ; but of these Mr. Herries was not aware until after the date of his last letter on the subject of the Finance Committee.

' Lord Goderich was informed by one of the most influential of his colleagues,[8] that in his judgment it was essential for the public interests that no time should be lost in representing to the Throne the unfavourable state of the public opinion with respect to the Government, and the apparent want of sufficient support from one branch at least of the Legislature (if not from both) to enable it to meet Parliament with any fair prospect of carrying on the public business with success. He was told that if he, Lord Goderich, did not take that course, his colleague, who was then

[8] Lord Lyndhurst.

advising him, would deem it incumbent upon him to adopt it himself.

'It appears by Mr. Huskisson's statement in reply on February 18, that a similar representation was made to him by two members of the Administration, and that he referred them to Lord Goderich as the proper quarter to which such a communication should be addressed.

'It was in this state of things, and with this crisis impending, that instead of taking to the King the resignation of Mr. Herries, freely and amicably offered, whereby one difficulty, at least, would have been removed from the execution of the proposed change in the Government, Lord Goderich put an end to his administration, on the ground of the differences between his two colleagues.

'In Lord Goderich's account of the event, these difficulties alone are mentioned as the cause of it. No allusion is made to any other.

'Mr. Herries, having in mind the facts and proceedings above stated, asserted that the termination of the Government was produced by the pressure of much more important circumstances, and that the contention about the Finance Committee, which but for the existence of those circumstances would have been easily obviated by the acceptance of his resignation, was, at the utmost, only the occasion of its accomplishment.

'Lord Goderich, by remarking in his statement on the postponement of Mr. Herries's final proceeding respecting the Finance Committee, without noticing at the same time the strange events which had occupied the interval, and whereby the Government itself had been suspended, gave occasion, unintentionally no doubt, to the imputation raised by others that Mr. Herries was influenced in his conduct respecting the Finance Committee by communications from a higher quarter. He has solemnly protested, and he now as solemnly repeats, that there is not the shadow of a foundation for the charge ; and that his determination, as expressed in his letter of December 21, was adopted upon his own judgment and conviction alone, uninfluenced by advice, suggestion, or communication from any quarter whatsoever.'

'Great George Street: March 1, 1828.'

The renewed and unqualified asseveration at the close of the foregoing paper ought to be amply sufficient without corroboration ; and we should abstain from attempting to give it any superfluous support, if 'the base statement' so positively contradicted had not been repeated in Lord Palmerston's 'Autobiography.'[9] The

---

[9] 'Huskisson blamed me for not having stood out ; he said if I had insisted upon the fulfilment of Goderich's promise that promise would not have been retracted, especially as it was spontaneously made, and Herries would not have been thrown like a live shell into the Cabinet to explode and blow us all up.

'At the appointed time he did explode. He picked a quarrel with Huskisson. . . .'—*Autobiography.*

Lord Palmerston does not say when the remarks attributed to Huskisson were made; but from the context it may be inferred that the conversation above related took place soon after Huskisson's return to England and the settlement of the dispute concerning the office of Chancellor of the Exchequer. This supposition, however, is inconsistent with the proved fact that Huskisson showed a very friendly disposition towards Mr. Herries in that matter. It is to be observed, moreover, that Huskisson did not urge the appointment of Lord Palmerston, whose name, indeed, was not once mentioned in the course of the negotiation which followed Huskisson's arrival. If, in spite of

old calumny having thus being revived, we are called upon to refute it.

As a preliminary observation, we have to remark that Lord Palmerston, sitting on the Treasury Bench, heard Mr. Herries, his colleague in the Cabinet, pledge his word of honour, in a tone of singular solemnity, to the truth of his denial; that he continued to be, both in office, and out of office, on very good and amicable (though not very intimate) terms with him; and that during the whole of the rest of Mr. Herries's life he never gave him the least reason to suppose that the personal esteem always professed by Mr. Herries for Lord Palmerston was not reciprocal.

We have here something very startling. Do what we may—turn, twist, shift, re-arrange these facts as we can—they drive us at last into a dilemma from which there is no possible escape. Either Lord Palmerston

logical sequence, we are to assume that Huskisson's tender reproach was addressed to Palmerston at a later period—that is to say, about the time of the break-up of the Goderich Cabinet—we shall be forced also to conclude, against all probability, that from Huskisson's memory every trace of transactions in which he had been actively engaged some four months previously had been entirely effaced. This is strange; still more extraordinary is it that Lord Palmerston likewise should have forgotten all that had happened to himself in August 1827. At that time it was certainly known both to Palmerston and to Huskisson that the reason why the understanding between Goderich and Palmerston could not be carried out was that the King positively put his veto on the proposed arrangement. If, therefore, Goderich's 'promise had not been retracted,' and he had persisted in opposing it to the King's decided refusal, the Prime Minister must necessarily have resigned and destroyed his half-formed Cabinet. It follows, therefore, that Huskisson, if he really used the words alleged, blamed Palmerston for not having prevented the consolidation of the Ministry, the impending dissolution of which he lamented. But so foolish a saying on the part of Huskisson seems impossible. Consequently we are justified in concluding that the words cited were not the words of Huskisson speaking to Palmerston, but those of Palmerston speaking to Bulwer.

contentedly sat in the same Cabinet, and frequently at the same table, with a man whom he believed to have been guilty, not only of the most odious treachery, but of the most revolting perjury, and during the space of more than twenty years met that man on a footing of friendly intercourse without ever manifesting towards him the abhorrence which such conduct must have inspired in the breast of any man of honourable feeling; —or he left recorded for posthumous publication, against a dead man, a monstrous accusation, in the truth of which he did not believe.

Having premised this much, we proceed to show the grounds on which, independently of Mr. Herries's denial, we declare the charge to be false.

1. Not a particle of evidence in support of it was ever put forward.

2. The papers produced and cited by us establish, beyond the possibility of doubt, the fact that during the negotiations between Lord Goderich and the King concerning Lord Holland in the first fortnight of December, Mr. Herries, like other members of the Cabinet not admitted into the Whig sub-Cabinet, was in total ignorance of what was going on ; that, until the 13th, when Lord Goderich's resignation was announced, he knew nothing of the Prime Minister's letter to the King, written under the direction of Lord Lansdowne and Mr. Huskisson; and that he was afterwards made aware of what had been done in this matter subsequently to Lord Goderich's return to power, not through any secret channel of communication with the Palace, but simply by another Cabinet Minister on

December 21, the day on which the letter alleged to
have been written in consequence of secret communications was addressed to Lord Goderich. But from
the King's point of view it was manifestly desirable
that those members of the Cabinet (Mr. Herries being
one of them) who were opposed to Lord Holland's
admission should be perfectly informed of what was
going on, in order that they might be able to help his
Majesty to resist the renewed demand. Nevertheless
they were not informed. And it is absolutely incredible
that if the letter of the 21st concerning the Finance
Committee was prompted by the King, no secret information should have been imparted to Mr. Herries on a
subject infinitely more interesting to the King than
Lord Althorp's nomination.

3. The form in which Mr. Herries's resignation was
offered to Lord Goderich was inconsistent with the
supposition of its having been concerted with the King
for the purpose of destroying the Government, in which
case it would have been, not conditional, but absolute
and immediate.

4. It is quite clear that both the Lord Chancellor
and Lord Bexley, who were in confidential and frequent communication with Mr. Herries, were at the
beginning of January under the impression that the
King was ignorant of the disputes in the Cabinet ; and
such a persistent deception as must have been practised
upon them both, if the Palmerston theory were true, is
wholly inconceivable.

5. In the latter part of December the King was
absorbed in preparations for the reception of Dom

Miguel, and it was well known that he was very unwilling to be disturbed in them by political business. So strongly was this felt, that Lord Bexley, in protesting against the Holland negotiation, told Lord Goderich that he reserved his determination as to any steps which he might think it right to take until the King's domestic engagements at Windsor should be terminated; and Mr. Herries also declared that he would postpone any further action which might break in improperly at that time upon His Majesty's arrangements. It is impossible that at that very moment he should, in concert with the King, have done anything calculated to produce an explosion which would most effectually have interfered with those arrangements.

6. On January 10, two days after the final dissolution of the Goderich Cabinet, Mr. Herries addressed to Sir William Knighton the following confidential letter :—

'Downing Street: January 10, 1828.

'My dear Sir William,—It is right that you should be in possession of the accompanying paper. It contains the whole story honestly told (and told by documents) of the subject on which the Whigs and I have been divided.

'The time must come, I presume, when it will be my duty to render an account to the King of my conduct in this affair. I will wait with patience for it, and not add to the troubles imposed upon his Majesty by any undutiful importunity on my part. Most truly yours,

'J. C. HERRIES.'

This authentic document is conclusive. No person of ordinary intelligence can read it, and still entertain the least doubt of the perfect truth of the writer's declaration in the House of Commons. It proves indisputably that, until some time after the Goderich Ministry had ceased to exist, the King received no information from Mr. Herries, either directly or indirectly, concerning the differences between him and his colleagues, and therefore entirely excludes any supposition of concerted action.

7. With regard to imaginary communications with the Tory leaders, the following letter, intended to be sent to the Duke of Wellington, is not less decisive.

'Downing Street: January 1828.

'My dear Lord Duke,—I transmit to you herewith a copy of my correspondence with Lord Goderich on a subject on which you have perhaps heard much from others. It is accompanied by a few observations necessary for the clear understanding of the circumstances which are referred to in it.

'I trust that your Grace will appreciate the motives which have induced me to maintain up to this time the strictest silence on this matter towards your Grace, although I could not but feel an earnest desire that no erroneous impression should be made upon your mind by the manner in which the subject of this correspondence has been treated in the public papers.

'I have judged it to be the most fair, the most -

---

[1] There is a rough draft as well as a fair copy signed and ready for transmission, which, however, apparently did not take place.

honourable, and the most delicate course towards all the parties who have been concerned in the transaction, to maintain the most scrupulous reserve upon it while the formation of a new Government was depending, and above all, to have no communication, direct or indirect, relating to it, either with your Grace or with any of the persons with whom or under whom I have heretofore had the satisfaction of acting in any political capacity.

'The time being now, however, come when that reserve is no longer required, nor proper, I transmit the correspondence to your Grace, with a strong conviction that you will find in it nothing to diminish that good opinion which your Grace has on so many occasions evinced in the most flattering manner of—Your most faithful, &c., &c.,   'J. C. HERRIES.'

Here we might close the case; but in order to leave nothing unsaid we will add this. Let us suppose that no declarations were made in the House of Commons, and that the testimony of no documents could be cited. We would still contend that the charge made in one form or another fifty years ago, and latterly brought forward again by Lord Dalling in Lord Palmerston's name, ought to be rejected by every impartial judge on account of its own inherent improbability, and of the enormous absurdities to which its admission must necessarily lead.

No free man becomes a traitor and exposes himself to ignominy and detestation, when he has nothing to gain, but much to lose, by his treachery.

An Eastern slave alone will commit acts of base turpitude, at great risk to himself, merely in obedience to the behest of a king. A silent clock may be carefully adjusted and regulated for the destruction of a vessel in mid-ocean; but no eloquence will persuade one of the chief officers of the ship to stow it away in his cabin—a course closely analogous to that which, according to Lord Palmerston, Mr. Herries was induced to take by George IV. If the King had urged the Chancellor of the Exchequer to blow up the Cabinet, that Minister (had he been capable of entertaining the proposal) would have replied, ' But I shall blow myself up along with my colleagues; and before doing so, I must be quite sure that I shall fall on my feet without being hurt by the explosion. Your Majesty must give me, if no more, at least assurance of safety.' It is morally impossible that such an agreement as that alleged could have been come to without a positive pledge on the part of the King that in any change Mr. Herries should be maintained in his then position, or should obtain an equivalent for it. But it is patent that no such bargain was struck, and that he received no assurance. For it is certain that, personally, he was in every respect a loser by the breaking up of the Goderich Administration—a loser in point of station, of consequence, of the means of acquiring increased reputation, and of emolument.

On the other hand, the King's motives, on the Palmerston hypothesis, are wholly unintelligible. As we have already observed there was nothing to prevent him from calling in the Duke of Wellington on the death of Mr. Canning. He need not have postponed for six months the construction of a Tory Government, interposing another Ministry only to have the trouble of getting rid of it by subtle contrivances. The Goderich Cabinet was a constant source of vexation and apprehension to him. Its internal dissensions, together with the harassing dictation and pretentious importunities to which he was almost incessantly subjected by some of its members, left him no peace and quiet. During the first, and during the last, months of its brief existence, he was always in hot water. He seems to have been obliged even to make a struggle for a tranquil Christmas dinner.[2] And we are expected to believe that, without the slightest necessity, he imposed upon himself this burden which made his life wretched, while, at the same time, he devised a cunning scheme for its removal after a period of extreme torment. We are gravely told that, in the process of its formation, the King took care to put a 'live shell' into the Cabinet, in order that, at a moment singularly inconvenient to himself, an explosion might destroy the Government, and enable his Majesty to do in January that which he could easily have done in August, with a saving of a world of annoyance. This is not all. A higher pinnacle of nonsense has yet to be reached.

The explosion of the 'live shell' was rendered unnecessary by the act of the Prime Minister himself, who, on December 11, as we have seen, blew up his

---

[2] Greville tells us that 'the King said he did not see why he was to be the only gentleman in his dominions who was not to eat his Christmas dinner in quiet, and he was determined he would.'

Cabinet without giving warning to anybody.[3] The King thereby became quite free to send for the Duke of Wellington and dismiss the ministers whom he disliked. Instead of doing so, he allowed Lord Goderich, after a week's retirement, to resume the station he had abandoned, and revive the Government, which, two days after its re-establishment, was to be again blown up—according to the Palmerston legend—at a signal from the King.

This is the culminating peak of absurdity. Having attained it, let us 'rest and be thankful,' in the confidence that our readers will agree with us in pronouncing the charge we have refuted to be, not only calumnious, but ridiculous and impossible.

[3] The silence of the *Autobiography* on this point is extraordinary.

CHAPTER VIII.

Cabinet changes—Correspondence with the Duke—Finance Committee—
Reform of the Sinking Fund—Dr. Bowring—Catholic emancipation—
Proposed Indian appointment — Board of Trade—Settlement of old
dispute with the United States—Parliamentary duties—Close of the
Wellington administration—Financial management of Tories and Liberals
compared.

WHEN the retirement of Mr. Huskisson and his friends,
precipitated by the inopportune rigidity of the Duke of
Wellington, made a partial redistribution of places in
the Cabinet necessary, Mr. Herries, who had correctly
described himself in a letter to Mr. Canning as belonging to the working class of politicians, addressed the
following letter to the Duke of Wellington, expressing
his desire to be removed to some office of more real
business than the Mint, where he felt that he was out
of his element :—

'Great George Street : May 28, 1828.

'My dear Lord Duke,—After having reflected
upon the plan which you showed me this morning for
the reconstruction of the Government, and bearing in
mind all the circumstances under which you have been
called upon at this time to make a new arrangement of
it, I feel that I should not be doing justice to the
interest which I take in the stability and success of
your Administration, nor to my own feelings of a more

personal nature, if I were not to draw your attention to my particular situation.

'The office which I now fill is a mere sinecure, and, connected as it is with a seat in the Cabinet, is such as might be held by any person who, by high rank or influential connections, though unqualified by official ability or experience, might add to the strength of your Government.

'My only means, if I have any, of being in any degree useful to you in the public service must consist in the efficient discharge of some public duties ; and I confess that I feel myself out of my proper position so long as I occupy an office suited to the station and influence which I do not possess, and unsuited to the exercise of any little ability which I may have acquired by the previous occupations of my official life.

'When my present office was conferred upon me, there were circumstances of a peculiar nature which precluded me from putting forward these considerations; but I feel it to be right, now that you are about to make a new distribution of the offices at your disposal, to put you in possession of my sentiments on the subject, and candidly to state that it would have given me more satisfaction if I had found that it would have accorded with your arrangements to place me in a situation of more labour and responsibility than that which I now hold.

'Having thus frankly expressed my sentiments on this subject, it only remains for me to assure your Grace that whatever may be your ultimate arrangements, and in whatever situation I may be placed, I shall use

my best endeavours to justify the confidence reposed in
me, and to prove how much I value the honour and
advantage of being connected with an Administration of
which your Grace is at the head.   Believe me, &c.,

                                   ' J. C. HERRIES.'

The Duke's reply was very friendly, though he was
not able immediately to make a new arrangement.

                                   ' London: May 29, 1828.

' My dear Mr. Herries,—I was not able to answer
your letter yesterday or this day; and I now steal a
moment from my rest to reply to you.

' Particular circumstances placed you in the office
of Chancellor of the Exchequer, for which you are
highly qualified; and another train of circumstances
rendered it necessary to remove you from it.   You are
now in the Cabinet, and holding an office which has
not much business connected with the Government;
and for that very reason your being in the Cabinet is
the more honourable to your character.   You are likewise in that situation in which, having not much
business to transact in your own immediate office, you
can materially assist the Government on a variety of
subjects with which you are well acquainted into which
they must make inquiries.   This you could not do if
employed in an office of which the business might be
sufficient to employ all your time.

' I entreat you then to be satisfied, and have
patience, and be assured that you must rise eventually
to offices of more business, though not of more importance, or more honourable to your character, than that
which you now hold.   Ever yours most faithfully,

                                   ' WELLINGTON.'

From the Duke's published correspondence we learn the fact, of which we should otherwise have been ignorant (there being no allusion to it in Mr. Herries's papers) that the King had proposed a new Ministerial list, in which, Mr. Goulburn being transferred from the Exchequer to the Colonies, his place was to be taken by Mr. Herries. In his reply the Duke expressed his entire concurrence in (to use Mr. Walpole's words) 'the King's estimation of the fitness' of the person recommended for the Finance department;[1] but gave particular reasons for concluding that 'the arrangement suggested would not answer'—in the first place because Mr. Goulburn was a West India proprietor, and secondly because the re-appointment of Mr. Herries to the post which he had before held might afford ground for the assertion that existing Ministerial difficulties were in some way connected with the breaking up of Lord Goderich's Administration, and 'occasion the secession of the Ministers who belonged' to it. In a memorandum apparently of about the same date as his letter to the King, the Duke states as a reason for not making any change in Mr. Herries's position, that it would 'remove him from Parliament and from the Finance Committee.'

This Committee, which had been the cause of so much strife, was appointed at the beginning of the Session of 1828, Sir Henry Parnell being put into the chair. Although both the Chancellor of the Exchequer

---

[1] 'There cannot be found a gentleman more highly qualified than he is for this office,' said the Duke of Wellington, who never said what he did not think.

and Mr. Huskisson were members of it, the management of the business on behalf of the Government was entrusted to the Master of the Mint.

Those who desire to understand the financial system of the country at this period would do well to consult the exhaustive statement made by him to the Committee, as Lord Althorp remarked in the House of Commons, 'in a very able, clear, and satisfactory manner.' In a debate in 1830 (March 12) Sir James Graham—a vehement adversary of the then Government, never very friendly to Mr. Herries, and at that time far from being so—said on this subject : 'I also place every reliance on the evidence and the statements made by the Right Honourable gentleman opposite, the Master of the Mint, in evidence before the Committee ; and I will go the length of saying that the clearest statement of the financial concerns of this country I have ever seen is that of the Right Honourable gentleman in the Fourth Report, which makes the whole of our complicated accounts clear to the plainest understanding, and contains many valuable suggestions which the extinction of the Committee will, I regret to say, prevent from being carried into effect.' And three years later, in a debate in the House of Commons on March 25, 1833, Sir James Graham, then in office, alluding to the same statement, used the strong expression—'which I shall never cease to consider as one of the most able financial statements ever made.'

The Fourth Report itself ('for which,' said Sir Henry Parnell, the chairman, 'the House and the country are indebted to the exertions of the Right

Honourable gentleman the Master of the Mint') was also drawn up by Mr. Herries.

The chief recommendations of that Report related to the Sinking Fund, on which point it was entirely in conformity with the views indicated in the Financial Memorandum already cited which was written by Mr. Herries in 1827.

The Act of 1823 (4 Geo. IV. c. 19) which modified previous arrangements, prescribed the annual payment of a fixed sum of 5,000,000*l.* (with accumulations of interest) towards the redemption of debt. The sums actually issued, pursuant to this Act, for that purpose were, in

					£
1823	.	.	.	.	5,059,210
1824	.	.	.	.	5,195,912
1825	.	.	.	.	5,528,528
1826	.	.	.	.	5,612,465
1827	.	.	.	.	5,762,987
					£27,159,102

This total amount exceeded, by 6,871,290*l.*, the aggregate surplus, for the same period, of Income over Expenditure (including, on both sides, advances for Public Works, &c., and repayments), which was 20,287,812*l.* Without the items mentioned, the surplus amounted to 22,741,820*l.*, or 4,417,282*l.* short of the Sinking Fund.

The surplus, inadequate as it was to meet the legal requirements of the Sinking Fund, must have been very considerably smaller but for the contributions derived from the wonderfully complicated contrivance known as the Dead Weight Annuity, and devised, primarily,

as the means of defraying the charge for Military and
Naval half-pay and pensions, but in reality also, 'with
a view of creating an addition to the income of the
State, whereby the surplus required to satisfy the
Sinking Fund of 5,000,000*l.* fixed by law might still
be provided, notwithstanding a considerable reduction
of the taxes then existing.'

On account of this annuity of 585,740*l.*, sold to the
Bank for 13,089,419*l.*, there were received, in the five
years specified above, 11,114,049*l.*, the aggregate amount
of the annual payments to the Bank having been on the
other hand 2,635,830*l.*　The difference was applied to
the reduction of debt, 'but the sale of the annuity was
itself a creation of debt, and it was therefore not correct
to call that a Sinking Fund, which only served to
extinguish in one shape a debt which it established in
another.'

It appeared that the maintenance of 'the semblance
of a Sinking Fund by this intricate contrivance' had
been, and must necessarily be in future, attended with
considerable expense ; and as the measure was 'wholly
useless as an expedient to supply a nominal amount
of Sinking Fund, the Committee had no hesitation in
recommending' its abandonment.

With regard to the future application of surplus to
the reduction of the National Debt, the Report states
that 'the Committee is impressed with a strong conviction of the sound policy of applying a surplus
revenue perseveringly, in those times during which no
extraordinary resources need be raised, in the reduction
of the debts accumulated to defray the expenses of

antecedent periods of difficulty and exertion. Without offering at present any opinion on the comparative advantages of defraying the charges of war by the immediate imposition of taxes to the amount of those charges, or by raising the required supplies by loans, the Committee consider that if a nation has been induced, for the sake of greater present facilities and safety, to provide for such exigencies by a system of borrowing, whereby a permanent annual charge has been created, that nation is bound, on the return of peace, to make every effort, consistent with a due regard to the other burthens upon the people, for the reduction of that charge. A course of policy founded upon the avowed principle of raising loans for the exigencies of the State in time of war, and of making no provision for diminishing the permanent charge of those loans in time of peace, must appear an abandonment of all consideration for the credit and safety of the country in the eventual occurrence of future difficulties and dangers.

'If the accumulated debt of each period of extraordinary exertion is to be handed down undiminished as a load upon those who are thereafter to meet the exigencies of other struggles and other difficulties, it is too obvious to require an argument that the time cannot be very distant (according to the ordinary vicissitudes of peace and war in the history of human affairs) when the combined weight of the past and present burthens must become too great for the most prosperous people to support, and the fabric of public credit must crumble under the accumulated pressure. . . .

'Impressed with these sentiments the Committee
would have recommended a perseverance in the resolution of 1819 to apply 5,000,000*l.* annually to the
gradual extinction of debt, if that measure could have
been accomplished by the application of a surplus
revenue, and without the necessity of borrowing or of
adding new burthens upon the country.

'But it is obvious . . . that there is at present no
clear surplus to that amount, nor any immediate prospect of such a surplus arising. . . . . The Committee
are of opinion that, instead of a fixed Sinking Fund,
the real surplus of revenue only should be appropriated
annually, in the mode hereafter stated, to the reduction
of debt.

.   .   .   .   .   .

'The Committee upon the whole are of opinion
that the following principles in the future regulation
of the Sinking Fund should be adopted : That . . . it
will be expedient, in estimating the Supply and Ways
and Means, to keep in view the necessity of a surplus
of not less than 3,000,000*l.* in each year, but that in
case the eventual annual surplus should not amount to
three millions, the deficiency ought not to be supplied
by borrowing.

'They are also of opinion that all Funded Debt
redeemed by the application of the real surplus Revenue
should be cancelled.'

.   .   .   .   .   .

The Report concludes with the observation that
while the Committee 'are deeply impressed with the
conviction that in the present state of the public

finances a severe economy in every branch of the national expenditure is imposed as a sacred duty upon the Government and upon Parliament, they derive from their inquiries the strongest confidence in the resources of the country to fulfil all its engagements, and to maintain unimpaired its high station in the world.'

The recommendations of the Committee were definitively carried into effect in the following year, 1829, by the Act, 10 Geo. IV. c. 27.

Upon the evidence of all the facts presented—that Mr. Herries proposed the constitution of a Committee of Financial Inquiry; that at the same time he dwelt upon the necessity of altering the then existing system of the Sinking Fund; that he was the member of the Government who laid before the Committee, when appointed according his suggestion, all the information relating to the general working of the mechanism of the finances which it required for its deliberations; and that finally he drew up the Report which embodied its most important general conclusions—we consider ourselves as fully warranted in claiming for him the credit of having been principally instrumental in bringing about the salutary financial reform above described.[2]

---

[2] It is somewhat remarkable that Mr. Spencer Walpole, who has devoted large space in his history to details more or less inaccurate concerning this question of the Sinking Fund, in order to convict Tory financiers of error, should have been able to find no more room than the corner of a foot-note for the mention of the useful labours of the Committee which, chiefly under the guidance of one particular Tory financier, rectified previous mistakes. This author has, with his customary carelessness, committed an extraordinary blunder in his account of the modification of the Sinking Fund system which was effected in 1823. He says: 'Vansittart applied a sum of money which he had not got, and which he had no prospect of getting, except by borrowing. Robinson, on the contrary, proportioned his Sinking Fund to his

The fashionable doctrine of the day among Liberals —a doctrine now repudiated—was the contrary of that maintained by the Tories. It was deemed impolitic for a nation, like the individual censured by a cynical wit, to 'muddle away its money in paying its debts.'[3] 'What real good,' Liberal economists scornfully asked, 'could be done by applying some three millions, or five millions, a year, towards the redemption of 800,000,000l.? A diminution of taxes to the same amount would afford us a much greater relief.'

When stripped of the pedantic varnish of sham science which covered it, this principle, once greatly in vogue, appears as nothing but the crude expression of selfishness, which says : ' By taking our money out of our pockets to pay our debts, instead of leaving it to fructify for our own benefit, we are depriving ourselves of present enjoyments for the benefit of posterity. But what is posterity to us ? Let us rather spend our

surplus, and devoted only the balance of income and expenditure to the reduction of debt.' It is manifest that the writer of this passage cannot have read, or understood, the Act of 1823 (Robinson being Chancellor of the Exchequer) founded upon Vansittart's resolutions of 1819, which were recited in the preamble. Its imperative directions required the annual payment of five millions—surplus or no surplus. And if Mr. Walpole had taken the trouble to inspect the public accounts referred to above he would have discovered the fact, opposed to his theory, that in 1826 the amount issued by Robinson, according to law, for the reduction of debt, did very largely exceed the balance of income over expenditure. ' *Et voilà comme on écrit l'histoire : puis fiez vous à messieurs les savans.*'

[3] Long after this phrase had been written the same quotation was used with reference to the same subject by a great popular orator in a speech at a public meeting; but he applied it, apparently, to the policy, not of the Liberals but of their opponents. It is certain, however, that Liberal luminaries, such as Mr. Joseph Hume, Mr. Poulett Thomson, Sir Henry Parnell, Lord Althorp, and others, always opposed and derided the persistent endeavours of 'stupid Tory' Governments to effect large reductions of debt. ' Base is the slave that pays,' was a Liberal, not a Tory, maxim.

money on cakes and ale without taking thought of future distress. Perish posterity, rather than that we should give up for it one crumb, or plum, of nice cake, or one drop of good ale. If posterity is crushed by the burdens bequeathed by us, with the addition of new ones imposed by its own necessities—so much the worse for it.'

In a debate on the Budget in 1828, Mr. Herries, in the course of a speech in which he refuted an accusation brought by Mr. Hume against Mr. Canning of having misled the House by inaccurate statements, took an opportunity of again expressing his opinion, and that of the Government, on the subject of the Sinking Fund, as to which he said : 'No one was more anxious than myself to enable the Finance Committee to arrive at the real principle on which it was founded, and to divest it of all the intricacy of borrowing on the one hand to discharge what was due on the other ; and indeed I may venture to say that the proposition of the measure originated with the members of the Government. At the same time, both on my own part and on the part of those who were members of the Government in the Committee with me, I must entirely disclaim any participation in the views of those who thought it was just, wise, and salutary utterly to abandon all endeavours to effect any reduction of the debt.[4] . . .

'The object with some is, not to maintain the surplus for the exclusive purpose of applying it to a

---

[4] It is well known that this was Lord Althorp's view. His avowed hostility to the principle of providing a surplus for the redemption of debt was one of the grounds on which Mr. Herries objected to his being made chairman of the committee.

Sinking Fund, but to render it occasionally available for other purposes ; and I contend that if once you do this, you involve (*sic*) the principle altogether. The majority of the Committee were in favour of keeping up a Sinking Fund of 5,000,000*l.* if it were possible ; and it was with great regret that they found it necessary to recommend that it should be reduced from 5,000,000*l.* to 3,000,000*l.* I fully concur in that proposal, and if 3,000,000*l.* actual surplus could not be raised, I should say, make the Sinking Fund even lower than that—in short, never have the Sinking Fund larger than the actual surplus of your income.' After some other remarks, he added : ' When gentlemen bring their accusations against the past times of war, and speak of Mr. Pitt in a spirit of so much condemnation, I think that they are bound to recall the circumstances under which that statesman brought forward the measure of the Sinking Fund ; he did so, no doubt, with the expectation that the war would only extend to a period of two or three years, and that, at the end of that time, the country would be in a state to rid itself of some of its burdens.'—(*Mirror of Parliament.*)

It was in this debate that Mr. Poulett Thomson broached his celebrated fructification theory, which is now, we suppose, wholly exploded.

The labours of the Committee, although very useful, were incomplete. Four reports were presented in the course of the Session of 1828. The first report merely conveyed a recommendation in six lines. The second, on the Ordnance Estimates, contains, among other general observations upon expenditure and retrenchment, the following : ' The Committee . . . unequivocally declare their full assent to the principle that no Government is justified in taking even the smallest sum of money from the people, unless a case can be clearly established to show that it will be productive of some essential advantage to them . . . and the Committee think that the Legislature of this country is more particularly bound never to deviate in the slightest degree from that principle in consequence of the great permanent burdens which the vast amount of the National Debt has imposed upon the people. . . . With regard to retrenchment, the Committee are sensible of the great difficulty which lies in the way of its accomplishment. . . . But the present circumstances of our finances render the attempt absolutely indispensable. . . .'

    .   .   .   .   .   .

It cannot be doubted that these remarks had the full concurrence of the Master of the Mint, the most active Ministerial member of the Committee. The words of the Report exactly represent the principles he always preached, and, so far as in him lay, always practised.

In the Third Report the subjects of Military and Naval Half-pay, Civil Superannuations, and Diplomatic Pensions—the regulations recommended for the granting of which last were adopted by the Civil List Committee in 1831 and established as they now exist, with some reductions of the amount in each class—were dealt with.

The Fourth and last Report we have already mentioned.

The Army, Navy, Colonial Establishments, and other branches of expenditure, were left for further inquiry. But, for some reason with which we are not acquainted, the Committee was not re-appointed. The Chancellor of the Exchequer in 1829 alleged as a ground for its postponement the pressure of other business ; but the Government had probably some other motive for their determination. It may at any rate be assumed that the Prime Minister and the Leader in the House of Commons were adverse to a continuance of the inquiry, which, according to letters written in 1827 by an intimate friend of the Duke of Wellington, was viewed with dislike by the Duke when the intended appointment of the Committee was announced by Mr. Canning. Its abandonment may be considered as an error of judgment, because, in spite of the large reductions of expenditure that were undoubtedly effected, it gave rise to unjust imputations against the Cabinet of want of sincerity in their economical professions.

In connection with the business of this Committee a long and curious correspondence took place between a man of note in later years, Dr.—afterwards Sir John—Bowring and the Master of the Mint. At the instance of the Finance Committee a Commission was appointed in 1828 to inquire into the system of Public Accounts, and Mr. Herries desired that Dr. Bowring—whose special qualifications were known to him, and against whom he had no prejudice on account of his Radical, or Benthamite, opinions—should, as one of the Com-

missioners, visit foreign countries—and Holland especially—for the purpose of investigating the methods
there pursued. But, owing to the decided hostility of
the Prime Minister and others, this intention could not
be entirely carried out. Mr. Herries, however, did his
utmost to promote what he considered as a very important object, giving Dr. Bowring all the assistance in
his power for the prosecution of inquiries which seem
to have been impeded by official obstacles abroad, and
perhaps by official spokes in the wheel at home. The
good disposition shown to him by one member of the
Government was always recognized very handsomely
by Dr. Bowring, who, four years later, when his friends
were in power, wrote as follows to Mr. Herries in opposition : ‘I cannot avoid this occasion of re-assuring
you of my sense of obligation for the part you then
took, being thoroughly persuaded that you did everything to prevent—and to mitigate—my *then* disappointment. It will be a subject of great delight to me if in
any future period of my existence I am able to testify
to you how much and how truly I am, my dear sir,
your obliged, &c.’

When the Duke of Wellington’s Cabinet was forced
by political necessity to bring forward the measure of
Catholic Emancipation which caused the rupture of the
Tory party, Mr. Herries was less embarrassed by his
previous conduct on this question than the two distinguished leaders of the Government, or than many of
his other colleagues. He had formerly voted against
the Catholic claims, but his opposition was always free
from passion or fanaticism. He certainly did not

entertain the notion which, according to Peter Plymley, had 'crept into the world, that difference of religion would make men unfit to perform together the offices of common and civil life; that Brother Wood and Brother Goose could not travel together the same circuit if they differed in creed, nor Cockell and Mingay be engaged in the same cause if Cockell was a Catholic and Mingay a Muggletonian.' He did not 'suppose that Huskisson and Sir Henry Englefield would squabble behind the Speaker's chair about the Council of Lateran, and many a turnpike bill miscarry by the sarcastical controversies of Mr. Hawkins Brown and Sir John Throckmorton upon the real presence.'

He cared very little for theological theory, but very much for priestly practice, which he believed to be still, as in all former ages, antagonistic to the reason, the civilization, and the freedom, of mankind.

He regarded the Catholic Question, not from a religious, but from a political point of view. Upon grounds of political expediency he considered the original exclusion of Papists from political functions as a rational measure; and he was not convinced that there had ceased to be good grounds for maintaining it —believing as he did that, although, where the Church was not concerned, a Catholic Member of Parliament might fulfil his duties quite as faithfully and loyally as a Protestant, whenever the interests of his Church came or appeared to come into conflict with the interests of the State, his allegiance to the Vatican would certainly overpower his sense of national obligation; and that, in dealing with many questions of political or social importance, his chief consideration would be, not how they might affect the welfare of the country, but how they might be viewed by an external authority.

On the other hand, insurrection appeared to him a far greater evil than any which could be apprehended from the admission of Catholics ; and, having to choose between prospective difficulties and the imminent peril of civil war, he could not hesitate in giving his voice for that course which public safety pointed out. The Coronation Oath, as an objection to legislative change, had absolutely no force in his eyes.

Few persons will now refuse to admit that the respectable, but inconvenient, scruples of George III.'s conscience, which prevented the settlement of the question at the beginning of this century are greatly to be regretted, and that it was impolitic to defer until the year 1828 an inevitable concession which might have been granted many years sooner. But, at the same time, it can hardly be denied, that the arguments constantly put forward by the Emancipationists, if now to be produced, would need considerable recasting before they could be read by the light of all the sayings and doings of the Vatican and its supporters during the last twenty or thirty years.

Half a century's experience of incessant agitation has demonstrated the vanity of the expectations fondly entertained of Irish tranquillity and content. It would be easy to show—facts in hand—that every single prediction, and every argument—except that of necessity—

in favour of emancipation, have been proved false by subsequent events.

In 1829 the following correspondence, which has a public as well as a personal interest, took place between Mr. Herries and Lord Ellenborough, then President of the now extinct Board of Control, who pressed him strongly and repeatedly to go out to India, and endeavour to effect the cure of the chronic disorder from which the finances of the Eastern Empire were at that time, as they are still, suffering. Every inducement to accept the offered post, in which perhaps he might have rendered great service to the State, was held out to him, but domestic considerations forced him to decline it.

'India Board: April 19, 1829.

'(Private.)

'My dear Herries,—Our Indian finances are in a bad state, and very much require your experienced hand to bring them round. The expense of collecting the revenue increases, the salaries of all the public officers increase, the manufactures of the country are undersold by ours, and India cannot pay its way. We must find a remedy for this, and none will be found until we can place one strong and practised mind at the head of the whole finance of the Empire.

'The first object is to diminish the unnecessary charges. I really believe we cannot increase the revenue until we diminish taxation, and by diminishing taxation enable the people to acquire wealth, and to rise elastically as the weight which now crushes them is removed.

'Whatever commerce we now have with India must be in great measure confined to the supply of the wants of the British residents. We should endeavour, not only to create in the body of the native population a taste for British manufactures, but to give them the means of gratifying their taste.

'There can be no profitable commerce with a pauper people.

'These opinions have pressed strongly upon my mind ever since I have been at the India Board ; but I am satisfied I made but little (*sic*) from hence.

'Would you undertake the general management of the finances of India, as a sort of Chancellor of the Exchequer to the Governor-General?   If you would do so you might, I am convinced, not only confer a very great benefit upon the public, but illustrate your own name much more than you could as Governor of any one of the Presidencies.

'If you should be inclined to look at the office as one which you might possibly undertake, I am disposed to think that I should have no great difficulty in inducing the Directors to make it worth your while to go to India.   You would live very much with the Governor-General, and as you would not be required to keep any establishment, I should think you might save 5,000*l.* or 7,000*l.* a year out of the 10,000*l.* or 12,000*l.* which we could manage to give you.

'Will you think of it ?

'You might depend upon being supported here. Lord W. Bentinck has lately appointed a Commission to inquire generally into the increase of expenditure, and if you would go you would just find the labours of the Commission finished, and all the materials ready to your hands.   A few years would enable you to redeem the errors of half a century, and to lay the foundation of a permanent system which might endure for as long a period as men can presume to look forward to.   Believe me, my dear Herries, very truly yours,

'ELLENBOROUGH.'

'Great George Street: April 20, 1829.

'My dear Lord Ellenborough,—I am just leaving London to pass a few days at Brighton, or I would have called on you to answer your letter by a personal communication rather than by a written one.

'Upon the first view of your proposition as it respects the office itself, I have great doubts of your being able so to constitute your Indian Chancellorship of the Exchequer as to effect your great object of regenerating the whole system of Indian finance without danger of interfering with some other very important objects of Indian government.

'I fear you would find it difficult to make such an office sufficiently substantive and independent for the accomplishment of such a task without making it too much so for the authority and influence of the Governor-General—which will hardly admit of any diminution. In short, I think your Finance Minister in India would be either a mere adviser of the Governor-General, and, as such, would have no substantive weight or power, or he would be a troublesome—perhaps a dangerous— check upon him.

' But these opinions are formed, as I said, upon the first view only of your plan. You are much better acquainted with the subject than I am, and have thought more upon it. My objections might possibly be over-ruled by you in a few minutes' conversation on the matter.

' But with respect to my undertaking such an office if it could usefully be instituted, there are personal and domestic reasons which would preclude my undertaking it, even if I could bring myself to agree in your much too favourable opinion of my fitness for it.

'If in any of the financial parts of your labours at home, either for preparing for the establishment of such an office, or on any other occasion, I can be of any service to you, I beg you to be assured that you may at all times freely command my services. Believe me, &c.

'J. C. HERRIES.'

' India Board : April 22, 1829.

' My dear Herries,—I should hardly venture to think of creating the office I spoke to you of unless I was certain of being able to place you in it, for I know no other man I think fit.

' Such an officer without talent, experience, and high station in England, all combined, would be incapable of doing good ; but with these qualities and with the support of the authorities at home he might do extensive good.

' Lord W. Bentinck wished to have a Vizir, and he does still.

' I am very much obliged to you for your kind

offers of assistance in the Financial Department. I may take advantage of them perhaps too largely. Believe me, &c.

'ELLENBOROUGH.'

It appears that the President of the Board of Control was in the habit of consulting his colleague, the Master of the Mint, on Indian matters. Thus we read in one letter : 'I am afraid I trouble you very much with my Indian business ; ' and in another, ' You will do me a great favour if you will read the accompanying memorandum and letter to Bombay on the subject of establishing a Government Bank there, and give me your opinion upon it. . . . I have thrown out the doubts which have arisen in my mind on reading the memorandum, but I have great hesitation in acting upon my own unassisted judgment in matters of this kind which are new to me, and I shall be disposed to defer to your opinion should it be against the validity of my doubts. A mass of papers was sent to me with the letter, which you shall have if you require them.'

Advice from the same quarter was sought by Lord Ellenborough many years afterwards, when he was Governor-General of India, and his correspondent a private individual, as we gather from this letter, which may not be out of place here, though written in 1842.

' My dear Lord Ellenborough,—Your letter about my son [5] was most gratifying to me. There is nothing

---

[5] Captain (afterwards Brevet-Major) William Robert Herries, 43rd Light Infantry and 3rd Light Dragoons, Aide-de-camp to the Governor-General. He was killed in action at Moodkee in 1845, when serving in the same capacity on the staff of the late Lord Hardinge.

I more desire than that he should continue to give satisfaction to you. The employment you are giving him will be of immense use to him.

'He writes to me in the strongest terms of your kindness and of his devotion to your service.

'I have been prevented by a continued absence from London from obtaining some information which I have sought for on the subject of the present system of control and check upon the current public expenditure in India. The defect of the system which you advert to lies, I have no doubt, in the want of a systematic supervision of the public outgoings in their earliest stages, whereby the mischief of a lax administration by the financial authorities, or a reckless profusion by civil or military servants who spend the public money, may be nipped in the bud. The ultimate examination or audit of the public accounts is not sufficient for that object. It comes too late for prevention and generally in such a shape that the highest authority cannot easily sift the mass of payments made with a view to general correction and improvement. In this country there has long (I think from the time of Godolphin) existed a department for advising the Treasury upon all *extraordinary* military expenditure if possible before it is incurred, and when the nature of the service will not admit of that, then as soon after the payments made as information of the accounts rendered will admit of. . . This has no doubt prevented a good deal of wasteful expenditure by Governors and military officers abroad, and Commissaries on foreign service. These Comptrollers of Army Accounts were until lately a separate

Board. The office is now merged in the Auditors of Public Accounts—one of whom is especially assigned to this service—that is, of advising the Treasury upon proposed incipient expenditure. I know not if you have any corresponding check in India. I should think it would be even more useful there than at home.

'Sir R. Peel is, no doubt, quite right in postponing to a future session any general explanations of Indian finance. It is highly desirable on every account to avoid at this time discussions upon that point and upon Indian policy in general. An Indian Budget and Indian debates will, I hope, be ushered in under more favourable auspices when you have been a twelvemonth at the head of the Indian Government.

'We have just learned by telegraph the arrival of the mail of June 1. . . . In the meantime I wish you heartily joy of the progress already made towards the restoration of the credit of our arms in Afghanistan. Yours, &c.

'J. C. HERRIES.'

In 1830, Mr. Vesey Fitzgerald, having been compelled by severe illness to retire, was succeeded in the office of President of the Board of Trade by Mr. Herries, who continued to hold together with it that of Master of the Mint.

During his tenure of office at the Board of Trade he had the satisfaction of contributing by active co-operation to the settlement of the long-vexed question of the commercial intercourse between the British West India Islands and the United States. After much amicable negotiation [6] between the British Government and Mr. MacLane, the American Minister—who renewed the discussions which had been carried on at intervals during many years—the dispute, injurious to both parties, was terminated by the removal of retaliatory restrictions on both sides, and the direct trade was at last opened to British and American vessels on a footing of equality by the repeal, on the one hand, of the American Acts of Congress of which Great Britain complained, and, on the other, of the British Orders in Council which were objected to by the United States.

This arrangement, which appears from the Duke of Wellington's correspondence to have been very reluctantly assented to by him, was facilitated by a considerable diminution of the import duties charged in the United States on several articles of British Colonial produce.

At the same time a measure was proposed to Parliament the object of which was to give, in accordance with then generally prevalent ideas, protection and encouragement to the trade of the North American Colonies with the West Indies by means of a new scale of discriminating duties in favour of certain articles imported from the former colonies into the latter.

In submitting it to the House of Commons on November 8, 1830, a few days before the adverse vote which overthrew the Duke of Wellington's Cabinet, Mr. Herries said : 'I have the gratification of being

[6] We believe that we should be justified in saying that the conduct of this negotiation devolved chiefly upon Mr. Herries, and that he deserves the credit of having brought it to a successful issue.

able to state that a topic of discussion between two
nations, which has occupied the longest time and was
of the most intricate character of any within memory,
and which has been subject to many varieties of pretension on both sides, has now been amicably, and I
trust for ever, terminated to the satisfaction of both
parties. . . . We have only to regret that the United
States having at length adopted and accepted these
terms, they had not done so at an earlier period. That
country has, however, now subscribed to them fully
and unconditionally, and I am bound to state—in fact
I should not be doing justice to the American Government were I not to do so—that it is impossible for any
Government to have conducted a negotiation involving
such important interests in a more friendly, civil, con-
ciliatory, straightforward, and therefore, I should say,
in a more wise and prudent manner than that pursued
by the United States. It would not become me to
express any strong opinion on a foreign Government,
did circumstances not render it indispensably necessary;
but having adverted to the many infructuous attempts
to settle this subject, I am bound to say that I believe
on this occasion neither party has had the slightest
reason to utter a complaint against the other on its
final adjustment, but that every real ground of satisfaction and confidence has been acted on. . . .

' The American Government have repealed those Acts
which contained the obnoxious proposals. . . . and lest
any ambiguity should arise, the most distinct explanations have been required on the one side and given on
the other. His Majesty's Government have adopted this

course in order to remove the possibility of *any after-claps, which I am sorry to say we have frequently had occasion to regret as arising out of treaties in the drawing up of which the closest eye had perhaps not been used.*' [7]

In the following year the measure proposed was taken up again and carried, with some alterations in the scale of duties, by Lord Grey's Government. Mr. Poulett Thomson, who, as Vice-President of the Board of Trade, had charge of the Bill in the House of Commons, while endeavouring to prove that his tariff was better than that of Mr. Herries, distinctly recognized the propriety—or necessity—of affording to the trade of the Northern Colonies the protection of discriminating duties, one of the alleged improvements of this new scheme being indeed a temporary increase of the protection so given.

Lord Palmerston was pleased to remark, in one of his letters preserved for the benefit of posterity, that 'Herries is entirely mute,' but this observation, like many others left on record by Lord Palmerston, had the defect of being untrue. A simple reference to the 'Mirror of Parliament' or to 'Hansard' shows that in the Sessions of 1828, 1829, and 1830, Mr. Herries took at least his fair share of the business of the House of Commons. He spoke not unfrequently, and on various subjects—on one occasion indeed in answer to a motion made by Lord Palmerston himself on the affairs of Portugal—but chiefly on those with which he was most perfectly acquainted. We may cite particularly a speech

---

[7] The italics are ours. Later Governments, too, have had occasion to regret after-claps arising out of treaties 'less accurate' than they ought to have been.

on the currency question (a matter of more importance to the English people than the constitution of Portugal and the tyranny of Dom Miguel) in opposition to a motion made by Mr. Attwood for the adoption of a double standard by making gold and silver coins a legal tender in the relative proportions established in 1717, and for the re-introduction of small notes.

In the course of the debate, Mr. Huskisson said : ' I am perfectly satisfied with the answer that my Right Honourable friend (Mr. Herries) made to this branch of the subject ; and, I will add, a more able or argumentative speech of the kind I never heard.' And Sir Robert Peel, commenting upon what Mr. Attwood had called his ' practical measure,' remarked that ' it would be almost waste of time to endeavour to show the absurdity of it, after the able and eloquent speech of my Right Honourable friend near me.'

The Wellington Cabinet, which was destroyed by the ricochet of a French revolution, and by the impolitic junction of advanced Tories with advanced Liberals, was, as well as its predecessor the Liverpool Ministry, held up to obloquy by the party in the ascendant in times of popular effervescence when defenders of bygone Tory Governments had no better chance of fair hearing than a Papist denounced by Titus Oates, or a British Ambassador accused of Turkophilism at a Bulgarian atrocity meeting. The prejudice created fifty years ago by those who had possession of the public ear has never since been entirely removed, and even now any mob-orator or pamphleteer can easily find ignorant listeners or readers ready to take upon trust his declamations against what he may please to call Tory misrule before the days of reform. But in one—and that the most important—branch of administration it can without much difficulty be demonstrated that Tory management was far more advantageous to the nation than that of the Liberals.

Let the railers at the old Tory system place side by side the financial results of its three last years, 1828, 1829, 1830, and those of the three last years of the ensuing Reform Governments, 1839, 1840, 1841. In the former triennial period they will find immense and most beneficial reductions of taxation terminating in a very large surplus (nearly three millions) bequeathed to the incoming Whigs, in whose unskilful hands it was immediately transmuted into a heavy deficit ; in the latter, a growing excess of expenditure culminating in enormous and dangerous deficiency left to be dealt with by a Conservative Government.

Or let the declaimers calculate how much lighter our burdens would now be than they are, if the diminution of the charge of the funded and unfunded debt had continued at the same rate as during the three years of the Wellington Administration—due allowance being made for subsequent additions of debt, and likewise for the relief derived from the simple expiration of annuities. In those years it amounted to 785,875*l.*, if actual payments be taken, or to 1,081,615*l.*, if the terminable and life annuities be converted into equivalent permanent annuities according to Mr. Finlaison's computation (Parliamentary Paper, 1831).

Another comparison may be made. In the last

eight Tory pre-Reform years, 1823–1830, without any deficit, the total real surplus (local advances and re-payments, as well as the sums received from and paid to the Bank under the ' Dead Weight ' arrangement, being eliminated from the accounts) which was applicable to the redemption of debt, amounted to 22,242,231*l*.,[8] while the aggregate net surplus (after deduction of the deficiencies of nine years) of the next *twenty* years, 1831–1850, was only 8,986,698*l*.

This is not all. The net remission of taxation in these eight Tory years exceeded qy nearly 37 per cent. that which was effected in the twenty Liberal and Peelian years; the totals being, respectively, 14,509,239*l*., and 10,598,761*l*.[9] The annual rate of such remission was, in the first period, 1,811,746*l*., and in the second, 529,938*l*. The yearly excess on the Tory side was therefore no less than 1,283,716*l*. To make the comparison complete, let the results above stated be put together thus :

	Eight Tory Years	Twenty Liberal, &c. Years
Surplus	22,242,231	8,986,698
Net Remission of Taxation .	14,509,239	10,598,761
Total	36,751,470	19,585,459
Tory Excess . . .	17,166,011	

The annual average was, for the eight years, 4,593,933*l*., and, for the twenty years, 979,272*l*.

---

[8] For reasons which would require too long an explanation, we believe that we have understated this surplus by more than a million.

[9] These results have been obtained from a table, the correctness of which may be assumed, in Mr. Giffen's *Essay on the Reduction of the National Debt*.

It must be remembered that, although in the first period there were some years of plenty and prosperity advancing by leaps and bounds until reckless speculation leapt and bounded into an abyss of bankruptcy, they were followed by others of deep depression and dire distress, agricultural, manufacturing, and commercial.

In order to remove the least suspicion of unfairness, let the most lauded portion of the twenty years above mentioned—namely the five years, 1842–1846 of the Peelian system—be set against five years, 1823–1827, of the pre-Reform system. It will be found that the net surplus of the former quinquennial period—7,483,815*l.* —was little more than half of that of the latter— 14,263,601—while the *gross* amount of taxes taken off in the five years 1842–1846, being 8,145,628*l.*, fell far short of the *net* reduction represented by 10,934,847*l.*, in the five years 1823–1827.

This may be added. In the ten years 1821–1830, the Tories, with an unreformed Parliament, diminished taxation to the extent of 17,107,007*l.*[1] In the thirty-six years following, successive administrations took off only 25,940,994*l.*, including the taxes imposed for the Crimean War.

In the face of all these facts it seems difficult to sustain the doctrine propounded by Liberal orators, as an article of faith not to be questioned, that bad finance is the necessary concomitant of Tory government, while the progress of the redemption of debt and of the reduction of taxation is always in direct ratio to the increase of democratic influence.

[1] 14,747,442*l.* (net) had been previously remitted since the Peace.

CHAPTER IX.

Tories in opposition—Herries's activity—Praed—Government influence at Harwich defied—Theory of Treasury ownership—Scurrility of Liberal press—Reform—Timber duties: defeat of the Ministry—Russian-Dutch loan: historical view; Herries's action—Duke of Wellington's attempt to form a Cabinet—Helpless condition of Conservative party—Croker and the 'Quarterly Review'—Reformed Parliament—Herries in Peel Cabinet—Goes to Italy—Parliamentary business—Metropolitan improvements—Stockdale and Hansard—Defeat of Melbourne Ministry on Herries's motion—His intervention with a Conservative journal in favour of Palmerston's policy solicited—Debates on the Budget of 1841—Huskisson's commercial policy elucidated.

DURING the dark period of the fortunes of the Tory party, reviled and proscribed after the transfer of power to the Whigs, no one was more active for its interests in various ways than Mr. Herries, whose exertions, which sometimes brought upon himself heavy pecuniary loss, were not a little useful in holding the party together at times when it seemed likely to go to pieces. His house was often resorted to for the discussion of plans and arrangements. He was one of the originators of the Carlton Club, the feeble precursor of which was a place of meeting for party purposes established to a great extent under his auspices in Charles Street, St. James's Square, and an object of much derision to enemies, who in their urbane style designated its habitual frequenters as 'the Charles Street gang.' Bearing no malice to the angry Tories by whose unwise coalition with its Liberal assailants the Cabinet to which he had belonged had been turned out of office, he busied himself in endeavouring to heal still rankling animosities and effect a reconciliation between the seceders and the leaders of the party. As a means of bringing them together again, and as a manifestation of renewed concord, it was proposed in the summer of 1831 that the 'Friends of the Constitution' should meet at a political banquet. There is in Mr. Herries's writing a rough draft of a paper for circulation on this subject with a list of 'noblemen and gentlemen connected with the landed, commercial, colonial, and other great interests of the Empire,' to be requested to act as stewards. To this suggestion the Duke of Wellington [1] returned a favourable reply.

'Walmer Castle: June 2, 1831.

'My dear Herries,—I have received your letter of yesterday, and I am very sorry that I shall not have the pleasure of seeing you here.

'I don't see any objection to the proposed dinner. Indeed, I conceive that such a meeting would have the effect of reviving the drooping spirits of the gentlemen of the country, if it should be well attended. But we must assume a good title, and must have good names as managers in order to be certain of being well attended.

'We ought to rest our pretensions to the confidence of the publick on our desire to protect and preserve

[1] Several letters on a variety of subjects from the Duke, who was very cordial towards Mr. Herries and often consulted him during many years, are preserved.

property and all the great establishments and interests of the country, rather than especially on our opposition to the Bill, or on the opinions of all or any of us upon Reform.

'Then for managers, &c., we ought to have moderate Reformers, great bankers and merchants [they were strongly represented on Mr. Herries's list] as well as noblemen and gentlemen. Believe me ever yours most sincerely,

'WELLINGTON.

'I understand that you are going down to Sir Robert Peel's, and you had better speak to him on this subject.'

Sir Robert's answer, in a letter of the same date, humorously pointing out all the possible inconveniences of the plan, was discouraging. A few days later he wrote again : 'I am sorry that the dinner is still in agitation. The object, I presume, is a formal party union with the ultra-Tories. This may be right or it may be wrong ; but at any rate it is a matter that requires in my opinion more consideration than the acceptance of a mere dinner engagement would render necessary ; and so far as the dining implies a new party connection it is a point on which everyone must be at liberty to decide for himself. I shall most certainly claim that privilege for myself individually. . . .'

Mr. Herries had a strong sense of the necessity, not sufficiently felt by others, of recruiting his party with young men of ability, and was always anxious that every encouragement should be given to rising talent ; but he found little or no disposition to second his views,

and he often lamented the disheartening tone of slight
or indifference which chilled enthusiasm and depressed
energy, if it did not, as was sometimes the case, convert
an adherent into an enemy. One of those whom he was
eager to assist in bringing forward in political life was
Winthrop Mackworth Praed, a convert from the early
errors of an undergraduate, whose loyal character, as
well as poetical genius, he greatly admired. The
following letter shows that Praed, returned in December
1830 for the Tory nomination borough of St. Germains,
a few weeks later than the election of his Cambridge
contemporary Macaulay for the Whig nomination
borough of Calne, owed his entrance into Parliament
in great measure to the exertions of Mr. Herries, who
never had any borough interest of his own. 'You
have heard that I am at last in the situation to which
your kindness more than anything else has contributed
to raise me. I am now about to return to town with
my new duties ; and I cannot set out without bespeak-
ing for myself a continuance of your goodwill. Until
you first honoured me by your notice, I never dreamed
of being where I am; and if I feel a little giddy
occasionally at my unlooked-for elevation, I trust the
same hand that lifted me up will be held out to keep
me steady.

'I have another inducement, however, to make me
venture upon writing to you. I know that I am
wretchedly awkward at expressing by word of mouth
my sense of personal obligation. And therefore I am
anxious, before I meet you again, to assure you that I
am very grateful for all you have done for me, and

that my old longings after distinction become doubly eager from the desire I feel to show myself not quite unworthy of your good word.

'I have always told my friends, and I have said as much to you, that I have been an overrated man, and that my services are likely to be scarcely worthy the asking. If it should prove so, I hope people will forget that you ever took up a blockhead, though I shall remember it myself with very useless gratitude. If I have better fortune than my fears prophesy, I shall indeed hold myself your debtor for the larger half of whatever success may be my lot in the career you have opened to me. . . . About the 13th I shall be settled in the Temple, and ready to work hard under your auspices. . . .'

Subsequent letters show how earnestly he acted up to his intentions, and how ardently he devoted himself to the cause which he had espoused. But instead of being welcomed as a valuable acquisition, Praed was received with repulsive coldness by the leader of the Conservative Opposition in the House of Commons. His attachment to Mr. Herries was never loosened, and he continued to look upon him as his best friend in the political world. This sentiment is strongly expressed in a letter in which, at the time of the canvass for the General Election of 1832, Praed bitterly complains of encouragement indirectly given to his opponent at St. Ives by some Tory magnates, and ends by saying, ' Pray forgive this long scrawl. I am furious, as you see ; and I shall grow cooler now that I have poured out my fury for the amusement of the only one of my political guides to whom I feel indebted for kindness, or in whom I trust for support. Whether chaired into Parliament or cheated out of it, I shall always be yours, &c.'

Out of office Mr. Herries successfully resisted during many years the efforts of the Liberal Government to eject him from the representation of Harwich, opposing to Ministerial influence, supposed to be all-powerful there, his own well-established personal influence. The organs of the Reform Administration propounded, with a crudeness unsurpassed by the most inveterate borough-monger, the theory of absolute ownership of the so-called Treasury boroughs ; and the holders of such seats, elected under the former Government, were summoned, in the terroristic style of the period, immediately to quit their wrongful occupancy. The more obnoxious of the two Tory members for Harwich in particular · was assailed, in the Whig 'Morning Chronicle' especially, with extraordinary virulence. A libellous attack in a letter from a correspondent—real or pretended—called for a denial, which was published in the discourteous manner too common half a century ago, of a specific allegation. The inadequacy of the reparation moved the injured person to address to the editor, Dr. Black, personally and not as an abstraction, the following dignified and decided remonstrance which seems to have led to apologies and to have prevented any repetition of the offence.

'By inserting the contradiction which appears in your paper of this day, to the only substantive assertion contained in the letter of "Interrogator," you have to that extent done an act of justice to me ; but you must permit me to state that I think you have failed to do the same justice to yourself by omitting to condemn and to repudiate the personal scurrility which pervades the letter containing that assertion.

' I write to you, Sir, under a belief impressed upon me by assurances from some persons acquainted with you that I am addressing a gentleman of good and honourable feelings, who would not, without disgust, see personal calumny or coarse personal vituperation employed in the prosecution of political controversy, and who would still less behold with approbation such discreditable means resorted to by anonymous assailants.

' I judge, from the manner in which the letter in question was inserted in your paper, that the writer of it must be entitled to some attention from you. If so I have a right to request you to inform him that if he will put any question to me in his own name and under that fair responsibility which he will then incur, he will find me quite ready to deal with his communications as may become them, and him, and me.

' But as there must, in all civilised society, be somewhere lodged a due responsibility for every insult offered by one individual to another, you will, I think, admit that the editor of a newspaper who publishes anonymous attacks on private character must be himself responsible for the offence if he refuses to disclose the name of the offender.

' I assure you, Sir, that this letter, addressed to you under the impression with respect to yourself which I have before stated, is written without any resentment, but with a very firm determination not to permit personal insult to be thrown upon me through the medium of a respectable paper such as yours with impunity. . . .'

It was not merely in newspapers that the doctrine of the indefeasible right of the Treasury to the representation of certain places was asserted.   In the House of Commons it was put forward in the most unqualified manner, and by the most advanced Reformers.   Mr. Hume complained that 'those who hold what are called Treasury boroughs voted against Ministers;' and Mr. O'Connell said, with regard to the same adverse vote, that 'it is seen that those members who form this Opposition hold their seats by the existence of Treasury boroughs which they represent, and which boroughs are known to belong to the Government. They who are the nominees of private individuals usually give up their seats when their opinions differ from those of their patrons.   Not so, however, in the case of the holders of the Treasury boroughs, who thus pursue at least a factious line of conduct.'

During many years, the utmost exertions were made in vain by the combined forces of the Treasury, the Admiralty, and the Woods and Forests, to turn Mr. Herries out.   Ministerial patronage and favours were, with hardly any attempt at decent disguise, bestowed for votes.   The Ministerial screw was applied with ruthless severity to electors directly or indirectly dependent upon the Crown.   No Tory Duke of Newcastle ever showed a more stern determination to ' do what he pleased with his own.'   All was of no avail. Falsehood, slander, promises, rewards, threats, punishment, were thrown away. The enemy could not be dislodged. In the teeth of the Whig Government, the limited constituency before, and the enlarged constituency after, the Reform Act, persisted in returning the Tory ex-Minister, at the General Elections of 1831, in the white heat of the Reform agitation, when popular intimidation, aided by the abuse of the King's name, in most places overpowered all resistance ; of 1832, when, in the delirium of Reform triumph, the Opposition minority was reduced to a lamentable rump ; of 1837 (at the election of 1834 he was in office), when the boundless affection of the nation for the young Queen was turned, with indecent disregard of constitutional principle, to the account of the waning—almost extinct—popularity of elderly Whig Ministers. At one of these elections a pleasant little surprise was prepared for the successful Tory candidate at Harwich by some of the Liberal party, exasperated by renewed defeat. As a clear manifestation of indignant public opinion, a plan, fortunately detected in time, was formed to make a salutary example of him by means of a noose to be thrown by dexterous Liberal hands over his head as he passed in the 'chairing' procession over a certain bridge (we are not acquainted with the topography), whereby he would be deftly hauled out of the chair, and flung into the river—a process which, if effectually completed, as intended, would necessarily have resulted in the instant death of the offending Tory member. Similar methods of combating erroneous opinions concerning the electoral franchise and the distribution of seats were not unusual.

In addressing his constituents on his election in 1831, Mr. Herries declared that, although strongly opposed to the measure proposed by the Government, he was not absolutely hostile to all Parliamentary Reform. This was true. He was often heard to express applause of Pitt's early endeavours to effect the reform of 'the rotten part of the Constitution;' although he also thought that the great statesman was wise in abandoning Reform when it became the watchword of the lovers of French revolutionary principles. He had no particular affection for Old Sarum. He had no great admiration of exclusive aristocratic influence. But what he above all things dreaded and detested was democratic despotism; and if he was mistaken in thinking that 'the Bill' would lead to its establishment, soon or late, he, at any rate, erred in very good company. On one point he was not mistaken. He did not share in the belief entertained by Lord John Russell and Mr. Secretary Stanley that the empirical creation of a uniform ten-pound franchise, resting neither on principle nor on antiquity, would prove the final settlement of the electoral question.

Although he did not frequently address the House, Mr. Herries was not 'entirely mute.' On some occasions he spoke with great effect, and it is a fact that the gravest embarrassments suffered by the Government on questions not relating to Reform were directly caused by his intervention. The defeat of the Cabinet, three days before the second reading of the Reform Bill in 1831, by a majority of forty-six on a proposed

alteration of the timber duties, was generally attributed
to his action, although the formal motion for the postponement of the Ministerial plan was in reality made
by Mr. Attwood. The Chancellor of the Exchequer
had previously announced his intention of proposing an
increase of the duty on Canadian timber for Budget
purposes. On March 18, 1831, without further notice,
he took a new departure, and suddenly submitted to
the House quite different resolutions for the reduction
of the duty on Baltic timber. In other words, he
substituted for a purely revenue question the entirely
distinct question of the protection to be afforded to
colonial and shipping interests. Mr. Herries opposed
the motion, not so much on its own merits, as on the
ground of its being a surprise ('a political trick,' he
called it), contending that, without time for deliberation,
the House could not fairly be called upon to decide
upon the new Ministerial scheme. It was in fact the
sudden change of front that he objected to—a legitimate
objection, by no means deserving the imputation of
factiousness thrown upon it by the Ministers and their
supporters.[2] It was asserted, as a reproach to the
members of the former Government—and particularly

---

[2] As might have been expected from the writer of a history the principal object of which seems to be the converse of that of Dr. Johnson's
Parliamentary Reporting—'that the Whigs should always have the worst of
it '—the action of the Opposition on this occasion is unfairly and incorrectly
represented by Mr. Spencer Walpole, as the passage in *Hansard* referred to
by himself is sufficient to show. But we are inclined to doubt whether he
ever looked at his own reference; and for this reason. Speaking of Lord
Althorp's change of plan, he says, 'This concession, however, failed to satisfy
the Protectionists.' This phrase is copied (not quoted) *verbatim et literatim*,
without the alteration of a comma, from an equally unfair account of the
same debate, in Sir Denis Le Marchant's *Memoir of Earl Spencer*.

to Mr. Herries—who voted against Lord Althorp's motion, that they had intended, if they had remained in office, to make a similar proposal. The Attorney-General even declared that they were pledged to do so. But the assertion was positively denied both by the President of the Board of Trade and the Chancellor of the Exchequer of the Duke of Wellington's Adminis-tration. The well-merited check which the Ministers met with might, in any other circumstances, have proved fatal to them ; but in view of the more important question of Reform which they had in hand, they, perhaps wisely, made up their minds to digest their discomfiture. But it is evident from Lord Grey's pub-lished correspondence with the King that ' the unto-ward event,' as he calls the vote on the timber duties in one letter, was considered as very seriously damaging to the Government. The feeling of their supporters, however, is exhibited in an article of the ' Times ' of March 20, which, scouting the supposition of the re-signation of the Cabinet, says, in the ' thorough ' style of English Reformers of the day—a style not very far removed from the *à la lanterne* formula of French reformers forty years before—' Canada is a respectable colony, and the shipowners are a respectable body ; but the British nation would rather see the Canadas swept for ever from the map of the Western world, with all the shipowners dangling from its red and yellow pines, than suffer the grand measure of Parliamentary regen-eration to be lost.'

A previous article in the same paper contains some curious observations, which might not be inapplicable to many discussions at the present day. 'It cannot be denied that the tone taken by some of the friends of the measure has been very offensive, and we may perhaps be allowed to take this opportunity of denouncing that parrot gabble about political economy, which is now so common in and out of Parliament. A person attends a few lectures of some pedant : he gets by rote a few abstract rules, and because he has acquired a little knowledge, just a degree above the nursery, he sets up for a statesman. . . . The coxcombs in question may waste as much paper as they please in scribbling, but they should not be suffered to meddle with public affairs. They injure every cause which they touch, and render contemptible every party which admits their fellowship. . . .'

On another, and a far more important, question relating to the legality of the continuance of payments on account of what is known by the name of the Russian-Dutch Loan, the Member for Harwich gave much trouble to the Whig Ministry.

The true history of the strange engagement, by which the people of this country have been saddled for a century with debts of the Russian Empire to Dutch bankers, was not known to Parliament either at the time when it was first sanctioned, or sixteen years afterwards when it was again the subject of discussion. It has been to a great extent revealed by the publication of the correspondence of Lord Castlereagh, Lord Liverpool, and the Duke of Wellington ; but some obscure points connected with it still need elucidation.

In the year 1788 [3] the Empress Catherine contracted with, or through, the house of Hope and Co. of Amsterdam, a loan of eighty million florins, for the purpose, as stated by Mr. Alexander Baring (whose authority on such a subject can hardly be contested) in the House of Commons on July 12, 1832, of providing the means of effecting the subjugation of Poland.   Mr. Whitbread said on May 26, 1815, that the loan was primarily intended for the Turkish war, which in 1791 nearly led to hostilities between Russia and Great Britain.   The interest due having for some years been left unpaid, the Russian Government, soon after the re-establishment of amicable relations with this country in 1812, expressed an earnest desire that Great Britain should assume the charge of this debt.[4]   So extravagant a request was very properly refused ; but in February 1814,[5] 'the intended aggrandizement of Holland suggested a new occasion on which Russia hoped to relieve herself of this incumbrance.'   When, in return for the sacrifices made, and to be made, by England for the common cause, Lord Castlereagh at Troyes asked for an engagement on the part of the Allies that they would promote the attainment of certain objects deemed most essential to her interests—the principal point insisted upon being the union of the Belgic Provinces with Holland—Austria and Prussia, readily recognizing the justice of the claim, promptly declared their acquiescence without any shabby shuffling.   But the conduct of

---

[3] The date is taken from *Fenn on the Funds*, a work of admitted authority.

[4] *Castlereagh Correspondence*, 3rd series, vol. i. Letter to Lord Clancarty.

[5] *Ibid.* Lord Castlereagh to Lord Liverpool, February 1814.

Russia was different.   She tried to drive a bargain, and make money out of the proposed arrangement.   'You will observe,' wrote Lord Castlereagh to Lord Clancarty, 'Austria is quite unqualified in her stipulation ; Prussia not less so in substance. . . . Russia alone has held back, not upon any objection, but from a desire to make conditions. . . . The object is to prevail upon Great Britain and Holland to take upon them jointly a debt of eighty millions of florins which Russia owes in Holland. . . . And why pay Russia rather than Austria and Prussia ?   It comes as a condition with the worse grace, after our recent gratuitous concession to Denmark, to fulfil a Russian engagement.'

Their sturdy importunity having been repelled, the Russian Government accepted the *Projet de Convention* after considerable delays.   But although Lord Castlereagh negatived the demand, he unfortunately did not discourage the hope that the resistance of the British Ministry might be overcome.   His colleagues, however, still remaining obdurate, the annexation of Belgium was settled in principle by the Treaty of Paris of May 30, 1814, without the desired concession which was afterwards untruly asserted to have been the condition *sine quâ non* of the Russian assent.

Between two and three months later, by a Convention with the Netherlands signed on August 13, Great Britain agreed to restore all the Dutch Colonies fairly conquered by British valour in a war unjustly waged against her by Holland, the vassal of France, with the exception of the Cape of Good Hope, Demerara, Essequibo, and Berbice, ceded to Great Britain, in consideration—so it was said—of an engagement, first, to pay to Sweden 1,000,000*l.* which Holland had previously been held liable to furnish; secondly, to advance a sum of 2,000,000*l.* for the defences of the Low Countries ; and thirdly, ' to bear equally with Holland such further charges as might be agreed upon between the high contracting parties and their allies towards the final and satisfactory settlement of the Low Countries in union with Holland, and under the dominion of the House of Orange, not exceeding, in the whole, the sum of 3,000,000*l.* to be defrayed by Great Britain.' [6]

This last prospective engagement had evidently in view the pressure brought to bear upon Holland by Russia.　But it was an engagement to Holland—not to Russia—and it did not bind this country to be a party to any special arrangement between the two States, although we were obliged to assist the former in the payment of the black mail likely to be levied upon her. Russia, however, was determined to drag England into the transaction she was bent on effecting for the liquidation of her outstanding debt ; and her pertinacity was rewarded with success.

Nothing can be more completely proved than the

[6] It seems worthy of notice that the French text of this very important article is much more complete and precise than the English version, which ought to be, but which is not, its exact equivalent. Among several other variations, there is a manifest difference between the opening words of the paragraph—' *A supporter, conjointement et en portion égale avec la Hollande* . . .'—and their intended counterpart—' To bear equally with Holland . . .' The word *conjointement* is not redundant. It has a distinct signification. Why, then, is it not rendered into English ?

Instances of similar divergence, whether arising from sheer carelessness, from linguistical deficiency, or from any other cause, are too common in treaties between Great Britain and other countries.

repugnance of Lord Liverpool (and presumably also of the Chancellor of the Exchequer, Mr. Vansittart) to the Russian scheme, which in his own name, and in that of his colleagues at home, he opposed, until at last their hands were forced by Lord Castlereagh, and perhaps also by the Duke of Wellington. In his letters of October 28, November 2, December 22, 1814, and January 6, 1815 (see Yonge's 'Life of Lord Liverpool,' and 'Supplementary Despatches of the Duke of Wellington'), the Prime Minister repeatedly and most earnestly exhorted Lord Castlereagh, then at Vienna, to abstain from any engagement with Russia as to the Dutch debt —a matter which the Cabinet evidently considered as one of great consequence. It seems very probable that these objections were alluded to in a despatch from Lord Castlereagh dated February 13, 1815, a selected extract from which was communicated to the House of Commons in 1847 by Lord Palmerston. All that the public has been permitted to know of the contents of that despatch is a plea for the policy of the arrangement to which the Cabinet was—justly, as we think— opposed.[7]

After his return to London, Lord Castlereagh, convinced of the utility, or necessity, of bribery, succeeded in inducing the Cabinet to adopt his views ; and

[7] Mr. Cooke, Under-Secretary of State for Foreign Affairs, who was with Lord Castlereagh at Vienna, took the same view of the matter as Lord Liverpool, to whom he wrote, on December 24, 1814: 'The only point I really fear for us is the Dutch Loan. Is it not capable of statement so as to affect our honour as a nation after Russian conduct and our protests against it ? . . . I think the subscribing the Polish arrangement, on other matters being adjusted, defensible, but adding six millions as a bonus very difficult to swallow.'—*Wellington Supplementary Despatches.*

the result was this instruction, sent on March 12, 1815,
to the Duke of Wellington.[8]

'I should hope, from the state of business at Vienna,
that your Lordship would find no great difficulty . . .
to prevail upon the Powers to sign at once a treaty
placing, by an early ratification, all the arrangements
already agreed upon [9] out of the reach of doubt. . . .
If you can effect this, you may give the Emperor of
Russia, in conjunction with the Dutch plenipotentiary,
an assurance that the half of the Dutch loan, under the
regulations as agreed upon [it does not appear what
they were, or when the agreement was come to] will be
defrayed by us ; it being understood that His Imperial
Majesty will act in concert with us in the other measures
remaining to be settled.

'I suggest a written assurance to remove doubts. .'
The giving of this assurance was made to depend upon
two conditions.   Therefore, the British Government
was still free to withhold it.   The Duke of Wellington,
on March 28, communicated to Count Nesselrode offi-
cially the words of Lord Castlereagh's despatch, with
the unaccountable omission of the important phrase
relating to future concert.   It must be supposed, however, that the understanding mentioned by Lord Castle-

[8] See *Supplementary Despatches of the Duke of Wellington*, vol. ix.

[9] They were those relating to Poland, Saxony, the reconstruction of
Prussia, the Kingdom of the Netherlands, Hanover, besides others of minor
importance.   But the definitive treaty which confirmed these arrangements
was not, in fact, signed until more than two months later.   Possibly an
equivalent may have been found in the Treaty of Alliance of March 25 against
Napoleon, binding the contracting parties to maintain the stipulations arising
out of the Treaty of Paris, which had been determined upon (by protocols)
and signed at the Congress of Vienna.

reagh was come to, although the practical value of the agreement is proved by the decisive evidence of Lord Clancarty, first British plenipotentiary at the Congress after the Duke of Wellington's departure, to have been *nil.* 'How the subject of the Dutch loan,' he wrote to Lord Castlereagh on May 19, 1815, 'has reached Lord Grey's ears, except through the Russian Chancery, I cannot guess; but sure I am that, so little has this Emperor kept faith with us, in aiding us in the concluding negotiations here, that he seems to me to have forfeited all claim to our future assistance.' This remonstrance came too late. On the day when Lord Clancarty's letter was written, the object which the Russian Government had at heart was secured by a convention signed in London between Russia, the Netherlands, and Great Britain, by which, after a preamble setting forth that the King of the Netherlands, being desirous, upon the final re-union of the Belgic Provinces with Holland, to render to the Allied Powers a suitable return for the heavy expense incurred by them in delivering the said territories from the power of the enemy; and the said Powers having agreed to waive their pretensions in favour of the Emperor of Russia . . .[1] the King of the Netherlands had resolved to execute with His Imperial Majesty a convention, to which His Britannic Majesty had agreed 'to be a

[1] Of the Allied Powers mentioned, the one who had principally 'incurred heavy expense in delivering, &c.,' was, without doubt, England. Therefore, if the averment of this preamble were true, it would result that England having a pretension to a 'suitable return' from the King of the Netherlands, waived that pretension in favour of Russia, and, at the same time, agreed with the Netherlands to pay money in satisfaction of that very pretension so assigned by herself. A singular arrangement truly!

party, in pursuance of engagements taken by his said Majesty, with the King of the Netherlands in a convention signed at London on the 18th day of August, 1814,' Great Britain and the Netherlands agreed respectively to take upon themselves a portion— amounting for each of them to 25,000,000 florins (or, according to a Parliamentary Paper,[2] 2,272,727*l.*)—of the capital and arrears of interest of the Russian loan (raised by accumulated arrears from 80,000,000, its original amount, to 100,000,000 florins), with an annual interest of five per cent., besides a yearly payment for Sinking Fund, of one per cent., which was liable to be increased to three per cent. on the demand of the Russian Government.[3]

But the fifth article of the convention contains the important proviso that all these obligations shall 'cease and determine, should the possession and sovereignty (which God forbid) of the Belgic Provinces at any time pass or be severed from the dominions of His Majesty the King of the Netherlands previous to the complete liquidation of the same.' Great value was attached to this stipulation by the British Government. It appears from a letter[4] addressed by Lord Castlereagh to Count Nesselrode, announcing the conclusion of the

---

[2] Laid before the House of Commons in 1815. In a later return, by a different calculation, the English equivalent of 25,000,000 florins is stated as 2,083,333*l.*

[3] It does not appear that under this one-sided convention either Great Britain or the Netherlands had the power of accelerating the redemption of the debt, the paying off of which at once would obviously have been advantageous to this country at least. But that would not have suited the views of Russia, whose bidding we bound ourselves to do.

[4] May 28, 1815. *Castlereagh Correspondence.*

convention, that Count Lieven, the Russian plenipotentiary, ' was desirous that the fifth article should have been confined in its operation to the part of the debt falling to the share of Holland '—the effect of such proposed limitation being that, in the event of the separation of Belgium, Holland would be relieved from the burthen assumed by her in consideration of the annexation, while England would still continue to be charged with the share she took for the sole purpose (ostensibly at least) of diminishing the pressure upon Holland. And this most absurd result, which the Tory Government in 1815 were determined to guard against, was actually brought about through the complaisance of Whig Ministers in 1832.

' But this change,' observed Lord Castlereagh in his letter, ' whilst it would have been at variance with all my arguments, as employed both at Vienna and since my return, to reconcile the Government to the measure, would have destroyed my whole case in Parliament, by enabling my opponents to describe the arrangement as one made not upon the principle of a fair equivalent with Holland, but as a gratuitous concession to Russia for an object that might not survive the present crisis.'

By an additional article in two paragraphs, which was kept secret until 1832, it was agreed, first, that in the event of a part of the Belgic Provinces being at any time severed from the dominions of His Belgic Majesty, a proportionate reduction only of the charge to be borne by the Netherlands and Great Britain should take place ; and, secondly, that the invasion or temporary occupation of those provinces by an enemy (words which do not occur in the first paragraph) should not be considered as determining any part of the stipulated payments, unless continued beyond the period of a year —a special provision obviously made for the eventualities of the coming campaign.

Presented to a puzzled Parliament, in connection with the Netherlands Colonial Treaty, and the Treaty with Sweden for the settlement of the wonderful affair of Guadeloupe (not the least of all the marvels of British diplomacy)—the three instruments forming together a bewildering labyrinth of cessions, retrocessions, cross compensations, and unintelligible transfers—this 'fantastical and incomprehensible plan,' as it was well termed by Mr. Baring (speech in the House of Commons, May 26, 1815), received, after a feeble opposition, the approval of the Legislature. And so it came to pass that the British nation, taking upon itself the liquidation of debts for funds employed in the extinction of the Polish nationality, became an accessory after the fact to that political crime.

The persistence by which Russia, after many rebuffs, attained her ends in this business, appears at first sight strange. In the case of Holland, some plausible pretext could be found for her demand, and, after all, the practical effect of the agreement was only the transfer of a loss sustained by a few Dutch capitalists through Russian insolvency to the whole body of the Dutch taxpayers. But upon England, Russia had no sort of claim, and it was not reasonable that English taxpayers should be compelled to indemnify Messrs. Hope and Co.

Why, it may be asked, did not the Russian Emperor, if unsatisfied with the lavish assistance furnished by England, simply solicit additional subsidies either in money or in stores for military purposes, instead of pressing for aid in an unusual, and a most objectionable form ?   The answer must be, that he wanted the power of borrowing; that so long as his debts remained unpaid he could have found no lenders; and that the credit of Great Britain afforded a much better security than that of the newly created Kingdom of the Netherlands. The explanation of the whole of this affair may, perhaps, be found in the fact that a few months after the signature of the convention of May 19, a new Russian loan was raised at Amsterdam.[5]

However vicious in principle, however onerous in practice, the engagement may have been, and whatever were the purposes for which it was wrung from the British Government, once taken, the honour of the nation required its strict fulfilment, but no more. To pay the uttermost farthing stipulated in the contract was a positive duty—to pay the thousandth part of a farthing beyond the covenant was degrading subserviency. The terms of the bond were precise. The Treaty, and the Act of Parliament which embodied and gave effect to it, had at least the merit—very rare in Acts of Parliament, and still more so in treaties—of accuracy and clearness of expression ; so that nothing was required for their interpretation but a sufficient knowledge of the English tongue. At length the case distinctly provided for in both instruments did arise. ' The

[5] In 1815. See *Fenn on the Funds.*

possession and sovereignty of the Belgic Provinces ' did ' pass,' and were ' severed from the dominions of His Majesty the King of the Netherlands ; ' and consequently the time arrived when, according to the positive words of the Treaty and the law, the payments were to ' cease and determine.' Nevertheless they were continued by the Government of which Lord Grey, who in 1815 had been vehement in his opposition to the Treaty, was the head.

From a very tardy communication to Parliament (in 1847) it appears that on January 25, 1831, a memorandum (' *Notice Confidentielle* ') was addressed to Lord Palmerston by the Russian plenipotentiaries Prince Lieven and Count Matuszewic containing, in reply apparently to some representation, the nature of which has not been made known, an elaborate plea for the unimpaired validity of the claims of Russia under the Convention of 1815, in spite of the actual separation of Belgium from Holland. It is inconceivable that so important a document should have received no answer from the British Secretary of State ; but none has ever been made public—a reticence on the part of the Foreign Office, which, common though it was under the Palmerston rule, is yet to be lamented for the sake of history, and also for the credit of British diplomacy.

The principal contention of the Russian plenipotentiaries was that the proviso contained in the fifth article of the convention had solely in view the possibility of foreign invasion and conquest, and was therefore not applicable to the case—never contemplated, as the plenipotentiaries asserted—of a separation brought about by internal revolution—an inference drawn from the additional article which in one place speaks of ' invasion or temporary occupation by an enemy.' But if acquiescence had not been thought more convenient than refutation, which would not have been difficult, the Foreign Office might have replied that the words cited occurred only in the second paragraph, which manifestly had in view a danger actually imminent at the moment when the convention was signed; and that the fact of their not being used either in the first paragraph of the additional article, or in the fifth article itself, in both of which severance was spoken of in general terms without any specification of the mode of its accomplishment, led reasonably to the conclusion that the operation of the fifth article was not meant to be limited to the particular case, provided for by the second paragraph of the additional article, of invasion by an enemy. It might have been added that the supposition of any such intended limitation was an improbable one, because what was important to the King of the Netherlands—the party primarily concerned, and upon whose obligation ours depended—was the fact, not the manner, of the separation of his Belgic Provinces, his acquisition of which was the sole ground for his assumption of a portion of the Russian debt, and the loss of which, from whatever cause ensuing, would leave him in the same position as if he had never possessed them.

On November 16, 1831, the day after the signature of the Treaty for the separation of Belgium from Holland, a new convention between Great Britain and

Russia relative to the Dutch loan was signed in London. In its preamble, containing several averments, the truth of which never was, or perhaps could have been, substantiated, not a word is said of the consideration for which the King of the Netherlands bound himself by the former Convention of 1815. He is not even mentioned as having been a party to that convention, which is spoken of as if it had been one simply between the other two Powers. Nor is there any allusion to the engagement in respect of the ceded Dutch colonies, which is stated in the preamble of the Convention of 1815 to have been the reason for British participation, and which must indeed be deemed to have been the only ground for it, unless that engagement is to be looked upon merely as a colourable pretence put forward to give the whole transaction a decent appearance, and veil the displeasing nudity of an agreement to throw some of the unsatisfied liabilities of a defaulting Czar upon the shoulders of the British people.

The King of the Netherlands being dropped out, by the new convention His Britannic Majesty bound himself to recommend to his Parliament to enable him to undertake to continue on his part the payments stipulated in the former one; and the Emperor of Russia, on the other hand, promised that if the arrangements agreed upon for the independence and neutrality of Belgium should be endangered, he would not contract any other engagement without a previous agreement with His Britannic Majesty and his formal assent. An entirely new departure was thus taken. The first treaty was based on the union of Belgium and Holland;

the second, on their separation. It was for the purpose of effecting ' the final and satisfactory settlement of the Low Countries in union with Holland and under the dominion of the House of Orange ' that Great Britain became a party to the former convention : it was in order to secure the independence of Belgium and, therefore, the ' final and satisfactory settlement of the Low Countries,' in separation from Holland and not ' under the dominion of the House of Orange,' that Great Britain concluded the latter.

This agreement amounted in effect to the sale of an Imperial policy. For a valuable consideration, the proud autocrat Nicholas alienated his eventual right of independent action in an European question of the first magnitude, putting himself under the control of Henry John, Viscount Palmerston, and his Lordship's lawful successors in Downing Street. It is, however, not to be believed that the Emperor would have entered into so humiliating a bargain, if he had been convinced that the purchase money was already his of right—that he was entitled to claim it purely and simply in virtue of a pre-existing contract. The convention of November 1831 would manifestly not have been signed, unless the Russian Government had been persuaded that the obligations created by the previous convention had ' ceased and determined.'

We now come to a further step in the process of mystification. On the meeting of Parliament in the following month, no allusion to the new convention or to any negotiations relating to the loan was made in the Speech from the Throne, although it announced the conclusion of the treaty (likewise unratified) for the separation of Belgium, which did not, as the former instrument did, require the sanction of Parliament for its execution. This curiosity of constitutional practice in the full tide of the Reform agitation seems to deserve notice. Motions for papers, &c., were soon made. One of these by Mr. Herries was for 'copies or extracts of any communications between his Majesty's Government and the Government of the King of the Netherlands relating to the payment of the Russian loan in Holland, after the separation, &c.' The return to the address was a very short one—*Nil.* If this statement had not been made upon the responsibility of the Secretary of State, it would appear absolutely incredible. It seems indeed passing strange that during the whole of the year 1831, while the question of the continued operation of the Convention of 1815 was pending, and was a subject of discussion between the Russian and British Governments, the Foreign Office should have been so reticent, or so little curious, as never to have endeavoured to ascertain the views of the co-partner of England concerning their joint engagement,—that the Netherlands Government should not have attempted to elicit the opinion of the British Government,—and that no interchange of observations on this important matter, in which they were equally interested, should have taken place.[6]

---

[6] Perhaps the terms of the motion were not sufficiently comprehensive to prevent evasion through technical subtleties. Persons who are not experts ought always to avoid the use of the word 'communication' in matters diplomatical, because by diplomatic persons it is frequently used in a '*non-natural*' sense.

After some preliminary discussions, the subject was brought formally before the House by Mr. Herries, who, on January 26, 1832, moved resolutions, the conclusion of which was—'that the application of the public money for the purpose of effecting any payments on the part of Great Britain, on account of the Russian loan in Holland, after the possession and sovereignty of the Belgic provinces had passed from the dominions of the King of the Netherlands, is contrary to the provisions of the Act 55 Geo. III. c. 115, and is unwarranted by any authority of Parliament.' Without discussing the very questionable wisdom of the Convention of 1815, or the possible expediency of its renewal with the sanction of Parliament, he rested his case entirely upon the legal and constitutional ground, that on an imaginative construction of a treaty, inconsistent with its plain terms, Ministers could not be justified in issuing money to a foreign power in direct opposition to the unambiguous and imperative words of an Act of Parliament prescribing the conditions under which the payments were to be made. In the conclusion of his speech he said—'I have not treated this as a party question; I have not had recourse to any of those taunts or asperities which too frequently are admitted into statements of this nature, both on one side and on the other. . . . I feel that the subject is one which must be discussed entirely by itself; . . . for it must be treated, not with reference to any party views or sentiments, but with reference to the authority of Parliament and the constitutional privileges of this House with regard to the distribution of the public money. Honourable gentle-

men who sit on the other side have been much in the
habit, particularly for some time past, of casting reflections in the way of comparison upon those who sit near
me, with respect to this very subject of the jealous
solicitude with which we should regard our control over
the public expenditure. We have been accused—too
frequently, because always unjustly—of great laxity on
this point in comparison with themselves. . . . It has
been attempted to be shown that there was a less
anxious solicitude in respect of public economy among
the members who now sit upon these benches, than
among those who sit upon the opposite ones. Now I
do not advert to that endeavour for the purpose of
reviving past discussions, or raising fresh animosity
between parties—but I advert to it for the purpose of
impressing upon gentlemen opposite that this is perhaps
almost the only opportunity that will be afforded us of
establishing a test by which to judge of their future
operations. . . . If you reject my motion you vote
away 5,000,000*l.* of public money. His Majesty's
Ministers have already voted it away ; and if you refuse
to second me, you sanction their grant. To all those
who are of opinion that this principle is of the highest
importance—that all directions for the expenditure of
the public money should be implicitly obeyed ; to all
those who believe that the assumption of the least
latitude in the observance of that high constitutional
principle is fraught with the greatest danger to the
constitution itself and the liberty of the subject, I
strongly recommend the most earnest consideration of
this question and motion before they venture to vote

against the latter. All those who think that eventually it might be right to concede such a grant—but who never will hear of its being conceded without Parliament being first consulted and its opinion being expressed upon it—I reckon upon as parties who will vote with me ; all those who from what they may now hear, or from their knowledge of this transaction as it now stands, are inclined to be convinced that we ought not at all events to make such a grant ; and that we are so far absolved from our engagements as to make it right that we should save this sum of money to the public till we are better advised (and I confess that I am one of these)—they, I say, will unquestionably vote for my proposition. . . .'

The Ministers, advised by the Law Officers of the Crown, and adopting the Russian theory without adducing a particle of evidence in support of it, contended that the obligations of Great Britain under the Convention of 1815 still subsisted, not being affected by the Belgian Revolution. The Whig Attorney-General took a high prerogative tone worthy of Mr. Attorney Noy, arguing that the King's right of making and interpreting treaties could not be limited by an Act of Parliament. But such a 'slavish doctrine,' better suited, as some modern Shippen might have exclaimed, to the meridian of St. Petersburg than to that of London, could not pass unchallenged by the Opposition, which had no lack of legal strength. Wetherall, Sugden, and Pollock, lawyers second to none in the House of Commons, or in Westminster Hall, vigorously supported the motion, and destroyed the unconstitutional sophistry of the Whig jurists. Lord Palmerston, clothed with all the authority of the Foreign Office, boldly confronted his adversaries with unfounded asseverations, of which let one serve as a specimen. Speaking of the conduct of Russia in the negotiation of the Convention of 1815, he said: ' Of her own accord—and this is important to the question—the payment of the loan was made contingent on the integrity of the kingdom of the Netherlands,—that is, Russia knew that it was a matter of paramount importance to England, that the union of the kingdoms of Belgium and Holland under one Monarchy should be observed inviolably by other nations ; and accordingly, Russia, solely with a view to manifest her ardent desire to co-operate with England, declared, in the terms of the treaty, that the loan should cease to be obligatory when a separation between Belgium and Holland took place. . . . And I ask, is this gratuitous generosity on the part of Russia to be now turned against herself by those in whose favour she volunteered it ?' This positive statement, made with all the weight of supposed official information, is proved, beyond the possibility of doubt, to have been contrary to the truth, by the evidence of Lord Castlereagh's letter, above cited, to Count Nesselrode, which shows that the condition alleged by Lord Palmerston to have been offered spontaneously by Russia, with ' gratuitous generosity' towards England, was in reality insisted upon by the British Government, and most unwillingly accepted by the Russian Plenipotentiary, who did his utmost to put it aside. But the House of Commons was ignorant of the existence of that letter.

The case made out against the Government was so strong that some of the most thoroughgoing Liberals— among others Mr. Joseph Hume, and Mr. O'Connell, who spoke as a lawyer—declared that it was impossible for them to resist the motion of censure. Even the Secretary at War, Sir Henry Parnell, preferring his convictions to his place, left the House refusing to vote with his colleagues. And on the final division the main resolution was rejected by only the small majority of twenty-four—a result which, though a formal absolution, was a virtual condemnation.

While the Ministers and the Crown lawyers in the course of this debate, as on a former occasion in answer to a question from Sir Robert Peel, affirmed with frequent and angry iterance that the old Convention still bound, and the Act of 1815 still enjoined, the Government to pay the interest on the loan, the House of Commons was studiously kept in ignorance of the fact that there lay concealed in a red box a new Convention absolutely inconsistent with the former one, which they declared to be still in force, and by its express words rendering necessary the new enactment which according to their emphatic assertions would be wholly supererogatory.

That the Reform Ministry were guilty of gross deception cannot be denied. But this is not the only imputation to which they are open. If, as they professed to believe, the honour of the British Crown required the uninterrupted discharge of all the liabilities incurred by the first Convention, then they did not act honourably towards the Emperor of Russia in imposing upon him an entirely new condition for their fulfilment of what they recognized as an honourable engagement—in compelling him to enter into a distasteful bargain for the continuance of a payment which, if their theory were true, they had no right to withhold.

The story of contradictions does not end here. The Auditor of the Exchequer, Lord Grenville, a statesman of the first rank, having expressed grave doubts as to the legality of any issue for the dividend falling due in January 1832, they were overcome by the opinion of the Law Officers that the money ought to be paid pursuant to the Act of 1815 ; but at the beginning of June—the, until then, hidden Convention of November 1831 being still unratified, and all the circumstances being therefore precisely the same as before—the Treasury informed Messrs. Hope that without the sanction of Parliament they had no authority to make any further payment. What was declared to be required by law in January, was declared to be contrary to law in July.

At last, seven months after its signature, the ratified Convention was brought to light, and laid before Parliament. In due course of time effect was given to it by an Act passed, not without many sharp debates, in which many hard facts and cogent arguments reminded the Whigs in the hour of their triumph that even they were fallible. On the Chancellor of the Exchequer's motion for going into Committee to take the new Convention into consideration on July 12, Mr. Herries, reviewing all the past transactions, pointing out the 'extraordinary discrepancies' between the information tardily given to the House 'and all the arguments, all the statements of His Majesty's Government on an antecedent step of this important question,' and adding to his former arguments against the conduct of Ministers those furnished by their own recorded admissions, moved the following resolution : ' That it appears. to this House that the payment made by the Commissioners of the Treasury on account of the interest due on the Russian loan in Holland in January last, when the obligation and authority to make any such payment had, according to the terms of the Convention with Holland and Russia, and of the Act of Parliament founded thereon, ceased and determined, and also when a new Convention with Russia, not then communicated to this House, had been entered into recognising the necessity of recurring to Parliament for power to continue such payments under the circumstances which had attended the separation between Holland and Belgium, was an application of the public money not warranted by law.'

But although the production of the new matter enabled the mover and his backers, Mr. Baring, Sir Charles Wetherall, Mr. Pollock (afterwards Lord Chief Baron) Sir Edward Sugden (Lord St. Leonards) Mr. Croker, and the leader of the Opposition, Sir Robert Peel—to show a far stronger case than in the previous discussion in January, the resolution of censure was negatived by the larger majority of forty-six, several of those in the Liberal ranks who had on the former occasion voted against, now voting for, the Government, while avowing that their opinions remained unchanged. Colonel Davies, one of the reformers, said that ' although he fully concurred in the general position of the right honourable gentleman the member for Harwich, it was impossible for him to vote for the resolutions. . . . He concurred with him in thinking that His Majesty's Ministers acted illegally in making the payment of January last, and that the Convention they have since made with Russia, acknowledging that that payment was contrary to law, has placed them in a worse situation than they were in before.' Observing that the question was so plain and simple that a child could understand it, and that he could find no ground on which Ministers could be entitled to act as they had done, the gallant and Liberal member wound up a series of arguments proving that their conduct was censurable with the declaration that he would not vote for their censure. Mr. Joseph Hume subsequently explained that he had ' voted for the Whigs though he believed them to be in the wrong,' and that ' it was his intention to support the Government, right or wrong,' a candid avowal which drew from Sir Robert Peel the remark : ' This I will venture to say, that if any unfortunate member for a rotten borough—for one of those condemned institutions which were so condemned because men supported Ministers against their consciences. . . . I say if any member of those condemned boroughs had avowed that he was ready to vote that black was white, and that what was illegal in January was legal in July, we should never have heard the last of the reprobation which would have been launched upon the head of that member for a borough constituency.'

It is worthy of observation, as an example of the

high-handed way in which Parliament was treated by
the Liberal Government, that in the whole course of the
debates concerning engagements imposing onerous and
durable charges upon the British people for the benefit
of a foreign potentate, no correspondence, no documen-
tary information throwing light upon the recent or upon
the previous transaction—not even the Russian memorandum, of which the Ministerial speakers, making it
their brief, used the very words—was produced.   The
communication of the bare Convention with Russia was
unaccompanied by a single elucidatory paper ; and
when Mr. Baring, on July 16, moved for those papers
which the House of Commons had a right to ask for,
the motion was met with a peremptory refusal, and
rejected by a ministerial majority of thirty-six.   Such
was the expression of Liberal views of the constitutional
relations of the Crown to the House of Commons just
after the passing of the Reform Bill.

The payment of the tribute to Russia by this nation,
whose deliverance from it the senior member for Harwich had so much at heart, will ' cease and determine '
in June 1915, when, at last, one hundred years after the
original imposition of the charge, the liabilities incurred
by the late Empress Catherine for iniquitous purposes
being extinguished by the operation of the Sinking Fund,
will no longer be a burden upon British tax-payers.
The total sum then paid for the satisfaction of sundry
Dutch creditors of Russia will have amounted to considerably more than double the maximum contribution
of 3,000,000*l.* which in 1814 Great Britain undertook to
make by her agreement with Holland.[7]

[7] The aggregate amount of our payments in respect of this loan from

Once again this subject was discussed in the House of Commons in 1847, when a motion was made by Mr. Hume,[8] for the discontinuance of these payments, on the quite untenable ground of the annexation of Cracow to Austria. On this occasion Lord Palmerston, having, as he said, caused enquiry to be made at the Record Office, laid upon the table a paper, in eleven pages (including four pages of translation) described as 'Correspondence relating to the Russian Dutch Loan, 1815 and 1831.' Its contents are the extract from Lord Castlereagh's despatch of February 13, 1815, and the 'Notice Confidentielle' of January 26, 1831, above mentioned. This is the whole of the information ever imparted by Lord Palmerston to the House of Commons concerning the correspondence of the Foreign Office on this matter, not a single paper of any kind signed by himself (except the Convention of 1831), nor any despatch addressed to him by a British representative at The Hague, or at

January 1, 1816, to December 31, 1871, was 5,445,406*l.* 8*s.* 8*d.* The capital redeemed was 1,166,666*l.* 13*s.* 4*d.*, leaving still to be paid off 916,666*l.* 13*s.* 4*d.*, bearing interest at five per cent.

[8] His speech (March 4, 1847) affords a good example of the historical ignorance which members of Parliament frequently display in debates on foreign questions. In stating his case, and in order to make it clear, he said : 'By the fourth article of the Treaty of Vienna an agreement was entered into between England, Russia, and Holland, respecting the Russian Dutch loan borrowed by Holland from Russia and payable upon two conditions.' It would be difficult to compress into the space of a single sentence a greater quantity of nonsense than that which is comprised in these words. For (1) the article cited contains no allusion whatever to England, to Holland, or to any loan ; (2) no agreement concerning the Russian Dutch loan is mentioned in any part of the Treaty of Vienna ; (3) the loan in question was borrowed, not by Holland from Russia, but by the latter in the former country ; (4) no loan was ever raised by Holland in Russia. But these absurdities were allowed to pass without notice. Perhaps they were not perceived.

St. Petersburg on the subject having been suffered to appear. A future generation may perhaps be better enlightened in 1915, when the suppressed papers of the Castlereagh and Palmerston periods being, possibly, allowed to emerge from the recesses of the Foreign Office, this nation may at last be enabled to learn the true and complete history of a century of debt imposed by Russian pressure upon British weakness.

It is necessary now to mention the course pursued by our co-partner in the transaction of 1815. Holland, interpreting the fifth article of the Convention of that year according to the simple and natural meaning of its words, ceased, in 1831, to pay her portion of the interest, &c., of the loan. But as she did not recognize the independence of Belgium until 1839, Russia maintained that up to that date, at all events, the payments were due. The question was under discussion for many years between the two Governments, and was finally settled in 1850 by a Convention, by which the Netherlands agreed to pay one million and a half of florins (the amount payable for about one year and a half—Great Britain paid in 1831, 1,056,250 florins) and received in return quittance in full of all claims—an arrangement implying an admission on the part of Russia that the interpretation put upon the Convention of 1815 by Holland and by the Tory Opposition in the British House of Commons (notably by the member for Harwich) was the true one; that the Russian interpretation adopted by the Whig Cabinet in England was a false one; and that the demands acceded to by the Government of Great Britain, but, with more spirit, rejected by the Government of the Netherlands, were groundless, extortionate, and fraudulent.

Enough, perhaps too much, has been said of the new way to pay old Russian debts.

A recently published letter from the Duke of Wellington to William IV, dated May 12, 1832, on the subject of the Duke's abortive attempt to construct a Reform Cabinet when Lord Grey resigned in consequence of the King's refusal to create a large batch of Peers, begins with the statement that ' The Duke of Wellington has seen in the course of this day some of the gentlemen mentioned by Your Majesty. The Duke is apprehensive that Mr. Herries as well as Mr. Goulburn will be unwilling to serve. . . .'

From this it would seem that Mr. Herries's name was suggested by the King, but that before any direct communication had been made to him, he manifested his determination to be no party to the proposed arrangement. He was frequently heard to speak of it afterwards in terms of the strongest condemnation, and there can be no doubt that he always looked upon the step taken by the Duke as a deplorable error of judgment. It may safely be assumed that, firm Constitutionalist as he was, he viewed with no favourable eye the subsequent negotiation by which the Sovereign induced the Duke and other Peers to pledge themselves to abandon their legislative duties in order to avert the risk of a forced increase of the Upper House.

The following letter dated May 23, 1832 (when the Reform Bill was in Committee of the House of Lords), from a friend of the Duke of Wellington has reference to this transaction.

'The Duke thought he could not do otherwise than assure the King that he, for one, would do nothing to embarrass him. Having said this, he now is positive that he cannot directly, or indirectly, take any part in the Bill, and indeed I don't think that he could with honour. . . . The Duke says that he was peculiarly circumstanced, but that this need not cause others to follow his example. He thinks it very hard that people will have no judgment of their own. I reply that, hard or not, the fact is that people look to him for an example, and follow the one he has set ; and that, inconvenient as this may be in an instance like the present, it would be quite impossible to have a Party and act upon a system if the great mass did not act as their chief does. Indeed I added that he would be the first to find fault if upon general subjects every one was acting for himself ; and that he could not be surprised if, at a moment of great distress, there was great con- fusion when the Party found itself without a leader. What is now to be done ? In the House of Commons Peel will not stir. . . . The Duke on his part has bound his honour not to embarrass the King. His particular friends in the House of Lords, such as Lords Aberdeen, Bathurst, and Rosslyn—will not move with- out him ; and indeed they seem to think that any attempt to improve the Bill would cause the immediate creation of Peers. . . . I come to the conviction that there is nothing to be done. You had better see Lord Ellenborough and consult with him. He will not quit his post.[9] He is active and intelligent and he will be able to let you know whether by any effort we could make there would be a possibility of rallying to such an extent as to alter the Bill on the third reading. . . . I hope you will have communicated with Lord Melbourne respecting the projects of the Political Unions. In the desperate state to which we are reduced, I would rather communicate with the Ministers themselves than be overtaken by the storm without striving to avoid it. Our leaders have left us. . . .'

In the previous year Mr. Herries had conveyed to the Home Office some secret intelligence probably of a similar nature to that above alluded to. On November 21, 1831, Mr. G. Lamb, Under-Secretary of State, wrote to him : 'I return you many thanks for the communication of Mr. ——'s letter which, I am sorry to say, is too much in consonance with other information from the same quarter. . . . I have immediately transmitted it to my brother [Lord Melbourne] accompanied with all the cautions which you wish to be observed in any communications with the quarter from which it comes, and there can be no doubt that it affords an opportunity for availing ourselves of a most valuable channel of information if dexterously used in the way you point out. I have only to assure you that it shall be considered as strictly confidential, and that I feel much obliged by the trust reposed in me, which can have no motive but the promotion of publick security and tranquillity.'

The following ' Rough sketch of a paper ' written

---

[9] He did not quit his post, and voted according to his convictions.

by Mr. Herries not long, apparently, before the passing
of the Bill, has no date.

'The question of Reform is now irrevocably decided.
All hope of any beneficial result from any combined
opposition to the measure in its present shape must be
abandoned ; and it therefore only remains for those who
have acted together as a party in opposing it to decide
what other steps they can or ought to take in order to
avert or mitigate its destructive consequences.

'Very great anxiety prevails among the principal
members and indeed throughout the whole body of
that Party to learn the determination or disposition of
their two leaders upon this point. Their opponents are
already active in the field for the ensuing elections, and
the Tory party must take their measures at once and
with great vigour, or give up all chance of forming any
considerable part of the new Parliament. . . . The
isolated endeavours of individual volunteers will effect
little in such a crisis as the present. Many generous
and resolute men will, no doubt, be found who will
spontaneously incur the expense and inconvenience of
contesting counties and boroughs upon Conservative
principles in opposition to Radical brutality. Some of
them may succeed ; but, unless there be a combined
effort, unless the majority of the Tory candidates be
invited, encouraged, and in some cases aided, by the
influence and the means of the Tory party acting under
the guidance of its acknowledged chiefs, the utmost that
can be expected from such individual exertions will be
the return of a fraction of that body—deprived of some
of its most active and experienced supporters, insufficient

in numbers or in weight to produce any effect in a Reformed House.

'Whether by a great combined exertion a more
successful result can be obtained is a question which
appears to require speedy attention and most deliberate
consideration. For this purpose is it not advisable—
is it not indeed urgently expedient—that the Duke of
Wellington and Sir Robert Peel should without delay
assemble the most influential of the Peers and Com-
moners who act with them, and, taking these persons
into council on the present most critical posture of our
affairs, should determine after mature deliberation what
course it may be best for the Tories as a body—if they
are to continue such—to pursue ? '

But they had almost ceased to be a body, and for all
practical purposes they had no leaders. Although, as
the writer of the above paper expected, ' many generous
and resolute men ' were found ready to come forward,
the ' combined effort ' which he desired was wanting.
There was no unity of action and little disposition
generally to make sacrifices for a common cause. ' I
hear that there is no idea of assisting any candidate with
money,' writes one very estimable candidate ; ' so Holmes
tells us and Bonham, and all who can be supposed to
have means of knowledge.' A letter from an intelligent
man with an illegible signature to Lord Aberdeen, and
by him communicated to Mr. Herries shows a dismal
prospect for the Conservatives on the eve of the General
Election at the end of 1832. ' It is impossible not to
be struck on the one hand with the great activity displayed in various parts of the country by the reforming

Whig and revolutionary parties ; and, on the other, with the torpor, listlessness, and Turkish waiting upon Providence displayed by the Conservative party. Truth to say, there seem but the two former parties in the field, displaying certainly all the incipient symptoms of that rancorous hostility which is likely to distinguish their hereafter bearing towards each other. Arise how it may, this apathy of the Conservative side is a fatal presage for the future. I have been led to think that it may be ascribed, not so much to want of faith in the cause, as to the utter inadequacy of the agents and agency (in former circumstances effective enough) to grapple with the new system. . . . .'

In the disorganised remnant of the Conservative Party after the election of the first reformed House of Commons there was a general feeling of despondency, which the attitude and tone of its leader was not calculated to lessen. Right or wrong, the belief was common that he wished to abandon his followers, whom he no longer seemed to care to direct or encourage. The complaint was universal that no one knew what were his views. Even those who had been most in his confidence found it difficult to obtain from him any clear indications of policy, as the following letter shows.

'January 4, 1833.

'My dear Herries,—Being desirous of eliciting from Peel his opinions and views as to the course which it would be most expedient for us to pursue in Parliament, I wrote to him when I was last at Cambridge. My letter stated what I considered to be the difficulties of our situation—suggested the importance of perfect union and complete concert with all who called themselves Conservative, as the only hope of keeping a party together, and urged that without a strong party, strong in union more than in numbers, there was no hope of our being of any use. I enclose you his reply which I received this morning. I agree with his general view, though I feel the difficulty of maintaining the neutral position which he recommends. I am sorry to see (what perhaps others would not observe) still an unwillingness to unite cordially with the Ultras, but this may easily be softened by our joint management. Of course the letter is for your private information, and when you have read it you will return it to me. I am obliged to divide it into two letters, as it is over weight for one. . . . Yours, &c.,

'H. GOULBURN.'

Even as to the Duke of Wellington's steadfastness, distrust, though quite unfounded, seems to have been felt in some quarters. Idle reports were circulated of his intention to give up politics and leave England. To Mr. Herries, who thought that such rumours were likely to have an injurious effect, the Duke wrote as follows :

'Belvoir Castle : January 5, 1833.

'My dear Herries,—Arbuthnot has shown me a letter from you on the subject of the paragraph in the 'Morning Post,' 'Standard,' &c., respecting my *Intention* of going abroad. It is difficult to judge what was the *Intention* of these Gentry in publishing such an article ; which, till I saw your letter, I considered a matter of indifference. It is still more difficult to contradict the existence of an *Intention* excepting from authority ; but as I never have had, so I never will have anything to say to any of the newspapers.

' But the *Intention* is supposed to exist because there has been a reduction of Establishments, servants, &c. This fact may be contradicted if it is judged necessary. In fact I have as many servants as I have ever had ; and more horses because I am in the habit of going out hunting more frequently than heretofore.

' No Establishment has been diminished, not even that for preserving Game ; notwithstanding that since the enactment of the Game Bill to put down poaching there has been such an increase of that crime, as that there is no Game to preserve.

' This is all that can be said upon the subject. But I would prefer to say nothing ; and to leave this Lye to take the usual course ; that is to be the wonder of nine days ; and to be the subject of various anonymous and abusive letters to myself; and then be forgotten, unless others should wish it to be contradicted by a contradiction of the facts. Believe me ever yours most sincerely,

' W.'

A letter received shortly before the meeting of the new Parliament from Sir Robert Peel exhibits a balance of inconveniences to be calculated.

' I have only this moment got your letter. . . . I hope it is true that the Radicals mean to declare war against the Government—I am adverse to any course of proceeding on our part which should justify the Govern-

ment in the eyes of the country in forming a cordial
union with the Radicals.   That I think would be
tantamount to positive destruction, because it would be
tantamount to the adoption of the views and principles
of the Radicals, and their practical enforcement through
the Crown and Government.

'At the same time I cannot advise us to make
any compromise of the principles which we have maintained by acquiescing in any declarations of opinion
which may be proposed in the address with one or other
of two views—either to compel us to such a compromise
or to expose our numerical weakness by refusing to
make it.   Of the two in my judgment the exposure of
our weakness will be the least evil.

'I hardly think it worth while to notice the very
foolish and mischievous reports countenanced, if not
propagated by our journals—of junctions with the
Government or at least coquetting with the Government
by individuals.   Disunion of the Conservative party on
any ground would be bad enough—but disunion on
the ground of individual accessions to a Government
constituted like the present would be an intolerable evil.

'The reports originate possibly in the surmise that
there are differences among the members of the Cabinet
—surmises for which the language of the ' Times,' and
the ' Globe' seem to afford ample foundation.   Whatever be their origin, they have none in any communication, direct or indirect, on any matter of public concern
with me or with any one to my knowledge.   Ever most
faithfully yours,

'R. P.'

About this time there began a series of letters from Mr. Croker concerning his political articles for the 'Quarterly Review.' On January 10, 1833, he wrote :

'Dear Herries,—. . . . I have obtained leave to show the enclosed to some one who can say whether it suits the views of our party—pray look at it—alter on the margin what you please. Your notes will only be seen by me. If the paper be altogether wrong, say so ; for we wish to keep the Review a good Tory on all points. When you have done, return the paper to my address at Mr. Murray's over the way [Mr. Herries then lived in Albemarle Street, opposite to the eminent publisher's]. Yours ever,

'J. W. CROKER.

'The article is nearly twice too long ; any omissions therefore which you would suggest would be very acceptable advice.'

Letters from the same writer asking for information or criticism were frequent during many years. One without date of year, says : 'Many thanks for your excellent advice, to which I shall give effect. . . . Lord George Seymour has called in with a report that the D. of W. is going to Ireland as L.L. If you hear that I am made Bishop of Waterford you may equally believe it. . . .'

Although the Conservative Opposition during the Sessions of 1833 and 1834 was impotent and disheartened, the member for Harwich did not desert his Parliamentary duties. He never spoke for the sake of speaking without a practical purpose, but on several questions of importance he expressed his opinions—as, for example, on the renewal of the Bank Charter Bill, when, together with Sir Robert Peel, he strenuously opposed the provision for making Bank notes a legal tender—on the Slavery Abolition Bill, when he strongly objected, not indeed to its principle, which he approved, or to the grant of 20,000,000*l.* as compensation, which he thought equitable, to the planters, but on constitutional grounds, from which he never swerved in the least, to the discretionary power given to the Government as to the mode of raising the money, asserting, as he always did, the absolute right of the House of Commons to determine the conditions of loans—and on various other subjects. He was once even imprudent enough to bring forward an Indian case, such as neither the House nor the public can ever be induced to pay attention to, advocating in a long speech the cause of the King of Oude against the Board of Control.

Among the changes introduced by the Whig Ministry, one important measure for the thorough reform of one of our most ancient institutions—the Exchequer— by the abolition of many offices become useless—those of Auditor, the Clerk of the Pells, the four Tellers,[1] with their subordinates — and the substitution of simpler forms in accordance with modern habits of

---

[1] A special exception was made by the Bill in the case of Lord Camden, whose office was retained as a mark of respect for the public spirit displayed by him in spontaneously giving up to the nation during many years considerable emoluments to which he was fully entitled, and amounting in the aggregate to upwards of a quarter of a million. He was a staunch Tory— a friend and disciple of Pitt.

business, for the antiquated and cumbrous machinery belonging to the times of the Norman Kings, with its tallies, grotesque notation, barbarous Latin jargon, and impracticable system of Roman numerals, received the cordial approval of Mr. Herries, at whose suggestion some improvements were made in the details of the Bill. He took an opportunity of pointing out, as Lord Granville Somerset had previously noticed, that in fact it was mainly founded upon the labours of a Royal Commission presided over by himself, which had been appointed in 1830, when the Duke of Wellington was in office, to enquire into the management of the Revenue. It appears, indeed, that the matter had been long under consideration ; for in the appendix to the Report of another Commission in 1831, there is a letter from the Clerk of the Pells in 1828, stating that early in the previous year he had received communications from the Chancellor of the Exchequer (Mr. Robinson) and the Secretary of the Treasury (Mr. Herries) directing his attention to the possible simplification of business, and reduction of establishment, which might be effected by the consolidation of existing offices.

The reform of the ancient procedure of the Exchequer was indirectly associated with the destruction of the ancient seat of the Legislature of England at the last moment of the existence of the first reformed House of Commons. The old tallies which represented the administrative history of this nation during many centuries having been doomed to the flames, lighted the fire which consumed the venerable Palace of Westminster, rich in the glorious memories of that Parliamentary history which long before the year 1832 was studied with admiration by the civilized world.

When Sir Robert Peel was hastily summoned from Rome to assume the direction of the Government at the end of 1834, he offered to Mr. Herries a seat, which was accepted, in his shortlived Cabinet, with the office of Secretary at War—a Department with the business of which Mr. Herries was, from old experience, well acquainted. He had not been long installed when he received (on January 5, 1835), from the new Prime Minister the communication of a confidential letter to the Duke of Wellington, expressing Sir Robert Peel's desire that the King's speech should, if possible, announce the fact that, notwithstanding all former reductions, the estimates of the year 1838 were lower than any preceding estimates since 1793, and that the head of each Department should commence without delay a consideration of what retrenchments could be made consistently with the true and permanent interests of the public service—but adding that he would not purchase the advantage of such a declaration by any reduction that could not safely be made.

The Premier's wishes were fully entered into by the Secretary at War, who yielded to no member of the House of Commons—not even to Mr. Joseph Hume himself, as he once told that gentleman in debate—in love of economy. It has already been shown how eager he was for retrenchment after the Peace, and again in 1827. Carrying out his own constant views he framed those Army Estimates for 1835, which many years afterwards were held up by the Manchester school as a model for perpetual imitation, and even now seem occasionally to be looked back upon with fond, but unavailing, regret. They were in fact lower than any estimates which have ever been voted since 1793, the first year of the Great Revolution War. Perhaps they were too low. Such, indeed, appears to have been, some years later, the impression of the Minister who presented them to Parliament. It must, however, be presumed that they were not laid before the House of Commons without the previous consideration and approval of the Duke of Wellington.

The following letters written during the progress of the General Election show what appeared to be the Ministerial prospects.

' January 10, 1835.

' My dear Peel,—The accounts from the boroughs this morning are not so good as those of yesterday. Out of 21 members returned we have only 7. The balance is therefore materially changed. It now stands thus : For, 138 ; Against, 133 ; Hopeful, 17 ; Doubtful, 3.

' Among our hopefuls and doubtfuls there are two or three respecting some of whom Bonham thinks you can give some account. . . . But the failure of the Lords and Secretary of the Admiralty is still the most pressing subject of difficulty. I have been so strongly impressed with it, that I wrote last night to Shaw to suggest to him the great importance of putting Sir George Cockburn into an Irish borough, if there were yet time for it, and any one were available for the purpose. It occurred to me that Kinsale might be so.

I hope I did right.   There was no time to be lost, and
I had no person to advise with here.   If you approve
of my suggestion, you will perhaps write to Shaw in
the same sense. . . .   Now that Grant has lost his
chance of a seat, may not Patrick Stewart be put on the
list of persons from which you will have to choose your
Chairman of Ways and Means?   I think he is in favour
with the House, and might be more easily carried than
a pure Tory. . . . Truly yours,　　　'J. C. HERRIES.'

'January 10, 1835.

' My dear Praed,—I despatched your servant yesterday with the " yes " which you said would suffice for
him.   That is not the usual answer carried away from
this office, I assure you.

' You have done admirably well, and it is with more
satisfaction than I can well express that I confess myself in the case of Yarmouth to have been a false
prophet, and a vain Croker.   I trembled for you.   I
thought it but fair to send your letter to Peel, who is at
Brighton. . . .

' We are doing quite as well as I expected in the
country.   We have a clear majority on the whole of the
returns up to this date, and I feel tolerably confident
that we shall maintain it to the end.   But it will be a
bare majority.   Truly yours,　　　'J. C. HERRIES.'

'January 11, 1835.

' My dear Herries,—I return Praed's letter.   He
has fought a good fight and his triumph is a very useful one.

'Bonham's calculations are the most flattering I have seen as to numbers. I am the last to despair of success in the great contest in which we are engaged.

'My confidence arises less from the returns themselves than from the conviction that we shall do all that can be reasonably and justly required, and that, in spite of clamour and menace, reason and justice will still prevail.

'A good infusion of ———s ———s and ———s is by no means to be deprecated. The violence of such empty, frothy fellows as Dr. ———, is of no disservice to a Government. Ever yours,

'ROBERT PEEL.'

Same date.

'I write one line to say that I quite agree with you as to Cockburn, and that I think the suggestion of Patrick Stewart worthy of the fullest consideration. . . In spite of returns, and occasional mishaps, I have a confidence in our success which arises mainly from this reflection :—If what we shall propose to the House of Commons will not satisfy—who are the men that will propose that something which is to satisfy?

'I do not hesitate to say that I feel that I can do more than any other man can who means his reforms to work practically, and who respects, and wishes to preserve, the British Constitution.

'I think this must ultimately prevail, and attract for us more support than we at present calculate upon.

'However, though God knows as utterly indifferent to the tenure of my present post as any man can be on all private grounds, I am very confident and very sanguine—and though this is not sufficient to ensure success, I am sure despondency and despair would at once prevent it. Ever yours, ' ROBERT PEEL.'

The attention of the Secretary at War seems not to have been confined to the business of his own department and the general policy of the Cabinet. Evidence of his having been consulted on administrative questions not connected with his office is afforded by a long letter, in many sheets, in answer to enquiries from Sir Robert Peel, on Exchequer Bills, their origin, nature, history, uses, and possible dangers, with some suggestions of an eventual change of system in their issue, for the sake of greater security. The following passages in this paper appear to have some historical interest.

' The counterbalancing objection to these advantages is the very great possible, though not probable, danger to which the Treasury is exposed by the existence of a debt professedly payable on the demand of the creditor without any means of making that payment if it should be actually demanded. The present practice is to advertise periodically the payment of all Exchequer Bills more than a twelvemonth old with an offer to the holders to give new Bills in lieu of money if they desire it. This is done in full confidence that the money will not be called for—and generally with the perfect certainty that, if it should be demanded, it would not be forthcoming at the Exchequer.

' The enormous danger that *may* arise under this system was exemplified at the period of the Panic in 1825. There is little doubt but that the shock to

Public Credit which produced such terrible results on that occasion was increased by the course which the Treasury was compelled to adopt with respect to Exchequer Bills. The period for advertising a large portion of them happened to fall in with the first indications of alarm and distress in the City. Exchequer Bills fell to a discount, and no doubt could be entertained that if the advertisement had been published in the usual manner, money would have been demanded for nearly the whole amount. In that case the Exchequer would have been bankrupt. Some delay consequently took place before an arrangement could be made with the Bank for meeting the emergency ; but the mere postponement of the advertisement became an additional source of alarm and pressure. . . .'

To the well-known history of the brief struggle which ended in the resignation of the Ministers there is nothing to be added. They gladly withdrew from an untenable position, into which they had been brought by circumstances not the consequences of their own acts. His own sentiments as well as those of all his colleagues on the termination of the hopeless contest were, no doubt, correctly expressed by Mr. Herries, when he wrote in a private letter on April 19 : ' We shall probably be out of office to-morrow ; and, so far as we are personally concerned, I am sure that there is not one of us who will not feel the release as a most welcome deliverance from a most painful burthen.'

A first visit to Italy, where he passed several months in the following year, afforded to Mr. Herries a pleasant and a wholesome change from House of Commons business, and the worry of party politics. The keen enjoyment which he derived from the study of art and antiquity, of which he was a true lover, without dilettantist affectation, was lessened only by the contemplation of the effects of misrule in many parts of the Peninsula, and especially at Rome, where his own observation, confirming him in the opinion he had always entertained, made him more than ever deplore the part taken by Great Britain in the restoration of the most odious and the most contemptible of all European Governments. 'Once overthrown,' he would say, 'it never ought to have been allowed to be set up again; and, if we could not prevent the re-establishment of such a system, at any rate we ought not to have had a hand in it.' Government by Priests appeared to him hardly, if at all, less offensive than government by mobs.

The duty of an Opposition, said Mr. Tierney, is threefold—always to oppose—never to propose—and to turn out the Government. That duty was upon the whole fairly well discharged by the Conservative adversaries of Lord Melbourne's Cabinet. But it can hardly be said that their proceedings—or indeed those of the Government—during the first three or four years at least, had a very interesting character. It may indeed be doubted whether any portion of our Parliamentary and political history since the accession of George III. is so little attractive to present readers as that which comprised the existence of the Melbourne Administration. To the general tediousness of the debates of the greater part of this period Mr. Herries contributed little or nothing, but, on the other hand, with perhaps more advantage to the public, he took a considerable share of Parliamentary work of a practically useful kind. He was one of the most active members of the Committee of 1838, and subsequent sessions, on Metropolitan Improvements—a subject in which he never ceased to take the most lively interest—to whose recommendations we owe the formation of many new thoroughfares, such as the prolongation of Oxford Street; the extension of Cannon Street; the line from Piccadilly to St. Martin's Lane; the enlargement of the approaches to London Bridge; and other additions to previously existing means of communication.

The greater part, if not the whole, of the second, the most comprehensive, Report of 1838, was written by Mr. Herries.

On the great Privilege question of Stockdale and Hansard, when the House of Commons, not venturing to punish the Lord Chief Justice of England and the other Judges whose decisions it condemned, or the Juries who had given verdicts adverse to its pretensions, visited with its wrath the Plaintiff in actions which it had more than once directed the Attorney-General to defend, the Plaintiff's solicitor, the solicitor's clerk, and the Sheriffs, who, under pain of attachment for default, had executed the judgment of the Court of Queen's Bench,—when night after night the subjects of debate were the hazardous shortness of the neck of one incarcerated Sheriff, and the perilous ' turgescence ' of the liver of the other—Mr. Herries, differing entirely from the Conservative leader, whom he respected and honoured, but would not blindly follow, and believing that the course pursued was arbitrary, illegal, unjust, subversive of judicial independence, dangerous to the liberty of the subject, and derogatory to the dignity of the House itself, voted repeatedly in the opposing minority, in the lists of which his name—the only one of the lay Conservative members of the rank of Privy Councillor—is to be found along with those of C. Cresswell, Sir W. Follett, W. E. Gladstone, T. Pemberton, Sir F. Pollock, Sir E. Sugden, F. Kelly, &c., &c., against the majority composed of Ministerialists, advanced Radicals, and Sir Robert Peel's supporters. Though he did not think himself called upon to attempt to add anything to the arguments of the eminent lawyers whose views he shared, his feeling on this question was very strong. He held the opinion that in the famous precedent case of Ashby and White Chief-Justice Holt and the House of Lords were in the right, and the House of Commons in the wrong. Being convinced that ' neither House of Parliament hath any power by any vote or declaration to create to themselves any new privilege that is not warranted by the known laws and customs of Parliament,' and applying to the present occasion the words of the Lords' resolutions of 1704, he came to the conclusion that ' The House of Commons . . . had assumed to themselves alone a legislative authority by pretending to attribute the force of a law to their declaration, had claimed a jurisdiction not warranted by the Constitution, and had assumed a new privilege to which they could have no title by the laws and customs of Parliament, and thereby, so far as in them lay, subjected the rights of Englishmen and the freedom of their persons to the arbitrary votes of the House of Commons.'   Arbitrary violence in any shape, whether exercised by the Crown or by the House of Commons, he abhorred.   The only mode of government which appeared to him tolerable was that of government by law—fixed, defined, known—and he refused to recognise the validity of any 'tyrant's plea,' under cover of which a bare majority of the House of Commons might destroy all securities for property, liberty, or even life, and substitute for English freedom, and English justice, the execrable despotism of a French Convention.   But although he was opposed to the claim of the House to make a privilege whatever it might at any time think proper to declare to be such, he at the same time thought that the absolute right of publication ought to be secured to Parliament by law. He therefore rejoiced at the rational termination of an unseemly conflict by an act of legislation which might have prevented it.

While this question was still pending, the existence, becoming more precarious every day, of the Melbourne Cabinet received from the member for Harwich the rudest shock which it had sustained since its temporary resignation in 1839.

The condition of the finances was deplorable, and there was no prospect of improvement.   Instead of having an annual surplus available for the reduction of debt, the country had fallen into a state of chronic deficit, which grew year by year, and the only remedy for which appeared to be increased taxation.   On February 13, 1840, Mr. Herries made a motion for accounts and estimates, to throw light upon the subject to which he forcibly drew the attention of the House. ' The finances of the country,' he said, ' now presented such an aspect, and things had now arrived at such a pass, that it became the imperative duty of a faithful House of Commons to look the affairs of the nation in the face . . . at a moment when their financial affairs were in a state which he did not scruple to designate as most dangerous. The duty which the House would have to perform was one of an extremely painful nature, and the painfulness of that duty was in no slight degree increased by the reflection that we were now in the twenty-sixth year of peace.' Admitting that his motion was unusual, he argued that it was justified by unusual circumstances. ' Was it too much to ask that light should be let in upon a state of things respecting which the public were as yet ignorant and uninformed? . . . .The conditions and prospects of the country were such as to render the information which he sought of immense importance. There existed with reference to it extreme solicitude in the public mind. There was no society into which he went where he did not hear en- quiries made, surmises hazarded, and a universal anxiety manifested ; there was no person with whom he con- versed that did not appear full of apprehension as to the prospects of the country.' He pointed out that in 1837 there had been a deficiency of 726,000*l.* ; in 1838, of 440,000*l.* ; in 1839, of 1,512,000*l.*, making a total of 2,678,000*l.* ; which he calculated would be raised at the end of 1840 to the aggregate deficit of certainly 4,678,000*l.*, or, probably, of nearly six millions. Such disastrous results he contrasted with those of the period of peace between 1817 and 1828, when by means of a large surplus income 'there had been a reduction of 3,500,000*l.* on the charge of the debt, while in the same time 26,000,000*l.* of taxes had been taken off;' and of that of the Duke of Wellington's Administration when the Chancellor of the Exchequer had reduced taxes to the amount of between 6,000,000*l.* and 7,000,000*l.* a year, and had still left a surplus revenue to his successor, Lord Althorp, of 3,000,000*l.* While he 'believed that there never existed a more solemn obligation on the House than at this time, to take proper steps to put a stop to the present financial embarrassments of the country,' he recommended the House, however, 'to guard themselves against forming an exaggerated or too gloomy view of the general state and situation of the country. . . . He believed that our resources were unimpaired, that, indeed, we were more competent than at any former period of our history to make great exertions. . . . He utterly repudiated the foolish saying that England was laid prostrate under the weight of its seven hundred millions of debt. . . .'

The motion was carried against the Government by a majority of ten, in which the names of two such decided Liberals as Mr. Grote and Mr. Hume appear. This defeat on a matter of primary importance was a 'heavy blow and a very great discouragement,' from which the tottering Cabinet never entirely recovered. From a Member of Parliament Mr. Herries received the following note of approval :—' It is impossible to write to you without congratulating you on Thursday last. I do so most sincerely. Notwithstanding a tearing cough, I listened to every word you said, and a more clear and conclusive statement, and one more damaging to our opponents I never heard. I believe that night to have been *le commencement de la fin.*'

Among a variety of letters of the year 1840, there appears the following curious note addressed to Mr. Herries a few days after the signature of the famous Quadruple Treaty of July 15, by one of the plenipotentiaries, an old acquaintance.

'Could you muzzle the ——'s [a Conservative journal] nonsense on the Eastern Question, which he does not understand? The writer of the two leading articles of yesterday and to-day does not see that he is playing the game of France and spoiling ours. . . .'

The veteran diplomatist knew the character of his correspondent, whose aid he solicited to prevent embarrassment to the policy of the Government. He knew that he was writing to a man who although strongly attached to his party, and a decided opponent of the Liberal Ministry, would never, like the Liberals during the whole of the great war, sacrifice national interests to party animosity. A question here presents itself. Is it not in the highest degree probable that the step taken by the foreign plenipotentiary to obtain the intervention of a leading member of the Conservative Opposition was made known to Lord Palmerston in the course of the frequent conversations which must have been held on the state of affairs ; if, indeed, the intention to take it was not previously communicated to his Lordship, who may possibly even have suggested the writing of the note ?

Taking the same view as his diplomatic friend, Mr. Herries lost no time in recommending the matter to the attention of a political manager, from whom he received the following answer :—

'Your correspondent is quite right in saying that the articles in question are playing the game of France, but not equally so, I suspect, in supposing that the writer does *not* understand the question. Whether he misstates I know not, but am satisfied that he does understand the question. Between ourselves, they come from a person who *has* some knowledge at least of the *French* policy on the Eastern affairs ; . . . but if *you* could satisfy me that the course taken by the paper (which commits only itself) is injurious to the Party, I have probably sufficient influence with —— to stop the course, or at least I would try it ; but, as at present advised, though approving Palmerston's policy, I see no harm that can arise from the paper's taking its own line. After all, however, when we talk of Party, does one remain, for any useful purpose?'

At the time when one of Lord Palmerston's political adversaries, moved by patriotic sentiments, showed his anxiety to silence some of the assailants of the Minister who was engaged at a most critical moment in defending the permanent interests of England, one of Lord Palmerston's own colleagues was, far more dangerously than the Conservative journal, 'playing the game of France,' and doing his best to 'spoil ours.' Lord Holland, a cosmopolite, whose patriotic sentiments were never so strong as his sympathies with foreigners of various sorts, was, indeed, at this moment ' a live shell in the Cabinet,' the intended explosion of which would have destroyed not only Lord Palmerston's position and policy, but together with them the credit of England and her power in the East.

Mr. Herries approved Lord Palmerston's policy in 1840, and did not believe that it would lead to war— from which, if necessary, he would not have shrunk then, or at any other time. His views do not seem to have been shared completely by the generality of his party, if the following passage in a letter written to him in October by the confidential manager before alluded to may be taken as an indication of prevalent Conservative opinion. 'With my general deference to your judgment, I yet entirely doubt the *possibility* of avoiding war.'

In the following year Mr. Herries took an active part in the long and agitated debates on the financial and commercial policy of the Government, which ended in its defeat by a majority of thirty-six. In the first debate, or conversation, upon the well-known Budget of 1841, he observed that ' although he would not enter into the general question as to the two first propositions respecting timber and sugar, yet after what he had heard from the President of the Board of Trade (Mr. Labouchere) he thought he went very nearly with him. As he understood that gentleman, his object was not to bring forward any sweeping or general measure of alteration in our commercial code. He did not embrace the views of the Import Duties Committee : he did not say, there should be no protection ; but he had endeavoured to arrive—whether he had or not was a question for future discussion—at that point which afforded the requisite degree of protection, consulting at the same time the interests of the consumer. And he could assure the right honourable gentleman that when he brought forward single cases in this way, as any demand for relief might arise, and founded on such principles, he would find no one more willing to give such propositions a fair and impartial consideration than himself.'

The following passages may also be quoted from a somewhat earlier speech in a debate concerning import duties in British colonies, as indications of the speaker's views on the subject of Protection. They likewise show what were, and always had been, his sentiments with regard to the commercial policy of Mr. Huskisson, towards whom systematic hostility has been falsely attributed to him by sundry diarists, letter-writers, and pamphleteers. Alluding to the Report of the Import Duties Committee, he said : ' He felt and admitted the actual necessity of carrying much further the enquiry whether there should or should not be a continuance of protecting duties. He begged to remind the House that Mr. Huskisson endeavoured, by the effect of his legislation, to adjust, not to abrogate, protecting duties. Mr. Huskisson endeavoured to find the point at which protecting duties were indispensably necessary, and he proposed to dispense with every shackle upon commerce that was not necessary. . . . For his own part, he felt bound to express the great satisfaction he felt upon every occasion when any measure proposed and carried into effect upon the legislation promoted by Mr. Huskisson produced the benefits which had been anticipated. He himself, so far as his humble endeavours went, had always acted with Mr. Huskisson in the promotion of the principles which that statesman entertained on this subject. He had never, on the subject of the principles of free trade, had any difference of opinion from that right honourable gentleman, and he could say, as all those who had acted with him could say—those who had been spoken of as illiberal, while Mr. Huskisson had been praised as liberal—. . . . that they had given a most cordial concurrence in all those measures which Mr. Huskisson had proposed. . . . Mr. Huskisson never was an indiscriminate promoter of free trade, and it was equally unjust to suppose that those who acted with him were not as liberal as he was in the view which he took in adapting our commercial system at the close of the war, and in a new state of things, to that of other countries, and in relieving our commerce from all those shackles that could possibly be dispensed with. . .'

Lord John Russell, following Mr. Herries, said that ' he wished to address a few observations to the House after the right honourable gentleman who had just sat down, because, interesting as this conversation rather than debate had been, there was no speech from which he had derived greater satisfaction than that of the right honourable gentleman. He agreed with him in his description of the general policy of Mr. Huskisson, although, perhaps, there was something to be added to that description. He was pleased, however, to hear that in that policy . . . . the colleagues of Mr. Huskisson had cordially concurred. . . . It was well known, too, that Mr. Canning. . . . eagerly supported the principles involved in those measures. The right honourable gentleman (Mr. Herries) opposite had himself declared his adherence to them; and he rejoiced to hear from testimony so valuable and undeniable that such principles were likewise to be found amongst the most enlightened of the party to which the right honourable gentleman belonged. . . .'

The language used by Lord John Russell, and by other distinguished members on the Ministerial side of the House, marks the importance of the political position which belonged to Mr. Herries in the judgment of his contemporaries. The Chancellor of the Exchequer (Mr. F. Baring) spoke of him as the individual who had more practical experience in financial matters than any other member. Mr. Charles Villiers, the able and consistent advocate of the repeal of the Corn Laws long before Mr. Cobden's appearance on the political stage, rising to reply to Mr. Herries in the sugar debate, said that 'he had listened to the right honourable member with great interest, for knowing that he had been connected with the finances of the country, and expecting that he might soon be so again, he was anxious to learn his views on the state of that financial emergency in which he had described the country to be placed. . . .' From these and many other expressions it was quite manifest that on the Ministerial side of the House Mr. Herries was looked upon as the person most likely to become the Chancellor of the Exchequer in a new Administration.

CHAPTER X.

Herries driven by evictions from Harwich : beaten by bribery at Ipswich ; not included in Peel Cabinet—Satisfactory assurances from Prime Minister—Correspondence with him and Goulburn—Herries out of office consulted by ministers—His correspondence with Sir R. Peel and Chancellor of the Exchequer on new plan of finance, &c.—Metropolis Improvements Commission—Thames Embankment, &c.

MR. HERRIES, who had contributed not a little assistance towards the discomfiture of the Melbourne Ministry, was not one of the great Conservative majority which in a new Parliament carried Sir Robert Peel triumphantly into power for the protection of British agriculture. He found that the Whig Government had at last become too strong for him at Harwich, where intimidation and eviction had done their work so surely as to render his re-election impossible without bribery, to which he never would resort. His principal supporter for many years —a gentleman of high respectability and considerable local influence—was driven away from the borough by the destruction of his business as a ship-builder, which he had for a long time carried on in premises belonging to the Crown. His steady adherence to the Tory member, whom the Government were bent on ejecting, after having procured for him, as well as others, a series of vexations, finally called forth a peremptory notice, enforced with needless harshness, to quit his shipyard, slips, dwelling-house, workshops, &c., &c. A copy of this document is extant, signed by the Postmaster-

General, two Commissioners of Woods and Forests, and two Lords of the Treasury. Such was the manner in which freedom of election was maintained by a Liberal Ministry seven years after the passing of the Reform Bill to secure the perfect representation of the people, undisturbed by undue influence and especially that of wicked Tory landlords. The Whig Government 'did what they pleased with their own.'

Banished from his old seat by the decree of those in power, Mr. Herries was induced by delusive calculations in a luckless hour to offer himself at the General Election as a candidate—in conjunction with the late Sir Fitzroy Kelly—for the borough of Ipswich, where, to their great surprise, the two Conservatives were defeated. But the election of their Liberal opponents was in the ensuing session declared void by reason of bribery. Upon this mischance Sir Robert Peel wrote to Mr. Herries on July 4 : 'I am very much disappointed at your failure, though not at all surprised that you should refuse to resort to the means by which alone success could have been obtained. From what I had heard before I left London, I had sanguine hopes of your success, though no part of them was founded on a favourable opinion of Ipswich voters. . . . I care little as to the loss of the seat compared with that of your valuable assistance and support. I now wish you had tried some constituency better qualified to form a just estimate of your value and qualifications as a representative than these Ipswich gentlemen.' From Mr. Goulburn also he received a letter full of expressions of friendly sympathy : 'I hope you cannot doubt my great regret at the issue of the

Ipswich election. I do not know what your own anticipations may have been, but I confess that my disappointment was aggravated by the result being so contrary to my previous expectations. I am in hopes that your disappointment in this quarter will not permanently exclude you from the House of Commons. For as far as regards myself I can truly say—and I think my feeling is only that of all those who have, like us, borne the heat and brunt of the day—that there is no one whose assistance and society I should more regret to lose in what I may at least call days of more prosperous fortune. . . .'

While the petition against the sitting members was pending, a strong desire was manifested in some quarters to compromise the matter in the manner fashionable among electioneering experts of the day. Many proposals, suggestions, and hints were made with that view to Mr. Herries, but he declined to enter into any arrangement. To Mr. Goulburn, then just installed in the Exchequer, in forwarding a letter concerning some revenue business from an Ipswich local politician, he wrote : 'The concluding paragraph of it adds to my conviction that Wason and Rennie will be ousted on petition. I have no doubt that if good Conservative candidates be sent down on the vacancy the two seats may be now secured. There is, however, a hankering after a compromise. I have already stated to you that I am no party to advising or encouraging such a proceeding in any shape, and least of all in one which might render me liable to the imputation of tripping up the heels of Kelly.' On the same subject he wrote, in

the latter part of 1841, to a Conservative gentleman at
Ipswich : 'I have, as you know, avoided making any
statement or declaration to you upon those intimations,
—not only while I was uncertain whether Mr. Kelly
was disposed to relinquish his claims upon the borough,
but even after I had understood from you that he had
positively declared that he would have nothing more to
do with it. The truth is that it did not appear to me
to be either necessary or becoming that I should say
anything of my own views or feelings on the subject
until some distinct proposition should be made to me.
. . . It is right, therefore, that you should know that
it is far from probable that I should be in a situation to
avail myself of the good wishes of the Conservative
Party at Ipswich in the event of a vacancy, and that you
must consequently be prepared to give your support
to some other, I hope, more influential and effective
representative on the right side of politics than myself. . . .' Endeavours were made to find a seat for him
elsewhere, and several places were suggested as offering
fair chances of success. If his party had been still in
opposition, it is probable that he would have taken the
advice of his friends and put himself forward as a
candidate on some suitable vacancy occurring. But
as matters then stood he thought that by doing so he
might bring himself into a false position.

Against general expectation, he was not included
in the list of the new Cabinet formed on Lord Melbourne's resignation in September, the sole cause of
his omission being, as Sir Robert Peel himself declared,
his absence from Parliament. What passed between

them on this subject is recorded in the following memorandum of a conversation on September 10.

'Mr. Herries waited on Sir R. Peel in consequence of a note received on the 8th making an appointment for this day.

'Sir R. Peel received him with the greatest cordiality, and, after a few commonplace general observations, entered upon the subject of the interview.

'He began by saying that he had been desirous of communicating the matter he was about to state at an earlier period, that he had even commenced a letter, which he found would be a long one if he explained himself so fully as he desired, but that his incessant and pressing occupations, some of them of the most harassing and perplexing kind, had prevented him from going on with it.   He then said that he had no doubt Mr. H. was perfectly aware of his earnest desire to have the benefit of his services and assistance in his new Government, and he assured him that he was fully prepared to have recommended him for an office with a seat in the Cabinet if the difficulty arising from his want of a seat in Parliament had not presented such an obstacle as he could not—circumstanced as he was with respect to other people—contrive to overcome.   He then said there were strong claims upon him on the part of Mr. ——, Lord ——, Lord ——, Mr. ——, &c. ; that if he had set aside a general rule of exception which existed in Mr. H.'s case, it would have been impossible for him to resist the various claims and pretensions put forward by those and other persons ; that it had cost him much to come to this decision, and he had done so very reluctantly and with considerable regret, but that he found himself really unable to do otherwise. He said that Mr. H. might be well convinced of his earnest desire to have removed this obstacle by seeing him provided with a seat in Parliament by the circumstance of his having sent the deputation from Bradford to him. . . He said that so strongly was he desirous of having Mr. H. for one of his colleagues, that he had been prepared to suggest to Sir —— to waive his pretensions on this occasion to facilitate an arrangement for Mr. H., and with a pretty good knowledge that he would have experienced no difficulty in that quarter. He then went on to say that it would be satisfactory to Mr. H. to know that the other members of the Cabinet (and he specifically mentioned Lord Stanley and Sir James Graham) would have been well pleased with any arrangement that should have placed Mr. H. among them. He said that some observations had been made— he forgot by whom—that a difficulty might arise from the placing of Lord Ripon and Mr. H. in the same Cabinet. He asked Mr. H. if any such objection would have existed on his part, and upon being answered in the negative, he stated that he had every reason to suppose that Lord Ripon was equally free from any feeling incompatible with their sitting in Council together with perfect cordiality.[1]

He added that he would at once frankly state that if any objection had been suggested by Lord Ripon to

---

[1] This obviously could not have been the case if Lord Ripon had believed that there was the least truth in Lord Palmerston's story about the imaginary blowing up of the Goderich Cabinet.

the admission of Mr. Herries into the Cabinet he should
in that case at once have declared that he would not
admit the objection, and that Lord Ripon could not be
a member of his Cabinet.[2]   He said that these statements
would convince Mr. Herries of the high estimation in
which he stood with him and of his sincere desire to have
him again for a colleague if the circumstances of his case
had allowed of it, and he added that he thought that such
declarations proceeding from him, and given in perfect
truth and sincerity, ought to be, and would be, sufficient
to remove from the mind of Mr. H.'s friends any unpleasant feelings which they might be induced to entertain by the mere view of the fact of Mr. Herries's not
being included in the recently formed arrangements.
He then asked Mr. Herries whether he intended to come
into Parliament (as Mr. H. understood), his words
being, 'I suppose you will come into Parliament.'   To
this it was answered Mr. H. did not exactly see the way
at present ; that his ability to come into Parliament
might with some constituencies depend a good deal
upon the position which he might happen to occupy
with relation to the Government.

Mr. H. then adverted to the borough of Ripon,[3]
and to his having suggested to Sir Robert Peel some
time back that Ripon and some other boroughs would
probably be at his disposal.   Sir R. Peel observed that
with respect to Ripon Sir George Cockburn had a

---

[2] This shows what was Sir Robert Peel's estimation of the relative value
of the two men.

[3] About to be vacated by Sir E. Sugden on his appointment as Lord-
Chancellor of Ireland.

peculiar claim, inasmuch as he had entertained an expectation of coming in upon a vacancy at Sandwich which it appeared was likely now not to occur. . . .

He then expressed his hope that Mr. H. would communicate with him as confidentially upon public matters as usual . . . and the interview terminated in the most friendly manner.'

It gave rise to the following correspondence:—

'September 11. 1841.

' My dear Peel,—I returned home too late to write to you by the post yesterday, or I should not have allowed it to depart without a few lines to assure you that my conversation with you had afforded me very great satisfaction in relieving my mind from an unpleasant though undefined misgiving as to the cause of my having heard nothing from you during the progress of your official arrangements.

' Your frank and friendly explanation has dispelled the vague surmises which had been haunting me ; and I have now the certainty that not only were you desirous of once more proposing me to the Crown for a Cabinet office, but that such an accession to your Councils would not have been unwelcome to any of your colleagues ; my want of a seat in Parliament being the only obstacle to your wishes in that respect.

' After these gratifying assurances from you upon a point of so much interest and importance to me, I shall pass into the retirement to which the unlucky result of the Ipswich election has alone consigned me, without any painful feeling except that of sincere regret that I am not able in the hour of success to rejoin those ranks in which, under your guidance, through many a year and many a turn of good and ill fortune to our common cause, I have witnessed all the good fights and good management which have ultimately led to it.

'I trust that I am not wrong in the understanding that I am at liberty to state to my own anxious and inquiring friends what have been your feelings and intentions in respect to my position, and what has been the only impediment to your acting upon them. Believe me, &c.,

'J. C. HERRIES.'

'Whitehall: September 18.

'My dear Herries,—You certainly are at liberty to mention to any of your relations or friends with whom you may deem it desirable to communicate upon the subject, that if on being recently called upon by Her Majesty to form an Administration, you had been a member of the House of Commons, I cannot doubt that I should have invited you to render the Government your valuable assistance as a member of it with a seat in the Cabinet.

'I do not believe that I should have met with the slightest impediment in the way of such an offer from any one of my present colleagues, and if I had, I should not have permitted it to prevail. Believe me, my dear Herries, with sincere regard, most faithfully yours,

'ROBERT PEEL.'

A few days later another communication took place.

'*September* 21.—A messenger from Sir Robert Peel arrived at $\frac{1}{2}$-past 5. I found him at my house on my return home at ½-past 6. He brought a letter desiring my immediate presence at Sir Robert's, on the subject of a proposal of a seat in Parliament.

'I returned with the messenger, and found Sir Robert at his house at 10 o'clock.

'He told me that the conduct of Sir E. Sugden had provoked a motion by Wilde to which it had been found necessary to give way, and that the writ for Ripon had consequently been moved. This he said had inconveniently precipitated his arrangements, and he now offered Ripon to me in such a manner that *an immediate decision* was *indispensably requisite*. I must go down this night, or to-morrow by the very first train, if I accepted the seat. He said that he had destined it for Sir George Cockburn, but that he was glad to offer it to me in the first instance, hoping that Cockburn might find an opening in some other place. . . . He pointed out in strong terms the advantages of Ripon as a seat—its certainty—its probable permanency—the terms on which it might be held, &c. In short, he said, it is the very best seat in England. He added, however, that the offer of the seat was to be considered as being unaccompanied by any other proposal. This I understood, and no doubt correctly, to intimate that he had no proposal to make to me respecting office.

'I told him that I was a great deal taken by surprise so far as Ripon was concerned, because in a former interview he had apprised me of a different destination for it. I said that I was sensible of his kindness in making me the offer, but that my present intention was to decline any seat under the immediate nomination of the Government at the present time, when I had so recently been left out of the official arrangements in the formation of it on the sole ground that I was not provided with one.

' He seemed surprised by my decision, and suggested various grounds to induce me to reconsider the matter. I thanked him heartily for his kindness on this occasion, and for that which he had expressed in assuring me that he had fully intended to associate me with him in his Cabinet if I had been in Parliament, and I expressed my earnest hope that nothing would occur to disturb the mutual regard between us. But I added that I felt so strongly that I should be in a false and very unsatisfactory position were I to occupy such a seat as Ripon while I was entirely unconnected with my former friends in office, that I must positively decline it. I assured him that I should always be ready to afford any assistance to him, and that I thought I could be more useful when out of Parliament than in it under such circumstances. . . .'

The views indicated above are brought out still more clearly in a communication to Mr. Goulburn.

'September 29, 1841.

' My dear Goulburn,—In the conversation which I had with you after I had declined the proposal to go to Ripon, you appeared to me to enter into the feelings which I then described as having actuated me, and I think you assented to the argument upon which my conclusion was built, though I do not remember that you expressly said so.

'I have since thought a good deal about that matter. The enclosed memorandum which I send you in confidence contains shortly my view of the subject. I am anxious that you should read it with a friendly attention, and that I should have the benefit of your judgment upon it. It is seldom that a man thinks very clearly or judges quite soundly when his feelings are strongly moved by the subject to which his thoughts are directed. I am the more anxious, therefore, to have your advice and opinion.

'You will see that the present object of my solicitude is that my separation in political life from those with whom I have so long and so cordially acted, may be effected in the manner least likely to occasion a severance in other respects.

'Do not think that I expect an immediate attention to this affair of mine. Let me hear from you at your leisure. . . . Most truly yours,   'J. C. HERRIES.'

Memorandum.

'The more I have reflected on the offer of the seat for Ripon from Sir Robert Peel, accompanied by the declaration, by way of caution, that it was not connected with any other proposal—by which I understood that no prospect of employment was held out to me—the more am I satisfied that it was right on my part to decline the favour thus proffered to me.

'My position is this : I was called into the higher departments of political life by Lord Liverpool from the lucrative permanent situation which I then filled, on.

the ground of my supposed experience and capacity
in public business.   From the period when that occurred
(now twenty years since) I have been in close and confidential connection with the party which I then joined,
and steadfastly devoted to the same political principles.
I have occupied some very prominent stations, both in
subordination to the Government and as forming a part
of it.   I have taken, on some occasions, a very forward,
and, at all times, a labouring, part in Parliament, in
concert with the chiefs of my party.   I have maintained
out of office, at a considerable cost, during more than
ten years, and at four elections, against all the power of
the Government, a seat theretofore invariably at the
disposal of the Treasury for the time being.   Driven at
length from thence by the overwhelming weight of that
power, I embarked, with every fair prospect of success,
in a contest at Ipswich, which proved unfortunate by
reason of the peculiar hostility of the Whigs to me ; and
I now find myself temporarily deprived of a place in
the House of Commons at the very time when the party
and the principles with which, and for which, I so long
have been fighting, have triumphantly prevailed.

' On the occasion of this great change every individual, so far as I know, having any fair claims to office,
or favour or distinction, high or low, has derived some
advantage from it, or received some public recognition
of his pretensions or services, except myself.   But I have
received the assurance that, had it not been for the unfortunate mischance of the lost election, and the consequent want of a seat in the House of Commons, a high
station in office would have been assigned to me.

'On my part it is perfectly true that I have not asked for office ; that I have urged no vain or selfish pretensions to employment ; and that, on the contrary, I have submitted myself entirely to the judgment of my leader to employ me or not, as to him might seem most expedient for the public service. I did so in perfect sincerity and good faith, prepared to abide, without objection or remonstrance, by the decision, be it what it might.

'But while I submit myself entirely to that determination, formed upon grounds of public expediency (not in any degree affecting my character), whereby I stand excluded from office, I am far from being indifferent to the effect which might be produced upon the estimation in which I have hitherto been held in public and private life by the manner of my retirement and the circumstances attending it. Any unfavourable misconstruction as to the cause of my official severance from the Conservative party might prove a thousandfold more painful to me than the mere fact of my being laid aside.

'It happens, unfortunately, that the most obvious conclusion with respect to my present insulated position is precisely that which has the smallest foundation in truth. It is supposed (and I know the fact from having been called upon to refute the error) that I have urged pretensions to a particular office, or at least to office of a certain rank, without which I would not be satisfied, and that a difference between me and Sir Robert Peel on that point has led to the result. This is as unfavourable to me as it is devoid of truth. Other conjectures equally unfounded have been made ; naturally enough,

because the real cause is not obvious, and indeed to
many persons, even when distinctly stated, it is not
easily intelligible. They will not understand how the
want of a seat in Parliament, which could be so easily
supplied now that my friends are in power, either by
them or by my own exertions, could so definitively have
closed the door against me. The vacancy at Ripon was
foreseen by every one even before the new Government
was formed, and if I had accepted the offer of that seat,
the very fact of my now filling it would have rendered
my separation from office more unaccountable. The
assurance, which I should have given to everyone, that
it was only because the vacancy did not actually exist at
the very moment when my former fellow-labourers were
called into employment again, would, if urged under
such circumstances as an explanation of my exclusion,
rather have tended, I think, to create than to remove
any unfavourable doubts. I should hardly have stood
clear and well in the public eye in such a position, and
with nothing more to offer than such an assurance
(strictly true though it be) to account for it. In short,
I do not see how I could at the present moment satisfactorily take a private station in Parliament under the
immediate auspices of the Government, but unconnected
with it, except on the clear and avowed understanding
that I had spontaneously renounced public employment, and was determined to retire from all public duties
beyond those of an individual member of the House of
Commons. That would undoubtedly be a high position,
and one which any man might be proud of. But it
is not mine, and I am not the man to assume a false

character, or to allow sentiments and pretensions to be
unduly ascribed to me not strictly in accordance with
the truth.

'What, therefore, remains for me, after so long a
period of active, and I hope not wholly unuseful service,
and after so great a sacrifice of personal interest as I
have made, except to abide quietly by my fireside, and
to watch with friendly anxiety the progress of a better
order of things in the hands of those who are now called
to the administration of public affairs?

'But I must take care that my retirement be not exposed to misconstruction, and that it bring no spot or
speck upon my good name. In this I confidently hope
for the assistance of all my friends in office, in concurrence with Sir R. Peel, who will, I am sure, do whatever may be most conducive to afford clear evidence
that my connection with his Government is not severed
by reason of any diminution of the good opinion or
goodwill towards me of those who compose it. It
would indeed be as little to their credit as to mine if
any mystery should hang over my separation from
them. After having so long been before the public I
must pass from official into private life as an upright
public servant, and as a gentleman and a man of honour
ought to do.'

Mr. Goulburn, in his reply, concluded thus : 'I can
truly say that I have never heard your exclusion from
office attributed to any other than the real cause, and
what our old friendship would make an imperative duty
on me is felt, I believe, by all your friends in the Government, that if any surmise to the contrary was to

reach them they would be prompt and eager in its refutation.' . . .

Although removed from active political life, Mr. Herries continued to be consulted, as he had been during the greater part of his existence, on many important questions, and his aid and advice, frequently sought, were always readily given. As we write we see before us a bulky packet of comparative financial statements and calculations for each of the Administrations since the Peace, enclosed in a letter to the Duke of Wellington, shortly before the meeting of the new Parliament.

'August 21, 1841.

' My dear Lord Duke,—I think the accompanying papers contain the answers to the several points on which you put questions to me, with the exception of the sugar, on which I hope you have received ample · information from the quarters in which I made inquiry.

' With respect to the prices of sugar, I find some of the best West Indians—Irving in particular, and I dare say Grant—beginning to be alarmed about the lowness of the price. They expect what they call bad times from the abundance of the supply. If there is reason for their fear in that respect, the argument becomes so much stronger against the framers of the Budget.

' My servant will return to me to-night, and if you wish for any further information that I can afford, you will perhaps send a line to me by him. Believe me, &c.,

'J. C. HERRIES.'

Not very long after the formation of Sir Robert

Peel's Government, we were present when the quiet of the retired politician was rudely disturbed by a hot and hurried Treasury messenger driven up to his door at full speed in a post-chaise—the bearer of a short but urgent missive from the Chancellor of the Exchequer, beginning with the ominous words, ' Peel and I are in a cleft stake,' and entreating that his friend would instantly repair to London for the purpose of trying to extricate them from that unpleasant position. Responding to this earnest appeal he hastened to town, where he learned that the difficulties, on account of which his help was wanted, had arisen out of a funding operation rendered necessary by the deficit bequeathed by the outgoing Whigs. It did not appear to the person called in that the embarrassment (which, in his opinion, might have been avoided) was a very serious one, and he suggested means for its removal. Then ensued a curious . incident. The two heads of the Treasury, closeted with a great capitalist, discussed the terms of a proposed arrangement, while in an adjoining room their concealed counsellor from the country sat apart for occasional consultation. He returned to his fields, wondering why he had been called away from them, and reflecting upon the much more difficult negotiations which in much more critical times he had often concluded with far less trouble, and without seeking any external aid.

On a far more important matter, his opinion was thought worth taking soon afterwards, as may be seen from the following paper in reply to a letter, dated November 5, 1841, from Sir Robert Peel, in which, referring to an interview with Mr. Herries on the same day, he encloses correspondence (returned uncopied), ' on the subject of some extensive scheme of finance for the purpose of supplying the existing and the contemplated deficiency by much more legitimate and satisfactory means than have been hitherto resorted to '—and adds, ' I shall be very much obliged by your careful perusal of these papers, and by the communication of your opinions on matters of such paramount importance.'

'November 8, 1841.

' My dear Peel,—A hasty glance at the papers which you sent to me on Friday night was sufficient to show me that great attention ought to be brought to the perusal of them, and being very pressingly engaged with the matters which had brought me to London, I was obliged to postpone, until my return hither, the careful consideration of these important documents. I return them herewith.

' Although they embrace several topics and some details of considerable interest, the main point to which all of these are subordinate is of such paramount importance that I think I shall best fulfil your wishes in confining my observations almost exclusively to it. The question for decision is, whether the existing insufficiency of the Revenue to meet the annual expenditure can be supplied in any manner more suitable to the present circumstances of the country than by the imposition of a tax on Income derived from Property? ' [4]

---

[4] From this passage and subsequent observations, as well as the words quoted above from Sir Robert Peel's own letter of November 5, it is manifest that the primary object which he had in view when he submitted the question so stated to the consideration of Mr. Herries was the restoration of the lost financial equilibrium. It cannot be doubted that the reimposition

' Your estimate of the actual deficiency for future years is 3,000,000*l.*, and, I presume, you contemplate the necessity of making provision to the extent of about 1,000,000*l.* beyond that as a surplus, indispensable for the sake of security and the maintenance of the public credit.

' I assume, of course, that all intention to dabble with the disastrous state of things by temporary expedients, involving the creation of new debt, is to be entirely rejected, as being a course bad in itself, and, moreover, peculiarly unfitted to the position of the present Government, and to the expectations that are entertained of it.

' Such being the case, I have no hesitation in declaring my firm conviction that no other safe and practicable expedient is open to you than a recourse to direct taxation, and that a Property Tax is the best

of a property or income tax was, at that time at least, contemplated as a means, in the first instance, of supplying the continuous deficiency of the Revenue which had to be made good. Sir Robert Peel's own words on bringing forward the measure in 1842 point to the same conclusion. But when Mr. Herries, in moving for a diminution of the income tax in 1851, asserted that such had been its original and principal purpose—observing at the same time that he knew the fact from having himself been consulted on the subject—he was contradicted in a somewhat too peremptory tone of authority. It had then become the fashion to treat as a matter of quite secondary importance the perilous financial condition of the nation at the beginning of 1842, described by Sir Robert Peel as the ' mighty and growing evil ' which he proposed to remedy, and to represent the income tax as having been from the outset devised solely, or chiefly, as an engine for effecting a complete change of fiscal policy.

It seems worthy of observation that in the passage above, ' a tax on income derived from property ' is spoken of. Whether in the original scheme brought under the cognizance of Mr. Herries the tax was intended to be so limited, or whether the words used by him implied a suggestion of his own, we have no means of knowing.

description of direct taxation that you can adopt under present circumstances.

'I have the less difficulty in arriving at this conclusion, because I have very long entertained the conviction that the burthens of this country, consisting in so large a degree of accumulated debt, ought to be defrayed, in a greater proportion than they have hitherto been since the Peace, by the contribution of accumulated wealth ; and that the very great preponderance assigned in our system of taxation to the duties derived from manufactures and consumption, was not only impolitic but unsustainable.

'I was so deeply impressed with this belief more than fifteen years ago that when I held the office of Chancellor of the Exchequer I had come to the determination, in entire concurrence with Huskisson and Lord Ripon, to propose a Property Tax by way of commutation for some of the then existing indirect taxes, which were most obstructive to the industry of the country, and consequently most detrimental to it in its then growing rivalry with the manufactures of the Continent, and also most obnoxious to the public feeling ; and therefore likely to be wrenched, sooner or later, out of the hands of any Government. The change of Ministry put an end to these intentions, but I have never ceased to think that they were right in principle ; and I am still convinced that by adopting such a course at that period the crisis in which we are now involved would have been averted. We should have anticipated the necessity under which we are now compelled to revert to direct taxation.

'I need not point out to you that our present insufficiency of public income does not arise from any really
extravagant or unforeseen excess of expenditure on the
one hand, nor from any decay of wealth or diminution
in the means of consumption or contribution to the
public revenue in the nation at large on the other.   If
the expenditure, such as it is even now, is compared
with the estimate formed by the Committee of Finance
in [1817 or 1828—the figures are uncertain], there is
nothing to complain of.   And if the actual produce of
the revenue be contrasted with the amount to which it
would have been reduced by the taxes taken off if consumption had remained stationary, the augmentation is
prodigious.

' It is, in truth, therefore, solely to the abandonment
of taxes that we owe the present deficiency ; and
although that abandonment may have been made in
some respects unnecessarily, and in others unskilfully,
by the late Government, I am still thoroughly persuaded
that no Government, however skilful or strong, could
have resisted, or, if they could, ought to have resisted,
the inducement to a large reduction of the indirect
taxation which the circumstances and the feelings of
the country created.

' Among the mistakes Lord Spencer, who may be
reckoned, perhaps, the very worst of the financial
managers who have had charge of the Exchequer,
committed, the greatest perhaps was the giving up of
the taxes on houses and windows (taxes upon property), and laying a duty upon raw cotton.   It was
moving exactly in the wrong direction.   Even the

unwise reduction of the Post Office revenue [5] was more justified upon principle than that measure. .

[5] In the judgment of the writer of this letter, as well as in that of Sir Robert Peel, to whom it was addressed, the change of the postal system introduced in 1840 was imprudent because it greatly increased the deficiency of the Revenue. This, and no other, was the ground of the opposition to the measure on the part of the Conservatives; and it is impossible to deny that their financial objections were well founded. The immediate loss of revenue was enormous. In the year ended January 5, 1839 (the last complete year under the old system), the net revenue of the Post Office was 1,659,509l., including 45,156l., the amount of postage charged on Government departments. In the year ended January 5, 1841 (the first year of the penny post), the net revenue was only 500,789l., including 90,761l. charged on Government departments. The real loss to the public, therefore, was 1,204,325l. Ten years later the net revenue was no more than 803,898l., from which being deducted 109,523l. for Government postage—a mere matter of account—there remained only 694,375l., falling short of the real receipts for profit of 1838 by 919,978l. As compared with the latter year, the returns for 1860, when the new system had been in operation for twenty years, still show a deficiency of 372,235l., not reduced to less than 174,374l. in 1862, after which date the Post Office accounts are made up on a different principle. But this is not the whole case; because, while these accounts previous to the last-mentioned year include, under the head of receipts, the postage charged in the United Kingdom for letters, &c. conveyed by British mail steamers, they exclude from the expenditure side the sums paid under contract for the conveyance of those mails. And, moreover, the actual cost of the manufacture of postage stamps has hitherto been defrayed, not by the Post Office, but by the Inland Revenue department.

However great, therefore, the advantages of cheap postage have been—and they are undeniable—to all classes of the community in other respects, the expectations of financial success held out by the promoters of the reform were delusive. It is incontestable that the adoption of the Rowland Hill system added very largely to the already dangerous deficit, which must have gone on growing until it had reached the most formidable proportions if the Liberal Government which carried the postal reform had remained long in office; because that Government was adverse to the application of the remedy —the only efficacious one—by which the evil was cured—the income tax.

Consequently, those who with Sir Robert Peel resisted the postal change when it was brought forward were fully justified in saying—before you throw away existing revenue, put an end to the existing deficit.

Persons who now deride an opposition which they attribute to Conservative factiousness or stupidity, and to official obstructiveness, would do well to take notice of the opinion strongly expressed against Rowland Hill's reform, sixteen years after its introduction, by Mr. McCulloch, a decided Liberal and an eminent economist, in his *Commercial Dictionary*. ed. 1856.

'But I should bore you, and very unnecessarily, if I were to pursue reflections upon this subject only tending to the same conclusion, that a Property Tax is the best expedient for restoring the balance of our income and expenditure. As I formerly thought that direct taxation should be substituted for indirect contributions to the public income, which I foresaw could not be preserved, so I am of opinion that it is the only proper mode of supplying the place of those duties now that they are wrested from you. It is still, in truth, only a substitution of the one for the other.

' I have already said that I should confine myself to a distinct statement of my opinion on the questions of overwhelming importance on which you have asked for it.

' There may be opportunities hereafter for remarks upon the detached observations (some of them of great value) which have been submitted to you by others.

'I will only say that, with respect to the House Tax, it is much easier to wish that it had never been abandoned than to suggest that it would be wise and practicable just now to re-establish it.

' With regard to the reduction in sugar' [that is to say, reduction of duty on British Colonial sugar], ' I confess that I entertain more than a doubt of the propriety of effecting it at present. Our expectations of a supply from the West and East Indies, sufficient to meet the entire consumption, have not, I believe, been realised; and, so long as the monopoly exists in favour of our own growers, with a supply at all within the consumption of the country, the remission of the duty would, in

a great degree, be a boon to the planter at the expense
of the Exchequer. If, hereafter, the produce should so
much exceed the consumption as to force prices at home
to a level with those on the Continent, then, indeed, it
may be an act of justice to the planter (since the benefit
of the bounty is taken from him) to make some reduction of the duty.

'Of the practical difficulty of framing an Act for the
imposition of a Property Tax [6] under existing circumstances, and of the skill and judgment and labour which
will be required for adjusting the burthens upon the
several descriptions of property and income, which ought
to be made in different proportions to contribute to it,
I am fully sensible.

'It will be an Herculean task, indeed, to prepare the
Act, and the fighting it through Parliament will be no
trifling undertaking. But I do not anticipate much
opposition in the House of Commons to the adoption
of the principle. On the contrary, I am led to believe
that you will have a great majority in favour of the
measure there.' . . .

That the views indicated in this paper really had
been seriously entertained by the writer at a much
earlier period, is proved by a passage in a speech delivered by him in the House of Commons in 1830, on

---

[6] The difficulty was immensely increased by the absence of records illustrative of the working of the former Act. All the old income tax returns,
&c. were unwisely destroyed in 1818, in compliance with a motion from
Mr. Brougham. The practical effect of this fiscal concession to public
opinion was that, on the renewal of the income tax in 1842, the fruits of
past experience were lost to those who had to frame the new Act and put
it in execution, public utility having been, neither for the first nor for the
last time, sacrificed to popular clamour.

Mr. Poulett Thomson's motion for a Committee for a Revision of Taxation ; when, referring to some previous remarks by Mr. Huskisson, he said : ' My right honourable friend, the member for Liverpool, on a former evening appealed to me, in confirmation of the assertion that I had long since been favourable to some change in taxation, by which its pressure might be transferred from one portion of the community to another. This undoubtedly is the case, and I concur with my right honourable friend in the principle, and would, under certain circumstances, be glad to see it carried into effect.'

He approved the renewal of the Income Tax in 1845 (when he was out of Parliament) for another period of three years ; and he thought that it was again warranted by the circumstances of the time in 1848. But in 1851, being in the House of Commons, he made a motion for a diminution of the tax, with a view to its gradual abandonment. This was no reversal of the policy he had recommended in 1841, and which he had intended to take up in 1828. The reasons which at those two periods had convinced him of the expediency, or necessity, of the imposition of an Income Tax no longer existed. The condition of the national finances was entirely changed. The distribution of fiscal burthens was widely different. Mr. Herries did not ask for the immediate and complete cessation of the Income Tax ; nor did he propose that a reduction of this charge should be compensated by the substitution of a corresponding amount of indirect taxation. The question at issue was not whether the Income Tax should be retained as the best means of repealing duties on articles of consumption, but whether a certain proportion (two-sevenths) of the then existing rate of Income Tax should, or should not, be still maintained, instead of another existing direct impost—the Window Tax—which Mr. Herries believed to be less generally obnoxious.

Another letter, written in the same month, relates to the Sugar question and the pending negotiations with Brazil. It very clearly marks the writer's views, which were opposed to monopoly on the one hand, and to any encouragement of slavery on the other.

' Sevenoaks: November 20, 1841.

' My dear Peel,—I return the *projet* of the Brazilian Treaty and the paper connected with it. I had intended to take them to you to-day, and to state verbally what occurred to me upon the subject. But I am prevented from leaving this place.

' In a former letter to you, I expressed much doubt with respect to the propriety of making a considerable reduction in the Sugar Duties generally, so long as the monopoly in favour of our own colonies continued to be effective by reason of the insufficiency of the supply from thence to meet the full demand for our home consumption. I understood at that time that such was the state of things, and I understand that it is still not expected that our sanguine expectations of an ample importation of British Possession sugar will be realised in the present year.

' But a new view of the case is presented by the proposal now under your consideration, and if foreign sugars are to be admitted upon such terms as will leave only a reasonable protection to the British grower, and thereby abolish his monopoly, the groundwork of my objection is removed, and the reduction of the Sugar Duty, coupled with the condition that the estimated loss of Revenue thereby to be created, is to be made good by an equivalent amount of new taxation, becomes a fair question of financial and commercial expediency. I assume, of course, that you are fully satisfied that, by the terms of your treaty with Brazil and the qualified character of the competition to be established between slave-grown and free-labour sugar, the objection on which we insisted so strongly last year [*last Session* should have been written], on the score of slavery, will be removed ; and that no danger to the successful progress of the measure of emancipation in our Colonies is to be apprehended from it. Upon that point I am hardly competent to form an opinion, and I need not suggest to *you* how important it will be to be able to establish it in argument consistently with the course pursued on our side against the propositions of the late Government.

' You are no doubt prepared to hear from them, that they also proposed to give to the consumer some benefit by an approach to competition between the sugars of our own labourers and those of Brazil; that they did so professedly with the view of enlarging our trade with that country, and of preparing for the renewal of our commercial treaty with it : but that their plan was to accomplish these objects not only without a loss of Revenue from sugar but with an augmentation of it; and that the additional benefit in the price of the article

(something more than a penny per lb.) which your plan
will confer upon the consumer beyond theirs, by the
reduction of the duty, must be purchased by the imposition of a new burthen, which may be found more onerous
to him, &c., &c. This is not my argument, but one
which will, I think, be used by a Whig Opposition by
way of appeal to the anti-Property Tax feelings of the
House.[7]

'I judge from the confidential paper which you
send me, that there is yet some uncertainty as to the
disposition of Brazil to accede to your propositions on
the subject of slavery; but I take it for granted that
you are fully satisfied that, if she does adopt them,
they will be effectual for their object. I should
otherwise have entertained some fears upon that
point.

'I am also led to suppose that the details of the
discriminating duties are as yet rather sketched out
than determined upon. On the rates of duty, I should
be unwilling to offer an opinion without more consultation than I could now venture to have with practical
men on the subject. The form in which it is proposed
to describe and enact the differential duties on sugar
appears to me to be susceptible of improvement by simplification; but that is altogether a minor consideration.

'Upon the whole, I shall be glad to see the principle of the proposed measure satisfactorily and successfully carried out. *The tendency of my opinions has always
been rather in opposition to the West Indian monopoly, more*

---

[7] This Sugar Question, as we know, was not brought forward by Sir
Robert Peel in 1842.

especially since the settlement with them on the emancipation of their slaves: and nothing but a clear conviction of the justice and weight of our anti-slavery argument against the Whig proposition of last Session would have induced me to enter so heartily as I did into opposition to it.[8]

' I shall be in London in the course of the week, and will take my chance of finding you at leisure.

'Believe me, &c.,

'J. C. HERRIES.'

On March 7, 1842, four days before Sir Robert Peel's celebrated financial statement was made in the House of Commons, a very long letter was addressed to the Chancellor of the Exchequer, commenting upon some points still under consideration. A few extracts from it may be worthy of perusal.

'Sevenoaks: March 7, 1842.

' My dear Goulburn,—You wished me to write to you after a little reflection on the two points which were mentioned when I saw you the other day, viz., the exemption of Ireland from the proposed tax on property, and the remission of the sugar duty.

' The first took me very much by surprise. I had always contemplated the re-imposition of a property tax (whether as the ultimate resource for meeting a public exigency, or as a commutation for other burthens) as being to be borne uniformly by all property of the same description in every part of the United Kingdom. And the more I have since thought upon

---

[8] The italics are those of the Editor. The passage is not underlined in the original draft.

the subject the less I can reconcile my judgment to the justice or policy of omitting Ireland from its due share of this assessment.

'It must, however, be observed, that I have not heard the arguments on the other side. You had no time to explain them to me when we met; and this is a subject upon which I cannot, until your plans are published, venture to invite discussion with other persons. I have therefore nothing to deal with but my own suggestions; and, as my opinions have long been fixed in favour of the extension of the tax to Ireland, the other side of the question has not had a fair chance in my cogitations.

'I know nothing but by conjecture of the feelings of the English landlords, capitalists, or professional men on such a subject; but I should apprehend that they would not easily be reconciled to bear the whole burthen of this imposition, by the consideration of the indirect taxes which you propose to create in Ireland; consisting chiefly of alterations, which will only bring Ireland more nearly to a level with England with regard to those taxes. . . .

'But these objections are all upon the surface, and must have been considered fully, together with many others, before you adopted your present resolution. The answers to them are, however, not equally obvious; and I must fairly confess to you that the only two points which you mentioned to me, viz. : 1st, The difficulty of establishing a machinery in Ireland for the collection of an Income Tax ; and 2ndly, That of persuading the Irish members to submit to it,—do not appear to me to be sufficient to outweigh considerations of so much magnitude.

' To the first of these I cannot attach much weight. It was urged long ago, and for many years, against the application of the Poor Laws to Ireland. It has been overcome in that matter, in which it was probably a more formidable obstacle than it would be found in the assessment of a Property Tax.

' The latter is, I daresay, the substantial impediment which you have to grapple with. I am far from being insensible to the embarrassment which it presents. I remember that Lord Londonderry bore testimony to the weight of it when there was a question, at the close of the war, of continuing a modified Property Tax instead of abandoning wholly that which then existed. He felt the difficulty of imposing it in Ireland ; but he also felt, if I mistake not, that without that condition it ought not to be re-imposed at all. My own belief is that at the present time, and under present circumstances, a good majority of the House of Commons would support you both in the imposition of a Property Tax, and in the extension of it to Ireland. . . .

' Now, with respect to the remission of a large proportion of the Sugar Duties.

' You know what my opinion is upon that subject, supposing that the supply from our Colonies and possessions be not greater than the average consumption of the United Kingdom, and consequently, that under their present monopoly of our home market, the planters would derive the chief benefit from the reduction of the duty. However much I may be a well wisher to the

East and West Indians, I am not prepared to make so great a sacrifice to them as that would be. On the other hand, supposing the colonial supply of sugar to be abundant, and the price in consequence to be regulated by the general European market—or supposing the projected treaty with Brazil to be brought to bear, so that a modified competition between foreign sugar and that of the Colonies would secure to the consumer the advantage of the reduction of duty—in either of these cases there can be no doubt that the remission of the tax upon sugar would be desirable. But you must bear in mind that in the present instance we have not the good fortune to be considering what concessions of taxation may be made from a surplus Revenue, but what are the fittest subjects for a *Commutation*. It is a question between Sugar Duty and Property Tax. I calculate roughly (but I have not seen your estimates and papers) that the duty proposed to be taken off sugar will be equivalent to about 1 per cent. of the Property Tax to be imposed. To the consumer it may make a difference in the price of the sugar of something more than 1*d*., and less than 1¼*d*., per lb. The point to be decided, therefore, is whether such a reduction of price in that article to the consumer generally is the best boon you can give to the community in compensation for the imposition of 1 per cent. on Income and Property.

'In determining upon that question, it should be borne in mind that the remission of Sugar Duty will have less influence on the interests of commerce and manufactures (except it be done in combination with a good Brazilian treaty) than the taking off of duties from raw materials of manufacture or supplies from foreign countries. This will be still more the case in consequence of the measures now in progress for the encouraging the intercourse between our colonies and other countries ; our own produce and manufactures will no longer possess the exclusive benefit of our colonial consumption. . . .

'But . . . I am hardly in a condition to compare the general advantages of a diminution of the Sugar Duties with that of other alterations of the tariff which you may not yet have determined to make. In the present state of my information I can only express a hope that it will not be preferred to a reduction of the charges on the importation of raw materials of our manufacture.

'All which is humbly submitted. Truly yours,
'J. C. HERRIES.'

A reference to Sir Robert Peel's financial speech on March 11, shows a remarkable coincidence between his arguments against the expediency of a reduction of Sugar duties, which, under existing circumstances would have benefited the British colonial producer alone, and those strongly urged against it—if unaccompanied by the admission of foreign competition—in the letters above cited. But it is evident from this correspondence that a reduction of some sort was originally contemplated as one of the measures to be proposed, and that the question was still undecided almost on the eve of the introduction of the famous budget.

That confidential communications of this kind were

habitual, may be assumed from a letter, dated February 28, 1844, to Mr. Herries from the Chancellor of the Exchequer, on the subject of the proposed reduction of the 3½ per Cents. and different plans for effecting it. 'I have deferred writing to you,' he says, 'because I have been in the hopes of seeing you, but as I cannot learn whether you intend being in London I think it better to ask for your advice by letter. . . .

'Would you be good enough to give me your opinion on this matter by return of post? Your experience in such matters makes you a better judge than most persons, and I should be unwilling to act without a previous knowledge of your views. . . . I find I am too late for the post, so I send this by a messenger in the morning.'

In the course of the Peel Administration, Mr. Herries rendered good service to the public as a member of the Royal Commissions on Metropolitan Improvements and Railway Termini. The first Report (1844) of the former Commission was chiefly devoted to the question of the Thames Embankment, part of which was originally projected by that great English artist, Sir Christopher Wren, who designed a commodious quay from Blackfriars to the Tower. To Sir Frederick Trench is due the credit of having proposed to Parliament a more extended plan for an embankment and public thoroughfare on the northern shore of the river between Westminster and London Bridges. His Bill for this purpose was brought forward, but afterwards dropped, in 1825. In 1840 the subject was submitted to the examination of a Committee of the House of

Commons which collected much valuable evidence, but went no further. The Royal Commission appointed by Sir Robert Peel studied all the different plans proposed, and strongly recommended the execution of the work in accordance with one of them particularly. Mr. Herries being entirely convinced of the utility and feasibility of the undertaking—although individually he preferred another plan (that of Mr. Walker) to the one selected—did his utmost to promote it, endeavouring to persuade the Government of the day to carry it out, and to enlist influential persons in support of the views of the Commission.[9] But the Prime Minister, whose countenance was necessary, threw cold water on the project ; and few could be made to feel the advantage of a scheme generally looked upon as an impracticable bore, detrimental to wharfingers and the owners of gardens, and not worth an additional tax of so many pence per ton of coals. More than twenty years were destined to elapse before the public hailed the accomplishment, on a greatly improved plan, of the noblest work of modern London ; but the efforts, though unsuccessful, of those who did not live to see its execution, deserve record and recognition.

[9] He continued his advocacy after Sir R. Peel's retirement.

CHAPTER XI.

1846—1852.

Return to Parliament, 1847—Monetary crisis—Bank Charter Act—Repeal
of the Navigation laws—Answer to Mr. Cobden's motion for reduction
of estimates—Derby Cabinet, 1852—Herries, President of the Board of
Control.

AT the beginning of 1846, a strong desire was expressed by the most prominent members of the surprised and derelict Conservative party that Mr. Herries,
whose principles were well known to them, should
return to Parliamentary life. But, though he entirely
disapproved the sudden change of the course of his
political friends in office, he felt no disposition to enter
into a conflict with them. To an obliging suggestion
from a distinguished person, that arrangements might
be made for the immediate fulfilment of the wishes of
those who were anxious that he should re-enter the
House of Commons, he replied : ' Your letter has found
me in a state of health and spirits little suited to the
arduous task which it suggests to me. Whoever may
be the friends, of whose wishes you are the kind inter-
preter, I beg sincerely to assure them and you that I
feel highly gratified by their too favourable opinion of
such public services as I should be able to render in
Parliament at the present most critical period. Had I
been a member of the House of Commons at this time,

I should, I trust, not have shrunk from the duty of freely discussing all the bearings of the fearful experiment which is about to be made upon the existing social and political constitution of this country : but I feel no desire to leave my present retirement to take part in such a fray; and the less so when I consider that I might be occupying a place which would be better filled by a younger and stouter combatant than myself at a time of such extraordinary difficulty and peril.'

Twelve months later he was again urged to come forward, by a letter from an active manager in the House of Commons, who wrote to him : 'I believe there is a great probability of a vacancy occurring within a few days of a seat, which I believe we can secure to you. I need hardly say that, if you were in the House, you would render great services to a large party.' . . .

To this invitation he replied : 'My long absence from the Carlton has been owing to long and severe illness, from which I am slowly recovering. I thank you much for your letter, and the very friendly terms in which you advert to the subject of it. I fear that you greatly overrate my power of rendering service to the good cause : but I shall, at all events, be very glad to meet you, and I will go to London on Friday for that purpose if I possibly can.'

   .   .   .   .   .   .

These communications, however, had no immediate result.

About the same time some correspondence took

place on the subject of Lord George Bentinck's proposed
measure 'for the prompt and profitable employment of
the people by the encouragement of railways in Ireland,' between the then leader of the Opposition and
Mr. Herries, who cordially approved the principle of the
Bill, while he suggested some alterations in its details.

'February 3, 1847.

'My dear Lord,—I beg to thank you for the perusal
of the draft of a Bill herewith returned, which I received
this morning only. . . . I have not been able to
bestow such attention upon it as it deserves. . . . I
have no hesitation, however, in stating that the general
scope of the measure appears to me to be excellent, and
that the detailed enactments suggested for the execution
of it appear generally to be sufficient for the purpose.

'If the principle of the measure should be adopted
by Parliament, the clauses in the Bill relating to the
mode of raising and applying the money required must,
of course, be left mainly in the hands of the Treasury.
That part of the [illegible] would present no practical
difficulty, and the money and [illegible] clauses might
perhaps be presented in a more simple form. . . . I
venture to express a doubt of the propriety of giving
authority to the Treasury to create and sell *Stock* for
the purpose. It is, I think, an unconstitutional course
that any permanent debt should be contracted, except
under conditions subject to the immediate control of
Parliament.[1] When that expedient was introduced into
the Savings Banks Bill I objected to it, and the then

---

[1] The writer always adhered inflexibly to this sound constitutional
doctrine.

Whig Government admitted the general principle of the objection, although they did not alter their course. Brokers care nothing for these matters.

'In the present case it seems to be unnecessary. The sum to be raised is comparatively small, and the Treasury might well make provision for this and other exigencies during the sitting of Parliament, either by a small loan or an increased [uncertain in the draft; some words appear to be omitted] credit of Exchequer Bills.

'It seems to me that *that* part of the task might well be left upon their shoulders.

'I am really sorry to be obliged to write so hastily on a subject of so much importance. I cannot conclude without expressing my sincere well wishes for your success in this very useful and highly important measure. Believe me, &c.,　　　'J. C. HERRIES.'

Lord George Bentinck wrote on the same day :—

'I am much obliged by the trouble so kindly taken by you in glancing over my Bill for me, and greatly encouraged by your approbation of it; the pretence for rejecting even its introduction is the disturbance it will create in the money market, and the dread that public securities may be lowered, and commerce and trade screwed down by another raising of the price of discounts by the Bank of England. To my mind such apprehensions are the most ridiculous that timidity and ignorance ever sowed in the mind of any visionary. But, nevertheless, I have gathered in private conversation with Lord John that the opposition to be raised.

against me will be mainly founded and built up upon this rotten ground.

'Now your opinion on all financial matters stands not only deservedly high with our Parliamentary friends, but would have great weight in the City, and a *pithy note* from you, giving a strong opinion upon this point, which I might be at liberty to read aloud in the House of Commons would, I think, have a stunning effect, and very likely turn the fortunes of the day. So valuable should I deem it, that if this note should fail to catch you before you leave town, or should catch you too late to give you time to answer it before you set out for Kent, I should very little regard the expense of an express to bring me such a note before five o'clock in the evening.

'I am much obliged for your general advice, which I will not fail to follow.' . . . .

The answer was to the following effect :

'I have only just now (in the afternoon) received your letter. I am very sure that you ascribe infinitely too much influence upon the public mind to any opinion of mine, and that no communication from me could have rendered such assistance to you in the House of Commons as you are kind enough to suppose it might have done. I must, however, candidly add that even if there had been time for me to convey such a communication to you, I should have been most reluctant to have had it put forward by you in the House, and with so much more importance attached to it than it could possibly have deserved.'

Yielding to repeated solicitations, Mr. Herries at length made up his mind to become a candidate for a seat at the general election of 1847, when he was returned, together with the Marquis of Granby, for the borough of Stamford, after a smart contest, of a local and personal, rather than a political, nature, with a Conservative opponent. His parliamentary revival is thus gracefully and justly noticed in a brilliant contemporary work.[2] 'Lord George Bentinck, however, gained an invaluable coadjutor by the reappearance of Mr. Herries in public life, a gentleman whose official as well as parliamentary experience, fine judgment, and fertile resource have been of inestimable service to the protectionist party.'

A protectionist—not a prohibitionist—he was then, as he always had been, but in a lower degree probably than the majority of the party to which he belonged. His desire was not to prevent, but, on the contrary, to favour competition; foreign competition with British industry, but also British competition with foreign industry. He was opposed to protective duties too high to admit the former, but he advocated the imposition of protective duties just high enough, but no higher, to make, according to his view, the latter possible. It has been seen, in the case of sugar, from his letters to Sir Robert Peel and Mr. Goulburn, that he objected to a diminution of duty on the produce of British colonies on the ground that it would have been in effect an augmentation of the protection then enjoyed by it, and which, deeming it excessive, he would have been willing

---

[2] *Lord George Bentinck: A Political Biography.* *By B. Disraeli*, p. 442.

to reduce considerably, but for the question of slavery. He believed that British agriculture, the ruin of which would, in his opinion, be a national calamity, stood in need of protection, because, owing to causes not removable either by legislation or by individual exertion, the unassisted competition of British producers with those of all other countries could not (as he thought) be permanently sustained.

Evidence is to be found in confidential communications from friends and supporters of a feeling of hostility on the part of some at least of the Peelites, who were anxious to prevent the election of Mr. Herries, and would have been glad if it could have been made void. But how little there was of personal animosity in his sentiments towards them may be seen from a letter to him from Croker, dated June 27, 1847, concerning an impending attack in the 'Quarterly Review' :—

'You will see that I have attended to *all* your suggestions, and omitted or altered everything that you had queried, much to the improvement of the article. I have also lowered a few expressions which you would have marked, no doubt, had you gone on marking. It is impossible not to feel indignation at the apostasy and at the mischief it has done, but personally I really have quite the reverse of ill-will or a desire to give pain, and so am very much obliged to you for your moderating hints.'

The warmth of Mr. Herries's reception on resuming his seat in the House of Commons was very gratifying. Sir Robert Peel took the first opportunity to 'express, in common with the House generally, his satisfaction at the return to this house of his right honourable friend, and his congratulations that, by his return, the House would have the benefit of his great intelligence and great practical experience.' By the occupants of the Treasury Bench, and especially by Lord John Russell, Prime Minister, Sir Charles Wood (Lord Halifax), Chancellor of the Exchequer (the frequent contests between whom and Mr. Herries were always characterised by the utmost courtesy), and Mr. Labouchere (the late Lord Taunton), he was invariably treated, in spite of strong opposition, not only with due civility, but with marked respect.

The monetary disasters of the autumn of 1847, and the extra-legal course taken by the Government in consequence of them, made the meeting of the new Parliament in November necessary, and required its immediate attention. The subject was one in which Mr. Herries took great interest. He believed that the crisis had been intensified, if not caused, by the restrictions imposed upon the Bank by the Act of 1844, from the operation of which he had always feared that dangerous embarrassment would arise. He predicted its recurrence, and he could not be persuaded that a law was a good one which involved the necessity of its own periodical violation by the assumption of a 'dispensing power' on the part of the Crown. He took an early opportunity of expressing his views in a debate on the Chancellor of the Exchequer's motion for a committee to inquire into the causes of the recent commercial distress. In doing so he said that 'he was satisfied that the day would come when Parliament would again be called upon to interfere.' He did not live to see the fulfilment of his prophecy ten years afterwards, in 1857, and again, with another interval of nine years, in 1866.

Lord John Russell, who replied particularly to Mr. Herries's speech, observing that in the course of the discussion some novel opinions had been thrown out, and there had been a great deal of discursive disquisition, said : ' I am happy to find, therefore, that in following the right honourable gentleman, I follow one who has kept himself within the limits of that which is properly the subject of debate, and who has given opinions which, whether I agree with them or not, at any rate must be listened to with the greatest respect, coming as they do from a person of his influence, his experience, and his knowledge both of the financial and the constitutional history of the country.' The person alluded to was reluctant to allow his name to be placed on the list of the committee, but consented to do so in compliance with the desire strongly manifested by the Chancellor of the Exchequer, who said that it would be a great public disadvantage if he should decline to serve on it. Soon after the Christmas holidays Mr. Herries brought the subject forward again by moving two resolutions, the first of which, approving the recommendation given by the Government to the Bank, was adopted, but the second, declaring the expediency of a suspension of the restrictions imposed by the Acts of 1844 and 1845, was rejected by a majority of 41. The motion came too late. The October panic had passed away, Consols were rising, and the pressure, no longer felt, was almost forgotten.

The repeal of the Navigation laws proposed for the

first time by the Government in 1848, and effected in 1849, was the most important question dealt with by the House of Commons during those sessions, or indeed during the whole existence of that Parliament. ' The resistance,' says Lord George Bentinck's illustrious biographer, ' was led with great ability by Mr. Herries, and the whole party put forward their utmost strength to support him.' In a fair and temperate spirit, as some of its best advocates admitted, he opposed the measure of the Government, believing that the abrogation of the ' Maritime Charter ' would expose to hazard that naval preponderance which it had been designed to secure, and to the maintenance of which, looking at the question from the point of view of national greatness, he made all other considerations entirely subordinate. But although he thought that it was rash to abolish the code which, modified indeed in some of its parts, had subsisted for two centuries, he never went to the extreme length of saying that no relaxation in any of its details ought ever to be allowed. He professed his readiness to assent, as he had done more than twenty years before, to such alterations as a change of circumstances might render necessary. His opinions were expressed in the resolution which, in concert with his friends, he moved on the 20th of May, 1848 : ' That it is essential to the national interests of this country to maintain the fundamental principles of the existing Navigation laws, subject to such modifications as may be best calculated to obviate any proved inconvenience to the commerce of the United Kingdom and its dependencies, without danger to our national strength.'

What he meant when he spoke of the 'fundamental principles of the existing Navigation laws,' he explained by quoting the words of Mr. Huskisson: 'The fundamental principle of the Navigation laws is that of giving by law in our foreign trade a preference to British shipping and British seamen, so far as we can do so consistently with our engagements and relations with other countries, and of confining our domestic trade, our coasting and colonial trade, as well as our fisheries, exclusively to ourselves.' . . . To these principles Mr. Huskisson firmly adhered. The legislative changes effected under his auspices, and in which Mr. Herries, then Secretary to the Treasury, was largely a collaborator, were no deviation from them. It was contended, with no little inconsistency, by many of those who at the same time most vehemently demanded the total repeal of the Navigation law, denouncing its artificial restrictions as injurious to commerce, to the consumer, and to the shipping interest itself, that hardly anything in reality remained of the detested statute. With varying metaphor it was said that the substance having been taken away by the legislation of Wallace and Huskisson, and by the reciprocity treaties, nothing was left but a shred, a rag, a shadow, the bark of the tree without its trunk, and from this strange fallacy was drawn, especially by Sir Robert Peel, an *argumentum ad hominem*, as illegitimate as such an argument commonly is, against Mr. Herries, who was twitted with his useless defence of the mere semblance of a protection, which he himself had helped to destroy. But such reasonings, however smart they may have appeared in debate, will not bear the test of candid examination. The so-called Reciprocity Acts of 1823 and 1824, and the treaties founded upon them, did not in fact touch the Navigation Act in the slightest degree. They dealt simply with the equalization of discriminating duties on ships and on the goods carried in them—charges not imposed by the Navigation Act, and which were not its necessary consequence. The amended Navigation Acts of 1822 and 1825 removed several of the former restrictions on the colonial trade, the long voyage trade, and the European carrying trade, some of which had no longer any meaning or importance, and others had been rendered inapplicable by altered political circumstances. One change indeed, by which the interdiction of importations of certain commodities from the Netherlands or Germany, was taken off, was nothing but a return to the Act of 1660. But after all these concessions to foreign navigation, the main provisions of the law were still in many respects intact. A Prussian vessel was enabled to carry Prussian produce from a Prussian port to certain ports in the British West Indies, and bring home colonial produce. But it could not carry a cargo of British goods from London to Jamaica, or a cargo of sugar from Trinidad to Liverpool. A Dutch ship might bring over to England from Amsterdam French wine previously imported into Holland, but not claret from Bordeaux, port wine from Oporto, or oranges from Palermo. The transformation of colonies into independent States required the adoption of new rules for the trade with the American Continent, but the old ones to a great extent subsisted for the import trade with Asia and Africa, which, for all practical purposes, was still a British monopoly, being confined to British ships or those of the country of origin *and* export. How then could it be pretended that the Navigation Act was reduced to a mere shadow ? To the *reductio ad absurdum* Mr. Herries replied by quoting Mr. Labouchere's words on introducing his bill in 1849 :—' The changes I am about to recommend are of a far more important and extensive description than any previously proposed to Parliament. . . . I do not disguise from myself that these alterations are of a very grave and serious character.' . . .

Although the result could not have been doubtful, the contest was vigorously sustained in the House of Commons, where Mr. Herries's motions were powerfully supported by Lord George Bentinck, Mr. Disraeli, Lord Granby, Mr. Walpole, and other speakers who were not afraid to fight a losing battle. In the House of Lords the Navigation law had no more eloquent defender than Lord Brougham. He often took counsel on this subject with Mr. Herries, at whose house he became a frequent visitor, and for whom he professed particular esteem ; his sentiments, which at an earlier period had been those of inveterate hostility,[3] having undergone an entire change.

---

[3] It was displayed both in and out of Parliament. Many bitter attacks in newspaper articles and reviews were known, or believed, to have proceeded from Brougham's pen. A passage in a letter written by him to Sir Robert Wilson in 1827 shows his *animus*. 'I fear such appointments as that ardent ultra [this Whig notion at that time was entirely erroneous] and concealed malignant Herries augur no great good to the *godly*.' The godly were of course the Whigs.—*Narrative of the Formation of Canning's Administration,* by General Sir Robert Wilson. Edited by the Rev. Herbert Randolph. 1872.

It must be conceded that the apprehensions of those who, adhering to the policy upheld by a long line of English statesmen, from Cromwell to Huskisson, and advocated by the greatest of English econom'sts, deprecated the abrogation of the law, famous in the history of England and of the world, ' for the encouragement of British Shipping and Navigation,' have not been realized, although it may be doubted whether, in all respects, their predictions have been proved to be erroneous by results. But their successful adversaries cannot justly refuse to admit that the maritime and commercial conditions of every region of the globe which existed prior to the year 1850, and in view of which the question was discussed, have since that time been wholly changed by the operation of causes not then foreseen. The requirements both of peaceful trade and of naval warfare at the present day are far removed from those of the year 1848.

All the calculations of the comparative cost of building and navigating British and foreign ships which were made at a time when the number of steam vessels was relatively insignificant, and wood was still the material principally employed, have been upset by the enormous increase of steam navigation, and of the use of iron in the construction of ships ; in both which respects our ability to defy foreign competition needs no demonstration.

The prodigious augmentation of traffic of all kinds between all countries, far exceeding that which previous experience could have warranted anyone in reckoning upon, has demanded a corresponding addition to the formerly available means of transport.

The unexpected access of Europeans to Japan; the extension of trade with China brought about by successful war; the creation of new centres of commercial activity consequent upon the gold discoveries of California and Australia; the opening of the Suez Canal by French enterprise in spite of the senseless opposition of Lord Palmerston to an undertaking beneficial to the world in general, but far more so to England in particular, of the impotent ill-will of British diplomacy, and of the prejudices instilled into the mind of the British public, led by persistent invective and insinuation to look upon the great work now placed in the category of 'British interests' of the first magnitude, as an engine malignantly designed for the destruction of the British Empire, and upon its ingenious and courageous promoter, as a deadly enemy bent on the ruin of all that was most sacred to a Briton: these extraordinary events, not even remotely referable to free trade in general, or to free trade in shipping, specifically, have given such an impulse to steam navigation on the largest scale as no man could have contemplated in 1848.

Another revolution not then to be imagined was the sudden displacement of American by British shipping: the result, not of fair competition in the ordinary course of trade, but of civil war, and of depredations exercised by 'volunteer cruisers' fitted out through the pernicious activity of English speculators.

In looking at comparative statistics of British navigation, it is well to remember that the conditions required, formerly and now, to constitute a British vessel are not the same. What was legally and technically described as a British ship under the old Navigation law, was such in reality. It was a vessel built in the United Kingdom or in some British dependency, owned by a British subject, navigated by a British master, and manned by a crew of which at least three-fourths were also British subjects. It is now possible for a ship to have a British register, and to be entitled to sail under British colours, which has been built in Norway, is owned by a Company the whole of whose capital belongs to Americans, commanded by a Dutchman, and manned with a 'scratch crew' of murderous mutineers of no known nationality, not one of whom speaks or understands the English tongue, or cares in the least for the parallelogram of red bunting with a particoloured corner, called the British ensign, which, manufactured perchance at Ghent, may have been purchased by a German bagman in a slop-shop at Antwerp. What is there British, except its register, about such a ship? Even the belaying pins with which, somewhere in the South Sea, the mate kills the captain, the boatswain the mate, the cook the boatswain, and the carpenter the cook, are probably not British made ; nor the knives with which, after scuttling the so-called British ship, the piratical crew cut each other's throats ; leaving the last survivor in possession of the only British articles on board—a bottle of whisky and a box of biscuits.

As to the genuine British seaman of the mercantile marine, some high naval authorities have held the opinion that his average quality has deteriorated since

the adoption of the modern system. But this is a
consideration which does not affect the question of cheap
conveyance, and consequently of cheap consumption,
long since recognized as the primary object of human
existence.

On Mr. Cobden's irrational motion (February 26,
1849) for a reduction of expenditure by ten millions in
order to bring it down to the standard of the estimates of
1835, without regard to all the changes which fourteen
years had brought about in modes of warfare, in arms,
in the numerical strength of continental armies, and in
the naval and military preparations of foreign Powers,
Mr. Herries, supporting the Government, animadverted
severely, but justly, upon the customary misrepresenta-
tions of the financial and economical agitators. 'The
Right Honourable gentleman, the Chancellor of the
Exchequer,' he said, 'had complimented the honourable
member for the West Riding on the moderation and
forbearance which had marked his observations. In
that compliment he (Mr. Herries) could not join; for
although the tone and language of the honourable
member were moderate and sufficiently tempered to
suit the atmosphere of that House, he (Mr. Herries)
could not forget that the speech of the honourable
member was, after all, but a repetition of that which
had been ringing in the public ear for the last six
months from Liverpool, from Manchester, and every
other scene of agitation, where the same things had been
said, though not exactly in the same terms. . . . The
honourable member was violent in one place, and
decorous in another; but if the honourable gentleman

was to have the privilege of using inflammatory and irritating language in one place, and sober and discreet language in another, he (Mr. Herries) would much prefer that he should give way to his violence and invective in that House, and reserve his decorous argumentation for those places where his audiences consisted of multitudes composed of more inflammable materials. . . . The honourable member had instituted a comparison between the expenditure of the Governments of England and France.   He (Mr. Herries) being thus provoked to follow the honourable gentleman in that contrast, was compelled to declare that he did not think he had studied that subject quite well enough to warrant him in coming, as he had done, to a conclusion in respect to the financial administration of the two nations unfavourable to that of England. . . . If they reviewed the financial progress of the English and French nations for the last twenty-eight years, they would see much more cause for congratulation than for blame or regret, in the comparative good management of our own Government, under the sanction of Parliament, when placed in contradistinction with that of France.' . . . He then gave a succinct statement of the expenditure of each country from 1820 to 1848 inclusive, showing, as the result of the comparison, that 'whilst in England they commenced in 1820 with 56,150,000*l.*, and ended in 1848 with 55,596,000*l.*; in France they commenced with 35,000,000*l.*, and ended with 72,000,000*l.* From 1824 the average amount was about 38,000,000*l.* until the year 1830. In that year a great change occurred.   There was a revolution.

Revolutions were expensive things—a fact which it would well become those who were disposed to promote them to bear in mind. In 1830 an enormous increase of expenditure was incurred for the revolution itself, whereby the amount of the Budget of 1831 was swelled to the sum of 60,000,000*l.* . . . . It was well deserving the attention of the House that the rapid expansion of public expenditure in France seemed to keep pace with the progressive infusion of more popular elements into her Government and Constitution ; and this remarkable circumstance suggested an observation on a doctrine which had been propounded to the good people of Manchester by the member for the West Riding, the effect of which was that the minute and progressive subdivision of property which prevailed in France, under the laws of that country, was an admirable safeguard against a propensity to war, by its tendency to arrest the expenditure by which war was always accompanied. . . . He (Mr. Herries) had been greatly surprised by the maintenance of such a doctrine in the face of history and experience. Why, let the honourable member but look at those papers to which he had just been referring, and then tell him what he meant by stating that this subdivision of property must have the effect of preventing war, because it prevented expenditure. Did he not know that this very subdivision of property and all this expanding expenditure had been going on together in France,[4] and that a great part of

---

[4] He might have added that the peasant proprietors of France were the mainstay of Bonapartism and Sacerdotalism. But he could not have predicted that a Second Em ire, created and supported by allied pea-

that expenditure was for the Algerine war—a war which had been forced upon the Government by the pressure from without ? . . . Let the honourable member then, whenever he again addressed the people of Manchester on the subject of agitating for a reduction of the national expenditure, and compared democratic with monarchical institutions—let him—if he chose to give the preference to democracy, tell his audiences that all history taught that if they must needs have republics and democracies in preference to such a monarchy as that under which we live, they must be well prepared to put their hands deep into their pockets to pay for the change. . . . The honourable member told the House of things past and things to come, and of his intense desire for the reduction of expenditure. In that he was not singular. Why, so was he (Mr. Herries) also for reduction. He was ready to go along with the honourable member if he would only go at a different pace. . . . With agitators he was not prepared to go— with an agitation that was based on no solid foundation he could not co-operate—an agitation, too, that was conducted in a spirit of hostility and hatred against particular classes. . . He would tell the honourable gentlemen

sant proprietors and priests, would bring ruin upon France by a war of aggression.

It might also have been suggested to Mr. Cobden as a matter for his consideration, whether the Corn Laws could have been repealed without conflict between town and country, if in 1846 the whole soil of the United Kingdom had been owned by the tillers thereof, numbering with their families many millions directly interested in the maintenance of high prices for agricultural produce, their sole means of subsistence ; and whether the minute subdivision of property which he desired would not inevitably be followed by a demand on the part of those millions for a return to agricultural protection.

opposite that they had no right to impute to him or to his friends any indisposition to retrenchment and economy. They were prepared to promote both to the utmost.'

.   .   .   .   .   .

The denial of the dogma that infinite subdivision of land among little cultivators is the true remedy for all maladies of the body politic was received with great indignation.   Mr. Herries was told that he was in favour of an increase of pauperism for the better preservation of peace, because he doubted the truth of the doctrine laid down by Mr. Cobden, and interpreted by another speaker, 'that the more property was divided in proportion to the population, as in France, the less danger was there of their institutions being disturbed.' This was said just one year after the revolution of February 1848, followed by months of ruinous anarchy, while the 'institutions' and society of England, where property was not 'divided as in France,' remained unshaken.   But concerning 'peasant proprietors' anything may be affirmed.

In spite of his constant desire to defer to the opinions of his friends in opposition, Mr. Herries was not always able to agree with them.   On one occasion, indeed, he felt compelled to express his dissent from a motion made by Mr. Henley, with the concurrence of many of the protectionist party, for a general reduction by ten per cent. of the salaries of civil servants, from the highest to the lowest, on the ground of an alleged decrease of the cost of living.   Being convinced that such a diminution of their scanty and well-earned incomes would inflict great suffering upon an immense number of meritorious functionaries, he voted with the Government against the proposal. In the course of his speech he pointed out the considerable reductions successively effected since 1815—the ratio of diminution having been much greater in salaries than in the number of officials. He also observed that when the price of wheat rose from 39s. in 1835 to 70s. in 1839, there was no proposition for an increase of salaries, and that their regulation by the price of corn, with a necessary alteration almost year by year— a system of corn salaries instead of corn rents—would be most detrimental to poor clerks with 90l. a year or less, who could not reduce their fixed charges for rent, insurance, and the like.

It is needless to follow the vicissitudes of the sessions of 1850 and 1851, the history of which is written in the Book of Hansard.

When Lord Palmerston's swift vengeance drove his late colleagues out of office in 1852, and Lord Derby was forced under adverse circumstances to undertake the formation of a new Cabinet, Mr. Herries accepted the post in it of President of the Board of Control. It was a very great disappointment to him that the place in the Cabinet which he was most qualified to fill—the Chancellorship of the Exchequer—could not be assigned to him. Lord Derby explained that there were special reasons which compelled him to unite the position of leader of the House of Commons with the office of Chancellor of the Exchequer in the present instance, and that this had been already arranged with Mr. Disraeli. But with that exception, and one or two others, he offered him his choice. So strongly did Mr. Herries feel upon the subject of the Exchequer, that he begged for a short time—though there was but little to spare—in order to consider what course he should pursue; and in the same afternoon he wrote to Lord Derby (whose great kindness, and even anxiety to satisfy him, he always acknowledged), offering to support the Government without office, or, if Lord Derby continued to think, as he had said in their interview, that it was of importance to the Government that he should be a member of it, he suggested that he might hold some honorary office without any serious duties attached to it.

In truth he felt that, at his time of life, and in his state of health, he could not undertake the administration of a department involving much labour, and that his intimate knowledge of our financial system, even in its minutest details, would enable him to deal with the Exchequer with the greatest ease.

But Lord Derby could not consent to either of these proposals, and, finally, it was left to Mr. Herries to decide between the Colonial office, the Board of Control (India Office), and the Board of Trade. He selected the India Office, being averse from the labour which he believed the Colonies would entail upon him.[5]

---

[5] There is much confidential correspondence betweeen Mr. Herries and Lord Derby, as well as other political personages, during the period from 1848 to 1853. It is of course too recent for publication; but the present Editor may, without indiscretion, remark that if it could be produced it would afford indisputable proof of the very high estimation in which Mr. Herries was held.

CHAPTER XII.

Work at the India Office—Correspondence on Burmese War, &c.—Exercise
of patronage—Letters to Croker and others—Recognition of French
Empire—Resignation of Derby Cabinet—Mr. Herries retires from Parliament—Letter from Brougham—Opinions of eminent public men—Death
—Liberal testimony—General view of Mr. Herries's political principles
and practice—Conclusion.

HE soon perceived that age had weakened the capacity
for continuous work which at an earlier period of his
life had been immense, and some premonitory attacks,
temporarily disabling him, warned him that he was endeavouring to do more than his strength would allow.
If the Cabinet had appeared to be firmly established he
would have sought rest in retirement, but, in the precarious state of its existence, a sense of duty to his
colleagues restrained him from abandoning the post he
had been persuaded to assume. His feeling of weariness
is expressed in a letter to a political friend of former
days :—' I rejoice to observe that you have lost none of
your warmth of attachment to the old school of politics
in which you and I were fellow-labourers " *a long time
ago.*" But a sad change has come over the spirit of
that dream. You are well out of the toil and turmoil
of a struggle with the augmented and augmenting
powers of Radicalism. I heartily wish I were in so
quiet a position as you are. The management of my
immense office is a hard task at my time of life, and

nothing but a conscientious devotion to a good cause would have induced me to undertake it. . . .'

But there is certainly no want of vigour or care perceptible in his correspondence, official or private.

The second Burmese War, the intelligence of the commencement of which reached England soon after the installation of the new Ministry, and the Parliamentary inquiry into the system of government in India previous to the expiration of the Company's charter, were the principal objects calling for the attention of the Indian Department during Mr. Herries's short administration of it. To other questions of permanent importance he devoted himself with the greatest solicitude. In particular, he earnestly pressed forward the construction of railways, and promoted the plans for the establishment of telegraphic communication, the honour of devising which belongs to Dr. O'Shaughnessy.

The following extracts from private letters,[1] written by Mr. Herries at this time show his views on these subjects, and his mode of treating them.

To the Duke of Wellington, March 4, 1852.

'In obedience to your wish expressed to me at the Levee, I send you the draft of the letter prepared by Lord Ellenborough in 1829 after consulting you on the possible renewal of the Burmese war, together with Lord Ellenborough's note suggesting a reference to it. . . .'

---

[1] The publication of the present Memoir has been retarded by the accidental discovery of a large volume containing this correspondence.

To the Earl of Ellenborough.

March 4.—'I am much obliged to you for your letter. I saw the Duke at the Levee, and I reminded him of his suggestions to you on the subject of a possible renewal of a Burmese War in 1829. He desired to have an opportunity of reading the draft of your despatch. I have accordingly sent it to him. I am anxiously waiting for the mail from India. As there is every disposition on the part of the Indian Government to avoid war, I am in hopes that nothing permanently mischievous may arise from the reported skirmish off Rangoon.'

To the Marquis of Dalhousie.

March 8.—' Your letter, addressed to Lord Broughton, dated January 23, has been placed by him in my hands, and affords me the first opportunity of opening a private and confidential correspondence with you, in my present official position, of which I avail myself with much pleasure. . . .

'. . . Although I entertain a strong expectation that under your prudent management the misfortune of a war with Ava will be avoided, I think it may be useful and interesting to you to refer to a despatch touching the possible danger of the renewal of a Burmese war, which you will find in your archives under date of September 29, 1829. It was sent out by Lord Ellenborough after a communication with the Duke of Wellington, from whom I have just received the note enclosed, after sending it to him for perusal. . . .'

April 8.—' Your letters by the last mail have been of great interest, and we await with much solicitude the result of your prompt and decisive measures for bringing the Burmese to reason. I do not in the least degree doubt the correctness of your conclusion, that nothing short of vigorous compulsion would produce that effect. . . .

' . . . With more discretion on the side of the naval negotiators, and a strict compliance with your instructions, the affair might perhaps have been terminated without having recourse to the strong measures which you are now forced to adopt. . . .

' I sincerely hope that you will not find it inconvenient, either to your health or to your private affairs, to accede to the request which Lord Derby has made to you, and which I also subsequently addressed to you through the Secret Committee (very much to the satisfaction of the Chairs), that you would consent to remain another year in the discharge of your high and most important functions. Under any circumstances a compliance with the request would have been essentially advantageous to the public service. The recent events and present prospect of affairs in India, greatly add to the importance of it. . . .'

May 24.—' Your letters by the last mail have put us in possession of all your proceedings and views up to the starting of the expedition against Rangoon. They afford no ground for hope that any answer would be received from Ava such as might authorise General Godwin to bring matters to a peaceful conclusion without striking a blow. I therefore expect to learn by the next arrival of the mail that Rangoon has fallen and Martaban also. The instructions which you have given to the General are in every respect approved of by Lord Derby and the whole of the Government here, of which I have the satisfaction of conveying to you an assurance by my secret despatch of this date.'

.   .   .   .

June 7.—' Your despatches of the 22nd and your private letter of the 24th, have brought us good tidings, and afforded much gratification to all of us. I heartily congratulate you on the complete success of an expedition prepared so immediately under your personal superintendence to carry out your own policy, in which the whole of the Government at home have unreservedly concurred, as I have already assured you. Although you were not sanguine at the date of your letter in the hope that the King of Ava might be wise enough to profit by the severe lesson which you have given him, I must confess that I am not without the belief and expectation that such a blow so promptly and so vigorously administered may have the effect of subduing even Burmese pride, and thereby lead to a speedy conclusion of the war. Heaven grant it may be so.

' The state of the health of the army is the only subject of anxiety to us. It does not appear from any accounts we possess whether the cholera, of which some cases had occurred, was of Rangoon origin, or carried with them by the troops from Madras or Calcutta. We are assured here by persons assuming to have knowledge by experience of the locality, that Rangoon is not invariably an unhealthy place. The reminiscences of our last military occupation of it are not decisive upon that point. In that instance there was a neglect of all those precautions and provisions for the health and comfort of the men which in this case you have so carefully attended to. . . .

.   .   .   .   .   .

'Our Committee, on the renewal of the "East Indian Territories" Act proceeds quietly and satisfactorily. There is a general inclination towards a maintenance of the present system with perhaps some— not very important—modifications.

'I took the liberty of communicating part of your letter to me to the Queen.'

.   .   .   .   .   .

June 8.—' I will attend immediately and with much interest to your despatches by the last mail on the subject of the electric telegraph. The papers are this day brought under my consideration. You may depend upon my warm support in the prosecution of your views, and on my giving all possible attention to Dr. O'Shaughnessy when he arrives. It is a matter of immense importance to the Government of India.'

June 23.—' It affords me much pleasure to be able to relieve your mind of one subject of solicitude, which appears (by your last letter of May 3) to occupy it. You were then under the impression that the Burmese War is unpopular here. But . . . I am able confidently to assure you that war with Ava stands in no disfavour in the public mind ; while, on the contrary, there certainly does prevail a very general admiration of the manner in which you have commenced and hitherto conducted it.   Your earnest endeavours to avoid it are duly appreciated.   We have published in an Extraordinary Gazette the documents relating to the capture of Rangoon and Martaban, and I trust that in the forthcoming Queen's Speech notice will be taken in becoming terms of approbation of your own share of these important achievements, as well as of the valour and discipline of the troops engaged in them.   They are, indeed, beyond all praise, considering the difficulties of the climate with which these brave fellows had to contend.

'The good health of the army and the favourable condition of the wounded are subjects of much gratification to all of us. . . .'

With reference to the two last letters, Lord Dalhousie wrote on August 7 :—'You have gratified me by the kind terms in which you have disabused my mind of the belief that this war is obnoxious in England. I do not affect to be insensible to any approbation which may be felt of my own share in the matter, or to be by any means indifferent to the expression of it, but I can also most unaffectedly declare that my chief care is that her Majesty's Government should, at the fitting time, give full praise and reward to the soldiers and sailors who have done their work so well.   They are noble fellows.   By my life they are noble fellows!

'Your very prompt and complete adoption of all our proposals regarding the electric telegraph has been most gratifying to us here.   Be assured it is a work whose importance and value to this country cannot be over-estimated.' . . .

To the Marquis of Dalhousie.

July 24.—' Your letters of June 2 have brought to us the satisfactory intelligence of the capture of Bassein.

' The movement upon that place was well planned and happily executed.

' The occupation of Bassein and the consequent command of the branch of the river on which it is situated, is an important addition to the possession of Rangoon and Martaban.

' General Godwin's opinion, confirmed by your own, on the impolicy of a forward movement under present circumstances is entirely acquiesced in here. I have submitted the papers to the Duke of Wellington. It is a remarkable circumstance that you should remain so entirely uninformed of the disposition or condition of the Court of Ava. There must be some special cause for the absence of information from thence. I am inclined to impute it to some convulsion in that Government, and I am not without hope that we may reap the benefit of their distracted councils in a concession which may relieve us from the necessity of a march upon Ava.

' Happen what may, I have no doubt but that you will make the Burmese pay our expenses. In the present state of our Indian finances, we can ill afford to incur extra charges for punishing their misconduct. I am aware of your anxious attention to the subject of the income and expenditure of India, and I trust you will permit me, in the course of the present recess, to open an unreserved correspondence with you on that important topic. . . . I have seen Dr. O'Shaughnessy, and am much pleased with him. I will do everything in my power to forward his business here, and to promote your intentions with respect to the electric telegraph system in India. We are doing what we can in pushing on the construction of your railways. I could not agree with the Directors on the question whether the Madras Railway should be executed by the East India Company itself, or by contract, as in the case of the others now in progress. The great advantage of inducing the investment of British capital, and the application of British enterprise to Indian improvements, taken in conjunction with the apparently successful progress (hitherto) of the contract system in the construction of the Bombay and Bengal railways, induced me to overrule the resolution of the Court of Directors in favour of the other course. . . .

'You will observe in our newspapers that great havoc has been made in the ranks of the late Parliament by the elections now nearly brought to a close. There are few of us who have not lost personal friends in the general slaughter ; and independently of all political bias there are some whose absence from Parliament I shall sincerely deplore.'

August 24.—'I have received your private letter of 3rd July. If you wrote to me by the preceding mail (which we fear is lost), I am without hope of ever seeing your letter. It is not in my power to write to you on this occasion as fully as I should have wished . . . by the next mail you may confidently expect a full and explicit communication of the views and decision of the Government upon the several alternatives set forth in your minute of the 30th of June,[2] concerning the ulterior measures to be pursued in the settlement of the Burmese question. . . . .'

To the Duke of Wellington.

September 2.—' Your paper of suggestions on the annexation of Pegu has been acted upon. I have drawn the instructions to the Governor-General accordingly, in concert with Lord Derby, and they are now with the Queen for approval. I thought it right to inform her Majesty that your advice had been taken by Lord Derby upon the subject.'

To Viscount Falkland.[3]

September 6.—'. . . . . You may be assured that there is, and always will be, a ready disposition on my part, and on that of the other members of H.M. Government, to repel unjust or injurious attacks upon the public servants abroad, as a duty to them upon general public grounds, independently even of the personal respect which they entertain for your Lordship and others who like you are discharging important duties in distant lands. . . . In a former letter to you I have adverted in just terms of approbation to the admirable celerity with which the orders of Lord Dalhousie were executed at Bombay in the preparation of the Naval Force required from thence for the expedition to Rangoon. The subsequent conduct of the Indian steamers in the Rivers of Pegu has been

----

[2] Papers presented to Parliament March 15, 1853, p. 37.
[3] Governor of Bombay.

sufficient, I trust, to dispel all prejudices which may have existed against your naval establishment.

'I have read with attention and interest your remarks upon the financial condition of your Lordship's Presidency. You are justly entitled to a full allowance for all the circumstances to which you advert, as necessary causes of the apparently unfavourable balance of the Income and Expenditure of Bombay. I am about to enter upon a full investigation of the financial condition of all the Presidencies, and you may be assured that the important facts to which you direct my attention will not be overlooked. . . .'

To the Marquis of Dalhousie.

September 7.—'I have received your private letters of the 14–15th June, and of the 14th July ; the earlier ones after the latter ; they were retarded by the failure of the Ajduha.

'I wrote by the last mail to inform you that we had received your important minute of the 30th June. I regretted that I could not by the same opportunity send you the opinions of the Government upon it. The mail which brought it arrived later than usual, and my colleagues were so dispersed that I was unable to lay before the Queen the draft of the instructions which you so earnestly and so naturally requested to receive in the most explicit terms, in time for the outgoing mail.

'Those instructions[4] will reach you when you receive this letter. The fullest consideration has been

---

[4] September 6. Papers presented to Parliament March 15, 1853, p. 52.

given to all the points adverted to in your Minute. Lord Derby thought it right to take the Duke of Wellington into our councils. . . . You will observe how entirely all your measures are approved of, and how cordially all your motives are concurred in by the Government at home. The only point on which we somewhat diverge—not from any of your positive views —but from a suggestion connected with your fifth and last proposed alternative—is one upon which I trust that you will ultimately agree with us.

'We see no practicable or safe termination of the warfare in which you are engaged with Burmah except by compelling the King of Ava to conclude it by a treaty such as may satisfy our interests and vindicate our honour, or by driving him from his capital and extinguishing his rule. We have, therefore, not adopted the course, rather hinted than expressly proposed in your minute, of confining our military operations to the expulsion of the Burmese from Pegu and then leaving them to do the worst they can against us.

'I see with satisfaction your determination to go yourself to Rangoon. Your presence cannot but have an excellent effect there. . . . On the whole we look forward with confident hope to the ultimate issue of the operations into which you have been compelled to enter. My own expectation is that they will put an end for ever to all danger and trouble on your eastern frontier, and open new and important sources of advantage to the commerce of this country and of India.'

To Sir J. W. Hogg, Bart., Chairman of the Court of Directors.

September 7.— . . . ' We differ very slightly from the Governor-General as to the *modus terminandi* of the war which he commenced with so much reluctance and has prosecuted with so much skill and vigour. Whatever may be thought of it by others, *I* look forward to great benefits to India to be ultimately derived from the ample punishment—perhaps the expulsion of the Burmese from our eastern frontier there. . . .'

To the Marquis of Dalhousie.

September 23.—'I have received your letter of the 7th August after your return from Rangoon. The information which it brings to us relating to the health and general good condition of the troops is so satisfactory that I have thought it right to communicate the contents of it to the Queen. I have also deemed it advisable to publish in the ordinary Gazette the despatches relating to the affair at Prome. It appears to be desirable, in order to prevent idle misrepresentation, to keep the public mind well informed upon the state of things in Burmah, and that it should be prepared by correct intelligence for the results to which your measures are inevitably tending. A great change has already taken place in the general feeling in this country respecting an extension of our Indian possessions eastward. Unless I am much mistaken there prevails at present a stronger disposition to deprecate too much forbearance and self-denial than to quarrel with conquest and aggrandisement in the quarter into which you have so successfully carried an unavoidable war. There would, I am confident, be an accusatory outcry of disappointment if Pegu were not to be added to our eastern Empire. I hope you will find our instructions sent out by the last mail as explicit as you could desire. The opinion of our great old Duke upon the subject, given at the request of Lord Derby, was perhaps the last advice of any political importance which he was called upon to give. He was peremptory upon the point of compelling the Burmese to cede Pegu by a definitive treaty, or driving them out of Ava; subject in the latter case to such further punishment as our sacrifices of men and money might justify and require. . . .

.   .   .   .   .   .

'The public mind is at this moment wholly engrossed here by the death of our great hero. Having been warmly attached to him myself during the last thirty years, I feel deeply and lament sincerely the loss of him. But his departure has been to me more a subject of regret than of surprise. The last letter which I received from him (a few days only before his death) was scarcely legible or intelligible.

'I have several important papers on your public affairs now under my consideration which I reserved on account of their magnitude for a day of leisure. . . . One of our first acts when Parliament meets must be the reappointment of the Committee on the renewal of the Indian Government Act. I do not anticipate any very serious opposition, but immense trouble, in obtaining the consent of Parliament to a continuation of it.   I trust that the late Government will concur with the present in the promotion of that object.   We worked harmoniously in the Committee in the last session. . . .'

October 8.—' I have received your letter of August 21.   It is full of interest, and presents altogether a very satisfactory prospect of the successful termination of the warfare into which you have been dragged by the insolent and impracticable Burmese. . . .

.   .   .   .   .   .

'I know nothing personally of General Godwin. But the good opinion which you have formed of him leads me to expect that once put in motion under your direction, and with the well-appointed army placed in his hands, his movements will be prompt and vigorous —such as appear to be especially required for the speedy success of the campaign which is before him, and the destruction of the enemy with which he has to cope. . . .'

To the Earl of Derby.

October 5.—' The mail from India, which reached me last night, brings intelligence which requires our immediate attention.

' The Governor-General has, somewhat hastily, as it appears to me, adopted a course with respect to his operations in Burmah which is indeed conformable to the suggestions thrown out towards the conclusion of his elaborate Minute, but which we did not approve of. I now send you his letter to General Godwin, showing the determination to which he had come after fully considering all that had been submitted to him by the military and naval commanders at Rangoon—whether it was in conformity with their opinions he does not state. . . .

'I also send you copies of his two latest private letters to me. In the last of these he does not enter into any explanation of his recent resolves.

' The receipt of our instructions, which (in conformity with his own especial and repeated request) are most explicit, on the question of policy upon which he applied for directions, and which he seems now to have decided for himself, will, I hope, have produced the effect of inducing him to alter his arrangements, if not his opinions, and to take vigorous steps for finishing the war which we have been forced to commence. There can be no satisfactory or final conclusion of the warfare in Burmah except by a treaty, or by the subjugation of the enemy. The Duke's memorandum leaves no doubt upon that point. It is fortunate that Dalhousie has made full preparations for carrying the war beyond the point at which he appeared disposed to stop when he wrote to Godwin. It is also satisfactory to know that the enemy is miserably unprepared to meet the pressure of a vigorous prosecution of the war. . . . They can look to no quarter for aid. On the side of Munipore they are threatened with hostility ; on the other side the Shans give them no countenance. . . . Their chief reliance is upon some tradition of a lucky spot near Ava!—a poor obstacle to oppose to the most efficient force and the best provided with all the requirements of war that has, perhaps, ever been put into the field by us in India.

'I am not sure that you have got a complete copy of these instructions [dated September 6]. I therefore send one. You will see that I incorporated *in toto* your paragraph. . . . I sent a copy to the Chancellor. I enclose his note of approval in returning it. The dispersion of our Cabinet rendered it impracticable for me to send it round to all its members. There was moreover no time for it. I now enclose for your consideration a sketch for a secret despatch, which I should be glad to send out by the mail which departs on Friday next.'

The Lord Chancellor's note above alluded to was as follows :—

'My dear Herries,—Although it is unimportant whether I approve or disapprove, yet I cannot withhold my approbation. It would be manifestly impolitic to stop short in the career of conquest at the point which you desire to retain, and then remain on the defensive. I admire the tone and composition of the paper itself. Yours, &c.,

'ST. LEONARDS.'

From General Godwin's 'Memorandum on the strength of the army I think requisite, to enable me to march into the heart of Burmah, and to subjugate it,' and from Sir John Littler's Minute of November 4 (both of which documents are published in the papers presented to Parliament), it is evident that the military authorities perceived no extraordinary difficulty in the execution of the instructions, which the Governor-General was determined not to carry out, for an advance upon Ava in the event of refusal or delay on the part of the King to treat for peace on the basis of the cession of Pegu.

Mr. Herries to the Earl of Derby.

October 22.—'I have prepared a secret despatch [October 23 : published in Burmah Papers] to Lord Dalhousie, in which I have noticed his change of plans, and the probability that he has been induced by the earlier advance of the force under General Godwin to anticipate in his Minute of August 10 our final instructions, which he justly observes he could not receive in time for a September movement of the troops. I have so worded it as to show that we adhere to those instructions, and to intimate our belief that they will square very well with the onward movement which he proposes to make, although our view of the ulterior policy to be pursued differs from that which is laid down in his Minute.'

To the Marquis of Dalhousie.

October 25.—'I heartily congratulate you on the state of your army. . . . Your letter of the 7.th is replete with good tidings, except in one particular, in which I sincerely sympathise with you. Your labour is enormous, and I fear that in such a climate it may prove distressing to you. But are you not in some measure the cause of this pressure ? If I mistake not, your indefatigable industry has heaped upon your single shoulders much of a weight distributed by your predecessors among others, and thus you are accumulating a burden which may hereafter break the back of one of your successors. . . .

'If you have had time to look at our newspapers you will have seen that my estimation of the public

feeling here on the subject of your war was quite correct. · The cry now is for conquest and annexation.
The mercantile and manufacturing interests begin to anticipate the advantages which they may derive from our
possession of the seaboard of Burmah. . . . Let us also
bear in mind that some other Power might have picked
a quarrel there, and have become a thorn in our side, if
we had not been compelled to establish ourselves in
Pegu. . . .'

November 8.—' Your last letter brings most cheerful
accounts of the health and conduct of the army in
Burmah. It would almost appear as if you had sent
them thither as to a kind of sanatorium. . . .

:   ' Your financial metamorphosis of an estimated deficiency into an actual surplus for the year 1850–51 is
so pleasing and so singular (in my long experience the
change has always been of a converse complexion), that
I can hardly receive it, even from you, without some
little apprehension, and mistrust of some possible draw-
back. However correct your statement no doubt must
be of the mere *cash* account, I am tempted to inquire
whether, as a *service account* the result will wear an
equally favourable aspect. Are there no postponements
of expected payments, and no accelerations of estimated
receipts . . . ? I need not recommend to your vigilant
mind an inquiry upon these points. I shall do what I
can here to obtain a clear view of the subject, before I
venture to crow *very loudly* in the House of Commons
upon it.[5]

[5] He seems to have felt that with regard to Indian estimates ' Confidence is a plant of slow growth in aged bosoms.' An expert in accounts, he

'We have had some startling occurrences in our exchange operations with India in this country. I readily yielded to the urgent request of the Chairs to lower the rate on which they offered bills when it was found that scarcely any could be got at 2*s.* the rupee. But I stickled for a reduction to 1*s.* 11½*d.* only. They however urged, and I yielded to them, the necessity of a further diminution, viz., to 1*s.* 11*d.* At that rate a torrent of bills was poured in, and we were compelled to put up the exchange again to 1*s.* 11½*d.*, and afterwards to 2*s.* The abundance of capital is wonderful, and the caprices of speculation are unfathomable. I rely in these matters greatly on the knowledge and experience of the Chairs, who sit in the very heart of the money market. . . .

'. . . In this case, however, they have all been at fault. . . .'

To Lord Raglan.

November 21.—'I return the extracts from General Godwin's letters. . . .

'I hope the day will soon arrive when I and others will be in a condition to do justice to General Godwin and the army in Parliament. . . . Nothing can have been better than the conduct of all the authorities, civil and military. in the preparation, dispatch, and management of the expedition to and at Rangoon. . . . The operations of the troops at the time when Godwin's

looked at them with caution, lest an apparent surplus should turn out to be a real deficit. Possibly he may have been convinced from long experience that the results of the incomings and outgoings of Indian finance belonged to the category of 'those things that no fellow can find out.'

letters were written, were wholly at the discretion of
Lord Dalhousie. He himself disclaimed the necessity
of any instructions from home in that respect : but no
mail went out without conveying to him cordial approval and encouragement. On the other hand, he *did*
apply for distinct instructions and directions respecting
the policy to be ultimately adopted in the prosecution
and termination of the war. They went out to him
full, distinct, and explicit, in the earliest possible reply
to his dispatch. We consulted the great Duke before
I framed them (with Lord Derby), and sent them to
the Queen for sanction. They not only give Dalhousie
full scope to do all that he contemplated, but they enjoin
him to do more. He is therefore anything but fettered
by the Government at home. But Dalhousie could not
receive these instructions before the middle of October.
His application for them was only dispatched from
India on the 3rd of July. . . .'

To the Marquis of Dalhousie.

December 23.—' As this is the last occasion of my
writing to you as President of the Board of Control, I
have much pleasure in availing myself of the opportunity to assure you of the gratification which your
confidential communications have afforded me. I shall
always reflect with much satisfaction on the harmony
and good understanding which have prevailed in our
correspondence, and upon the light which it has thrown
upon the zeal, activity, and judgment which have been
constantly displayed in the discharge of your most
arduous duties in the government of India ; to which I

shall at all times be ready to bear my humble testimony whether in or out of Parliament. I have written a short secret letter[6] to you this mail, with which I trust you will be satisfied. I have avoided touching upon any controversial topics, and have confined myself to the notice of your proposed *modus operandi*, which will I hope, practically accomplish the end of our instructions.

' The wretched and barbarous Court of Ava appears to be in such a state of impotency that even a moderate degree of pressure ought to be sufficient to reduce it to submission, while you have prepared the means of subjecting it to much more than a moderate degree of coercion.

.   .   .   .   .   .

' But I feel that I am trespassing upon the province of my successor. Whoever he may be [Sir Charles Wood succeeded him ; but the new Cabinet was not formed at the date of this letter], he cannot be half so content to assume the office as I am to relinquish it. I harnessed myself again in the public service with great reluctance, and only in compliance with the wishes and entreaties of my political friends, who had strong claims upon my humble services. I can now sing my *nunc dimittis* with hearty satisfaction, and enjoy my retirement with a satisfied conscience.'

Nothing could have been more handsome than the manner in which Lord Dalhousie appears to have been treated by the Government, to which he was well known to be strongly opposed in political opinions. 'Dalhousie,' Mr. Herries wrote in one of his letters to Lord

---

[6] December 23. *Burmah Papers*, p. 96.

Derby, ' is no friend to our party.'   But, for the public interest, the Prime Minister urged the Governor-General to remain at his post, and the President of the Board of Control cordially supported the request.   Both the private correspondence of Mr. Herries and the published despatches written by him in the name of the Secret Committee, testify the earnest desire of the Government to afford to Lord Dalhousie the utmost encouragement. On the other hand, it can hardly be affirmed that he displayed an equal readiness to act in conformity with their views.   And the day may perhaps come, when native insolence, or foreign intrigue, in Burmah, will make Englishmen regret that the bold and decisive policy inculcated by the Derby Cabinet twenty-eight years ago, was not then carried into effect.[7]

A general belief erroneously prevailed that the Indian patronage of the President of the Board of Control was almost boundless.   Mr. Herries, sharing probably the fate of his predecessors and successors, before the introduction of the system of competition, was speedily overwhelmed with applications, far beyond his means of complying with them—for cadetships, admissions to

[7] Letters written by Mr. Herries in 1853 contain the following passages : ' In my last short despatch of December 1852, in reply to Dalhousie's long, feeble, and inconclusive objections to those instructions (which he nevertheless professed it to be his duty to obey), I approved of the measures which he proposed to take, because I observed that they would, if carried out, fulfil the object of those instructions. . . . If our orders had been frankly and promptly carried into effect, Ava would have been in our possession before this time, and the war and its expenses at an end. . . . He (Dalhousie) is a difficult man to manage. . . . We should have been in Ava long before this time if our instructions had been obeyed. In the present state of China that might have been of the greatest consequence ; for we should have been in immediate and close river communication with its western provinces. . . .'

Addiscombe or Haileybury, and the like—a certain number of which, in accordance with usage, were placed at his disposal not long before he quitted office. Three cases in which he had the gratification of rendering services to individuals on public grounds, are of sufficient interest to deserve mention. The first was an appointment asked for by the Duke of Wellington in one of his latest letters, which could not easily be deciphered. The Duke made an earnest request on behalf of a young friend, observing at the same time with some bitterness, that similar applications on his part had been constantly neglected in other quarters.

The answer was as follows :—

' September 2, 1852.

' My dear Lord Duke,—It will gratify me exceedingly to put at your disposal the first nomination to an appointment at Haileybury which will be at mine. No patronage has yet been assigned to me. It is in November that the nominations to writerships are distributed. The holder of my office is generally put upon the same footing as the Chairman of the Directors. It will give me very sincere pleasure to do justice to your wishes. . . .'

In the second instance alluded to, Mr. Herries was able at the last moment, but not apparently without some difficulty, to secure a nomination of some kind for a grandson of Lord Nelson, recommended to his care by an exalted and patriotic personage.

To art also due honour was rendered. After the greatest of British warriors on sea and on land, a famous British tragedian must be named.

To W. C. Macready, Esq.

' My dear Sir,—I am very glad to find that my offer
of an Addiscombe Cadetship for your son is acceptable
to you. I believe it is the best mode of entering into
the East India military service. It therefore affords
me much satisfaction that I am enabled by this appointment not merely to meet the wishes of a friend, but at
the same time to testify my sense of the just claim to
public patronage of a gentleman who has so largely
contributed, as you have, to the gratification and improvement of the public. Believe me, &c.,

' J. C. HERRIES.'

In another instance, one of the much coveted appointments to what were called direct cavalry cadetships was given, in preference to many well recommended
applicants, to the son of a distinguished officer now
living, solely on account of the military services of his
father—then only a Captain, but well known to the
public—with whom the President of the Board of
Control was not personally acquainted.

Among the miscellaneous correspondence of this
time there are some letters to and concerning Mr.
Herries's much maligned old friend Croker, on literary
and historical matters. One of them, in answer to
queries about some transactions alluded to as ' Charles
Fox's dealing with Irish Pells,' says :—' I can recollect
nothing (if indeed I ever knew anything) of the matter
to which you call my attention. I put the inquiry into
hands which I thought might gather some information

for me, but I have just now received the answer—*nil*. .
It occurs to me while I am writing that Monteagle
might ferret out some information. . . .

'I admire your fortitude and perseverance, and most
heartily wish that they were not put to so severe a
test.'

To Lord Monteagle, with whom, in or out of office,
he had for many years maintained excellent relations,
Mr. Herries wrote on this subject :—'I send you a letter
from Croker asking for information which I cannot get
for him. It occurs to me that you might perhaps be
able to refer me to some source of knowledge on the
subject which would be useful to him. His fortitude
and energy in his wretched condition are admirable.'
There is something curious in this application from a
veteran Tory to an ex-Whig Minister and a former
contributor to the 'Edinburgh Review,' for materials
to be used by a 'Quarterly' Reviewer, a Tory of
Tories, respecting—perhaps against—Fox.

Another letter throws considerable doubt on an
historical point supposed to be certain, and completely
disproves assertions connected with it too confidently
made by some writers.

'November 9, 1852.

'My dear Croker,—My recollections, imperfect as
they are, all tend to negative the stories which I have
heard and read about the compromise between Lord
Liverpool and George IV. for the disposal of the library
of George III. I believe them to be without foundation.

'There may have been some private discussion
between the King and his Minister on the subject of

these books, which some officious and half-informed
intriguer may have converted into the substantial
allegations which have obtained a sort of credit (partly,
if I mistake not, through the 'Quarterly Review') in
the public mind. But I doubt the existence even of
such a slight foundation as that. I never heard Lord
Liverpool mention it, although at that period he was
very unreserved in his morning conversations with
myself and Arbuthnot touching his communications
with the King.

' The application of money from the French
Indemnity Fund towards the works going on at
Buckingham House had no connection whatever with
the library. I myself had the conduct of that affair,
and conducted the defence of it in the House of Commons when it was attacked by M. A. Taylor.

' I believe Nash had nothing to do with the affair of
the books. . . . Truly yours,
                                             ' J. C. H.

' I hope your pulse and hearing continue in their
amended state.'

It is probably this letter which is alluded to in a
foot-note to an article on the British Museum in the
'Quarterly Review' for December 1852, saying :—'We
have received a strong remonstrance, accompanied with,
as it seems to us, very strong evidence, against the
whole and every part of the anecdote related in our
number for December 1850, relative to the motives and
manner of the transfer by George IV. of his father's
library to the museum. We took the anecdote from
the original and full edition of the Handbook for Spain ;

but think Mr. Ford must have been misled by some of the loose talkers among his Majesty's Whig ex-friends.'[8]

A letter of an earlier date relates to the politics of the day.

'My dear Croker,—I have just had time to cast my eye over your excellent article. But I have done better for you. I have induced Derby to do the same, and I send you the note I have just received from him.

'Your view is surely the correct one. What we are now threatened with is a coalition of which ultra-democracy is a powerful ingredient, and of which it promises to become the predominating element. . . . Yours, &c.,

'J. C. H.'

[8] The story alluded to here, and which has since been repeated, was to the effect that George IV. having entered into negotiations for the sale of his father's library to the Emperor of Russia, was deterred by the strong remonstrances of his ministers from carrying them into effect; and that although he made a merit of the presentation of the Royal collection of books to the British Museum, he stipulated for a sum, to be paid to him out of the money received as indemnity from France, equivalent to the amount which he would have obtained by the projected sale. As to the alleged application of the French indemnity funds, the evidence of Mr. Herries, who was perhaps better acquainted than any other person with everything relating to the receipt, transfer, and disposal of every penny of them, is absolutely conclusive. It proves that the assertion, in whatever quarter it may have originated, was nothing but a simple lie, invented no doubt for party purposes. We may add, although corroboration is superfluous, that we have inspected several ponderous bundles of papers concerning the French indemnity, without the discovery of the least trace of any allusion to the supposed bargain with the King. On the other point, that of the representations said to have been necessary on the part of the King's ministers, Mr. Herries's negative testimony does not of course exclude their possibility; but it seems in the highest degree improbable that both he, who was in confidential communication both with the Prime Minister and with Sir William Knighton, the King's Private Secretary, and his predecessor as Secretary of the Treasury, Mr. Arbuthnot, should have remained in total ignorance of such a transaction if it had really occurred.

One of the last acts of the first Derby Cabinet was the unavoidable recognition of that Second Empire declared to be synonymous with peace, but which brought a sword. The fact is merely alluded to here because it affords an opportunity of stating that the person whose actions and opinions we are endeavouring faithfully to record, although he accepted this political necessity, looked upon the great December crime with all the abhorrence which it could not fail to arouse in the mind of every man to whom law, justice, truth, honour, humanity, and freedom were not vain words void of sense. He would not have been induced by any consideration to cover with fulsome adulation the successful adventurer at whose feet this nation soon precipitated itself in a torrent of sycophancy.[9]

After the resignation of the ministry and the formation of the coalition Government presided over by Lord Aberdeen, Mr. Herries ceased to feel much inclination for party contentions, and acted independently during the last year of his parliamentary life. In the debates on the India Government Bill, some parts of which he opposed, he joined with the Ministers in resisting Lord Stanley's motion for suspension. He agreed with his successor in office, Sir Charles Wood, as to the principle of the continuance of the political functions of the East India Company, although he was well aware of defects requiring remedy.

[9] Several letters written at a subsequent period manifest on the part of Mr. Herries towards Napoleon III., whom he always designates by the initials L. N. B., the greatest distrust. He was not the only person who thought that the nephew had all the selfishness and all the perfidy, without a spark of the genius, of the uncle.

The system of double government has been destroyed, and is perhaps generally condemned ; but it is open to doubt whether the new Imperial rule is in all respects superior to it in efficiency. Experts in Indian matters may be found who declare that the former method ensured a more thorough sifting of important questions, and a more complete despatch of business, than the present machinery. They also say that the Council of the Secretary of State for India is no more a reality than the Secret Committee was, in whose name the President of the Board of Control addressed his instructions to the Governor-General. Persons who are not experts may be excused if they are unable to discern in recent occurrences any clear proof that all is for the best under the best of all possible Indian Governments, and if they observe that in the later history of the old Charter no such administrative monstrosity can be perceived as the financial mystification which crowned the edifice of Lord Lytton's Viceroyalty.

Warned by failing health that he could no longer sustain the fatigue of constant attendance to the duties of the House of Commons, at the end of the session of 1853 Mr. Herries resigned his seat, and finally closed his public career. On doing so he addressed this letter to the Speaker, Mr. Shaw Lefevre (Lord Eversley) :—

' My dear Mr. Speaker,—I cannot take my leave of Parliament, and subside, as I do from mere weariness and exhaustion, into private life, without a farewell word to yourself, and an expression of my personal thanks for the courtesy, kindness, and assistance which I so often experienced from you, and especially at the time when I took a more active part in the business of the House, when that assistance was invaluable.' . . .

Among many friendly letters which were addressed to him on this occasion, the following was not the least remarkable, coming, as it did, from a former enemy :—

'Brougham: August 29, 1853.

'Dear Mr. Herries,—I saw with regret your retirement from Parliament, but you are the best judge how far it was fitting.

'I cannot help mentioning to yourself what I have often stated to others—because it may be satisfactory to you—I mean the very strong opinion once and again expressed to me by my friend, A. Baring, afterwards Ashburton. He said you were, of all the men he had ever seen in the financial department—and I think he added transacted business with—by far the most competent. He was by no means apt to be easily pleased with the extent and accuracy of any one's knowledge. Believe me sincerely yours,

'H. BROUGHAM.'

The opinion repeatedly expressed by so well qualified a judge as the first Lord Ashburton, and, apparently, endorsed by Lord Brougham, may to many persons seem more important than the contrary opinion of Mr. Spencer Walpole. It agrees in a striking manner with George the Fourth's 'estimate of fitness' which provokes a sneer from that writer at the King and the Minister. Alexander Baring's observation of 'the financial department' embraced a long period, and the administration of many Chancellors of the Exchequer, for he was born in 1774, and sat in the House of Commons from 1812 to 1835, when he was raised to the Peerage.

His view coincided also with that manifested more than once to a permanent public servant of high rank (on whose authority we state the fact) by (then) Lord John Russell, who declared that, as he believed, Mr. Herries knew more of the finances of this country than any other man in England.

To a kind letter from his old friend, Mr. Goulburn, Mr. Herries replied: 'I am much obliged to you for your letter. It brought pleasantly to my mind the recollection of old times, when we commenced together our political career under good old Tory auspices, and [something illegible] real, not radical, liberality.

'I was sorry to hear from our common friends that you had been so unwell in the Spring, and, like myself, much absent from Parliament on that account.

'I retired when I found that it was seriously detrimental to my health to attempt to give regular attendance in the House of Commons. I do not say what I might have done to struggle against the difficulty, if there had been any personal or public inducement to stimulate the exertion or the sacrifice. In the absence of any such motive I have subsided quietly into private life, with a calm conscience and a hearty disposition to enjoy it.

'I heartily wish you the same peaceful quietus when it shall be your turn to follow my example.'

Mr. Croker wrote to him thus on August 15 : 'Thanks for your letters (the paper is not yet come).

My object is to examine what colonies can be worth, over which we have no control.'   [This refers to a former letter asking for information ' as to the military and naval expenses of our colonies.'] . . .

' I had heard some days ago of your intended retirement from Parliament and public life. I am not, as Juvenal was, " digressu veteris *confusus* amici." . . . It is perhaps, on the whole, better that you should eclipse yourself. . . . I hope it may succeed as well with you as it did with me. I have had twenty years of quiet, and I may add happiness, and, till the last two years, of health, since I ceased to be M.P., which may now be interpreted member of *Pandemonium* ; in my day it was only *Purgatory*.

' I should like very much to know what are your speculations on *parties*. I begin to be interested *for* Aberdeen, for I see not who is to succeed him. Graham seems to me to stand the most forward for the succession, but what between his boldness of language and timidity in action, I should be afraid, for him and for us, of some great catastrophe ; but he is, I think, the cleverest administrator in the Cabinet. . . .'

Though he had done with party politics, Mr. Herries lost none of his interest in national concerns. He anxiously watched, but without any confidence in the result, the efforts of the Government to control Russian arrogance by pacific diplomacy, directed by Lord Clarendon, an old friend, for whom, though politically opposed, he never ceased to entertain the most sincere regard. He lamented the feebleness of Lord Aberdeen, which allowed the country without preparation to 'drift' into a war the Minister neither dared to make ready for, nor knew how to avert.   If he applauded the tardy resolution of the Cabinet to employ the only means by which Russian aggression ever has been checked—force—he deplored the want of forethought which exposed our arms to the risk of humiliation ; and, remembering as he did, the stern solemnity of the hour of Nelson's last departure,[1] he was saddened by the vulgar exhibition of buffoonery, swagger, and bombastic braggadocio, which made ' the judicious grieve' on the sailing of the worst manned fleet that within human memory had left a British port to encounter an enemy.   But manners and language were not more different than times and men.   If the careless levity which marked the despatch of the Baltic expedition was unlike the earnest exertion, the terrible determination, of the eve of Trafalgar ; if the sorry fustian of the Reform Club banquet, and the vainglorious vapouring of the Copenhagen address, were lamentably out of keeping with the simple grandeur of the famous signal of October 21 ; it was equally true that Napier was not Nelson, any more than Aberdeen was Pitt, or Nicholas Napoleon.

Mr. Herries died suddenly on April 24, 1855.

The following notice of this event is to be found in a newspaper, 'The Examiner,' representing opinions the very antipodes of those of the deceased.

---

[1] Mr. Herries was probably on duty at Nelson's funeral, as a Lieutenant of the Light Horse Volunteers, which corps held on that occasion the highly honourable post of the front of the Admiralty, where the coffin was deposited on January 8, 1806, and whence the procession started on the following morning.

' The journals of the week contain the announce-
ment of the death of the Right Hon. J. C. Herries at
the age of seventy-seven.   He was one of the few sur-
vivors of that race of public men whose services may
be dated from the beginning of the century ; he
was a sincere and upright politician ; and his career,
spent in the discharge of many important and varied
duties, was .honourable and useful.   Those who,
like ourselves, were opposed to him and his political
views, could not fail to esteem in him the rare quality
of consistency ; and to his own party the withdrawal
of his wise and moderate counsels must be a severe loss.
He was respected by all who knew how to respect an
uncompromising integrity, and his strong sagacity made
him always invaluable as an adviser.   Mr. Herries
entered Parliament in middle life,[2] and had not the gifts
of an orator.   He was neither a frequent nor a brilliant
speaker : and when his speeches made an impression on
the House, it was owing to the matter and not to the
manner of them.   It was therefore to the force of his
intellect, to his clear judgment, and to his honourable
character, that his position as a public man was due ;
but those who had the privilege of knowing him in
private life, knew in him all the fine qualities of the
understanding joined to those of the heart, with a
benevolence which never ceased to exercise itself upon
all around him.   Among his intellectual qualities a
discerning and liberal taste in literature and art was
conspicuous ; and he was an accomplished scholar both
in the dead and living languages of Europe. . . .'

[2] At the age of forty-five—considerably past the ' *mezzo del cammin.*'

These remarks appeared in the radical 'Examiner.' The spirit of candour they breathe towards a political adversary—very different from the uncandid tone of systematic detraction perceptible in another quarter— is highly honourable to the editor of the paper at that time, Mr. John Forster, whose advanced Liberal sentiments are well known.

There is reason to believe that Mr. Herries was at some period more justly appreciated by members—and those not the least important—of the party to which he was opposed, than by some of the party to which he belonged.   And yet he served his party well and constantly in 'either fortune'—in adversity as in prosperity —in the broken line of a discomfited minority, as well as on the Treasury bench supported by a compact majority.   He never sailed under false colours, or was afraid to show his own.   He had no taste for a patent reversible flag suitable for all uses ; nor did he try to wash down his 'true blue' into a neutral tint.   But although he steadfastly adhered to his principles—the result of reflection, not the product of emotion—he did not push them to extreme and dangerous consequences. At no time 'passion's slave,' he eschewed violent courses, and deprecated rash resolutions.   What he desired was the maintenance of lawful authority, good government, for the benefit of all classes, according to law, subject to the constitutional control of Parliament —but of Parliament alone—and unswayed by the capricious clamour of ignorant multitudes guided by ambitious men for their own ends.   But while he detested political agitation, and objected to unnecessary changes made merely for love of novelty and excitement, he was always friendly to salutary remedies of real defects, and ready to promote well-considered measures, whether legislative or administrative, of practical improvement.[3] Having no superstitious veneration for antiquity, he would gladly have concurred in the removal of many of its relics which he did not admire. In particular he would have hailed with satisfaction law reforms much larger than any attempted in his time, or likely to be effected in the present generation ; for he was not convinced of the superlative wisdom of our system of jurisprudence, civil or criminal. He was, what he professed to be, a moderate, rational, governmental—not transcendental—Tory. The toryism to which he addicted himself was that of the school of Pitt, whom he considered as incomparably the greatest of English statesmen—not that of the school of Bolingbroke, whom he did not look upon as a model for imitation. Had he lived in the early years of the eighteenth century, he would probably have been called a Whig—as an adherent of the Revolution Settlement.[4] He had no fancy for anachronous revivals. Revived Stuartism was repugnant to his reason. Revived Laudism excited his scorn. In no sense of the word a

---

[3] In a letter from him, dated August 25, 1853, the following words occur:—'. . . My steadfast Toryism, and opposition to organic changes in the British Constitution . . . while I promoted all the measures for the extension and liberation of commerce introduced by Huskisson and Liverpool and Canning—those truly liberal improvers and anti-Radical reformers. . . .'

[4] Like his forefathers. According to family tradition his grandfather was injured by the Jacobites in 'the '45' on account of his 'Hanoverian' proclivities.

High Churchman, he viewed with strong dislike the uprising of Sacerdotalism described as the 'Oxford movement,' and condemned the prelatical pusillanimity, or connivance, which favoured the Romeward course. In matters of Ecclesiastical polity he was, in truth, a sound Erastian. The Church, connected with the State, upheld by the State, but subordinate to the State, and controlled by the State, was valued by him as a preservative institution very beneficial in its action, if judiciously directed. But when he spoke of the Church, he meant the *Protestant Church of England by law established*—a Church regulated by, and subject to, the law of the land. He did not mean an anti-Protestant Church, beyond the law, above the law, hostile to the law, claiming by virtue of a supernatural authority attributed to itself by itself, a right of independent action as '*libera Chiesa*' in, no longer, '*libero Stato*,' over which, and over a prostrate laity, a legion of parochial popelings should reign supreme.

He thought that the bases of the foreign policy of the Crown should be the scrupulous fulfilment of all its own engagements, with an inflexible resolution to require the observation of all engagements towards itself; the preservation of a general equilibrium as the only security for peace, and for the independence of all nations; and the vindication, in all parts of the world, at all times, at all hazards, of British honour and interests, which he would never have been prepared to sacrifice to all ' the aspirations ' of all ' the nationalities ' and all ' the races.' An ethnological and philological foreign policy, regardless of history, geography, strategy, public faith, or state interest, and necessarily involving, if carried to its legitimate consequences, the dismemberment of almost every State in Europe, beginning with the United Kingdom itself, seemed to him fit only for discussion in an assembly of lunatics. Not being able to admit that Welshmen ought to be absolved from their allegiance to the English Crown because Sussex farmers, as a general rule, could not comprehend the mysteries of Eisteddfod, he did not understand why it should be deemed iniquitous on the part of a foreign sovereign to retain under his sceptre persons speaking divers languages, and classified by learned professors under different ethnographical denominations.

Such were, as we believe, in general terms, his political opinions, as gathered from private conversation more than from his public utterances, which, indeed, were not very frequent. Coming into Parliament too late in life to acquire skill in the art of political speaking, he did not add to the too large number of those who unsuccessfully attempt oratorical display. He never quite overcame the diffidence which commonly restrains men of mature years who have not practised debating when young. It very often happened, besides, that he was prevented from taking part in the discussion of important questions by an affection, destroying his power of making himself heard, to which he was continually liable. Nevertheless, when he addressed the House he generally did so with effect, from knowledge of the subject of which he had to treat. One remark may be added. Some writer once described him satirically as 'the man of figures,' and he was skilled in their use.

But in his speeches he did not abuse them. It is observable that he was comparatively sparing of statistics in what may be called the statistico-commercial period of our parliamentary history, the student of which is startled by the appearance of their formidable masses filling up the columns of Hansard with arithmetical eloquence. Every sentence a sum, every parenthesis a percentage, the reports of five speeches out of six must be reckoned, rather than read, through. From simple addition there is but a step to compound multiplication of a painful kind ; and he is fortunate who does not, in the course of two pages, find himself exposed to double rule of three in its most virulent aspect.

In the transaction of public business, it is not to be denied that in the judgment of his contemporaries of different parties Mr. Herries showed ability of a very high order ; and of his constant efforts to secure or increase the efficiency of the public service sufficient proof has been furnished in the preceding pages.

We have completed the unwelcome task forced upon us by attacks which it was our sacred duty to repel. In vindicating the memory which has been unjustly assailed by others we cannot pretend to have been free from bias, but we are not conscious of having been guilty of exaggeration or unfairness. Nothing has been intentionally overcoloured, nothing thrown into the shade. There has been neither invention nor concealment in our narrative. For all that we have advanced we have shown what we believe to be solid grounds. If the necessities of our defence, and a firm determination to tell the truth, the whole truth, nothing but the truth, have compelled us sometimes to disturb popular notions, and to exhibit facts detrimental to established reputations, we have done so with regret, but without fear. Refutation, not apology, was the object we had in view. It was not our purpose with bated breath to deprecate hostility and sue for condonation, but to overthrow calumny, and encounter malice with the genuine records of a long and spotless life.

We lay them before the public, whose impartial judgment we confidently await upon the question, whether we have, or have not, succeeded in proving that the injurious assertions we undertook to meet were wholly false, and that, far from deserving the aspersions of his slanderers, John Charles Herries was justly entitled to the fame of a most faithful, zealous, and able servant of the Crown and the Nation.

' E questo fia suggel, ch' ogni uomo sganni.'

INDEX.

THE END.

LONDON: PRINTED BY
SPOTTISWOODE AND CO., NEW-STREET SQUARE
AND PARLIAMENT STREET

50, ALBEMARLE STREET, LONDON.
November, 1880.

MR. MURRAY'S
GENERAL LIST OF WORKS.

ALBERT MEMORIAL. A Descriptive and Illustrated Account of the National Monument erected to the PRINCE CONSORT at Kensington. Illustrated by Engravings of its Architecture, Decorations, Sculptured Groups, Statues, Mosaics, Metalwork &c. With Descriptive Text. By DOYNE C. BELL. With 24 Plates. Folio. 12*l*. 12*s*.

———————— HANDBOOK TO. Post 8vo. 1*s*.; or Illustrated Edition, 2*s*. 6*d*.

———————— (PRINCE) SPEECHES AND ADDRESSES. Fcap. 8vo. 1*s*.

ALBERT DÜRER; his Life, with a History of his Art. By DR. THAUSING, Keeper of Archduke Albert's Art Collection at Vienna. Translated from the German. With Portrait and Illustrations. 2 vols. Medium 8vo. [*In the Press*.

ABBOTT (REV. J.). Memoirs of a Church of England Missionary in the North American Colonies. Post 8vo. 2*s*.

ABERCROMBIE (JOHN). Enquiries concerning the Intellectual Powers and the Investigation of Truth. Fcap. 8vo. 3*s*. 6*d*.

ACLAND (REV. CHARLES). Popular Account of the Manners and Customs of India. Post 8vo. 2*s*.

ÆSOP'S FABLES. A New Version. With Historical Preface. By REV. THOMAS JAMES. With 100 Woodcuts, by TENNIEL and WOLF. Post 8vo. 2*s*. 6*d*.

AGRICULTURAL (ROYAL) JOURNAL. (*Published half-yearly.*)

AIDS TO FAITH: a Series of Essays. Miracles; Evidences of Christianity; Prophecy and Mosaic Record of Creation; Ideology and Subscription; The Pentateuch; Inspiration; Death of Christ; Scripture and Its Interpretation. By various Authors. 8vo. 9*s*.

AMBER-WITCH (THE). A most interesting Trial for Witchcraft. Translated by LADY DUFF GORDON. Post 8vo. 2*s*.

APOCRYPHA: With a Commentary Explanatory and Critical, by various Writers. Edited by REV. PROFESSOR WACE. 2 Vols. Medium 8vo. [*In the Press*.

ARISTOTLE. See GROTE, HATCH.

ARMY LIST (THE). *Published Monthly by Authority.*

———————— (THE NEW OFFICIAL). *Published Quarterly.* Royal 8vo. 15*s*.

ARTHUR'S (LITTLE) History of England. By LADY CALLCOTT. *New Edition, continued to* 1872. With 36 Woodcuts. Fcap. 8vo. 1*s*. 6*d*.

ATKINSON (DR. R.) Vie de Seint Auban. A Poem in Norman-French. Ascribed to MATTHEW PARIS. With Concordance, Glossary and Notes. Small 4to. 10*s*. 6*d*.

AUSTIN (JOHN). LECTURES ON GENERAL JURISPRUDENCE; or, the Philosophy of Positive Law. Edited by ROBERT CAMPBELL. 2 Vols. 8vo. 32*s*.

———————— STUDENT'S EDITION, compiled from the above work, by ROBERT CAMPBELL. Post 8vo. 12*s*.

———————— Analysis of. By GORDON CAMPBELL. Post 8vo. 6*s*.

ADMIRALTY PUBLICATIONS; issued by direction of the Lords
Commissioners of the Admiralty:—
A MANUAL OF SCIENTIFIC ENQUIRY, for the Use of Travellers.
Fourth Edition. Edited by ROBERT MAIN, M.A. Woodcuts. Post
8vo. 3s. 6d.
GREENWICH ASTRONOMICAL OBSERVATIONS, 1841 to 1847,
and 1847 to 1877. Royal 4to. 20s. each.
GREENWICH ASTRONOMICAL RESULTS, 1847 to 1877. 4to. 3s.
each.
MAGNETICAL AND METEOROLOGICAL OBSERVATIONS, 1844
to 1877. Royal 4to. 20s. each.
MAGNETICAL AND METEOROLOGICAL RESULTS, 1848 to 1877.
4to. 3s each.
APPENDICES TO OBSERVATIONS.
1837. Logarithms of Sines and Cosines in Time. 3s.
1842. Catalogue of 1439 Stars, from Observations made in 1836-
1841. 4s.
1845. Longitude of Valentia (Chronometrical). 3s.
1847. Description of Altazimuth. 3s.
Description of Photographic Apparatus. 2s.
1851. Maskelyne's Ledger of Stars. 3s.
1852. I. Description of the Transit Circle. 3s.
1853. Bessel's Refraction Tables. 3s.
1854. I. Description of the Reflex Zenith Tube. 3s.
II. Six Years' Catalogue of Stars, from Observations. 1848
to 1853. 4s.
1860. Reduction of Deep Thermometer Observations. 2s.
1862. II. Plan of Ground and Buildings of Royal Observatory,
Greenwich. 3s.
III. Longitude of Valentia (Galvanic). 2s.
1864. I. Moon's Semi-diameter, from Occultations. 2s.
II. Reductions of Planetary Observations. 1831 to 1835. 2s
1868. I. Corrections of Elements of Jupiter and Saturn. 2s.
II. Second Seven Years' Catalogue of 2760 Stars. 1861-7. 4s.
III Description of the Great Equatorial. 3s.
1871. Water Telescope. 3s.
1873. Regulations of the Royal Observatory. 2s.
1876. II. Nine Years' Catalogue of 2263 Stars. (1861-67.) 4s.
Cape of Good Hope Observations (Star Ledgers): 1856 to 1863. 2s.
————————————————— 1856. 5s.
——————————— Astronomical Results. 1857 to 1858. 5s.
Cape Catalogue of 1159 Stars, reduced to the Epoch 1860. 3s.
Cape of Good Hope Astronomical Results. 1859 to 1860. 5s.
—————————————————— 1871 to 1873. 5s.
————————————— —— 1874 to 1876. 5s. ch.
Report on Teneriffe Astronomical Experiment. 1856. 5s.
Paramatta Catalogue of 7385 Stars. 1822 to 1826. 4s.
REDUCTION OF THE OBSERVATIONS OF PLANETS. 1750
1830. Royal 4to. 20s. each.
——————————————— LUNAR OBSERVATIONS. 1750
to 1830. 2 Vols. Royal 4to. 20s. each.
——————————— 1831 to 1851. 4to. 10s. each.
—— ———————— GREENWICH METEOROLOGICAL OBSERVA-
TIONS. Chiefly 1847 to 1873. 5s.
ARCTIC PAPERS. 13s. 6d.
BERNOULLI'S SEXCENTENARY TABLE. 1779. 4to. 5s.
BESSEL'S AUXILIARY TABLES FOR HIS METHOD OF CLEAR-
ING LUNAR DISTANCES. 8vo. 2s.
ENCKE'S BERLINER JAHRBUCH, for 1830. *Berlin*, 1828. 8vo. 9s.
HANSEN'S TABLES DE LA LUNE. 4to. 20s.
HANNYNGTON'S HAVERSINES.
LAX'S TABLES FOR FINDING THE LATITUDE AND LONGI-
TUDE. 1821. 8vo. 10s.
LUNAR OBSERVATIONS at GREENWICH. 1783 to 1819. Compared
with the Tables, 1821. 4to. 7s. 6d.

Admiralty Publications—*continued.*

MACLEAR ON LACAILLE'S ARC OF MERIDIAN. 2 Vols. 20s. each.

MAYER'S DISTANCES of the MOON'S CENTRE from the PLANETS. 1822, 3s.; 1823, 4s. 6d. 1824 to 1835. 8vo. 4s. each.

———— TABULÆ MOTUUM SOLIS ET LUNÆ. 1770. 5s.

———— ASTRONOMICAL OBSERVATIONS MADE AT GÖTTINGEN, from 1756 to 1761. 1826. Folio. 7s. 6d.

NAUTICAL ALMANACS, from 1767 to 1883. 2s. 6d. each.

———— SELECTIONS FROM, up to 1812. 8vo. 5s. 1834-54. 5s.

———— SUPPLEMENTS, 1828 to 1833, 1837 and 1838. 2s. each.

———— TABLE requisite to be used with the N.A 1781. 8vo. 5s.

SABINE'S PENDULUM EXPERIMENTS to Determine the Figure of the Earth. 1825. 4to. 40s.

SHEPHERD'S TABLES for Correcting Lunar Distances. 1772. Royal 4to. 21s.

———— TABLES, GENERAL, of the MOON'S DISTANCE from the SUN, and 10 STARS. 1787. Folio. 5s. 6d.

TAYLOR'S SEXAGESIMAL TABLE. 1780. 4to. 15s.

———— TABLES OF LOGARITHMS. 4to. 60s.

TIARK'S ASTRONOMICAL OBSERVATIONS for the Longitude of Madeira. 1822. 4to. 5s.

———— CHRONOMETRICAL OBSERVATIONS for Differences of Longitude between Dover, Portsmouth, and Falmouth. 1823. 4to. 5s.

VENUS and JUPITER: Observations of, compared with the Tables *London*, 1822. 4to. 2s.

WALES AND BAYLY'S ASTRONOMICAL OBSERVATIONS. 1777. 4to. 21s.

———— REDUCTION OF ASTRONOMICAL OBSERVATIONS made in the Southern Hemisphere. 1764—1771. 1788. 4to. 10s. 6d.

BARBAULD (Mrs.). Hymns in Prose for Children. With 100 Illustrations. 16mo. 3s 6d.

BARCLAY (BISHOP). Selected Extracts from the Talmud, chiefly illustrating the Teaching of the Bible. With an Introduction. Illustrations. 8vo. 14s.

BARKLEY (H. C.). Five Years among the Bulgarians and Turks between the Danube and the Black Sea. Post 8vo. 10s. 6d.

———— Bulgaria Before the War; during a Seven Years' Experience of European Turkey and its Inhabitants. Post 8vo. 10s. 6d.

———— My Boyhood : a True Story. A Book for Schoolboys and others. With Illustrations. Post 8vo. 6s.

BARROW (John). Life, Exploits, and Voyages of Sir Francis Drake. Post 8vo. 2s.

BARRY (Canon). The Boyle Lectures, 1877-78. The Manifold Witness for Christ. Being an Attempt to Exhibit the Combined Force of various Evidences, Direct and Indirect, of Christianity. 8vo. 12s.

———— (Edw.), R.A. Lectures on Architecture, delivered before the Royal Academy. 8vo. [In Preparation.

BATES (H. W.) Records of a Naturalist on the Amazons during Eleven Years' Adventure and Travel. Illustrations. Post 8vo. 7s. 6d.

BAX (Capt.). Russian Tartary, Eastern Siberia, China, Japan, and Formosa. A Cruise in H.M.S. Dwarf. Illustrations. Cr. 8vo. 12s.

BELCHER (Lady). Account of the Mutineers of the 'Bounty,' and their Descendants; with their Settlements in Pitcairn and Norfolk Islands. Illustrations. Post 8vo. 12s.

BELL (Sir Chas.). Familiar Letters. Portrait. Post 8vo. 12s.

———— (Doyne C.). Notices of the Historic Persons buried in the Chapel of St. Peter ad Vincula, in the Tower of London, with an account of the discovery of the supposed remains of Queen Anne Boleyn. With Illustrations. Crown 8vo. 14s.

BERTRAM (Jas. G.). Harvest of the Sea: an Account of British Food Fishes, including Fisheries and Fisher Folk. Illustrations. Post 8vo. 9s.

BIBLE COMMENTARY. The Old Testament. Explanatory and Critical. With a Revision of the Translation. By Bishops and Clergy of the Anglican Church. Edited by F. C. Cook, M.A., Canon of Exeter. 6 Vols. Medium 8vo. 6l. 15s.

Vol. I. 30s. — Genesis. Exodus. Leviticus. Numbers. Deuteronomy.

Vols. II. and III. 36s. — Joshua, Judges, Ruth, Samuel, Kings, Chronicles, Ezra, Nehemiah, Esther.

Vol. IV. 24s. — Job. Psalms. Proverbs. Ecclesiastes. Song of Solomon.

Vol. V. 20s. — Isaiah. Jeremiah.

Vol. VI. 25s. — Ezekiel. Daniel. Minor Prophets.

———— The New Testament. 4 Vols. Medium 8vo.

Vol. I. 18s. — Introduction. St. Matthew. St. Mark. St. Luke.

Vol. II. 20s. — St. John. Acts.

Vol. III. — Romans, Corinthians, Galatians, Philippians, Ephesians, Colossians, Thessalonians, Philemon, Pastoral Epistles, Hebrews.

Vol. IV. — St. James, St. John, St. Peter, St. Jude, Revelation.

———— The Student's Edition. Abridged and Edited by John M. Fuller, M.A., Vicar of Bexley. (To be completed in 6 Volumes.) Vols. I. to III. Crown 8vo. 7s. 6d. each.

BIGG-WITHER (T. P.). Pioneering in South Brazil; Three Years of Forest and Prairie Life in the Province of Parana. Map and Illustrations. 2 vols. Crown 8vo. 24s.

BIRCH (Samuel). A History of Ancient Pottery and Porcelain: Egyptian, Assyrian, Greek, Roman, and Etruscan. With Coloured Plates and 200 Illustrations. Medium 8vo. 42s.

BIRD (Isabella). Hawaiian Archipelago; or Six Months among the Palm Groves, Coral Reefs, and Volcanoes of the Sandwich Islands. Illustrations. Crown 8vo. 7s. 6d.

———— Unbeaten Tracks in Japan: Travels of a Lady in the interior, including Visits to the Aborigines of Yezo and the Shrines of Nikko and Ise. With Map and Illustrations. 2 Vols. Crown 8vo. 24s.

———— A Lady's Life in the Rocky Mountains. Illustrations. Post 8vo. 10s. 6d.

BISSET (Sir John). Sport and War in South Africa from 1834 to 1867, with a Narrative of the Duke of Edinburgh's Visit. With Map and Illustrations. Crown 8vo. 14s.

BLUNT (Lady Anne). The Bedouins of the Euphrates Valley. With some account of the Arabs and their Horses. With Map and Illustrations. 2 Vols. Crown 8vo. 24s.

———— A Pilgrimage to Nejd, the Cradle of the Arab Race, and a Visit to the Court of the Arab Emir. With Illustrations from the Author's Drawings. 2 Vols. Post 8vo.

BLUNT (Rev. J. J.). Undesigned Coincidences in the Writings of
the Old and New Testaments, an Argument of their Veracity. Post 8vo. 6s.
———— History of the Christian Church in the First Three
Centuries. Post 8vo. 6s.
———— Parish Priest; His Duties, Acquirements, and Obliga-
tions. Post 8vo. 6s.
———— University Sermons. Post 8vo. 6s.
BOSWELL'S Life of Samuel Johnson, LL.D. Including the
Tour to the Hebrides. Edited by Mr. Croker. *Seventh Edition.*
Portraits. 1 vol. Medium 8vo. 12s.
BRACE (C. L.). Manual of Ethnology; or the Races of the Old
World. Post 8vo. 6s.
BREWER (Rev. J. S.). English Studies. New Sources of English
History. Contents. Green's History. The Royal Supremacy.
Hatfield House. The Stuarts. Shakespeare. How to Study English
History. Ancient London. 8vo.
BOOK OF COMMON PRAYER. Illustrated with Coloured
Borders, Initial Letters, and Woodcuts. 8vo. 18s.
BORROW (George). Bible in Spain; or the Journeys, Adventures,
and Imprisonments of an Englishman in an Attempt to circulate the
Scriptures in the Peninsula. Post 8vo. 5s.
———— Gypsies of Spain; their Manners, Customs, Re-
ligion, and Language. With Portrait. Post 8vo. 5s.
———— Lavengro; The Scholar—The Gypsy—and the Priest.
Post 8vo. 5s.
———— Romany Rye—a Sequel to "Lavengro." Post 8vo. 5s.
———— Wild Wales: its People, Language, and Scenery.
Post 8vo. 5s.
———— Romano Lavo-Lil; Word-Book of the Romany, or
English Gypsy Language; with Specimens of their Poetry, and an
account of certain Gypsyries. Post 8vo. 10s. 6d.
BRITISH ASSOCIATION REPORTS. 8vo.

York and Oxford, 1831-32, 13s. 6d.	Cheltenham, 1856, 18s.
Cambridge, 1833, 12s.	Dublin, 1857, 15s.
Edinburgh, 1834, 15s.	Leeds, 1858. 20s.
Dublin, 1835, 13s. 6d.	Aberdeen, 1859, 15s.
Bristol, 1836, 12s.	Oxford, 1860, 25s.
Liverpool, 1837, 16s. 6d.	Manchester, 1861, 15s.
Newcastle, 1838, 15s.	Cambridge, 1862, 20s.
Birmingham, 1839, 13s. 6d.	Newcastle, 1863, 25s.
Glasgow, 1840, 15s.	Bath, 1864, 18s.
Plymouth, 1841, 13s. 6d.	Birmingham, 1865. 25s.
Manchester, 1842, 10s. 6d.	Nottingham. 1866, 24s.
Cork, 1843. 12s.	Dundee, 1867. 26s.
York, 1844, 20s.	Norwich, 1868, 25s.
Cambridge, 1845. 12s.	Exeter, 1869. 22s.
Southampton, 1846, 15s.	Liverpool, 1870, 18s.
Oxford, 1847, 18s.	Edinburgh, 1871, 16s.
Swansea, 1848, 9s.	Brighton, 1872. 24s.
Birmingham, 1849, 10s.	Bradford, 1873, 25s.
Edinburgh, 1850, 15s.	Belfast, 1874, 25s.
Ipswich, 1851, 16s. 6d.	Bristol, 1875, 25s.
Belfast, 1852, 15s.	Glasgow, 1876. 25s.
Hull, 1853, 10s. 6d.	Plymouth, 1877, 24s.
Liverpool, 1854, 18s.	Dublin. 1878. 24s.
Glasgow, 1855, 15s.	Sheffield. 1879, 24s.

BRUGSCH (Professor). A History of Egypt, under the
Pharaohs. Derived entirely from Monuments, with a Memoir on the
Exodus of the Israelites. Translated by Philip Smith, B.A., with
new preface and notes by the author. Maps. 2 vols. 8vo.

BUNBURY (E. H.). A History of Ancient Geography, among the
   Greeks and Romans, from the Earliest Ages till the Fall of the Roman
   Empire. With Index and 20 Maps. 2 Vols. 8vo. 42s.
BURBIDGE (F. W.). The Gardens of the Sun: or A Naturalist's
   Journal on the Mountains and in the Forests and Swamps of Borneo and
   the Sulu Archipelago. With Illustrations. Crown 8vo.
BURCKHARDT'S Cicerone; or Art Guide to Painting in Italy.
   Translated from the German by Mrs. A. Clough. New Edition, revised
   by J. A. Crowe. Post 8vo. 6s.
BURN (Col.). Dictionary of Naval and Military Technical
   Terms, English and French—French and English. Crown 8vo. 15s.
BUTTMANN'S Lexilogus; a Critical Examination of the
   Meaning of numerous Greek Words, chiefly in Homer and Hesiod.
   By Rev. J. R. Fishlake. 8vo. 12s.
BUXTON (Charles). Memoirs of Sir Thomas Fowell Buxton,
   Bart. With Selections from his Correspondence. Portrait. 8vo. 16s.
   Popular Edition. Fcap. 8vo. 5s.
——— (Sydney C.). A Handbook to the Political Questions
   of the Day; with the Arguments on Either Side. 8vo. 5s.
BYLES (Sir John). Foundations of Religion in the Mind and
   Heart of Man. Post 8vo. 6s.
BYRON'S (Lord) LIFE AND WORKS :—
   Life, Letters, and Journals. By Thomas Moore. *Cabinet
   Edition.* Plates. 6 Vols. Fcap. 8vo. 18s.; or One Volume, Portraits.
   Royal 8vo., 7s. 6d.
   Life and Poetical Works. *Popular Edition.* Portraits.
   2 vols. Royal 8vo. 15s.
   Poetical Works. *Library Edition.* Portrait. 6 Vols. 8vo. 45s.
   Poetical Works. *Cabinet Edition.* Plates. 10 Vols. 12mo. 30s.
   Poetical Works. *Pocket Ed.* 8 Vols. 16mo. In a case. 21s.
   Poetical Works. *Popular Edition.* Plates. Royal 8vo. 7s. 6d.
   Poetical Works. *Pearl Edition.* Crown 8vo. 2s. 6d.
   Childe Harold. With 80 Engravings. Crown 8vo. 12s.
   Childe Harold. 16mo. 2s. 6d.
   Childe Harold. Vignettes. 16mo. 1s.
   Childe Harold. Portrait. 16mo. 6d.
   Tales and Poems. 16mo. 2s. 6d.
   Miscellaneous. 2 Vols. 16mo. 5s.
   Dramas and Plays. 2 Vols. 16mo. 5s.
   Don Juan and Beppo. 2 Vols. 16mo. 5s.
   Beauties. Poetry and Prose. Portrait. Fcap. 8vo. 3s. 6d.
CAMPBELL (Lord). Lord Chancellors and Keepers of the
   Great Seal of England. From the Earliest Times to the Death of Lord
   Eldon in 1838. 10 Vols. Crown 8vo. 6s. each.
——————— Chief Justices of England. From the Norman
   Conquest to the Death of Lord Tenterden. 4 Vols. Crown 8vo. 6s. each.
——————— Life and Letters: Based on his Autobiography,
   Journals, and Correspondence. Edited by his daughter, Mrs. Hard-
   castle. 2 Vols. 8vo.
——————— (Thos.) Essay on English Poetry. With Short
   Lives of the British Poets. Post 8vo. 3s. 6d.
CARNARVON (Lord). Portugal, Gallicia, and the Basque
   Provinces. Post 8vo. 3s. 6d.
——————— The Agamemnon : Translated from Æschylus.
   Sm. 8vo. 6s.

CARNOTA (Conde da). Memoirs of the Life and Eventful Career of F.M. the Duke of Saldanha; Soldier and Statesman. With Selections from his Correspondence. 2 Vols. 8vo. 32s.

CARTWRIGHT (W. C.). The Jesuits: their Constitution and Teaching. An Historical Sketch. 8vo. 9s.

CAVALCASELLE'S WORKS. [See Crowe.]

CESNOLA (Gen.). Cyprus; its Ancient Cities, Tombs, and Temples. Researches and Excavations during Ten Years' Residence in that Island. With 400 Illustrations. Medium 8vo. 50s.

CHILD (Chaplin). Benedicite; or, Song of the Three Children; being Illustrations of the Power, Beneficence, and Design manifested by the Creator in his Works. Post 8vo. 6s.

CHISHOLM (Mrs.). Perils of the Polar Seas; True Stories of Arctic Discovery and Adventure. Illustrations. Post 8vo. 6s.

CHURTON (Archdeacon). Poetical Remains, Translations and Imitations. Portrait. Post 8vo. 7s. 6d.

CLASSIC PREACHERS OF THE ENGLISH CHURCH. St. James's Lectures.

  — 1877, Donne, by Bishop of Durham; Barrow, by Prof. Wace: South, by Dean Lake; Beveridge, by Rev. W. R. Clark; Wilson, by Canon Farrar; Butler, by Dean Goulburn. With Introduction by J. E. Kempe. Post 8vo. 7s. 6d.

  — 1878, Bull, by Rev. W. Warburton; Horsley, by Bishop of Ely; Taylor, by Canon Barry; Sanderson, by Bishop of Derry; Tillotson, by Rev. W. G. Humphry; Andrewes, by Rev. H. J. North. Post 8vo. 7s. 6d.

CLIVE'S (Lord) Life. By Rev. G. R. Gleig. Post 8vo. 3s. 6d.

CLODE (C. M.). Military Forces of the Crown; their Administration and Government. 2 Vols. 8vo. 21s. each.

  — Administration of Justice under Military and Martial Law, as applicable to the Army, Navy, Marine, and Auxiliary Forces. 8vo. 12s.

COLERIDGE'S (Samuel Taylor) Table-Talk. Portrait. 12mo. 3s. 6d.

COLONIAL LIBRARY. [See Home and Colonial Library.]

COMPANIONS FOR THE DEVOUT LIFE. A Series of Lectures on well-known Devotional Works. Crown 8vo. 6s.

De Imitatione Christi, Canon Farrar.	Theologia Germanica. Canon Ashwell.
Penseés of Blaise Pascal. Dean Church.	Fénélon's Œuvres Spirituelles. Rev. T. T. Carter.
S. François de Sales. Dean Goulburn.	Andrewes' Devotions. Bishop of Ely
Baxter's Saints' Rest. Archbishop of Dublin.	Christian Year. Canon Barry.
S. Augustine's Confessions. Bishop of Derry.	Paradise Lost. Rev. E. H. Bickersteth.
Jeremy Taylor's Holy Living and Dying. Rev. Dr. Humphry.	Pilgrim's Progress. Dean Howson
	Prayer Book. Dean Burgon.

CONVOCATION PRAYER-BOOK. (See Prayer-Book.)

COOKE (E. W.). Leaves from my Sketch-Book. Being a Selection from Sketches made during many Tours. With Descriptive Text. 60 Plates. 2 Vols. Small folio. 31s. 6d. each.

COOKERY (Modern Domestic). Founded on Principles of Economy and Practical Knowledge. By a Lady. Woodcuts. Fcap. 8vo. 5s.

CRABBE (Rev. George). Life and Poetical Works. With Illustrations. Royal 8vo. 7s.

CRAWFORD & BALCARRES (Earl of). Etruscan Inscriptions. Analyzed, Translated, and Commented upon. 8vo. 12s.

CRIPPS (Wilfred). Old English Plate : Ecclesiastical, Decorative, and Domestic, its Makers and Marks. With a Complete Table of Date Letters, &c. Illustrations. Medium 8vo. 21s.

———— Old French Plate ; Furnishing Tables of the Paris Date Letters, and Fac-similes of Other Marks. With Illustrations. 8vo. 8s. 6d.

CROKER (J. W.). Progressive Geography for Children. 18mo. 1s. 6d.

———— Boswell's Life of Johnson. Including the Tour to the Hebrides. *Seventh Edition*. Portraits. 8vo. 12s.

———— Historical Essay on the Guillotine. Fcap. 8vo. 1s.

CROWE and CAVALCASELLE. Lives of the Early Flemish Painters. Woodcuts. Post 8vo, 7s. 6d.; or Large Paper, 8vo, 15s.

———— History of Painting in North Italy, from 14th to 16th Century. Derived from Researches in that Country. With Illustrations. 2 Vols. 8vo. 42s.

———— Life and Times of Titian, with some Account of his Family, chiefly from new and unpublished records. With Portrait and Illustrations. 2 vols. 8vo. 42s.

CUMMING (R. Gordon). Five Years of a Hunter's Life in the Far Interior of South Africa. Woodcuts. Post 8vo. 6s.

CUNYNGHAME (Sir Arthur). Travels in the Eastern Caucasus, on the Caspian and Black Seas, in Daghestan and the Frontiers of Persia and Turkey. With Map and Illustrations. 8vo. 18s.

CURTIUS' (Professor) Student's Greek Grammar, for the Upper Forms. Edited by Dr. Wm. Smith. Post 8vo. 6s.

———— Elucidations of the above Grammar. Translated by Evelyn Abbot. Post 8vo. 7s. 6d.

———— Smaller Greek Grammar for the Middle and Lower Forms. Abridged from the larger work. 12mo. 3s. 6d.

———— Accidence of the Greek Language. Extracted from the above work. 12mo. 2s. 6d.

———— Principles of Greek Etymology. Translated by A. S. Wilkins, M.A., and E. B. England, M.A. 2 vols. 8vo. 15s. each.

———— The Greek Verb, its Structure and Development. Translated by A. S. Wilkins, M.A., and E. B. England, M.A. 8vo. 12s.

CURZON (Hon. Robert). Visits to the Monasteries of the Levant. Illustrations. Post 8vo. 7s. 6d.

CUST (General). Warriors of the 17th Century—The Thirty Years' War. 2 Vols. 16s. Civil Wars of France and England. 2 Vols. 16s. Commanders of Fleets and Armies. 2 Vols. 18s.

———— Annals of the Wars—18th & 19th Century. With Maps. 9 Vols. Post 8vo. 5s. each.

DAVY (Sir Humphry). Consolations in Travel ; or, Last Days of a Philosopher. Woodcuts. Fcap. 8vo. 3s. 6d.

———— Salmonia ; or, Days of Fly Fishing. Woodcuts. Fcap. 8vo. 3s. 6d.

DARWIN (CHARLES) WORKS:—

JOURNAL OF A NATURALIST DURING A VOYAGE ROUND THE WORLD. Crown 8vo. 9s.

ORIGIN OF SPECIES BY MEANS OF NATURAL SELECTION; or, the Preservation of Favoured Races in the Struggle for Life. Woodcuts. Crown 8vo. 7s. 6d.

VARIATION OF ANIMALS AND PLANTS UNDER DOMESTICATION. Woodcuts. 2 Vols. Crown 8vo. 18s.

DESCENT OF MAN, AND SELECTION IN RELATION TO SEX. Woodcuts. Crown 8vo. 9s.

EXPRESSIONS OF THE EMOTIONS IN MAN AND ANIMALS. With Illustrations. Crown 8vo. 12s.

VARIOUS CONTRIVANCES BY WHICH ORCHIDS ARE FERTILIZED BY INSECTS. Woodcuts. Crown 8vo. 9s.

MOVEMENTS AND HABITS OF CLIMBING PLANTS. Woodcuts. Crown 8vo. 6s.

INSECTIVOROUS PLANTS. Woodcuts. Crown 8vo. 14s.

EFFECTS OF CROSS AND SELF-FERTILIZATION IN THE VEGETABLE KINGDOM. Crown 8vo. 12s.

DIFFERENT FORMS OF FLOWERS ON PLANTS OF THE SAME SPECIES. Crown 8vo. 10s. 6d.

THE POWER OF MOVEMENT IN PLANTS. Woodcuts. Cr. 8vo.

LIFE OF ERASMUS DARWIN. With a Study of his Works by ERNEST KRAUSE. Portrait. Crown 8vo. 7s. 6d.

FACTS AND ARGUMENTS FOR DARWIN. By FRITZ MULLER. Translated by W. S. DALLAS. Woodcuts. Post 8vo. 6s.

DE COSSON (E. A.). The Cradle of the Blue Nile; a Journey through Abyssinia and Soudan, and a Residence at the Court of King John of Ethiopia. Map and Illustrations. 2 vols. Post 8vo. 21s.

DENNIS (GEORGE). The Cities and Cemeteries of Etruria. A new Edition, revised, recording all the latest Discoveries. With 20 Plans and 200 Illustrations. 2 vols. Medium 8vo. 42s.

DENT (EMMA). Annals of Winchcombe and Sudeley. With 120 Portraits, Plates and Woodcuts. 4to. 42s.

DERBY (EARL OF). Iliad of Homer rendered into English Blank Verse. With Portrait. 2 Vols. Post 8vo. 10s.

DERRY (BISHOP OF). Witness of the Psalms to Christ and Christianity. The Bampton Lectures for 1876. 8vo. 14s.

DEUTSCH (EMANUEL). Talmud, Islam, The Targums and other Literary Remains. With a brief Memoir. 8vo. 12s.

DILKE (SIR C. W.). Papers of a Critic. Selected from the Writings of the late CHAS. WENTWORTH DILKE. With a Biographical Sketch. 2 Vols. 8vo. 24s.

DOG-BREAKING, with Odds and Ends for those who love the Dog and Gun. By GEN. HUTCHINSON. With 40 Illustrations. Crown 8vo. 7s. 6d.

DOMESTIC MODERN COOKERY. Founded on Principles of Economy and Practical Knowledge, and adapted for Private Families. Woodcuts. Fcap. 8vo. 5s.

DOUGLAS'S (Sir Howard) Theory and Practice of Gunnery.
Plates. 8vo. 21s.

———————— (Wm.) Horse-Shoeing; As it Is, and As it Should be.
Illustrations. Post 8vo. 7s. 6d.

DRAKE'S (Sir Francis) Life, Voyages, and Exploits, by Sea and
Land. By John Barrow. Post 8vo. 2s.

DRINKWATER (John). History of the Siege of Gibraltar,
1779-1783. With a Description and Account of that Garrison from the
Earliest Periods. Post 8vo. 2s.

DUCANGE'S Mediæval Latin-English Dictionary. Re-arranged
and Edited in accordance with the modern Science of Philology, by Rev.
E. A. Dayman and J. H. Hessels. Small 4to. [In Preparation.

DU CHAILLU (Paul B.). Equatorial Africa, with Accounts
of the Gorilla, the Nest-building Ape, Chimpanzee, Crocodile, &c.
Illustrations. 8vo. 21s.

———————— Journey to Ashango Land; and Further Pene-
tration into Equatorial Africa. Illustrations. 8vo. 21s.

DUFFERIN (Lord). Letters from High Latitudes; a Yacht
Voyage to Iceland, Jan Mayen, and Spitzbergen. Woodcuts. Post
8vo. 7s. 6d.

———————— Speeches and Addresses, Political and Literary,
delivered in the House of Lords, in Canada, and elsewhere. 8vo.

DUNCAN (Major). History of the Royal Artillery. Compiled from the Original Records. Portraits. 2 Vols 8vo. 18s.

———————— English in Spain; or, The Story of the War of Succession, 1834-1840. Compiled from the Reports of the British Commissioners. With Illustrations. 8vo. 16s.

EASTLAKE (Sir Charles). Contributions to the Literature of
the Fine Arts. With Memoir of the Author, and Selections from his
Correspondence. By Lady Eastlake. 2 Vols. 8vo. 24s.

EDWARDS (W. H.). Voyage up the River Amazon, including a
Visit to Para. Post 8vo. 2s.

EIGHT MONTHS AT ROME, during the Vatican Council, with
a Daily Account of the Proceedings. By Pomponio Leto. Translated from the Original. 8vo. 12s.

ELDON'S (Lord) Public and Private Life, with Selections from
his Correspondence and Diaries. By Horace Twiss. Portrait. 2
Vols. Post 8vo. 21s.

ELGIN (Lord). Letters and Journals. Edited by Theodore
Walrond. With Preface by Dean Stanley. 8vo. 14s.

ELLESMERE (Lord). Two Sieges of Vienna by the Turks.
Translated from the German. Post 8vo. 2s.

ELLIS (W.). Madagascar Revisited. Setting forth the Perse-
cutions and Heroic Sufferings of the Native Christians. Illustrations.
8vo. 16s.

———————— Memoir. By His Son. With his Character and
Work. By Rev. Henry Allon, D.D. Portrait. 8vo. 10s. 6d.

———————— (Robinson) Poems and Fragments of Catullus. 16mo. 5s.

ELPHINSTONE (Hon. Mountstuart). History of India—the
Hindoo and Mahomedan Periods. Edited by Professor Cowell.
Map. 8vo. 18s.

———————— (H. W.). Patterns for Turning; Comprising
Elliptical and other Figures cut on the Lathe without the use of any
Ornamental Chuck. With 70 Illustrations. Small 4to. 15s.

ELTON (Capt.) and H. B. COTTERILL. Adventures and
Discoveries Among the Lakes and Mountains of Eastern and Central
Africa. With Map and Illustrations. 8vo. 21s.

ENGLAND. [See ARTHUR, CROKER, HUME, MARKHAM, SMITH, and STANHOPE.]

ESSAYS ON CATHEDRALS. Edited, with an Introduction. By DEAN HOWSON. 8vo. 12s.

FERGUSSON (JAMES). History of Architecture in all Countries from the Earliest Times. With 1,600 Illustrations. 4 Vols. Medium 8vo.
Vol. I. & II. Ancient and Mediæval. 63s.
Vol. III. Indian & Eastern. 42s. Vol. IV. Modern. 31s. 6d.

—————— Rude Stone Monuments in all Countries; their Age and Uses. With 230 Illustrations. Medium 8vo. 24s.

—————— Holy Sepulchre and the Temple at Jerusalem. Woodcuts. 8vo. 7s. 6d.

—————— Temples of the Jews and other buildings in the Haram Area at Jerusalem. With Illustrations. 4to. 42s.

FLEMING (PROFESSOR). Student's Manual of Moral Philosophy. With Quotations and References. Post 8vo. 7s. 6d.

FLOWER GARDEN. By REV. THOS. JAMES. Fcap. 8vo. 1s.

FORBES (CAPT. C. J. F. S.) British Burma and its People; sketches of Native Manners, Customs, and Religion. Cr. 8vo. 10s. 6d.

FORD (RICHARD). Gatherings from Spain. Post 8vo. 3s. 6d.

FORSYTH (WILLIAM). Hortensius; an Historical Essay on the Office and Duties of an Advocate. Illustrations. 8vo. 7s. 6d.

—————— Novels and Novelists of the 18th Century, in Illustration of the Manners and Morals of the Age. Post 8vo. 10s. 6d.

FORSTER (JOHN). The Early Life of Jonathan Swift. 1667-1711. With Portrait. 8vo. 15s.

FRANCE (HISTORY OF). [See JERVIS — MARKHAM — SMITH — Students'—TOCQUEVILLE.]

FRENCH IN ALGIERS; The Soldier of the Foreign Legion— and the Prisoners of Abd-el-Kadir. Translated by Lady DUFF GORDON. Post 8vo. 2s.

FRERE (SIR BARTLE). Indian Missions. Small 8vo. 2s. 6d.

—————— Eastern Africa as a Field for Missionary Labour. With Map. Crown 8vo. 5s.

—————— Bengal Famine. How it will be Met and How to Prevent Future Famines in India. With Maps. Crown 8vo. 5s.

GALTON (F.). Art of Travel; or, Hints on the Shifts and Contrivances available in Wild Countries. Woodcuts. Post 8vo. 7s. 6d.

GEOGRAPHY. [See BUNBURY—CROKER—SMITH—STUDENTS'.]

GEOGRAPHICAL SOCIETY'S JOURNAL. (Published Yearly.)

GEORGE (ERNEST). The Mosel; a Series of Twenty Etchings, with Descriptive Letterpress. Imperial 4to. 42s.

—————— Loire and South of France; a Series of Twenty Etchings, with Descriptive Text. Folio. 42s.

GERMANY (HISTORY OF). [See MARKHAM.]

GIBBON (EDWARD). History of the Decline and Fall of the Roman Empire. Edited by MILMAN, GUIZOT, and Dr. WM. SMITH. Maps. 8 Vols. 8vo. 80s.

—————— The Student's Edition; an Epitome of the above work, Incorporating the Researches of Recent Commentators. By Dr. WM. SMITH. Woodcuts. Post 8vo. 7s. 6d.

GIFFARD (EDWARD). Deeds of Naval Daring ; or, Anecdotes of
the British Navy. Fcap. 8vo. 3s. 6d.

GILL (CAPT. WILLIAM), R. E.   The River of Golden Sand.
Narrative of a Journey through China to Burmah With a Preface by
Col. H. Yule. C.B. Maps and Illustrations. 2 Vols. 8vo. 30s.

—————— (MRS.). Six Months in Ascension. An Unscientific Account of a Scientific Expedition. Map. Crown 8vo. 9s.

GLADSTONE (W. E.). Rome and the Newest Fashions in
Religion. Three Tracts. 8vo. 7s. 6d.

—————————— Gleanings of Past Years, 1843-78. 7 vols. Small
8vo. 2s. 6d. each. I. The Throne, the Prince Consort, the Cabinet and
Constitution. II. Personal and Literary. III. Historical and Specu-
lative. IV. Foreign. V. and VI. Ecclesiastical. VII. Miscellaneous.

GLEIG (G. R.). Campaigns of the British Army at Washington
and New Orleans. Post 8vo. 2s.

—————— Story of the Battle of Waterloo. Post 8vo. 3s. 6d.

—————— Narrative of Sale's Brigade in Affghanistan. Post 8vo. 2s.

—————— Life of Lord Clive. Post 8vo. 3s. 6d.

—————————— Sir Thomas Munro. Post 8vo. 3s. 6d.

GLYNNE (SIR STEPHEN R.). Notes on the Churches of Kent.
With Preface by W. H. Gladstone, M.P. Illustrations. 8vo. 12s.

GOLDSMITH'S (OLIVER) Works. Edited with Notes by PETER
CUNNINGHAM. Vignettes. 4 Vols. 8vo. 30s.

GOMM (FIELD-MARSHAL SIR WM. M.), Commander-in-Chief in
India, Constable of the Tower, and Colonel of the Coldstream Guards,
1784—1879. His Life, Letters, and Journals. Edited by F. C. Carr
Gomm. With Portrait. 8vo.

GORDON (SIR ALEX.). Sketches of German Life, and Scenes
from the War of Liberation. Post 8vo. 3s. 6d.

—————————— (LADY DUFF) Amber-Witch : A Trial for Witchcraft. Post 8vo. 2s.

—————— French in Algiers. 1. The Soldier of the Foreign
Legion. 2. The Prisoners of Abd-el-Kadir. Post 8vo. 2s.

GRAMMARS. [See CURTIUS ; HALL ; HUTTON ; KING EDWARD ;
LEATHES ; MAETZNER ; MATTHIÆ ; SMITH.]

GREECE (HISTORY OF). [See GROTE—SMITH—Students'.]

GROTE'S (GEORGE) WORKS :—

    HISTORY OF GREECE. From the Earliest Times to the close
of the generation contemporary with the Death of Alexander the Great.
Library Edition. Portrait, Maps, and Plans. 10 Vols. 8vo. 120s.
Cabinet Edition. Portrait and Plans. 12 Vols. Post 8vo. 6s. each.

    PLATO, and other Companions of Socrates. 3 Vols. 8vo. 45s.

    ARISTOTLE. With additional Essays. 8vo. 18s.

    MINOR WORKS. Portrait. 8vo. 14s.

    LETTERS ON SWITZERLAND IN 1847. 6s.

    PERSONAL LIFE. Portrait. 8vo. 12s.

GROTE (MRS.). A Sketch. By LADY EASTLAKE. Crown 8vo. 6s.

HALL'S (T. D.) School Manual of English Grammar. With
Copious Exercises. 12mo. 3s. 6d.

—————— Manual of English Composition. With Copious Illustrations and Practical Exercises. 12mo. 3s. 6d.

—————— Primary English Grammar for Elementary Schools.
Based on the larger work. 16mo. 1s.

HALL's (T. D.)—*continued.*

———— Child's First Latin Book, comprising a full Practice of Nouns, Pronouns, and Adjectives, with the Active Verbs. 16mo. 2s.

HALLAM'S (HENRY) WORKS :—

THE CONSTITUTIONAL HISTORY OF ENGLAND, from the Accession of Henry the Seventh to the Death of George the Second. *Library Edition,* 3 Vols. 8vo. 30s. *Cabinet Edition,* 3 Vols. Post 8vo. 12s. *Student's Edition,* Post 8vo. 7s. 6d.

HISTORY OF EUROPE DURING THE MIDDLE AGES. *Library Edition,* 3 Vols. 8vo. 30s. *Cabinet Edition,* 3 Vols. Post 8vo. 12s. *Student's Edition,* Post 8vo. 7s. 6d.

LITERARY HISTORY OF EUROPE DURING THE 15TH, 16TH, AND 17TH CENTURIES. *Library Edition,* 3 Vols. 8vo. 36s. *Cabinet Edition,* 4 Vols. Post 8vo. 16s.

HALLAM'S (ARTHUR) Literary Remains; in Verse and Prose. Portrait. Fcap. 8vo. 3s. 6d.

HAMILTON (GEN. SIR F. W.). History of the Grenadier Guards. From Original Documents, &c. With Illustrations. 3 Vols. 8vo. 63s.

———— (ANDREW). Rheinsberg: Memorials of Frederick the Great and Prince Henry of Prussia. 2 Vols. Crown 8vo. 21s.

HART'S ARMY LIST. (*Published Quarterly and Annually.*)

HATCH (W. M.). The Moral Philosophy of Aristotle, consisting of a translation of the Nichomachean Ethics, and of the Paraphrase attributed to Andronicus, with an Introductory Analysis of each book. 8vo. 18s.

HATHERLEY (LORD). The Continuity of Scripture, as Declared by the Testimony of our Lord and of the Evangelists and Apostles. 8vo. 6s. *Popular Edition.* Post 8vo. 2s. 6d.

HAY (SIR J. H. DRUMMOND). Western Barbary, its Wild Tribes and Savage Animals. Post 8vo. 2s.

HAYWARD (A.). Sketches of Eminent Statesmen and Writers, with other Essays. Reprinted from the "Quarterly Review," with Additions and Corrections. Contents: Thiers, Bismarck, Cavour, Metternich, Montalembert, Melbourne, Wellesley, Byron and Tennyson, Venice, St. Simon, Sevigné, Du Deffand, Holland House, Strawberry Hill. 2 Vols. 8vo.

HEAD'S (SIR FRANCIS) WORKS :—

THE ROYAL ENGINEER. Illustrations. 8vo. 12s.

LIFE OF SIR JOHN BURGOYNE. Post 8vo. 1s.

RAPID JOURNEYS ACROSS THE PAMPAS. Post 8vo. 2s.

BUBBLES FROM THE BRUNNEN OF NASSAU. Illustrations. Post 8vo. 7s. 6d.

STOKERS AND POKERS; or, the London and North Western Railway. Post 8vo. 2s.

HEBER'S (BISHOP) Journals in India. 2 Vols. Post 8vo. 7s.

———— Poetical Works. Portrait. Fcap. 8vo. 3s. 6d.

———— Hymns adapted to the Church Service. 16mo. 1s. 6d.

HERODOTUS. A New English Version. Edited, with Notes and Essays, Historical, Ethnographical, and Geographical, by CANON RAWLINSON, SIR H. RAWLINSON and SIR J. G. WILKINSON. Maps and Woodcuts. 4 Vols. 8vo. 48s.

HERRIES (RT. HON. JOHN). Memoir of his Public Life during the Reigns of George III. and IV., William IV., and Queen Victoria. Founded on his Letters and other Unpublished Documents. By his son, Edward Herries, C.B. 2 vols. 8vo.

HERSCHEL'S (CAROLINE) Memoir and Correspondence. By MRS. JOHN HERSCHEL. With Portraits. Crown 8vo. 7s. 6d.

FOREIGN HANDBOOKS.

HAND-BOOK—TRAVEL-TALK. English, French, German, and Italian. 18mo. 3s. 6d.

———————— HOLLAND AND BELGIUM. Map and Plans. Post 8vo. 6s.

———————— NORTH GERMANY and THE RHINE,— The Black Forest, the Hartz, Thüringerwald, Saxon Switzerland, Rügen, the Giant Mountains, Taunus, Odenwald, Elass, and Lothringen. Map and Plans. Post 8vo. 10s.

———————— SOUTH GERMANY,—Wurtemburg, Bavaria, Austria, Styria, Salzburg, the Alps, Tyrol, Hungary, and the Danube, from Ulm to the Black Sea. Maps and Plans. Post 8vo. 10s

———————— PAINTING. German, Flemish, and Dutch Schools. Illustrations. 2 Vols. Post 8vo. 24s.

———————— LIVES AND WORKS OF EARLY FLEMISH Painters. Illustrations. Post 8vo. 7s. 6d.

———————— SWITZERLAND, Alps of Savoy, and Piedmont. In Two Parts. Maps and Plans. Post 8vo. 10s.

———————— FRANCE, Part I. Normandy, Brittany, the French Alps, the Loire, Seine, Garonne, and Pyrenees. Maps and Plans. Post 8vo. 7s. 6d.

———————— —— Part II. Central France, Auvergne, the Cevennes, Burgundy, the Rhone and Saone, Provence, Nimes, Arles, Marseilles, the French Alps, Alsace, Lorraine, Champagne, &c. Maps and Plans. Post 8vo. 7s. 6d.

———————— MEDITERRANEAN—its Principal Islands, Cities, Seaports, Harbours, and Border Lands. For travellers and yachtsmen. Maps and Plans. Post 8vo.

———————— ALGERIA AND TUNIS. Algiers, Constantine, Oran, the Atlas Range. Maps and Plans. Post 8vo. 10s.

———————— PARIS, and its Environs. Maps and Plans. 16mo. 3s. 6d.

———————— SPAIN, Madrid, The Castiles, The Basque Provinces, Leon, The Asturias, Galicia, Estremadura, Andalusia, Ronda, Granada, Murcia, Valencia, Catalonia, Aragon, Navarre, The Balearic Islands, &c. &c. Maps and Plans. Post 8vo. 20s.

———————— PORTUGAL, Lisbon, Porto, Cintra, Mafra, &c. Map and Plan. Post 8vo. 12s.

———————— NORTH ITALY, Turin, Milan, Cremona, the Italian Lakes, Bergamo, Brescia, Verona, Mantua, Vicenza, Padua, Ferrara, Bologna, Ravenna, Rimini, Piacenza, Genoa, the Riviera, Venice, Parma, Modena, and Romagna. Maps and Plans. Post 8vo. 10s.

———————— CENTRAL ITALY, Florence, Lucca, Tuscany, The Marches, Umbria, &c. Maps and Plans. Post 8vo. 10s.

———————— ROME AND ITS ENVIRONS. Maps and Plans. Post 8vo.

———————— SOUTH ITALY, Naples, Pompeii, Herculaneum, and Vesuvius. Maps and Plans. Post 8vo. 10s.

———————— PAINTING. The Italian Schools. Illustrations. 2 Vols. Post 8vo. 30s.

———————— LIVES OF ITALIAN PAINTERS, FROM CIMABUE to Bassano. By Mrs. Jameson. Portraits. Post 8vo. 12s.

———————— NORWAY, Christiania, Bergen, Trondhjem. The Fjelds and Fjords. Maps and Plans. Post 8vo. 9s.

———————— SWEDEN, Stockholm, Upsala, Gothenburg, the Shores of the Baltic, &c. Maps and Plan. Post 8vo. 6s.

HANDBOOK—DENMARK, Sleswig, Holstein. Copenhagen, Jutland, Iceland. Maps and Plans. Post 8vo 6s.

——————— RUSSIA, St. Petersburg, Moscow, Poland, and Finland. Maps and Plans. Post 8vo. 18s.

——————— GREECE, the Ionian Islands, Continental Greece, Athens, the Peloponnesus, the Islands of the Ægean Sea. Albania, Thessaly, and Macedonia. Maps, Plans, aud Views. Post 8vo. 15s.

——————— TURKEY IN ASIA—Constantinople, the Bosphorus, Dardanelles, Bronsa, Plain of Troy, Crete, Cyprus, Smyrna, Ephesus, the Seven Churches, Coasts of the Black Sea, Armenia, Euphrates Valley, Route to India, &c. Maps and Plans. Post 8vo. 15s.

——————— EGYPT, including Descriptions of the Course of the Nile through Egypt and Nubia, Alexandria, Cairo, and Thebes, the Suez Canal, the Pyramids, the Peninsula of Sinai, the Oases, the Fyoom, &c. In Two Parts. Maps and Plans. Post 8vo. 15s.

——————— HOLY LAND—Syria, Palestine, Peninsula of Sinai, Edom, Syrian Deserts, Petra, Damascus; and Palmyra. Maps and Plans. Post 8vo. 20s. *.* Travelling Map of Palestine. In a case. 12s.

——————— INDIA. Maps and Plans. Post 8vo. Part I. Bombay, 12s. Part II. Madras, 15s.

ENGLISH HAND-BOOKS.

HAND-BOOK—ENGLAND AND WALES. An Alphabetical Hand-Book. Condensed into One Volume for the Use of Travellers. With a Map. Post 8vo. 10s.

——————— MODERN LONDON. Maps and Plans. 16mo. 3s. 6d.

——————— ENVIRONS OF LONDON within a circuit of 20 miles. 2 Vols. Crown 8vo. 21s.

——————— ST. PAUL'S CATHEDRAL. 20 Illustrations. Crown 8vo 10s. 6d.

——————— EASTERN COUNTIES, Chelmsford, Harwich, Colchester, Maldon, Cambridge, Ely, Newmarket, Bury St. Edmunds, Ipswich, Woodbridge, Felixstowe, Lowestoft, Norwich, Yarmouth, Cromer, &c. Map and Plans. Post 8vo. 12s

——————— CATHEDRALS of Oxford, Peterborough, Norwich, Ely, and Lincoln. With 90 Illustrations. Crown 8vo. 18s.

——————— KENT, Canterbury, Dover, Ramsgate, Sheerness, Rochester, Chatham, Woolwich. Maps and Plans. Post 8vo. 7s. 6d.

——————— SUSSEX, Brighton. Chichester, Worthing, Hastings, Lewes, Arundel, &c. Maps and Plans. Post 8vo. 6s.

——————— SURREY AND HANTS, Kingston, Croydon, Reigate, Guildford, Dorking, Boxhill, Winchester, Southampton, New Forest, Portsmouth, Isle of Wight, &c. Maps and Plans. Post 8vo. 10s.

——————— BERKS, BUCKS, AND OXON, Windsor, Eton, Reading, Aylesbury. Uxbridge, Wycombe, Henley, the City and University of Oxford. Blenheim, and the Descent of the Thames. Maps and Plans. Post 8vo.

——————— WILTS, DORSET, AND SOMERSET, Salisbury, Chippenham, Weymouth, Sherborne, Wells, Bath, Bristol, Taunton, &c. Map. Post 8vo. 10s.

——————— DEVON, Exeter, Ilfracombe, Linton, Sidmouth, Dawlish, Teignmouth, Plymouth, Devonport, Torquay. Maps and Plans. Post 8vo. 7s. 6d.

HAND-BOOK—CORNWALL, Launceston, Penzance, Falmouth, the Lizard, Land's End, &c. Maps. Post 8vo. 6s.

———— CATHEDRALS of Winchester, Salisbury, Exeter, Wells, Chichester, Rochester, Canterbury, and St. Albans. With 130 Illustrations. 2 Vols. Cr. 8vo. 36s. St. Albans separately, cr. 8vo. 6s.

———— GLOUCESTER, HEREFORD, AND WORCESTER, Cirencester, Cheltenham, Stroud, Tewkesbury, Leominster, Ross, Malvern, Kidderminster, Dudley, Bromsgrove, Evesham. Map. Post 8vo.

———— CATHEDRALS of Bristol, Gloucester, Hereford, Worcester, and Lichfield. With 50 Illustrations. Crown 8vo. 16s.

———— NORTH WALES, Bangor, Carnarvon, Beaumaris, Snowdon, Llanberis, Dolgelly, Cader Idris, Conway, &c. Map. Post 8vo. 7s.

———— SOUTH WALES, Monmouth, Llandaff, Merthyr, Vale of Neath, Pembroke, Carmarthen, Tenby, Swansea, The Wye, &c. Map. Post 8vo. 7s.

———— CATHEDRALS OF BANGOR, ST. ASAPH, Llandaff, and St. David's. With Illustrations. Post 8vo. 15s.

———— NORTHAMPTONSHIRE AND RUTLAND— Northampton, Peterborough, Towcester, Daventry, Market Harborough, Kettering, Wallingborough, Thrapston, Stamford, Uppingham, Oakham. Maps. Post 8vo. 7s. 6d.

———— DERBY, NOTTS, LEICESTER, STAFFORD, Matlock, Bakewell, Chatsworth, The Peak, Buxton, Hardwick, Dove Dale, Ashborne, Southwell, Mansfield, Retford, Burton, Belvoir, Melton Mowbray, Wolverhampton, Lichfield, Walsall, Tamworth. Map. Post 8vo. 9s.

———— SHROPSHIRE AND CHESHIRE, Shrewsbury, Ludlow, Bridgnorth, Oswestry, Chester, Crewe, Alderley, Stockport, Birkenhead. Maps and Plans. Post 8vo. 6s.

———— LANCASHIRE, Warrington, Bury, Manchester, Liverpool, Burnley, Clitheroe, Bolton, Blackburn, Wigan, Preston, Rochdale, Lancaster, Southport, Blackpool, &c. Maps and Plans. Post 8vo. 7s. 6d.

———— YORKSHIRE, Doncaster, Hull, Selby, Beverley, Scarborough, Whitby, Harrogate, Ripon, Leeds, Wakefield, Bradford, Halifax, Huddersfield, Sheffield. Map and Plans. Post 8vo. 12s.

———— CATHEDRALS of York, Ripon, Durham, Carlisle, Chester, and Manchester. With 60 Illustrations. 2 Vols. Cr. 8vo. 21s.

———— DURHAM AND NORTHUMBERLAND, Newcastle, Darlington, Gateshead, Bishop Auckland, Stockton, Hartlepool, Sunderland, Shields, Berwick-on-Tweed, Morpeth, Tynemouth, Coldstream, Alnwick, &c. Map. Post 8vo. 9s.

———— WESTMORLAND AND CUMBERLAND—Lancaster, Furness Abbey, Ambleside, Kendal, Windermere, Coniston, Keswick, Grasmere, Ulswater, Carlisle, Cockermouth, Penrith, Appleby, Map. Post 8vo.

₊ MURRAY'S MAP OF THE LAKE DISTRICT, on canvas. 3s. 6d.

———— SCOTLAND, Edinburgh, Melrose, Kelso, Glasgow, Dumfries, Ayr, Stirling, Arran, The Clyde, Oban, Inverary, Loch Lomond, Loch Katrine and Trossachs, Caledonian Canal, Inverness, Perth, Dundee, Aberdeen, Braemar, Skye, Caithness, Ross, Sutherland, &c. Maps and Plans. Post 8vo. 9s.

———— IRELAND, Dublin, Belfast, the Giant's Causeway, Donegal, Galway, Wexford, Cork, Limerick, Waterford, Killarney, Bantry, Glengariff, &c. Maps and Plans. Post 8vo. 10s.

HOME AND COLONIAL LIBRARY. A Series of Works adapted for all circles and classes of Readers, having been selected for their acknowledged interest, and ability of the Authors. Post 8vo. Published at 2s. and 3s. 6d. each, and arranged under two distinctive heads as follows:—

CLASS A.

HISTORY, BIOGRAPHY, AND HISTORIC TALES.

1. SIEGE OF GIBRALTAR. By JOHN DRINKWATER. 2s.
2. THE AMBER-WITCH. By LADY DUFF GORDON. 2s.
3. CROMWELL AND BUNYAN. By ROBERT SOUTHEY. 2s.
4. LIFE OF SIR FRANCIS DRAKE. By JOHN BARROW. 2s.
5. CAMPAIGNS AT WASHINGTON. By REV. G. R. GLEIG. 2s.
6. THE FRENCH IN ALGIERS. By LADY DUFF GORDON. 2s.
7. THE FALL OF THE JESUITS. 2s.
8. LIVONIAN TALES. 2s.
9. LIFE OF CONDÉ. By LORD MAHON. 3s. 6d.
10. SALE'S BRIGADE. By REV. G. R. GLEIG. 2s.
11. THE SIEGES OF VIENNA. By LORD ELLESMERE. 2s.
12. THE WAYSIDE CROSS. By CAPT. MILMAN. 2s.
13. SKETCHES OF GERMAN LIFE. By SIR A. GORDON. 3s. 6d.
14. THE BATTLE OF WATERLOO. By REV. G. R. GLEIG. 3s. 6d.
15. AUTOBIOGRAPHY OF STEFFENS. 2s.
16. THE BRITISH POETS. By THOMAS CAMPBELL. 3s. 6d.
17. HISTORICAL ESSAYS. By LORD MAHON. 3s. 6d.
18. LIFE OF LORD CLIVE. By REV. G. R. GLEIG. 3s. 6d.
19. NORTH - WESTERN RAILWAY. By SIR F. B. HEAD. 2s.
20. LIFE OF MUNRO. By REV. G. R. GLEIG. 3s. 6d.

CLASS B.

VOYAGES, TRAVELS, AND ADVENTURES.

1. BIBLE IN SPAIN. By GEORGE BORROW. 3s. 6d.
2. GYPSIES OF SPAIN. By GEORGE BORROW. 3s. 6d.
3 & 4. JOURNALS IN INDIA. By BISHOP HEBER. 2 Vols. 7s.
5. TRAVELS IN THE HOLY LAND. By IRBY and MANGLES. 2s.
6. MOROCCO AND THE MOORS. By J. DRUMMOND HAY. 2s.
7. LETTERS FROM THE BALTIC. By A LADY.
8. NEW SOUTH WALES. By MRS. MEREDITH. 2s.
9. THE WEST INDIES. By M. G. LEWIS. 2s.
10. SKETCHES OF PERSIA. By SIR JOHN MALCOLM. 3s. 6d.
11. MEMOIRS OF FATHER RIPA. 2s.
12 & 13 TYPEE AND OMOO. By HERMANN MELVILLE. 2 Vols. 7s.
14. MISSIONARY LIFE IN CANADA. By REV. J. ABBOTT. 2s.
15. LETTERS FROM MADRAS. By A LADY. 2s.
16. HIGHLAND SPORTS. By CHARLES ST. JOHN. 3s. 6d.
17. PAMPAS JOURNEYS. By SIR F. B. HEAD. 2s.
18 GATHERINGS FROM SPAIN. By RICHARD FORD. 3s. 6d.
19. THE RIVER AMAZON. By W. H. EDWARDS. 2s.
20. MANNERS & CUSTOMS OF INDIA. By REV. C. ACLAND. 2s.
21. ADVENTURES IN MEXICO. By G. F. RUXTON. 3s. 6d.
22. PORTUGAL AND GALICIA. By LORD CARNARVON. 3s. 6d.
23. BUSH LIFE IN AUSTRALIA. By REV. H. W. HAYGARTH. 2s.
24. THE LIBYAN DESERT. By BAYLE ST. JOHN. 2s.
25. SIERRA LEONE. By A LADY. 3s. 6d.

*** Each work may be had separately

c

HOLLWAY (J. G.). A Month in Norway. Fcap. 8vo. 2*.

HONEY BEE. By Rev. Thomas James. Fcap. 8vo. 1*.

HOOK (Dean). Church Dictionary. 8vo. 16*.

———— (Theodore) Life. By J. G. Lockhart. Fcap. 8vo. 1*.

HOPE (A. J. Beresford). Worship in the Church of England.
8vo. 9*., or, *Popular Selections from.* 8vo. 2*. 6d.

HORACE; a New Edition of the Text. Edited by Dean Milman.
With 100 Woodcuts. Crown 8vo. 7*. 6d.

HOUGHTON'S (Lord) Monographs, Personal and Social. With
Portraits. Crown 8vo. 10*. 6d.

————————————— Poetical Works. *Collected Edition.* With Portrait. 2 Vols. Fcap. 8vo. 12*.

HOUSTOUN (Mrs.). Twenty Years in the Wild West of Ireland,
or Life in Connaught. Post 8vo. 9*.

HUME (The Student's). A History of England, from the Invasion of Julius Cæsar to the Revolution of 1688. New Edition, revised,
corrected, and continued to the Treaty of Berlin, 1878. By J. S.
Brewer, M.A. With 7 Coloured Maps & 70 Woodcuts. Post 8vo. 7*. 6d.

HUTCHINSON (Gen.). Dog Breaking, with Odds and Ends for
those who love the Dog and the Gun. With 40 Illustrations. Crown
8vo. 7*. 6d.

HUTTON (H. E.). Principia Græca; an Introduction to the Study
of Greek. Comprehending Grammar, Delectus, and Exercise-book,
with Vocabularies. *Sixth Edition.* 12mo. 3*. 6d.

HYMNOLOGY, Dictionary of. See Julian.

INDIA in 1880. By Sir Richard Temple. 8vo.

IRBY AND MANGLES' Travels in Egypt, Nubia, Syria, and
the Holy Land. Post 8vo. 2*.

JAMES' (Rev. Thomas) Fables of Æsop. A New Translation, with
Historical Preface. With 100 Woodcuts by Tenniel and Wolf.
Post 8vo. 2*. 6d.

JAMESON (Mrs.). Lives of the Early Italian Painters—
and the Progress of Painting in Italy—Cimabue to Bassano. With
50 Portraits. Post 8vo. 12*.

JAPAN. See Bird, Mossman, Mounsey, Reed.

JENNINGS (Louis J.). Field Paths and Green Lanes in Surrey
and Sussex. Illustrations. Post 8vo. 10*. 6d.

———————— Rambles among the Hills in the Peak of Derbyshire
and on the South Downs, from Petersfield to Beachy Head. With
sketches of people by the way. With Illustrations. Post 8vo.

JERVIS (Rev. W. H.). The Gallican Church, from the Con-
cordat of Bologna, 1516, to the Revolution. With an Introduction.
Portraits. 2 Vols. 8vo. 28*.

JESSE (Edward). Gleanings in Natural History. Fcp. 8vo. 3*. 6d.

JEX-BLAKE (Rev. T. W.). Life in Faith : Sermons Preached
at Cheltenham and Rugby. Fcap. 8vo. 3*. 6d.

JOHNSON'S (Dr. Samuel) Life. By James Boswell. Including
the Tour to the Hebrides. Edited by Mr. Croker. 1 vol. Royal
8vo. 12*. *New Edition.* Portraits. 4 Vols. 8vo. [*In Preparation.*

JULIAN (Rev. John J.). A Dictionary of Hymnology. A
Companion to Existing Hymn Books. Setting forth the Origin and
History of the Hymns contained in the Principal Hymnals used by the
Churches of England, Scotland, and Ireland, and various Dissenting
Bodies, with Notices of their Authors. Post 8vo. [*In the Press.*

JUNIUS' HANDWRITING Professionally investigated. By Mr. CHABOT, Expert. With Preface and Collateral Evidence, by the Hon. EDWARD TWISLETON. With Facsimiles, Woodcuts, &c. 4to. £3 3s.

KERR (ROBERT). Small Country House. A Brief Practical Discourse on the Planning of a Residence from 2000l. to 5000l. With Supplementary Estimates to 7000l. Post 8vo. 3s.

————— Ancient Lights; a Book for Architects, Surveyors, Lawyers, and Landlords. 8vo. 5s. 6d.

————— (R. MALCOLM) Student's Blackstone. A Systematic Abridgment of the entire Commentaries, adapted to the present state of the law. Post 8vo. 7s. 6d.

KING EDWARD VITH's Latin Grammar. 12mo. 3s. 6d.

————————————— First Latin Book. 12mo. 2s. 6d.

KING (R. J.). Archæology, Travel and Art; being Sketches and Studies, Historical and Descriptive. 8vo. 12s.

KIRK (J. FOSTER). History of Charles the Bold, Duke of Burgundy. Portrait. 3 Vols. 8vo. 45s.

KIRKES' Handbook of Physiology. Edited by W. MORRANT BAKER, F.R.C.S. With 400 Illustrations. Post 8vo. 14s.

KUGLER'S Handbook of Painting.—The Italian Schools. Revised and Remodelled from the most recent Researches. By LADY EASTLAKE. With 140 Illustrations. 2 Vols. Crown 8vo. 30s.

————— Handbook of Painting.—The German, Flemish, and Dutch Schools. Revised and in part re-written. By J. A. CROWE. With 60 Illustrations. 2 Vols. Crown 8vo. 24s.

LANE (E. W.). Account of the Manners and Customs of Modern Egyptians. With Illustrations. 2 Vols. Post 8vo. 12s

LAWRENCE (SIR GEO.). Reminiscences of Forty-three Years' Service in India; including Captivities in Cabul among the Affghans and among the Sikhs, and a Narrative of the Mutiny in Rajputana. Crown 8vo. 10s. 6d.

LAYARD (A. H.). Nineveh and its Remains. Being a Narrative of Researches and Discoveries amidst the Ruins of Assyria. With an Account of the Chaldean Christians of Kurdistan; the Yezedis, or Devil-worshippers; and an Enquiry into the Manners and Arts of the Ancient Assyrians. Plates and Woodcuts. 2 Vols. 8vo. 36s.
  。 A POPULAR EDITION of the above work. With Illustrations. Post 8vo. 7s. 6d.

————— Nineveh and Babylon; being the Narrative of Discoveries in the Ruins, with Travels in Armenia, Kurdistan and the Desert, during a Second Expedition to Assyria. With Map and Plates. 8vo. 21s.
  。 A POPULAR EDITION of the above work. With Illustrations Post 8vo. 7s. 6d.

LEATHES' (STANLEY) Practical Hebrew Grammar. With the Hebrew Text of Genesis i.—vi., and Psalms i.—vi. Grammatical Analysis and Vocabulary. Post 8vo. 7s. 6d.

LENNEP (REV. H. J. VAN). Missionary Travels in Asia Minor. With Illustrations of Biblical History and Archæology. With Map and Woodcuts. 2 Vols. Post 8vo. 24s.

————— Modern Customs and Manners of Bible Lands in Illustration of Scripture. With Coloured Maps and 300 Illustrations. 2 Vols. 8vo. 21s.

LESLIE (C. R.). Handbook for Young Painters. With Illustrations. Post 8vo. 7s. 6d.

————— Life and Works of Sir Joshua Reynolds. Portraits and Illustrations. 2 Vols. 8vo. 42s.

LETO (Pomponio). Eight Months at Rome during the Vatican
Council. With a daily account of the proceedings. Translated from
the original. 8vo. 12s.

LETTERS From the Baltic. By a Lady. Post 8vo. 2s.

———————— Madras. By a Lady. Post 8vo. 2s.

———————— Sierra Leone. By a Lady. Post 8vo. 3s. 6d.

LEVI (Leone). History of British Commerce: and Economic
Progress of the Nation, from 1763 to 1878. 8vo. 18s.

LEX SALICA; the Ten Texts with the Glosses and the Lex
Emendata. Synoptical'y edited by J H. Hessels With Notes on
the Frankish Words in the Lex Salica by H. Kern, of Leyden. 4to. 42s.

LIDDELL (Dean). Student's History of Rome, from the earliest
Times to the establishment of the Empire. Woodcuts. Post 8vo. 7s. 6d.

LISPINGS from LOW LATITUDES; or, the Journal of the Hon.
Impulsia Gushington. Edited by Lord Dufferin. With 24 Plates. 4to. 21s.

LIVINGSTONE (Dr). Popular Account of his First Expedition
to Africa, 1840-56. Illustrations. Post 8vo. 7s. 6d.

———————— Second Expedition to Africa, 1858-64. Illustrations. Post 8vo. 7s. 6d.

———————— Last Journals in Central Africa, from 1865 to
his Death. Continued by a Narrative of his last moments and sufferings.
By Rev. Horace Waller. Maps and Illustrations. 2 Vols. 8vo. 15s.

———————— Memoirs of his Personal Life. From his unpublished Journals and Correspondence. By Wm. G. Blaikie, D.D.
With Map and Portrait. 8vo.

LIVINGSTONIA. Journal of Adventures in Exploring Lake
Nyassa, and Establishing a Missionary Settlement there. By E. D.
Young, R.N. Maps Post 8vo. 7s. 6d.

LIVONIAN TALES. By the Author of "Letters from the
Baltic." Post 8vo. 2s.

LOCKHART (J. G.). Ancient Spanish Ballads. Historical and
Romantic. Translated, with Notes. Illustrations. Crown 8vo. 5s.

———————— Life of Theodore Hook. Fcap. 8vo. 1s.

LOUDON (Mrs.). Gardening for Ladies. With Directions and
Calendar of Operations for Every Month. Woodcuts. Fcap. 8vo. 3s. 6d.

LYELL (Sir Charles). Principles of Geology; or, the Modern
Changes of the Earth and Its Inhabitants considered as Illustrative of
Geology. With Illustrations. 2 Vols. 8vo. 32s.

———————— Student's Elements of Geology. With Table of British
Fossils and 600 Illustrations. Third Edition, Revised. Post 8vo. 9s.

———————— Geological Evidences of the Antiquity of Man,
including an Outline of Glacial Post-Tertiary Geology, and Remarks
on the Origin of Species. Illustrations. 8vo. 14s.

———————— (K. M.). Geographical Handbook of Ferns. With Tables
to show their Distribution. Post 8vo. 7s. 6d.

LYTTON (Lord). A Memoir of Julian Fane. With Portrait. Post
8vo. 5s

McCLINTOCK (Sir L.). Narrative of the Discovery of the
Fate of Sir John Franklin and his Companions in the Arctic Seas.
With Illustrations. Post 8vo. 7s. 6d.

MACDOUGALL (Col.). Modern Warfare as Influenced by Modern
Artillery. With Plans. Post 8vo. 12s.

MACGREGOR (J.). Rob Roy on the Jordan, Nile, Red Sea, Gen-
nesareth, &c. A Canoe Cruise in Palestine and Egypt and the Waters
of Damascus. With Map and 70 Illustrations. Crown 8vo. 7s. 6d.

MAETZNER'S English Grammar. A Methodical, Analytical, and Historical Treatise on the Orthography, Prosody, Inflections, and Syntax. By Clair J. Grece, LL.D. 3 Vols. 8vo 36s.

MAHON (Lord), see Stanhope.

MAINE (Sir H. Sumner). Ancient Law: its Connection with the Early History of Society, and its Relation to Modern Ideas. 8vo. 12s.

———— Village Communities in the East and West. 8vo. 12s.

———— Early History of Institutions. 8vo. 12s.

MALCOLM (Sir John). Sketches of Persia. Post 8vo. 3s. 6d.

MANSEL (Dean). Limits of Religious Thought Examined. Post 8vo. 8s. 6d.

———— Letters, Lectures, and Reviews. 8vo. 12s.

MANUAL OF SCIENTIFIC ENQUIRY. For the Use of Travellers. Edited by Rev. R. Main. Post 8vo. 3s. 6d. (Published by order of the Lords of the Admiralty.)

MARCO POLO. The Book of Ser Marco Polo, the Venetian. Concerning the Kingdoms and Marvels of the East. A new English Version. Illustrated by the light of Oriental Writers and Modern Travels. By Col. Henry Yule. Maps and Illustrations. 2 Vols. Medium 8vo. 63s.

MARKHAM (Mrs.). History of England. From the First Invasion by the Romans. Woodcuts. 12mo. 3s. 6d.

———— History of France. From the Conquest by the Gauls. Woodcuts. 12mo. 3s. 6d.

———— History of Germany. From the Invasion by Marius. Woodcuts. 12mo. 3s. 6d.

———— (Clements R.). A Popular Account of Peruvian Bark and Its introduction into British India, Ceylon, &c., and of the Progress and Extent of its Cultivation. With Maps. Post 8vo.

MARRYAT (Joseph). History of Modern and Mediæval Pottery and Porcelain. With a Description of the Manufacture. Plates and Woodcuts. 8vo. 42s.

MARSH (G. P.). Student's Manual of the English Language. Edited with Additions. By Dr. Wm. Smith. Post 8vo. 7s. 6d.

MASTERS in English Theology. The King's College Lectures, 1877. Hooker, by Canon Barry; Andrews, by Dean Church; Chillingworth, by Prof. Plumptre; Whichcote and Smith, by Canon Westcott; Jeremy Taylor, by Canon Farrar; Pearson, by Archdeacon Cheetham. With Introduction by Canon Barry. Post 8vo. 7s. 6d.

MATTHIÆ'S Greek Grammar. Abridged by Blomfield, Revised by E. S. Crooke. 12mo. 4s.

MAUREL'S Character, Actions, and Writings of Wellington. Fcap. 8vo. 1s. 6d.

MAYO (Lord). Sport in Abyssinia; or, the Mareb and Tackazzee. With Illustrations. Crown 8vo. 12s.

MEADE (Hon. Herbert). Ride through the Disturbed Districts of New Zealand, with a Cruise among the South Sea Islands. With Illustrations. Medium 8vo. 12s.

MELVILLE (Hermann). Marquesas and South Sea Islands. 2 Vols. Post 8vo. 7s.

MEREDITH (Mrs. Charles). Notes and Sketches of New South Wales. Post 8vo. 2s.

MICHAEL ANGELO, Sculptor, Painter, and Architect. His Life and Works. By C. Heath Wilson. Illustrations. Royal 8vo. 26s.

MIDDLETON (CHAS. H.) A Descriptive Catalogue of the Etched Work of Rembrandt, with Life and Introductions. With Explanatory Cuts. Medium 8vo. 31s. 6d.

MILLINGTON (REV. T. S.). Signs and Wonders in the Land of Ham, or the Ten Plagues of Egypt, with Ancient and Modern Illustrations. Woodcuts. Post 8vo. 7s. 6d.

MILMAN'S (DEAN) WORKS:—

HISTORY OF THE JEWS, from the earliest Period down to Modern Times. 3 Vols. Post 8vo. 18s.

EARLY CHRISTIANITY, from the Birth of Christ to the Abolition of Paganism in the Roman Empire. 3 Vols. Post 8vo. 18s.

LATIN CHRISTIANITY, including that of the Popes to the Pontificate of Nicholas V. 9 Vols. Post 8vo. 54s.

HANDBOOK TO ST. PAUL'S CATHEDRAL. Woodcuts. Crown 8vo. 10s. 6d.

QUINTI HORATII FLACCI OPERA. Woodcuts. Sm. 8vo. 7s. 6d.

FALL OF JERUSALEM. Fcap. 8vo. 1s.

———— (CAPT. E. A.) Wayside Cross. Post 8vo. 2s.

———— (BISHOP, D.D.,) late Metropolitan of India. His Life. With a Selection from his Correspondence and Journals. By his Sister. Map. 8vo. 12s.

MIVART (ST. GEORGE). Lessons from Nature; as manifested in Mind and Matter. 8vo. 15s.

— ———— The Cat. An Introduction to the Study of Backboned Animals, especially Mammals. With numerous Illustrations. 8vo.
                [In the Press.

MOORE (THOMAS). Life and Letters of Lord Byron. *Cabinet Edition.* With Plates. 6 Vols. Fcap. 8vo. 18s.; *Popular Edition,* with Portraits. Royal 8vo. 7s. 6d.

MORESBY (CAPT.), R.N. Discoveries in New Guinea, Polynesia, Torres Straits, &c., during the cruise of H.M.S. Basilisk. Map and Illustrations. 8vo. 15s.

MOSSMAN (SAMUEL). New Japan; the Land of the Rising Sun; its Annals during the past Twenty Years, recording the remarkable Progress of the Japanese in Western Civilisation. With Map. 8vo. 15s.

MOTLEY (J. L.). History of the United Netherlands: from the Death of William the Silent to the Twelve Years' Truce, 1609. Portraits. 4 Vols. Post 8vo. 6s. each.

———————— Life and Death of John of Barneveld, Advocate of Holland. With a View of the Primary Causes and Movements of the Thirty Years' War. Illustrations. 2 Vols. Post 8vo. 12s.

MOZLEY (CANON). Treatise on the Augustinian doctrine of Predestination. Crown 8vo. 9s.

MUIRHEAD (JAS.). The Vaux-de-Vire of Maistre Jean Le Houx, Advocate of Vire. Translated and Edited. With Portrait and Illustrations. 8vo. 21s.

MUNRO'S (GENERAL) Life and Letters. By REV. G. R. GLEIG. Post 8vo. 3s. 6d.

MURCHISON (SIR RODERICK). Siluria; or, a History of the Oldest rocks containing Organic Remains. Map and Plates. 8vo. 18s.

———————— Memoirs. With Notices of his Contemporaries, and Rise and Progress of Palæozoic Geology. By ARCHIBALD GEIKIE. Portraits. 2 Vols. 8vo. 30s.

MURRAY (A. S.). A History of Greek Sculpture, from the Earliest Times down to the Age of Phidias. With Illustrations. Roy. 8vo.

MUSTERS' (Capt.) Patagonians; a Year's Wanderings over Untrodden Ground from the Straits of Magellan to the Rio Negro. Illustrations. Post 8vo. 7s. 6d.

NAPIER (Sir Wm.). English Battles and Sieges of the Peninsular War. Portrait. Post 8vo. 9s.

NAPOLEON at Fontainedlrau and Elba. Journal of Occurrences and Notes of Conversations. By Sir Neil Campbell. Portrait. 8vo. 15s.

NARES (Sir George), R.N. Official Report to the Admiralty of the recent Arctic Expedition. Map. 8vo. 2s. 6d.

NASMYTH and CARPENTER. The Moon. Considered as a Planet, a World, and a Satellite. With Illustrations from Drawings made with the aid of Powerful Telescopes, Woodcuts, &c. 4to. 30s.

NAUTICAL ALMANAC (The). (*By Authority.*) 2s. 6d.

NAVY LIST. (Monthly and Quarterly.) Post 8vo.

NEW TESTAMENT. With Short Explanatory Commentary. By Archdeacon Churton, M.A., and the Bishop of St. David's. With 110 authentic Views, &c. 2 Vols. Crown 8vo. 21s. *bound.*

NEWTH (Samuel). First Book of Natural Philosophy; an Introduction to the Study of Statics. Dynamics. Hydrostatics, Light, Hea', and Sound, with numerous Examples. Small 8vo. 3s. 6d.

———————— Elements of Mechanics, including Hydrostatics, with numerous Examples. Small 8vo. 8s. 6d.

———————— Mathematical Examples. A Graduated Series of Elementary Examples in Arithmetic, Algebra, Logarithms, Trigonometry, and Mechanics. Small 8vo. 8s. 6d.

NICOLAS (Sir Harris). Historic Peerage of England. Exhibiting the Origin, Descent, and Present State of every Title of Peerage which has existed in this Country since the Conquest. By William Courthope. 8vo. 30s.

NILE GLEANINGS. See Stuart.

NIMROD, On the Chace—Turf—and Road. With Portrait and Plates. Crown 8vo. 5s. Or with Coloured Plates, 7s. 6d.

NORDHOFF (Chas.). Communistic Societies of the United States; including Detailed Accounts of the Shakers, The Amana, Oneida, Bethell, Aurora, Icarian and other existing Societies; with Particulars of their Religious Creeds, Industries, and Present Condition. With 40 Illustrations. 8vo. 15s.

NORTHCOTE'S (Sir John) Notebook in the Long Parliament. Containing Proceedings during its First Session, 1640. Edited, with a Memoir, by A. H. A. Hamilton. Crown 8vo. 9s.

OWEN (Lieut.-Col.). Principles and Practice of Modern Artillery, including Artillery Material, Gunnery, and Organisation and Use of Artillery in Warfare. With Illustrations. 8vo. 15s.

OXENHAM (Rev. W.). English Notes for Latin Elegiacs; designed for early Proficients in the Art of Latin Versification, with Prefatory Rules of Composition in Elegiac Metre. 12mo. 3s. 6d.

PALGRAVE (R. H. I.). Local Taxation of Great Britain and Ireland. 8vo. 5s.

PALLISER (Mrs.). Mottoes for Monuments, or Epitaphs selected General Use and Study. With Illustrations. Crown 8vo. 7s. 6d.

PARIS (Dr.) Philosophy in Sport made Science in Earnest; or, the First Principles of Natural Philosophy inculcated by aid of the Toys and Sports of Youth. Woodcuts. Post 8vo. 7s. 6d.

PARKYNS' (Mansfield) Three Years' Residence in Abyssinia: with Travels in that Country. With Illustrations. Post 8vo. 7s. 6d.

PEEL'S (Sir Robert) Memoirs. 2 Vols. Post 8vo. 15s.

PENN (Richard). Maxims and Hints for an Angler and Chess-player. Woodcuts. Fcap. 8vo. 1s.

PERCY (John, M.D.). Metallurgy. Fuel, Wood, Peat, Coal, Charcoal, Coke. Fire-Clays. Illustrations. 8vo. 30s.

———— Lead, including part of Silver. Illustrations. 8vo. 30s.

———— Silver and Gold. Part I. Illustrations. 8vo. 30s.

PERRY (Rev. Canon). Life of St. Hugh of Avalon, Bishop of Lincoln. Post 8vo. 10s. 6d.

PHILLIPS (John). Geology of Yorkshire, The Coast, and Limestone District. Plates. 2 Vols. 4to. 31s. 6d. each.

———— (Samuel). Literary Essays from "The Times." With Portrait. 2 Vols. Fcap. 8vo. 7s.

POPE'S (Alexander) Works. With Introductions and Notes, by Rev. Whitwell Elwin. Vols. I., II., VI., VII., VIII. With Portraits. 8vo. 10s. 6d. each.

PORTER (Rev. J. L.). Damascus, Palmyra, and Lebanon. With Travels among the Giant Cities of Bashan and the Hauran. Map and Woodcuts. Post 8vo. 7s. 6d.

PRAYER-BOOK (Illustrated), with Borders, Initials, Vignettes, &c. Edited, with Notes, by Rev. Thos. James. Medium 8vo. 18s. cloth ; 31s. 6d. calf ; 36s. morocco.

———————— (The Convocation), with altered rubrics, showing the book if amended in conformity with the recommendations of the Convocations of Canterbury and York in 1879. Post 8vo. 5s.

PRINCESS CHARLOTTE OF WALES. A Brief Memoir. With Selections from her Correspondence and other unpublished Papers. By Lady Rose Weigall. With Portrait. 8vo. 8s. 6d.

PRIVY COUNCIL JUDGMENTS in Ecclesiastical Cases relating to Doctrine and Discipline. With Historical Introduction, by G. C. Brodrick and W. H. Fremantle. 8vo. 10s. 6d.

PSALMS OF DAVID. With Notes Explanatory and Critical by the Dean of Wells, Canon Elliott, and Canon Cook. Medium. 8vo.

PUSS IN BOOTS. With 12 Illustrations. By Otto Speckter. 16mo. 1s. 6d. Or coloured, 2s. 6d.

QUARTERLY REVIEW (The). 8vo. 6s.

RAE (Edward). Country of the Moors. A Journey from Tripoli in Barbary to the Holy City of Kairwan. Map and Etchings. Crown 8vo. 12s.

RAMBLES in the Syrian Deserts. Post 8vo. 10s. 6d.

RASSAM (Hormuzd). British Mission to Abyssinia. With Notices of the Countries from Massowah to Magdala. Illustrations. 2 Vols. 8vo. 28s.

RAWLINSON'S (Canon) Herodotus. A New English Version. Edited with Notes and Essays. Maps and Woodcut. 4 Vols. 8vo. 48s.

———————— Five Great Monarchies of Chaldæa, Assyria, Media, Babylonia, and Persia. With Maps and Illustrations. 3 Vols. 8vo. 42s.

———————— (Sir Henry) England and Russia in the East ; a Series of Papers on the Political and Geographical Condition of Central Asia. Map. 8vo. 12s.

REED (Sir E. J.) Iron-Clad Ships; their Qualities, Performances, and Cost. With Chapters on Turret Ships, Iron-Clad Rams, &c. With Illustrations. 8vo. 12s.

——— Letters from Russia in 1875. 8vo. 5s.

——— Japan : Its History, Traditions, and Religions. With Narrative of a Visit in 1879. Illustrations. 2 Vols. 8vo. 28s.

REJECTED ADDRESSES (THE). By JAMES AND HORACE SMITH. Woodcuts. Post 8vo. 3s. 6d.; or Popular Edition, Fcap. 8vo. 1s.

REMBRANDT. A Descriptive Catalogue of his Etched Work ; with Life and Introductions. By CHAS. H. MIDDLETON, B.A. Woodcuts. Medium 8vo. 31s. 6d.

REYNOLDS' (SIR JOSHUA) Life and Times. By C. R. LESLIE, R.A. and TOM TAYLOR. Portraits. 2 Vols. 8vo. 42s.

RICARDO'S (DAVID) Political Works. With a Notice of his Life and Writings. By J. R. M'CULLOCH. 8vo. 16s.

RIPA (FATHER). Thirteen Years at the Court of Peking. Post 8vo. 2s.

ROBERTSON (CANON). History of the Christian Church, from the Apostolic Age to the Reformation, 1517. 8 Vols. Post 8vo. 6s. each.

ROBINSON (REV. DR.). Biblical Researches in Palestine and the Adjacent Regions, 1838—52. Maps. 3 Vols. 8vo. 42s.

——— (WM.) Alpine Flowers for English Gardens. With 70 Illustrations. Crown 8vo. 7s. 6d.

——— Sub-Tropical Garden. Illustrations. Small 8vo. 5s.

ROBSON (E. R.). SCHOOL ARCHITECTURE. Remarks on the Planning, Designing, Building, and Furnishing of School-houses. Illustrations. Medium 8vo. 18s.

ROME (HISTORY OF). See GIBBON—LIDDELL—SMITH—STUDENTS'.

ROYAL SOCIETY CATALOGUE OF SCIENTIFIC PAPERS. 8 vols. 8vo. 20s. each. Half morocco, 28s. each.

RUXTON (GEO. F.). Travels in Mexico; with Adventures among Wild Tribes and Animals of the Prairies and Rocky Mountains. Post 8vo. 3s. 6d.

ST. HUGH OF AVALON, Bishop of Lincoln ; his Life by G. G. PERRY, Canon of Lincoln. Post 8vo. 10s. 6d.

ST. JOHN (CHARLES). Wild Sports and Natural History of the Highlands of Scotland. New, and beautifully Illustrated Edition. Crown 8vo. 15s. Cheap Edition, Post 8vo. 3s. 6d.

——— (BAYLE) Adventures in the Libyan Desert. Post 8vo. 2s.

SALDANHA (DUKE OF), Soldier and Statesman, Memoirs of the Eventful Career of. By the CONDE DA CARNOTA. Portraits and Maps. 2 Vols. 8vo. 32s.

SALE'S (SIR ROBERT) Brigade in Affghanistan. With an Account of the Defence of Jellalabad. By REV. G. R. GLEIG. Post 8vo. 2s.

SCEPTICISM IN GEOLOGY; and the Reasons for It. An assemblage of facts from Nature combining to refute the theory of "Causes now in Action." By VERIFIER. Woodcuts. Crown 8vo. 6s.

SCOTT (SIR GILBERT). Lectures on the Rise and Development of Mediæval Architecture. Delivered at the Royal Academy. With 400 Illustrations. 2 Vols. Medium 8vo. 42s.

——— Secular and Domestic Architecture, Present and Future. 8vo. 9s.

SCHLIEMANN (DR. HENRY). **Troy and Its Remains.** A Narrative of Researches and Discoveries made on the Site of Ilium, and in the Trojan Plain. With 500 Illustrations. Medium 8vo. 42s.

————— **Discoveries on the Sites of Ancient Mycenæ** and Tiryns. With 500 Illustrations, Medium 8vo. 50s.

————— **Ilios;** A Complete History of the City and Country of the Trojans, Including all Recent Discoveries and Researches made on the Site of Troy and the Troad in 1871–3 and 1878–9. With an Autobiography of the Author. With nearly 2000 Illustrations. Imperial 8vo. 50s.

SCHOMBERG (GENERAL). **The Odyssey of Homer,** rendered into English blank verse, Books I—XII. 8vo. 12s.

SEEBOHM (HENRY). **Siberia in Europe;** a Naturalist's Visit to the Valley of the Petchora in North-Eastern Russia. With notices Birds and their migrations. With Map and Illustrations. Crown 8vo.

SELBORNE (LORD). **Notes on some Passages in the Liturgical** History of the Reformed English Church. 8vo. 6s.

SHADOWS OF A SICK ROOM. Preface by Canon LIDDON. 16mo. 2s. 6d.

SHAH OF PERSIA'S Diary during his Tour through Europe in 1873. Translated from the Original. By J. W. REDHOUSE. With Portrait and Coloured Title. Crown 8vo. 12s.

SHAW (T. B.). **Manual of English Literature.** Post 8vo. 7s. 6d.

————— **Specimens of English Literature.** Selected from the Chief Writers. Post 8vo. 7s. 6d.

————— (ROBERT). **Visit to High Tartary, Yarkand, and Kashgar** (formerly Chinese Tartary), and Return Journey over the Karakorum Pass. With Map and Illustrations. 8vo. 16s.

SIERRA LEONE; Described in Letters to Friends at Home. By A LADY. Post 8vo. 3s. 6d.

SIMMONS (CAPT.). **Constitution and Practice of Courts-Martial.** 8vo. 15s.

SMILES' (SAMUEL, LL.D.) WORKS :—

    BRITISH ENGINEERS; from the Earliest Period to the death of the Stephensons. With Illustrations. 5 Vols. Crown 8vo. 7s. 6d. each.

    LIFE OF A SCOTCH NATURALIST (THOS. EDWARD). Illustrations. Crown 8vo. 10s. 6d.

    LIFE OF A SCOTCH GEOLOGIST AND BOTANIST (ROBERT DICK). Illustrations. Crown 8vo. 12s.

    HUGUENOTS IN ENGLAND AND IRELAND. Crown 8vo. 7s. 6d.

    SELF-HELP. With Illustrations of Conduct and Perseverance. Post 8vo. 6s. Or in French, 5s.

    CHARACTER. A Sequel to "SELF-HELP." Post 8vo. 6s.

    THRIFT. A Book of Domestic Counsel. Post 8vo. 6s.

    DUTY. With Illustrations of Courage, Patience, and Endurance. Post 8vo. 6s.

    INDUSTRIAL BIOGRAPHY; or, Iron Workers and Tool Makers. Post 8vo. 6s.

    BOY'S VOYAGE ROUND THE WORLD. Illustrations. Post 8vo. 6s.

SMITH'S (DR. WM.) DICTIONARIES:—

    DICTIONARY OF THE BIBLE; its Antiquities, Biography, Geography, and Natural History. Illustrations. 3 Vols. 8vo. 105s.

Smith's (Dr. Wm.) Dictionaries—*continued.*

Concise Bible Dictionary. With 300 Illustrations. Medium 8vo. 21s.

Smaller Bible Dictionary. With Illustrations. Post 8vo. 7s. 6d.

Christian Antiquities. Comprising the History, Institutions, and Antiquities of the Christian Church. With Illustrations, 2 Vols. Medium 8vo. 3l. 13s. 6d.

Christian Biography, Literature, Sects, and Doctrines; from the Times of the Apostles to the Age of Charlemagne. Medium 8vo. Vols. I. & II. 31s. 6d. each. (To be completed in 4 Vols.)

Greek and Roman Antiquities. With 500 Illustrations. Medium 8vo. 28s.

Greek and Roman Biography and Mythology. With 600 Illustrations. 3 Vols. Medium 8vo. 4l. 4s

Greek and Roman Geography. 2 Vols. With 500 Illustrations. Medium 8vo. 56s.

Atlas of Ancient Geography—Biblical and Classical. Folio. 6l. 6s.

Classical Dictionary of Mythology, Biography, and Geography. 1 Vol. With 750 Woodcuts. 8vo. 18s.

Smaller Classical Dictionary. With 200 Woodcuts. Crown 8vo. 7s. 6d.

Smaller Greek and Roman Antiquities. With 200 Woodcuts. Crown 8vo. 7s. 6d.

Complete Latin-English Dictionary. With Tables of the Roman Calendar, Measures, Weights, and Money. 8vo. 21s.

Smaller Latin-English Dictionary. 12mo. 7s. 6d.

Copious and Critical English-Latin Dictionary. 8vo. 21s.

Smaller English-Latin Dictionary. 12mo. 7s. 6d.

SMITH'S (Dr. Wm.) ENGLISH COURSE:—

School Manual of English Grammar, with Copious Exercises. Post 8vo. 3s. 6d.

Primary English Grammar. 16mo. 1s. 6d.

Manual of English Composition. With Copious Illustrations and Practical Exercises. 12mo. 3s. 6d.

Primary History of Britain. 12mo. 2s. 6d.

School Manual of Modern Geography, Physical and Political. Post 8vo. 5s.

A Smaller Manual of Modern School Geography. Post 8vo. 2s. 6d.

SMITH'S (Dr. Wm.) FRENCH COURSE:—

French Principia. Part I. A First Course, containing a Grammar, Delectus, Exercises, and Vocabularies. 12mo. 3s. 6d.

French Principia. Part II. A Reading Book, containing Fables, Stories, and Anecdotes, Natural History, and Scenes from the History of France. With Grammatical Questions, Notes and copious Etymological Dictionary. 12mo. 4s. 6d.

French Principia. Part III. Prose Composition, containing a Systematic Course of Exercises on the Syntax, with the Principal Rules of Syntax. 12mo. [In the Press.

Student's French Grammar. By C. Heron-Wall. With Introduction by M. Littré. Post 8vo. 7s. 6d.

Smaller Grammar of the French Language. Abridged from the above. 12mo. 3s. 6d.

SMITH'S (Dr. Wm.) GERMAN COURSE :—

GERMAN PRINCIPIA. Part I. A First German Course, containing a Grammar, Delectus, Exercise Book, and Vocabularies. 12mo. 3s. 6d.

GERMAN PRINCIPIA. Part II. A Reading Book ; containing Fables, Stories, and Anecdotes, Natural History, and Scenes from the History of Germany. With Grammatical Questions, Notes, and Dictionary. 12mo. 3s. 6d.

PRACTICAL GERMAN GRAMMAR. Post 8vo. 3s. 6d.

SMITH'S (Dr. Wm.) ITALIAN COURSE :—

ITALIAN PRINCIPIA. An Italian Course, containing a Grammar, Delectus, Exercise Book, with Vocabularies, and Materials for Italian Conversation. By Signor Ricci, Professor of Italian at the City of London College. 12mo. 3s. 6d.

SMITH'S (Dr. Wm.) LATIN COURSE :—

THE YOUNG BEGINNER'S FIRST LATIN BOOK : Containing the Rudiments of Grammar, Easy Grammatical Questions and Exercises, with Vocabularies. Being a Stepping stone to Principia Latina, Part I, for Young Children. 12mo. 2s.

THE YOUNG BEGINNER'S SECOND LATIN BOOK : Containing an easy Latin Reading Book, with an Analysis of the Sentences, Notes, and a Dictionary. Being a Stepping-stone to Principia Latina, Part II., for Young Children. 12mo. 2s.

PRINCIPIA LATINA. Part I. First Latin Course, containing a Grammar, Delectus, and Exercise Book. with Vocabularies. 12mo. 3s. 6d.
₊ In this Edition the Cases of the Nouns, Adjectives, and Pronouns are arranged both as in the ORDINARY GRAMMARS and as in the PUBLIC SCHOOL PRIMER, together with the corresponding Exercises.

APPENDIX TO PRINCIPIA LATINA Part I. ; being Additional Exercises, with Examination Papers. 12mo. 2s. 6d.

PRINCIPIA LATINA. Part II. A Reading-book of Mythology, Geography, Roman Antiquities, and History. With Notes and Dictionary. 12mo. 3s. 6d.

PRINCIPIA LATINA. Part III. A Poetry Book. Hexameters and Pentameters; Eclog. Ovidianæ; Latin Prosody. 12mo. 3s. 6d.

PRINCIPIA LATINA. Part IV. Prose Composition. Rules of Syntax with Examples, Explanations of Synonyms, and Exercises on the Syntax. 12mo. 3s. 6d.

PRINCIPIA LATINA. Part V. Short Tales and Anecdotes for Translation into Latin. 12mo. 3s.

LATIN-ENGLISH VOCABULARY AND FIRST LATIN-ENGLISH DICTIONARY FOR PHÆDRUS, CORNELIUS NEPOS, AND CÆSAR. 12mo. 3s. 6d.

STUDENT'S LATIN GRAMMAR. For the Higher Forms. Post 8vo. 6s.

SMALLER LATIN GRAMMAR. For the Middle and Lower Forms. 12mo. 3s. 6d.

TACITUS, Germania, Agricola, &c. With English Notes. 12mo. 3s. 6d.

SMITH'S (Dr. Wm.) GREEK COURSE :—

INITIA GRÆCA. Part I. A First Greek Course, containing a Grammar, Delectus, and Exercise-book. With Vocabularies. 12mo. 3s. 6d.

INITIA GRÆCA. Part II. A Reading Book. Containing Short Tales, Anecdotes, Fables, Mythology, and Grecian History. 12mo. 3s. 6d.

SMITH'S (DR. WM.) GREEK COURSE—*continued.*
>   INITIA GRÆCA. Part III. Prose Composition. Containing the Rules of Syntax, with copious Examples and Exercises. 12mo. 3s. 6d.
>   STUDENT'S GREEK GRAMMAR. For the Higher Forms. By CURTIUS. Post 8vo. 6s.
>   SMALLER GREEK GRAMMAR. For the Middle and Lower Forms. 12mo. 3s. 6d.
>   GREEK ACCIDENCE. 12mo. 2s. 6d.
>   PLATO, Apology of Socrates, &c. With Notes. 12mo. 3s. 6d.

SMITH'S (DR. WM.) SMALLER HISTORIES:—
>   SCRIPTURE HISTORY. Woodcuts. 16mo. 3s. 6d.
>   ANCIENT HISTORY. Woodcuts. 16mo. 3s. 6d.
>   ANCIENT GEOGRAPHY. Woodcuts. 16mo. 3s. 6d.
>   ROME. Modern Geography. Woodcuts. 16mo. 3s. 6d.
>   GREECE. Woodcuts. 16mo. 3s. 6d.
>   CLASSICAL MYTHOLOGY. Woodcuts. 16mo. 3s. 6d.
>   ENGLAND. Woodcuts. 16mo. 3s. 6d.
>   ENGLISH LITERATURE. 16mo. 3s. 6d.
>   SPECIMENS OF ENGLISH LITERATURE. 16mo. 3s. 6d.

SMITH (GEO.). Life of John Wilson, D.D. (of Bombay), Fifty Years Missionary and Philanthropist. Portrait. Post 8vo. 9s
——— (PHILIP). History of the Ancient World, from the Creation to the Fall of the Roman Empire, A.D. 476. 3 Vols. 8vo. 31s. 6d.

SOMERVILLE (MARY). Personal Recollections from Early Life to Old Age. Portrait. Crown 8vo. 12s.
——————— Physical Geography. Portrait. Post 8vo. 9s.
——————— Connexion of the Physical Sciences. Portrait. Post 8vo. 9s.
——————— Molecular & Microscopic Science. Illustrations. 2 Vols. Post 8vo. 21s.

SOUTHEY (ROBT). Lives of Bunyan and Cromwell. Post 8vo. 2s.

STAEL (MADAME DE). *See* STEVENS.

STANLEY'S (DEAN) WORKS:—
>   SINAI AND PALESTINE, in connexion with their History. Maps. 8vo. 14s
>   BIBLE IN THE HOLY LAND; Extracted from the above Work. Woodcuts. Fcap. 8vo. 2s. 6d.
>   EASTERN CHURCH. Plans. 8vo. 12s.
>   JEWISH CHURCH. From the Earliest Times to the Christian Era. 3 Vols. 8vo. 38s.
>   EPISTLES OF ST. PAUL TO THE CORINTHIANS. 8vo. 18s.
>   LIFE OF DR. ARNOLD, OF RUGBY. Portrait. 2 vols. Cr. 8vo. 12s.
>   HISTORY OF THE CHURCH OF SCOTLAND. 8vo. 7s. 6d.
>   MEMORIALS OF CANTERBURY CATHEDRAL. Post 8vo. 7s. 6d.
>   WESTMINSTER ABBEY. Illustrations. 8vo. 15s.
>   SERMONS DURING A TOUR IN THE EAST. 8vo. 9s.
>   MEMOIR OF EDWARD, CATHERINE, AND MARY STANLEY. Cr. 8vo. 9s.
>   CHRISTIAN INSTITUTIONS. Essays on Ecclesiastical Subjects. 8vo.

STEPHENS (REV. W. R. W.). Life and Times of St. John Chrysostom. A Sketch of the Church and the Empire in the Fourth Century. Portrait. 8vo. 12s.

STEVENS (Dr. A.). Madame de Staël; a Study of her Life and Times. The First Revolution and the First Empire. 2 Vols. Cr. 8vo.

STRATFORD de REDCLIFFE (Lord). The Eastern Question. Being a Selection from his Writings during the last Five Years of his Life. With a Preface by Dean Stanley. Post 8vo.

STREET (G. E.). Gothic Architecture in Spain. Illustrations. Royal 8vo. 30s.

———————————————————— Italy, chiefly in Brick and Marble. With Notes on North of Italy. Illustrations. Royal 8vo. 26s.

STUART (Villiers). Nile Gleanings: The Ethnology, History, and Art of Ancient Egypt, as Revealed by Paintings and Bas-Reliefs. With Descriptions of Nubia and Its Great Rock Temples, 58 Coloured Illustrations &c. Medium 8vo. 31s. 6d.

STUDENTS' MANUALS :—

Old Testament History; from the Creation to the Return of the Jews from Captivity. Maps and Woodcuts. Post 8vo. 7s. 6d.

New Testament History. With an Introduction connecting the History of the Old and New Testaments. Maps and Woodcuts. Post 8vo. 7s. 6d.

Ecclesiastical History. The Christian Church during the First Ten Centuries; From its Foundation to the full establishment of the Holy Roman Empire and the Papal Power. Post 8vo. 7s. 6d.

English Church History, from the accession of Henry VIII. to the silencing of Convocation in the 18th Century. By Canon Perry. Post 8vo. 7s. 6d.

Ancient History of the East; Egypt, Assyria, Babylonia, Media, Persia, Asia Minor, and Phœnicia. Woodcuts. Post 8vo. 7s. 6d.

Ancient Geography. By Canon Bevan. Woodcuts. Post 8vo. 7s. 6d.

History of Greece; from the Earliest Times to the Roman Conquest. By Wm. Smith, D.C.L. Woodcuts. Crown 8vo. 7s. 6d.
 ** Questions on the above Work, 12mo. 2s.

History of Rome; from the Earliest Times to the Establishment of the Empire. By Dean Liddell. Woodcuts. Crown 8vo. 7s. 6d.

Gibbon's Decline and Fall of the Roman Empire. Woodcuts. Post 8vo. 7s. 6d.

Hallam's History of Europe during the Middle Ages. Post 8vo. 7s. 6d.

History of Modern Europe, from the end of the Middle Ages to the Treaty of Berlin, 1878. Post 8vo.   [In the Press.

Hallam's History of England; from the Accession of Henry VII. to the Death of George II. Post 8vo. 7s. 6d.

Hume's History of England from the Invasion of Julius Cæsar to the Revolution in 1688. Revised, corrected, and continued down to the Treaty of Berlin, 1878. By J. S. Brewer, M.A. With 7 Coloured Maps & 70 Woodcuts. Post 8vo. 7s. 6d.
 ** Questions on the above Work, 12mo. 2s.

History of France; from the Earliest Times to the Establishment of the Second Empire, 1852. By H. W. Jervis. Woodcuts. Post 8vo. 7s. 6d.

English Language. By Geo. P. Marsh. Post 8vo. 7s. 6d.

English Literature. By T. B. Shaw, M.A. Post 8vo. 7s. 6d.

Specimens of English Literature from the Chief Writers. By T. B. Shaw. Post 8vo. 7s. 6d.

Modern Geography; Mathematical, Physical and Descriptive. By Canon Bevan. Woodcuts. Post 8vo. 7s. 6d.

Moral Philosophy. By Wm. Fleming. Post 8vo. 7s. 6d.

Blackstone's Commentaries on the Laws of England. By Malcolm Kerr. Post 8vo. 7s. 6d.

STANHOPE'S (Earl) WORKS :—
- History of England from the Reign of Queen Anne to the Peace of Versailles, 1701-83. 9 vols. Post 8vo. 5s. each.
- Life of William Pitt. Portraits. 3 Vols. 8vo. 36s.
- British India, from its Origin to 1783. Post 8vo. 3s. 6d.
- History of "Forty-Five." Post 8vo. 3s.
- Historical and Critical Essays. Post 8vo. 3s. 6d.
- French Retreat from Moscow, other Essays. Post 8vo. 7s 6d.
- Life of Belisarius. Post 8vo. 10s. 6d.
- Life of Condé. Post 8vo. 3s. 6d.
- Miscellanies. 2 Vols. Post 8vo. 13s.
- Story of Joan of Arc. Fcap. 8vo. 1s.
- Addresses on Various Occasions. 16mo. 1s.

SUMNER'S (Bishop) Life and Episcopate during 40 Years. By Rev. G. H. Sumner. Portrait. 8vo. 14s.

SWAINSON (Canon). Nicene and Apostles' Creeds; Their Literary History ; together with some Account of "The Creed of St Athanasius." 8vo. 16s.

SYBEL (Von) History of Europe during the French Revolution. 1789—1795. 4 Vols. 8vo. 48s.

SYMONDS' (Rev. W.) Records of the Rocks; or Notes on the Geology, Natural History, and Antiquities of North and South Wales, Siluria, Devon, and Cornwall. With Illustrations. Crown 8vo. 12s.

TALMUD. See Barclay; Deutsch.

TEMPLE (Sir Richard). India in 1880. 8vo.

THIBAUT'S (Antoine) Purity in Musical Art. Translated from the German. With a prefatory Memoir by W. H. Gladstone, M.P. Post 8vo. 7s. 6d.

THIELMANN (Baron). Journey through the Caucasus to Tabreez, Kurdistan, down the Tigris and Euphrates to Nineveh and Babylon, and across the Desert to Palmyra. Translated by Chas. Heneage. Illustrations. 2 Vols. Post 8vo. 18s.

THOMSON (Archbishop). Lincoln's Inn Sermons. 8vo. 10s. 6d.

———— Life in the Light of God's Word. Post 8vo. 5s.

———— Word, Work, & Will : Collected Essays. Crown 8vo. 9s.

TITIAN'S LIFE AND TIMES. With some account of his Family, chiefly from new and unpublished Records. By Crowe and Cavalcaselle. With Portrait and Illustrations. 2 Vols. 8vo. 42s.

TOCQUEVILLE'S State of Society in France before the Revolution, 1769, and on the Causes which led to that Event. Translated by Henry Reeve. 8vo. 14s.

TOMLINSON (Chas.); The Sonnet; Its Origin, Structure, and Place in Poetry. With translations from Dante, Petrarch, &c. Post 8vo. 9s.

TOZER (Rev. H. F.) Highlands of Turkey, with Visits to Mounts Ida, Athos, Olympus, and Pelion. 2 Vols. Crown 8vo. 24s.

———— Lectures on the Geography of Greece. Map. Post 8vo. 9s.

TRISTRAM (Canon). Great Sahara. Illustrations. Crown 8vo. 15s.

———— Land of Moab ; Travels and Discoveries on the East Side of the Dead Sea and the Jordan. Illustrations. Crown 8vo. 15s.

TRURO (Bishop of). The Cathedral : its Necessary Place in the Life and Work of the Church. Crown 8vo. 6s.

TWENTY YEARS' RESIDENCE among the Greeks, Albanians, Turks, Armenians, and Bulgarians. By an ENGLISH LADY. Edited by STANLEY LANE POOLE. 2 Vols. Crown 8vo. 21s.

TWISS' (HORACE) Life of Lord Eldon. 2 Vols. Post 8vo. 21s.

TYLOR (E. B.) Researches into the Early History of Mankind, and Development of Civilization. 3rd Edition Revised. 8vo. 12s.

———— Primitive Culture; the Development of Mythology, Philosophy, Religion. Art, and Custom. 2 Vols. 8vo. 24s.

VIRCHOW (PROFESSOR). The Freedom of Science in the Modern State. Fcap. 8vo. 2s.

WELLINGTON'S Despatches during his Campaigns in India, Denmark, Portugal, Spain, the Low Countries, and France. 8 Vols. 8vo. 20s. each.

———————— Supplementary Despatches, relating to India, Ireland, Denmark, Spanish America, Spain, Portugal, France, Congress of Vienna, Waterloo and Paris. 14 Vols. 8vo. 20s. each. *₊* An Index. 8vo. 20s.

———————— Civil and Political Correspondence. Vols. I. to VIII. 8vo. 20s. each.

———————— Speeches in Parliament. 2 Vols. 8vo. 42s.

WHEELER (G.). Choice of a Dwelling; a Practical Handbook of Useful Information on Building a House. Plans. Post 8vo. 7s. 6d.

WHITE (W. H.). Manual of Naval Architecture, for the use of Naval Officers, Shipowners, Shipbuilders, and Yachtsmen. Illustrations. 8vo. 24s.

WHYMPER (EDWARD). The Ascent of the Matterhorn. With 2 Maps and 100 Illustrations. Medium 8vo. 10s. 6d.

WILBERFORCE'S (BISHOP) Life of William Wilberforce. Portrait. Crown 8vo. 6s.

———————— (SAMUEL, LL.D.), Lord Bishop of Oxford and Winchester; his Life. By Canon ASHWELL, D.D. With Portrait. Vol. I. 8vo. 15s.

WILKINSON (SIR J. G.). Manners and Customs of the Ancient Egyptians, their Private Life, Laws, Arts, Religion, &c. A new edition. Edited by SAMUEL BIRCH, LL.D. Illustrations. 3 Vols. 8vo. 84s.

———————— Popular Account of the Ancient Egyptians. With 500 Woodcuts. 2 Vols. Post 8vo. 12s.

WILSON (JOHN, D.D.), of Bombay, Fifty Years a Philanthropist and Missionary in the East; his Life. By GEORGE SMITH, LL.D. Portrait. Post 8vo. 9s.

WOOD'S (CAPTAIN) Source of the Oxus. With the Geography of the Valley of the Oxus. By COL. YULE. Map. 8vo. 12s.

WORDS OF HUMAN WISDOM. Collected and Arranged by E. S. With a Preface by CANON LIDDON Fcap. 8vo. 3s. 6d

YORK (ARCHBISHOP OF). Collected Essays. Contents.—Synoptic Gospels. Death of Christ. God Exists. Worth of Life. Design in Nature. Sports and Pastimes. Emotions in Preaching. Defects in Missionary Work. Limits of Philosophical Enquiry. Crown 8vo. 9s.

YULE (COLONEL). Book of Marco Polo. Illustrated by the Light of Oriental Writers and Modern Travels. With Maps and 80 Plates. 2 Vols. Medium 8vo. 63s.

———————— A. F. A Little Light on Cretan Insurrection. Post 8vo. 2s 6d.

BRADBURY, AGNEW, & CO., PRINTERS, WHITEFRIARS.